KAYOS

EFFECT

An
Unfortunate
Lineage

VOLUME
II

A Novel

Also Available
by **Delaine Christine** through
Kimerah Publishing

KAYOS

EFFECT

An
Unfortunate
Lineage

VOLUME
II

A Novel

Delaine Christine

Kayos Effect
An Unfortunate Lineage Volume II

ISBN-13: 978-1950563067

Original Publication 2015 As The Beginning: The Blackthorne Saga, Book One. Re-published in 2018 with updates under the same title

Book and Cover Design by DC Johnson
Model Pic by Olena Zaskochento, used with permission
Scenic Cover Image by Roman Krochuk
Interior Model Image by Badmanproduction, used with permission

Kimerah Publishing, Elkhart, IN

Printed in the United States of America.

The Prophecy
Continues...

A choice to make, one right one wrong.
We will know for sure before long.

Two years from now it must begin
Or the millennium will see much sin.

Fifteen years we must then wait
If not start now twill be too late...

PROLOGUE

Don't skip me.
You'll wish you hadn't.

That's right folks, it's me again, Vortigern Black, your ever illusive and always mysterious narrator of Terrible Karisma and the An Unfortunate Lineage series. I'm back again to help connect some of the dots for you folks with this here inspirational tale.

To start you should know that the author and I have been arguing feverishly for months. She seems to think that at the beginning of this book I should be updating you on what transpired in the first volume of this series.

But I disagree.

Why should I repeat myself?

Why should I tell you that in the last story, Kahner RavenCroft returned home with a woman and three children in tow after having been gone for fifteen years working undercover with the CIA? I would argue that telling you all this would be like giving away the fact that the woman in question, Sable Kryder, aka Kalysta Radford, wound up pregnant by Kahner and is now experiencing his ability to know a person's thoughts as a result. Or that he convinced her to marry him. And that Sable was the estranged wife of Lionel Radford; a wife beater and a bully whose drug cartel has managed to go global and whose brother, has a high ranking official within the CIA in his pocket. Seriously, what would be the point in convincing you to go back and pick up book one if you hadn't already, if I tell you all this now? Sort of ruins it, don't you think?

What do you think the author's response was to my way of thinking? She said, and I quote, "It's a romance, Vortigern. Everybody knows it wouldn't be a love story if they didn't come together in the end, and besides, there is pertinent information in the last book that won't get re-iterated here otherwise."

I'll tell you what, the woman is so tightly wound, it would take a dozen valium, a slingshot, and a rubber ball to bring her down from the ladder she's perched on. But that's just my opinion.

I suppose there may well be some merit to getting you back up to speed on what's been happening. As the author of this story argued, not everyone may have read the first one yet. To which I asked her, why the heck not? For I am Vortigern Black, an attractive individual with a vast intellect and a worldly view who works deep, deep undercover, and happens to be the teller of this tale. Who wouldn't want to read about me?

Or, wait, that is… what I'm narrating – you know – this truly unfortunate lineage. That's what I meant to say. Who wouldn't want to read about the RavenCrofts? Or rather, this time around it'd be the Blackthorne's, I guess.

Hahaha.

Oops.

Moving on...

The author was also – not so – kind enough to point out that I really wasn't needed to impart any nuggets of my vast wisdom for this part of the An Unfortunate Lineage series. Mostly because I, as she put it, "...Was not present throughout this portion so it's not necessary."

Phooey. That doesn't mean I don't have things to say.

Have you noticed so far that the author also happens to be a pain in my butt? Unfortunately, she may well have a point. So, while rolling my eyes in disgust, I am to tell you that you likely won't be hearing anything more from me until the next volume. I was asked though to share two important pieces of information before we start the story.

Out of spite, I'm going to give you three, mostly because I like that number better than two. Hehe.

One, if you are discovering this novel first, then you might want to consider backing up and starting with the first book in the series, Terrible Karisma. You can read Kayos Effect and enjoy it a great deal, but you will miss a bit of the larger picture.

Two, if you have come straight off of reading the first book then you already know I am deep, deep undercover, as I've said previously, and I won't be telling you who I am.

That's right. This is a mystery, within a mystery. A suspenseful thriller with a bit of fantasy. A chaotic depiction of a family drama and a universal love story all rolled into one. Even though I was not present during this part of the story you are still getting your next clue as to who I, Vortigern Black, really am. The clue of which was within what I just said.

I wasn't present within the Blackthorne's tale.

That means – drumroll please...

You can eliminate every single character within this story.

That's a lot of suspects.

And three, this tale revolves solely around the Blackthorne family, who are related by blood to the RavenCroft's and are, therefore, also gifted. But this family of six adults and their father, Rafe Blackthorne, were raised with Christian beliefs and values rather than the secular ones their cousins and Uncle have, so this story will have more of a religious tone to it. No worries people. We'll get back to the RavenCroft's in the next volume. In order to tell you more of their story we need to impart the Blackthorne's tale as well, for they are all linked to the same unfortunate lineage.

From what I gather, the Blackthornes make it a point to use their abilities to help others whenever they can. No, they are not superhero's who run around wearing spandex, tights, and underwear outside of their clothes. They are human, however, so they tend to make poor choices, just like the RavenCrofts, you, or me.

That is ... *you* anyway.

I don't make bad choices for *I* am perfect.

Remember now people, this will be the only time you'll get to hear from me until the next volume. Though I know that saddens you greatly, try and keep in mind I'll be back in the next volume.

Oh, and by the way, you may notice as you read that there are some uncanny similarities and parallels between Dante Blackthorne's story and Kahner RavenCroft's. The author and I thought it important to mention that there is a reason for it which won't likely be explained until much later. My saying this next part won't make a whole lot of sense but, not even I have all the answers yet.

But somehow the author seems to know.

Which is odd.

Because I'm the one who gave her this story.

Or, at least ... I thought I did.

Chapter 1

The day started like any other weekday.

Astraia O'Kahner woke to the sound of her husband's alarm at four in the morning and began her daily ritual along with him.

Grabbing two mugs from the cupboard, she quickly poured coffee into one, adding sugar and cream for Dylan. Pouring the other cup, she added a teaspoon of honey, and raised the mug to her lips, allowing the scent of the lightly sweetened brew to awaken her senses with its caffeine-infused aroma.

Sipping appreciatively at her coffee, she grabbed up the other mug with her free hand and carried it into the bathroom, where her husband was just now stepping into the shower.

"If you keep dawdling, you're going to make yourself late again." She laughed and handed him the mug. Moaning in annoyance, he took a swig of coffee, wincing as it scalded his mouth. He handed the mug back, and she set it down next to the sink.

"Why do I have to go to work again?" he asked, as was his habit most mornings.

Chuckling, Astraia responded as usual. "Because the kids like a roof over their heads and food on the table and…"

"Clothes on their backs, electricity, heat, water. I know. You don't have to tell me twice." He smiled out at her from the shower door.

"That's funny, seems like I have to tell you that almost every morning." Astraia gave him a weak smile back, annoyed to be having the same repetitive conversation. Knowing what was coming next, she braced herself.

Dylan reached out and pulled her to him. Holding her close, he kissed her on the lips and murmured in her ear.

"You have no idea how much I love you." Releasing her from his hold, he guided her out of the shower as Astraia quietly returned with a meek, "me too," and extricated herself from the bathroom.

Walking through their bedroom to the kitchen, she hugged herself tightly, rubbing her arms in that way she did when she'd become agitated. She felt hollow inside and didn't understand why.

Dylan was a good man, and he treated her well. Better than her ex-husband ever had. He didn't talk down to her or beat her like some men could. Nor did he make her feel bad for being overweight and he frequently told her he loved her. So why was it that every time he told her he loved her, she felt like such a liar telling him she loved him back?

Noticing her hands were beginning to shake again, as they always did when she became anxious, Astraia clenched them together, then shook them vigorously.

Feeling the panic trying to seize her, she closed her eyes and inhaled deeply, desperate to fend off the anxiety attack she sensed was trying to overcome her. Sighing heavily in distress, Astraia rubbed at her eyes and began to pray silently.

Lord, what's wrong with me?

Am I incapable of loving my husband?

I know I loved him in the beginning, for I wouldn't have married him otherwise.

And why do I become so anxious when I think on the subject?

Help me Lord, please. Lead me to the answers I seek.

Help me to squelch this intense fear growing inside me.

Managing to pull herself together, she took a deep breath and ended her prayer. Still a bit anxious, she began pulling eggs and sausage from the fridge and dropped bread into the toaster. The repetitive daily motions helped to ease any remaining anxiety she was experiencing. While she worked at making Dylan's breakfast and preparing his lunch for the day, she couldn't help but wonder why, after six years of marriage, she was once again experiencing the panic attacks.

The more she contemplated on it the more her mood began to deteriorate. To boost her spirits, she made the conscious decision to let the notions go for now.

Be positive! Think positive, Astraia thought for she knew that God was with her. Just yesterday she had read in Deuteronomy 31:8 that, the Lord himself would lead her and be with her. The verse told of how God would not fail her or abandon her and to not lose courage or be afraid.

A sense of calm overcame her, and she smiled softly while buttering the bread for Dylan's sandwich. Deciding she needed to take a few minutes for devotions this morning, regardless of whether she had the time or not, she noticed Dylan poke his head out of the bedroom door.

"Any chance breakfast is ready? I'm starving." He yawned while towel drying his hair.

"Yup, it's good to go. Lunch too." Astraia smiled brightly, handing over to him the sausage and egg sandwich and lunch bag. Her expression quickly changed to exasperation as she watched him leave the towel on the kitchen floor where he had dropped it. Stepping on the towel as he walked through the kitchen to the living room, eating his breakfast as he went, Dylan talked through mouthfuls.

"Have you seen my work boots?"

Astraia sighed inwardly. She turned her back to him and rolled her eyes.

"Same place as you always leave them." Glancing back, she saw Dylan looking at her questioningly. Pointing towards his computer desk with the knife she'd been using, she went on. "They're near your computer desk, silly."

Nodding that he heard, he went straight to his desk and sat down. Laying his food on the desk, he grabbed one of his boots and began putting it on.

"What you got planned for today?" He looked up at her as he finished lacing his boots.

"The usual; job hunting, updating resumes and writing cover letters. I need to get Sayleena off to kindergarten, of course, then the twins to preschool. After that, I'll make my plasma donation, go grocery shopping then pick the boys up. I'll need to hit the library for some books for the kids first, then bring them home for lunch and start some laundry. Then, I'll fix the boys bed, straighten the house, vacuum and then go get Sayleena from the bus stop. Why do you ask?"

"I noticed our comforter is getting pretty dirty."

"Right," Astraia said dryly. "Your point?"

"My point is; it needs to be taken to be washed." The tenor of his voice made him sound as though he were humoring her.

"No problem." She took a deep, weary breath, trying hard to maintain her good spirits. "Wonder Woman shall try and fit that in between dropping off the boys and her plasma donation."

Dylan grabbed up his lunch and keys, after shouldering on his work coat.

"Thanks. I'll see you later, Wonder Woman."

Bending down he gave her a quick peck on the cheek, smacked her bottom and strode out of the front door, allowing the screen door to bang on his way out.

Wincing at the loud noise, hoping it hadn't awakened the children; Astraia gently closed the door the rest of the way. Sighing, on a wave of relief, she walked back into the kitchen to finish packing her daughter's lunch. As she leaned against the kitchen sink, she watched as Dylan pulled out of the driveway.

Astraia knew he wanted her to find a new job soon, but she wasn't looking forward to going back to work. Closing her eyes, she recalled how stressful working a full-time job, being a mom, and taking care of everything else had been. The relief she'd experienced the day the General Manager at Acostco had pulled her into his office and told her he had to let her go due to cutbacks had been huge. The chance to get a break after having worked since she was thirteen was exciting to her.

She remembered coming home that day and going through their bills. Discovering they had been spending over eight hundred dollars on childcare for Saruman and Storman to attend daycare, Astraia was left with barely four hundred dollars after paying the school. So she'd approached Dylan with the idea of being a stay at home mom. After all, why pay someone else to raise their kids? She could make up some of that by continuing to donate plasma to Octapharma twice a week.

To her surprise, Dylan had been very upset by the idea. It was still an extra four hundred dollars a month, even more with her plasma donations. That allowed them to go out to eat, buy movies, computer games and toys for the kids. She'd been appalled by his priorities and made the mistake of reminding him of a promise he'd made to her when they had first found out she was pregnant with Sayleena. This issue had been a bone of contention between them for years. He'd said then that she could be a stay-at-home mom, and he'd make sure they were taken care of. They had fought daily about it since she'd been laid off.

Throwing the washcloth, she'd been using at the counter, Astraia strode over to her laptop on the table. Her mood was starting to diminish again the more she thought about the most recent fight of the night before.

The reality was that since she'd been out of work things had become much simpler and the children were happier. *She* was happier. When she'd been working, she couldn't keep up on everything. Laundry piled up and they had to dig through clean piles to find clothes for the day because she never had time to put them away. She would forget various activities or appointments for the kids and the house would go weeks before she'd be able to vacuum and she frequently found herself paying bills late even when they had the money.

Astraia oversaw the finances, care and upkeep on the house and vehicles, planning meals, doing the shopping, cleaning, laundry, dishes, meal preparations and taking care of all three of her children's needs, as well as her husband's. She knew many of these responsibilities were typically shared in other households when both parents worked.

Dylan, on the other hand, would come home from work, sit down in front of the television or PS2, and play games all night, ignoring the kids and, for that matter, her.

That was before she'd been laid off. She still had all those chores now and was expected to be canvassing the city to find work again. So not working still meant that her days were full, just nowhere near as chaotic.

Before, she couldn't even breathe. Instead, now she rarely had time to herself and that, at least, was much more acceptable. Adding a full-time job to the mix would make life that much more difficult again. She'd never have time to spend with the kids.

Half-heartedly glancing over the want ads in the jobs section of their local online listings, she yawned and glanced at the clock, then her Bible on the table. Taking another sip of coffee, she added taking the comforter to the Laundromat to her 'To do' list. Then she reached for her Bible. Determining her spiritual need outweighed the need to look for work, she opened it to the marked section of Deuteronomy.

Astraia was unsure how she'd managed to get through her days before she started doing devotions in the morning a year ago. Having become a Christian at a young age, she'd fallen away from the Lord nearly fifteen years before and was gradually trying to find her way back. Knowing it was going to be a long day, she sensed she needed God's word to help her get through it.

- - -

Swinging into the gas station on the way to work, Dylan parked his gray 86' Crown Victoria on the far side of the station, instead of at the pump since he didn't need to gas up.

Often treating himself to a large cup of cappuccino and a donut on the way to work, he tended to frequent this one. It had the best donuts in the area.

Pulling out his wallet, he counted the bills he had left for the week. Noticing he'd be short a few dollars to be able to stop every day, he tapped on the wheel in frustration.

The last time he'd pulled cash from the account for donuts and coffee Astraia had gone ballistic. She asked him what the point was of her getting up so early in the morning to fix him breakfast if he was just going to stop for donuts every day. From then on, he'd made it a point to deposit his paycheck himself, rather than having his company do it for him. That way he could take the cash he wanted without her knowing. Dylan figured, for as hard as he worked, he deserved to be able to spend it as he saw fit.

Deciding he needed a cigarette before heading inside, he pulled one from its pack and lit it with a flick of his silver-plated lighter. Stepping out of the car, he leaned his tall frame against the hood as he took his first drag.

Shivering lightly, he happened to glance, in a furtive manner, over his shoulder, suspecting he knew why the sensation had rolled down his back. Noticing the same nondescript Chevy truck from the day before parked in the alley behind the business next door, he grunted softly. Pretending to ignore the hulking frame of a man with black hair exiting the vehicle as another car pulled up next to it, he took another long drag of his cigarette and blew it out.

Dylan had been thinking for some time now that he needed to make a change. He loved his wife, but this scraping by was getting on his nerves. He figured his wife should be working, rather than sitting at home on her duff doing nothing all day.

Rolling his shoulders and pretending to stretch, he watched out of the corner of his eye as the big guy was met by a black man with a goatee. He had noticed lately men were meeting there more frequently and knew from experience what that likely meant.

Shaking his head, he pondered his options. Dylan couldn't help but wonder at his own stupidity. When he'd met Astraia, she had told him her father's name was Andrew Morris, and that he was into cigarettes. Thinking she'd meant he was the owner of the nation's leading cigarette manufacturer, Morris & Harding Group, he'd pursued her voraciously and married her as quickly as possible. In his excitement, he'd missed the fact she had meant her father was simply a smoker too, just as he was. So instead of marrying a potential heiress to a small fortune, he'd married a data entry clerk at a local parts and lumber store.

Sighing heavily, he marveled at where he'd come from, and what he'd gotten himself into. In the end, he supposed it was all right for she was kind of pretty and being in her presence always made him feel better about the kind of man that he used to be. Even after their daughter was born, he'd managed to find some contentment with the life they were leading. It wasn't until the boys were born that he had started to feel restless and desperate because that's when things had gotten tight financially. But the last straw was when Astraia lost her job and announced she wanted to be a stay-at-home mom.

Harrumphing as he noticed the man with the goatee grin and produce a package from under his arm, Dylan dropped his cigarette and squashed it out with the heel of his boot. Nodding his head, he strolled toward the front door. He realized he would have to decide one way or another real soon. There was a potential out presenting itself. The only thing left to decide was whether he took his family with him or left them behind.

Chapter 2

The store seemed busier than normal for a Thursday morning.

More people meant more difficulty getting through the aisles, which prevented Astraia from being able to rush through the grocery shopping as she usually did.

Glancing down at her watch, she realized she was starting to run short on time. She needed to find her last few items and get checked out quickly or she would be late picking up her twin boys, Saruman and Storman, from preschool.

Astraia wheeled her cart down the cereal aisle, searching for the section with the large bags of generic shredded wheat. Finding what she needed, she tossed the bag under the cart, accidentally bumping the cart in the process while nearly running down the man standing next to her. Rattled by her already harried morning, she barely looked up from her list as she apologized.

"I'm so sorry, I..." Stopping mid-sentence, she was startled to find herself looking up into the most unusual eyes she'd ever seen. Framed by black eyelashes and well-formed eyebrows were a pair of amazing, crystal-clear blue eyes. Almost translucent in nature, like a pair of sparkling diamonds with the barest hint of blue they evoked a sense of calm – of peace. Lost in the brilliant light of his eyes she imagined, in a daze, that they were likely more pronounced by his tanned skin and jet-black hair. Standing easily a foot taller than her, the man was quite large and clearly well built.

Astraia was accustomed to being around a tall man, as her own husband was big in his own right at six foot. But this guy was easily four inches taller than her husband and broader built. The muscles in his arms visibly flexed under the fabric of his shirt when he'd grabbed hold of the cart to steady it. She also noted how the shirt stretched taught against his massive chest. His waist tapered, as did Dylan's, only this man did not have what her husband commonly referred to as his winter fluff. All this paled in comparison to the captivating eyes which had captured her attention in the first place. She was speechless.

"Never realized how hazardous shopping could be." Dante Blackthorne said with a smile, unaware that the gesture was making him appear even more handsome to her. Letting go of the cart, he leaned out of the way of another shopper attempting to move past him. Though conscious of the other shoppers around him, his eyes never swayed from her heart-shaped face. Her deep blue eyes had surprised him at their intensity for there was a light that seemed to shine within them.

He was rarely surprised by anything.

Realizing she had been staring at him the whole time, Astraia's cheeks flushed. She intentionally tore her eyes away from his.

"Sorry about that." She laughed nervously.

Patting her chest gently with her hand, to ward off her heart's sudden pounding, Astraia accidentally dropped her list. Before she could grab it, he deftly bent down and picked it up. Taking her spare hand in his, he laid the list in the palm of her hand, curling her fingers in so she held it tightly.

The instant his hand touched hers, Dante felt a numbing, almost tingling, sensation in the palm of his hand. Startled by what he felt, he glanced first at his hand, then back at her. Seeing the same surprised look register in her face, his gaze narrowed upon her thoughtfully. He could tell she was struggling to maintain her composure. Chuckling inwardly, he sensed her common interest.

Inhaling sharply, she stuttered a thank you, then looked away hastily and tore down the aisle.

Dante couldn't help but chortle out loud. Her arm bumped a couple of cereal boxes, causing them to fall to the floor. Clearly, she had been embarrassed by her response; so much so that she didn't even stop to pick the boxes up.

Astraia shook her head in dismay, refusing to look back in humiliation. Heat flooded her face once again, though this time finding its way around her neck and up the back of her head. Agitated and embarrassed, she went straight to the checkout line, forgetting she had two more items on her list.

While standing in line, she became distracted from her reaction to the man when she noticed a young woman checking out in front of her struggling with her two small children. The little boy in the front of the cart couldn't have been more than eighteen months old. He kept reaching for the peanut butter at the register. The other little boy was clearly giving his mother a hard time over a candy bar he wanted.

Astraia couldn't help but sympathize with her. She watched as the extremely harassed mother reached into her giant purse for her wallet and dropped her keys. Her son snatched them up and refused to give them back unless she bought the candy. At the same moment, the cashier finished ringing up the few items she had at the register.

"That'll be twenty-five dollars and sixty-eight cents please," the clerk said, while she finished bagging the items.

The woman handed the cashier her debit card and proceeded to grab hold of her son to get her keys.

"That's enough, Cody. Mama needs her keys," she heard the woman say, as the impatient cashier attempted to get her attention.

"Miss? I'm sorry but it's declining your card."

Distracted, the woman didn't hear at first but then finally caught on that there was a problem.

"I'm sorry. What did you say?"

"Your card, Miss, it's been declined. Do you want to try another card?" The teenage girl operating the register snapped her gum and stared at her, waiting for a response

The woman appeared confused, and at a loss. She glanced at her wallet, and then at the card the clerk had extended to her, taking it back. She shook her head in frustration.

"No, I don't. That's all I've got." The woman's voice shook and her hands were trembling. Her son stopped jumping up and down on the cart and looked at her, realizing something was wrong.

"Mama? Are we not buying groceries *again* this week?" he asked in a worried tone, loud enough for those around to hear. The scene had drawn the attention of the other cashier and customers in both lines. The young mother was becoming very upset, and the teenage cashier seemed unsympathetic to her plight.

"I don't understand. There's supposed to be thirty dollars left, can you please try it again?" There was a note of panic in her voice. The cashier looked at her doubtfully. Appearing annoyed, she took the card back and tried again.

Astraia recalled the items she'd seen at the register. They were necessities most people required during the week: milk, eggs, bread, and peanut butter. There had been a two cans each of fruits and veggies, cereal, a couple pounds of hamburger and four boxes of Hamburger Helper. Hastily pulling her own wallet from her purse, she stepped forward towards the woman, watching as the cashier handed the card back once again while apologizing with little to no empathy in her tone.

"I'm sorry. It still won't work."

"Here, try this one." Astraia handed her card off to the cashier. Grabbing the candy bar the child had been begging for, she tossed it on the counter. "And add this too, please."

The teenager reached out automatically and accepted the card, looking back and forth between the two women as she rang up the candy.

"What are you doing?" The young woman blinked, her mouth parting in surprise.

The cashier rang up the purchase with Astraia's card, had her sign the receipt, and then handed the candy bar over to the young mother who accepted it with a stunned look on her face.

Turning towards the woman and her son, Astraia patted her on the shoulder and said, "I've been where you're at. Just promise that one day when things get better - and they will get better - you'll pay it forward."

"We got groceries, Mommy! And candy," the little boy piped up excitedly.

"Thank you so much!" The frazzled mother wheeled her cart away, looking a bit dazed by her good fortune.

Pulling her groceries from her cart, Astraia tossed them on the counter. The cashier began ringing up her grocery items. Taking a moment to survey her own purchases, she realized that her gesture of goodwill might cause her own bill to exceed her limit.

Leaning over the counter, she whispered to the cashier as she handed her the large package of toilet paper and paper towels.

"Do me a favor and have someone put this back for me."

The teenager's eyes grew wide, as she took the items from Astraia, and set them on the floor behind her counter. Turning back to the register, she finished ringing up the purchases.

Astraia tapped her fingers on the counter, all the while silently praying that she hadn't gone over her own account limit.

Noticing her nervous behavior the cashier asked her rather loudly as she swiped her card. "Are you gonna have enough to cover your own stuff?"

"We'll see." Astraia shrugged and smiled weakly.

"Why would you do that, then?" The girl asked with wide-eyed surprise while they waited for the registers response. They both seemed to sigh with relief as the card was accepted and the cashier handed her the receipt to sign.

"That woman had no ring on her hand which means she's likely a single mom who's just barely getting by. She wasn't intending to buy candy or junk but only food she and her kids needed for the week."

Astraia put her card back in her wallet and shoved it back in her purse. Seeing the teenager's confused expression, she went on. "Look, she needed help and I was able to help her out. If the roles were reversed, I'd hope someone would do the same for me. Wouldn't you?"

"But you had to put stuff back to do it. Don't you need it?"

"Eventually, yes, but we'll be fine until next week."

The teenager cocked her head and smiled back at Astraia, then placed her last grocery bag in the cart.

"Wow. You know what? I hope I get someone like you behind me if that ever happens to me someday."

"Hopefully, it'll never happen to you." Astraia smiled back at her. Taking her copy of the receipt, she pushed her cart out of the way, realizing at that moment that they'd drawn an audience. Glancing over at the other register she saw the handsome man she'd nearly mowed down in the aisle watching her curiously with his mesmerizing eyes. The customers and cashier from that line had also apparently been listening, for many smiled at her as she left.

She could feel the heat suffuse her face as she blushed, more at his attention than anyone else's. Looking away quickly, she attempted to rush out of the store.

Surprised by the sudden reaction to his attention and blatant good looks, she became distracted and flustered. She felt guilty for having the encounter but managed to regain her composure by the time she was wheeling her cart out of the grocery store.

The unusually cool Florida air was just what she needed, she thought, as she buttoned her jacket unnecessarily while waiting for cars to pass. The wind picked up, causing her long blonde hair to blow in her face briefly, impairing her ability to see clearly.

Pushing the cart along the crosswalk, the right front wheel slid unexpectedly, getting caught on a large pothole. Her right leg banged the rear of the cart, causing the pant leg of her jeans to snag on it. The sudden jarring motion resulted in the cart tipping over, taking Astraia with it.

Falling partially under the cart, she found herself in a mess of grocery bags and run-away cans of food. The hard pavement scraped the palm of her hands and her leg ached where she'd been pinned.

"Are you all right, Miss?"

Dazed and a little disoriented, Astraia felt the weight of the cart being yanked off her. She heard a car engine revving nearby, sparking a note of alarm within her. In the same instant, she was being lifted off the ground by the same man she'd nearly run down in the store.

Startled by the sudden motion and no longer anxious over the car's proximity, she found she was unable to speak at first. He had her by the waist. Her belly firmly pressed up against his side. The man released his hold on her cart. He began brushing the dirt off her face and out of her hair while he still held her in place.

He spoke again, his voice gentle and deep.

"Miss? Are you all right?" Dante looked down at her, the concern now evident in his voice and entrancing eyes.

Stuttering, she finally found her voice. "I, uh, yes. I'm sorry. I'm Astraia O'Kahner. I'm fine," she said breathlessly, thinking she sounded awfully stupid and wondering why she had given him her name. Staring, as though transfixed by his clear blue eyes, it took her a moment to realize she held his rapt attention as well. They both were unaware of the people around them expressing concern and aiding in returning her items to her bags.

Dante's mouth spread into a wide grin at her words as his eyes twinkled merrily. "Astraia, that's very pretty.

Most people call me Kastle," he responded without thinking. "And are you sure you're okay? Can you walk all right?" he asked finally, gesturing to her torn pant leg while still holding her to his side.

Feeling silly and a little out of sorts being so intimately close to him, she took a deep breath to help regain her composure a bit.

"Yes, I think so. Thank you." She felt him release his hold on her, just enough, to allow her to slide down the length of him. As she found her footing again, he took hold of her left hand briefly to help steady her. Noticing him glance around them, she realized suddenly that there had been several people who had aided in returning all her groceries to her cart.

"Thank you, everyone. Thank you so much."

Feeling the tiny diamond ring on the finger of her left hand, Dante's face fell suddenly in disappointment. Realizing she was married, he felt foolish for allowing himself to become interested in her and guilty for having held her so close for so long. Of course, she was married. It explained why she had been so embarrassed by her reaction to him. A pretty woman like that, with a heart like hers, was bound to have been snatched up already.

Astraia felt her hand being released abruptly, and the handsome man began backing away from her with an odd expression on his face.

"Sorry." Dante apologized, irritated that he sounded so flustered. "If you are all right then," he said crisply. Nodding toward her, he felt an overwhelming sickening sensation flood into his gut as he spoke. Staring at her briefly, he suddenly realized what he had just done. Reaching up towards his face in alarm, it occurred to him he'd failed to put his brown colored contacts in before leaving for the store this morning. He'd told her his name was Kastle, his alias, rather than Dante. Unsure what the possible ramifications of that would be, he grabbed up his bag from the ground and swiftly turned away.

What had he been thinking? What had he done? He was in the middle of an undercover operation right now. How could he have possibly managed to slip up so badly?

Astraia watched for a second as he walked away. Then, grabbing hold of her cart again, she guided it this time around the offending pothole, limping slightly as she went.

There was no point in daydreaming over a man like that. He was handsome, true. His eyes had riveted her, and his touch on her skin, her face, had sent a shiver up her spine. None of this made any difference though, because Astraia was married and had three children who needed her. Regardless of her inner turmoil, she loved her family, and would never do anything to destroy what she had. Refusing to allow temptation to rule her, she proceeded on to her car.

Shaking her head to clear the fantasies, Astraia couldn't imagine that this Kastle guy would have ever taken a second look at her if it weren't for her spilling her cart. After all, at five foot three inches tall, and what felt like about fifty pounds of extra weight on her since having the kids, she didn't imagine she was his type anyway. Men like that went for women with long legs, shapely figures, and beautiful faces. All of which, Astraia knew full well, she was not.

- - -

Watching the scene unfold, the angel called Maleeka frowned over at his counterpart. They stood together, unaffected by the wind blowing around them. Garbed in white pants, a snug fitting long sleeved t-shirt, and wide leather belt with scabbard attached, the one called Woreash narrowed his gaze at the man curiously.

Still holding his sword in hand, he observed as the man lifted the woman from the ground with one arm and nodded with approval. The wise eyes that met Maleeka's gaze were filled with light, as he stood with his sword still unsheathed.

"Are you sure she's the one?" Maleeka asked with uncertainty.

"Oh, yes. Did you not see what she did at the register?" Woreash asked of his friend. "Her generosity will serve to go a long way today. And it has taught the woman who received the gesture, as well as those who witnessed it, a great lesson." Staring at him, Woreash saw Maleeka nod, his long dark mane of hair rustling around his baggy shirt sleeves.

Like Woreash, he was wearing all white and had a thick braided leather belt with scabbard hanging from his waist. In contrast, however, Maleeka had the habit of dressing in blousy, loose-fitting pants that were somewhat reminiscent of the long skirts of old. He didn't like to be constrained by clothing at all, but as they were on occasion seen by human eyes, it was necessary for the sake of mankind's sanity.

"She has a kind heart. Not even he moved to step in."

"He would have, had she not," Woreash replied, shrugging absently. "Yes, we've found her exactly where the Lord said she would be." Woreash was pleased their search was over, and none too soon, for time was running out.

"But is it too late? Tomorrow is the deadline and she is married to another. You know as well as I that He would never allow..." Seeing Woreash shaking his head vigorously, Maleeka looked back at the man and woman as they went their separate ways.

"What do you know that I don't?" Maleeka asked suddenly.

Woreash sighed sadly. "She is not legally bound to him by man's law, for he is not who he says he is."

A look of surprise crossed Maleeka's face before becoming thoughtful. "She is still bound to him by the flesh."

Shaking his head Woreash said grimly, "He's on the list, Maleeka. Something, it would seem, is already in motion. There's a decision to be made today that will affect her one way or another. How she responds will determine all their fates, as well as her children's."

Eyes widening, Maleeka stared at Dante as he disappeared. He'd noticed his reaction to her, so it was clear there was already something there.

"This cannot be a coincidence." Maleeka was hopeful. He glanced again at his partner.

"I agree, but in the end, it is still up to her. They must come together of their own accord. We cannot influence them, especially in this instance." Woreash said while sheathing his sword.

"Those pesky demons are getting aggressive lately." Maleeka's tone became testy as he watched Astraia limp the rest of the way to her car. "That one would have had that car run her down if you hadn't killed it. Think it was one of Zalman's gang?"

One of the devil's many commanders, the demon Zalman had become extremely unpredictable of late.

Frowning, Woreash nodded. "Yes, I have seen him among Fallen's ranks. Regardless, I took care of him and now we know for sure."

"So it would seem. Why else would the demons be intent upon causing the death of this one otherwise." Maleeka extended a hand towards the woman. "Normally they are content with merely tormenting the humans unless they pose a threat."

They both watched her as she struggled with the groceries. Managing to finally unload her cart, she stood, debating whether there was time to return it to the stall. In that same instant, Maleeka appeared suddenly next to her and spoke near her ear.

"Return it only if you'll make it on time, Little Star."

"I hate leaving the carts out everywhere, but being late for the boys would be worse," Astraia said aloud. She pushed the cart out of the way near the front of her vehicle.

Turning, as Woreash appeared by his side, Maleeka laid his hand on the hilt of his sword. Nodding in the direction of the woman gingerly stepping into her car, Woreash instructed accordingly.

"You stay with her. I'll follow him. I expect we will meet up again soon."

"Woreash, if this does not go as we want, it could be a very long time before God will allow us the chance to right this wrong again. Have you any word…?"

"No. For now, we shall simply have to see how this plays out."

With those final words, Woreash disappeared, and Maleeka took a seat next to Astraia in her car. Starting the ignition, she sighed heavily, then glanced wearily at the clock on her dashboard. Oblivious to Maleeka's presence, she backed up and proceeded on her way to her children's preschool.

Chapter 3

Scrubbing vigorously at the casserole pan, Astraia wished for the second time that night that she'd taken the time to line the dish with aluminum foil. Flustered, and mad at both the dish and Dylan, she threw the S.O.S. pad into the sink. Water splashed across her chest and face.

"Calm down, Honey. I didn't mean…"

Cutting her husband off before he could finish, she turned and pointed at him, flinging water across the room in the same motion.

"No, Dylan. I won't calm down," she vented while trying hard not to smirk and take satisfaction in seeing him wipe his hand across his face. "I'm tired of this. Something has got to give. I cannot keep doing everything around here," she declared, gesturing toward the house in general, "and be expected to work a full-time job! It's too much."

"Honey, listen to me." Dylan crossed the room and took her firmly by the shoulders. "When you start your new job, I promise I'll help out more around the house. I *am* capable of doing a load of laundry now and then." He grinned mischievously and wrinkled his eyes while waggling his eyebrows at her.

Dylan was clearly attempting to add levity, while also trying to get her to do what he wanted at the same time. It was the same old manipulation game he'd been using ever since they'd gotten married. But Astraia had finally become wise to his ways.

Shaking her head, she knocked his arms away angrily. "Oh, no you don't. I am not falling for it this time."

"Falling for what?" He gestured plaintively towards her with outstretched arms, his facial expression deliberately set to appear confused.

Astraia knew better.

"Dylan O'Kahner, don't you dare make me promises that you and I both know you won't keep." She spat the words out angrily.

Her husband had the good sense to look at her in surprise.

Silence filled the room.

In the background, she could hear her three children playing in the boys' bedroom down the hall.

She glared at him defiantly, her hands balled in fists on either side of her.

"That's all you ever do. You make promises, then you break them." Her voice trembled in anger. "You tell me you're going to do something and you don't do it. Like this past weekend when you said you'd join us for church, and then couldn't be bothered to get out of bed. If it were just me it wouldn't bother me so much, but you promised them, Dylan!" She snarled quietly, gesturing to the living room and down the hall. Seeing him shaking his head her eyes narrowed.

"Yes, you did. That very night before, you swore you would attend, and then you broke your promise. I'm sick of it." Shaking, she went on. Tears were starting to well in her eyes. "Honestly, Dylan, I'm beginning to believe you're actually physically incapable of making a promise and keeping it."

With a heavy sigh, her husband sat down in his chair at the table. He glanced around the small room while rubbing his temple, not meeting his wife's gaze. After a moment, he finally looked up at her, as if seeing her for the first time.

Noting her drawn and tired expression, he could see how weary she was of their fighting. Tired of the same old debate, he thought quickly, seeking a change of subject to distract her.

"How long exactly have you been unhappy?"

Taken aback by the unexpected question, she didn't answer right away. Realizing what he was doing she sighed in frustration.

"Don't try and change the subject. This discussion isn't about whether I'm happy. It's about whether I should have to go back to work. And I'm telling you, I need a break." Exasperated and tired of constantly having to keep the conversation on the topic, Astraia limped over to the table, and gently slid into a chair across from him. She had been favoring her right leg most of the day, after the incident with the cart.

Crossing her arms in front of her on the table, she began pulling the wrap off her arm from her plasma donation that day. It was so tight this time it was starting to hurt. Wadding the bandages up in a ball, she tossed it in the trash, then leaned down and rested her head on her arms. After a moment, she drew her head up slowly, wearily, and met his gaze. Apparently, he had been watching her the whole time.

"Dylan, why are you so insistent that I overextend myself like this? Do you have any comprehension of what my days are like? Or do you just take for granted that everything is going to get done?"

Leaning back in his chair, Dylan raised his arms above his head. Frustrated by her constant nagging, he was becoming irritated with her. Why should he be the only one working? His wife acted as though she was being overworked or something. She was just a housewife for heaven's sake. What all could she possibly have to do in a day?

"Tell you what, Astraia. You remember that list you asked me to make the other night? The one of all the current responsibilities we have?"

Astraia nodded slowly, wondering where he was going with this.

"Did you finish yours?"

"Yes. Why?" she asked suspiciously.

"I finished mine and it's almost half a page," he said proudly, as though half a page was a lot. Getting up, he took the few short steps to his desk and grabbed a letter-sized tablet of paper that had been laying there. "Let's compare them, and if your list is longer than mine, then you don't have to work anymore and I'll never ask you to get a job again." Smiling confidently, as if he'd just won an argument, Astraia couldn't help but burst out laughing at the sight of him standing there looking pleased with himself.

"You're on! And I'm holding you to that, buddy," she responded. Walking over to her desk, she took her own pad of paper from the file drawer. Tossing it on the table in front of him, she continued, "There you go; four and a half pages. I only did the front side, as I figured it would be easier for you to look through."

Stunned, he looked down at her list, leafing through it.

"You're kidding me, right?"

"Nope." She placed her hands on the table and leaning in closer to him. "And I didn't even list job hunting."

- - -

The unusually cool Florida breeze flowed in from the window, as Astraia burrowed deeper under the warm blankets of her bed. Rolling onto her back, she stretched languorously under the covers.

Astraia debated whether to get up and finish closing the bedroom window. Dylan liked having a bit of a chill in the air when he slept, but he wasn't home yet. The draft coming from the window was not only cold but, she noted, was attempting to extinguish the dozens of candles she'd lit around the room.

Making the decision to brave the cold, she stood quickly, shivering as she held her arms close to her body, and made a beeline for the window. After shutting it completely, she dove for the covers.

Wisps of her long, wavy blonde hair tickled her nose as they fell across her forehead once she had found a comfortable position. Pushing her hair away from her face, Astraia giggled, remembering her husband's last words when he left the house an hour before.

"Put them to bed, Astraia. Put them all to bed and I'll be back with cake and champagne before you know it. I'll show you how to really relax," he said as he winked.

Smiling as she rolled over, she lay in bed remembering the conversation of only a few hours earlier.

Recalling how Dylan had spent the better part of fifteen minutes going over her list of chores, he had sat in stunned silence, staring at her. She remembered how he'd looked at her when his face fell upon the list again. Standing, leaving her list on the table, he shook his head as if disgusted, and walked away. Grabbing his coat, he'd headed outside, taking his cigarettes with him. It was a long while before he returned. By then, she'd finished with the dishes, straightened and swept the kitchen, and was calling the kids from their bedrooms for their bath time.

Astraia marveled at how she'd been brave enough to just walk right past him as he stood in the hallway after returning inside. Instead of stopping and attempting to make amends with him, like she would normally do, she'd proceeded on to the bathroom to start bath water for the boys.

She was stripping them down to their birthday suits when Dylan came down the hall and stood in the bathroom doorway. He watched her quietly for a while. After a bit, his gaze started to make her a little uneasy.

"How is it you haven't filed for divorce already?" he'd asked quietly.

It had taken Astraia several moments to realize her husband was finally beginning to understand how much he took her for granted. Not waiting for an answer, he continued.

"You're so much stronger than I am, Astraia. I know at times I'm a hard man to love. I know I don't make it easy. Were I in your shoes, I couldn't do what you do. From the looks of that list, you don't even need me."

"I do need you, Dylan. I may be able to do all those things, but I could never provide for them the one thing that you give us." she'd said, pointing towards their boys.

"What's that?"

"Security," she responded simply. Wincing inwardly at the look that crossed Dylan's face, Astraia wished she could say he'd completely taken it the wrong way but that wouldn't be true.

Chuckling in disgust, Dylan inquired, "So you keep me around for the money?"

Astraia giggled and covered her face with her hands. His question had been absurd, and she couldn't help but laugh out loud.

"Right, because we're rich," she had said derisively, rolling her eyes in the process. "Our bankruptcy closed only a year ago. If it were only about the money, we wouldn't still be married. It's more than that, and I think you know it. Besides, I don't believe in divorce."

Looking at her quizzically, he'd asked, "How can you say that? You've been divorced before."

"You know full well the circumstances behind that. The marriage was based on a lie. Manuel never wanted or loved me. He was illegal and just wanted residency."

Tossing the washcloth in the water, Astraia sat for a moment, watching her boys play in the water with a dark expression on her face. Any time the subject of her previous marriage came up it always put her in a mood. After a moment, she'd continued, while still watching them play and not looking at him. Astraia had known she would need to choose her words carefully.

"I'm not going to try to justify my decision to divorce him. That said, I take my wedding vows seriously. I would still be married to him today if I thought he'd felt the same way about his vows. But he didn't, it was all a sham. The case officer at INS said I wasn't even legally married to him."

Seeing her husband wincing, Astraia could only imagine the haunted expression she must have on her face. In the process of her divorce, she'd learned that her ex-husband was still married to his supposed ex-wife, who still lived in Mexico with his daughter. That bit of news had sent her into depression for an entire year, once the dust had finally settled.

The age-old ache in her heart, though dulled by time, had returned once again, reminding her of the shame and embarrassment she'd experienced at Manuel's hand. The knowledge she'd been with him for three and a half years, sleeping in his bed as his wife, and hadn't been legally married, still hurt deeply.

Dylan pondered her words. "So you would have stayed with him even though you didn't love him?"

"I never said I didn't love him."

"But I thought..."

Standing, Astraia had faced him finally. "Knowing me as well as you do, Dylan, do you honestly think I would have married him if I hadn't loved him?"

"I suppose not." Pausing, he then asked the question she knew would be coming. "Does that mean you still love him?"

The way he'd looked at her at that moment, she could almost believe he had been worried about what her answer might be.

Astraia knew what he was hoping to hear; a simple no. But instead, she'd looked him directly in the face and answered his question with a question of her own.

"How could I possibly still love someone who would lie to me repeatedly? After a while, all you're left with is an empty hole in your heart."

She remembered waiting to see what his reaction would be. Whether he'd understand the parallel she'd made to their relationship. Instead, he'd smiled at her brightly, completely missing the point she'd been trying to make.

"I understand now. I guess the point I'm trying to make is this. You fix holes in our walls and repair headboards on beds. You change the tires and oil on our vehicles and you can even reseed the lawn all by yourself. You're doing things that you shouldn't have to be doing. Things that I should be doing for you, right?"

Astraia needed to look away from him. She dropped back down on her knees and began finishing the boy's bath.

"Right," she'd said simply, choking back a sob, hoping he wouldn't notice.

That's when she'd heard him take a deep breath.

"I promise, Honey, things are going to change around here. You aren't going to have to work so much anymore."

Feeling him bend down behind her, Dylan wrapped his arms around hers, pinning her in a hug so she couldn't move.

"Babe, you don't just need a break. You deserve a paid vacation, a chance to relax."

Announcing he would return with cake and champagne, Dylan left shortly thereafter.

Her husband seemed genuine when he spoke, as though he meant what he'd said. She remembered feeling a spark of hope inside and thinking that maybe, just maybe, for once, he wasn't lying to her again. Was it possible he was making her a promise he might keep?

Astraia had been touched by the gesture and was excited about his promises of relaxation, for she knew what that meant. A full body massage, something that he rarely gave her, but was, oh, so good at giving. They had been fighting for a couple weeks now, so neither one of them had been in the mood to initiate any kind of intimacy with the other, until now.

Giggling again like a schoolgirl as she yawned, Astraia wondered briefly at what was taking him so long to return, for there was a store just down the road.

Lord, he's made so many promises and broken them. Please let him keep his promise this time. I honestly don't think I can handle another broken promise right now, she prayed before drifting off to sleep.

Chapter 4

Agent Kastle, aka Dante Blackthorne, sped down the main road toward the O'Kahner residence in their sports utility vehicle, while banging on the wheel in frustration.

To say that the operation had gone south was mild. It had tanked like a sinking submarine.

Not only had a civilian gotten in the middle of his operation, but he'd gotten shot as well. Taken a bullet he wasn't meant to have taken.

Add to that the unfortunate issue of their identities being mixed up, and Kastle had a mess. One he was desperately trying to fix before things got worse, and the man's family had to pay the same price he had.

Alone in the vehicle, Kastle groaned aloud as he once again marveled at the unnerving coincidence of who the civilian wound up being. After pulling the man's ID from the wallet he had on him Kastle found out the man's last name had been O'Kahner. Thinking it odd to run into two different individuals on the same day with the same last name, Kastle tried Googling the man but found he was a ghost. Taking a chance, he looked up Astraia O'Kahner instead, managing to locate her Facebook account. That was when he learned that the man lying dead of a gunshot wound before him was the husband of the woman he'd met at the store that very morning. The discovery was both surprising and infuriating. Of all the people to find their way into the middle of their operation, it had to be that sweet woman's husband.

Slapping his hand against the wheel one more time for good measure, Kastle growled into thin air. They had been so close to bringing down Kobi Radford and his lousy drug cartel, which spanned seven countries, and this guy, Dylan, had to screw the whole thing up by killing the man's younger brother. And they still hadn't quite figured out why Dylan had been there, and how he had figured out about them in the first place.

Turning into the mobile home park, Kastle glanced in his rearview mirror and noticed a black Honda Pilot behind him. Pulling out a burner phone from his jacket, he punched in a number.

"That you back there?" His agitation was palpable.

"It's me. We aren't going to have a lot of time."

"Got enough to get them out?"

"It's going to be tight but a well-planned accident bought us another couple minutes."

"Understood."

Kastle ended the call and slid the phone back in his pocket as his GPS beeped at him, signaling that he'd reached his destination. Pulling into the driveway, he parked next to a gray 86' Crown Victoria. The SUV was barely in park when he leaped out and kicked the door shut, not taking the time to lock it.

God, I know I haven't prayed in a while, but if you could help me save this woman and her children I would be eternally grateful. They don't deserve this, Lord. Help me keep them safe, he prayed frantically.

Seconds later, Agent Jericho Henley had Agent Ricardo Pegueros pulled up behind both vehicles and jumped out. Stepping out from the driver's seat, Pegueros gave a mock salute to Kastle after he leaned over the hood.

"So, the rumors are false." Agent Pegueros said, speaking with a strong Spanish accent. "Good to see you're not dead."

"Get the car seats switched while we get them out. The doors are unlocked." Kastle told him. Not amused by his partner's poor sense of humor, he turned on his heel, dismissing Agent Pegueros's statement.

Smirking while walking around the Cherokee, Agent Pegueros did as he was told.

The other two men dashed for the front door. Kastle took hold of the house key Dylan had marked for him and quickly let themselves into the house, quietly closing the door behind them. Fully registering his surroundings, he made a beeline for the kitchen, with Henley trailing behind him.

Kastle could smell the familiar scent of lavender wafting from what appeared to be the master bedroom. Sensing Agent Henley sidle up quietly next to him, he noticed him pointing towards the soft faint light coming from under the doorway, just past the kitchen. In that same instant, the door opened suddenly and for a second they both stopped dead in their tracks.

While Kastle had the good sense to look away in discomfort, Henley, on the other hand, continued to stare at the naked woman standing in the doorway. Oblivious to the two men, Astraia stretched unabashedly, in what should have been the privacy of her dark kitchen.

Realizing Henley was gawking inappropriately at her, Kastle was about to move to cover her when they heard her speak.

"Dylan, it's after midnight," she could be heard to say softly in a tired voice. She stifled a yawn with the back of her hand. Clearly, the woman was expecting her husband. "Are you just now...?"

Tensing, Astraia suddenly registered that there were two men standing in her kitchen and neither one was her husband. Her voice stopped abruptly and her breath came up short. Her face registered shock. She was suddenly very aware of her state of undress, and she froze in a blind panic. Just as alarming was the realization that she recognized one of them as he stepped cautiously toward her, arms outstretched. He was the same man who'd saved her from the grocery cart earlier that morning. Only the closer he came she realized his eyes seemed different somehow.

Seeing the recognition in her eyes, Kastle spanned the remaining space between them in two quick strides. Squelching her startled cry by covering her mouth with one hand, he brought her up hard against him with the other. He was all too aware of her soft body against his chest but he couldn't allow this to distract him. It was imperative that he make her understand the severity of the situation and get her dressed quickly.

"Mrs. O'Kahner, I know you're scared, but we're not here to hurt you. My name is Agent Franclin Kastle, I work for the CIA." He spoke quickly, carrying her further into her bedroom. "Can I trust you won't scream if I release my hand and cover you?"

Nodding her head vigorously, Astraia trembled against him as he reached around to the dresser, grabbing an old flannel shirt he saw there and spun her around so she faced away from him. Wrapping it around her back, he tucked her arms into the sleeves, pulling the shirt together in the front for her to button it.

Once covered, he motioned for the other agent to enter the room. Seeing Agent Henley, Astraia appeared as though she were ready to bolt from the room. Taking hold of her arms gently, but firmly, Kastle set her on the bed while she finished buttoning her shirt with shaking fingers.

"Agent Jericho Henley, I'm with Homeland Security."

Astraia watched in confusion and renewed anxiety, as the second man produced identification from his jacket for her to see.

"It's not our intent to frighten you but we are running out of time, and I need you to listen very carefully."

Kastle canvassed the small room as Agent Henley spoke, noting the candles nearly burned down to their wicks. Wincing internally, it occurred to him that she had been waiting for her husband for some time.

"You are, Astraia Crystal O'Kahner?"

"Yes, that's me. What's this about?" she asked nervously. Her voice cracked as she pulled her shirt down from where it was cropping up. "Are you guys serious with this? Cause if this is a prank it's in very poor taste. My husband will not be amused, and he'll be home any minute."

"I assure you this is not a prank." Agent Henley glanced at Agent Kastle.

"Are you sure about that?" Astraia asked, first glaring at Henley, then at the second man. Seeing Agent Henley's confused expression, she explained her reticence at believing him. "Come on, Frank Castle is an Agent of S.H.E.I.L.D. and a character in a Marvel comic called the Punisher," she exclaimed as she pointed at the man called

Franclin Kastle while eyeing him with disbelief. Seeing the man roll his eyes, she noticed they were brown, rather than the shimmering pale blue she'd seen earlier in the day. "You can't seriously expect me to believe...."

Kastle glared at Henley then growled. "I told you this wasn't a good idea. We don't have time for this."

"Mrs. O'Kahner, this is very real. Agent Kastle, show her your badge," Henley said urgently.

"I'm telling you I'm changing my name. They never believe me." Exasperated, he pulled out his identification for her to see. Not for the first time, Kastle was swearing inwardly at his father's rather poor taste at humor, having given him this new name and identity fifteen years prior.

Staring down at his badge, Astraia noted the name was spelled differently than in the comic series. Eyebrows raised, she stared up at Agent Kastle suspiciously.

"How do I know that's a real badge? And your eyes are different." Pointing towards him, she gazed up at him suspiciously in the dim light. "You know what? I think you guys should come back when my husband gets home, which will be any minute, by the way. He's not the kind of man you want to mess with."

"Colored contacts, I had them in earlier today," Kastle replied in explanation, intentionally sounding nonchalant. He noted Agent Henley's curious gaze. "The badge is real and Dylan's not coming home," he finished after exchanging meaningful glances with Agent Henley.

Alarmed by what he'd said Astraia just stared, her heart in her throat. The agent called Kastle had spoken with such finality, it made her cringe. Glancing between the two men, she suddenly felt anxious and was becoming increasingly self-conscious at wearing nothing but a shirt.

"Why won't he be...?"

Agent Henley raised a hand to halt her and proceeded to explain. "For security reasons, I am not at liberty to go into detail about the evening's events. What I can tell you is that your husband found himself in the wrong place, at the wrong time tonight, and was killed."

Astraia's eyes grew wide. She gasped and her hands flew to her mouth. While Henley continued to explain, Kastle proceeded to rummage quickly through her dresser drawers.

"You and your children are now in great danger. You are persons of interest to the men who killed him." Henley nodded towards Kastle's huge frame. "For that reason, you and your family are officially being placed in protective custody. Agent Kastle will be handling your protection and security along with Agent Pegueros of whom you will meet shortly." Tucking his badge back into his pocket, Henley noticed Astraia appeared visibly relieved at hearing this, and yet, at the same time, angry.

"You and your children will assume new identities and be relocated."

"That's absurd!" Astraia's voice shook. Trembling upon hearing the alarming news, she watched in dismay as Agent Kastle tossed undergarments at her.

"If I'm to believe what you say…"

"Before he died, Dylan said not to tell you he was sorry," Kastle said out of the blue. He turned to look at her, gaining her attention. "He said you'd never believe it, from such a hard man to love like him anyway."

Gasping, Astraia's eyes grew even wider, and her hands flew to her mouth once again. Tears streamed down her cheeks at the realization that what they were telling her was true. Her children had just lost their dad. Though he may not have been the easiest man to love or live with, he *was* her husband, and he'd always been good to her.

Overcome with grief, she wiped at her eyes and tried hard to pay attention to what the agent was saying.

Seeing both belief and sadness in her eyes, Kastle took an uneasy breath and kept searching through her things for a pair of pants. He couldn't shake the feeling that they were running out of time, fast.

"We need to get you and your children safely relocated." Agent Henley tried to reassure her while reaching out to take a hold of her arm. "Let's go."

Jumping away from Henley, Astraia crawled up onto the bed. Standing as far back as possible, she looked down upon them, appearing visibly shaken for some reason by Henley's advance.

Standing only a few feet from her, Kastle eyed her with concern before speaking up. His features were obscured by the gloom and shadows of the candles. "Astraia, you're perfectly safe with me. No one is going to hurt you while I'm around." He spoke with reassurance while glancing over at Agent Henley. Then he reached out to her as if trying to calm a child. "But there are men on their way, as we speak, who are intent on killing you and your children. We need to get you out now. It's past time to go."

Kastle looked at her evenly, the seriousness of the situation clear in his eyes. Reaching out to her, he helped her down from the bed, handing her the undergarments she'd dropped in the process. Overwhelmed by Kastle's size and proximity, Astraia took a shaky breath and released it. Embarrassed, she accepted her undergarments from him with trembling fingers.

"Can I at least grab…?"

"No." Henley cut her off and turned towards the bedroom door, anxious to get moving.

Taking her firmly by the arm, Kastle tried to guide her towards the door, but she shook him off.

"I *need* pants," Astraia stated flatly, squaring her shoulders. Feeling a lump forming in her throat at all the things she'd be leaving behind, she decided she didn't care in the end. All that mattered was her kids and a pair of pants.

"Please," she begged almost plaintively. Astraia glanced up, catching the glint in Agent Kastle's brown eyes.

Nodding his approval, Henley left the bedroom as she reached for her bottom dresser drawer to find a pair of jeans.

"Grab them, quick, and let's get your children." Kastle stood in the bedroom doorway, his face turned towards the kitchen to allow privacy as he waited.

Suddenly he tensed, the muscles in his jaw clenching as he put his hand to the cord extending from his ear. The next thing she knew, Agent Franclin Kastle was leaping across her bed after her. No longer able to see or hear Agent Henley, she didn't fully understand what was happening at first.

"We're out of time. When they walk through that door it is imperative that they believe I am your husband and that I have been here all night. Do you understand?" he asked gruffly. He proceeded to yank off his shirt. Kicking his shoes off at the same time, he decided to leave his jeans on for the sake of propriety.

He could see the fear in Astraia's eyes, along with acceptance as she nodded her head in assent.

"I've got this Henley. Go!" She heard him whisper harshly, before pulling the earpiece out. Then he tucked it under the pillow along with his gun. "What are you willing to do to protect your children? How far would you be willing to go?"

Astraia could hear the urgency in the agent's voice even though it was calm. Unshed tears brimmed from her eyes as he searched her face, seeking a signal from her.

"Just tell me what to do." Astraia's voice shook as she trembled. Kastle watched with admiration when she lifted her chin with resolve.

Flicking the blankets down toward the end of the bed, he picked her up with ease and placed her in it. Hastily crawling in after her, he pulled the blankets up over them, kneeling over her as he did so.

Astraia's eyes grew wide, believing she understood what his plan was, as he positioned himself over her. Panic welled in her throat but she forced it down. Wriggling awkwardly beneath him, she attempted to gain a more comfortable position. Fear overwhelmed her senses, preventing rational thought, and her ability to pray for protection.

Seeing her eyes widen, Kastle realized what she thought he intended to do to her. Vigorously shaking his head, he tried to quell her growing anxiety. "You misunderstand. My job is to protect you, not take advantage of you, so there's no need to be intimate. They'll think I'm your husband since we're in bed together and that they've made a mistake," he said, preparing himself mentally for Kobi's men to arrive.

Glaring up at him, she let out a strangled laugh. "It'll never work. They will never believe we are married," she said emphatically, her voice rising with panic as she spoke.

Astraia understood she needed these men to believe Agent Kastle was her husband, and she knew there was no way that would happen unless they did catch them in the act. She believed she was too fat, and unattractive, for that to be possible otherwise.

"You have to make love to me." She said finally, sounding frightened as she voiced the inappropriate demand.

Both startled and shocked by her suggestion, he could see the distress on her face and in her eyes.

"Franc, please." She whimpered the agent's first name desperately. Tears streamed down her face. While she pleaded with the man above her, a war waged within her. The fear, of what could happen to her children if he refused outweighed the fear she was experiencing at the notion of committing adultery at that moment. Reaching around him, she tried to pull him closer.

"This is dangerous. It's been way too long … and I could hurt you." He attempted to distance himself while eyeing her warily. His facial expression was pinched, and his muscles tensed as he looked back into her eyes. Recalling the inappropriate thoughts, he'd had of her earlier in the day, he struggled to maintain what little control he had. What she was suggesting was tempting but he knew it would be wrong. It went against everything he'd been taught growing up and everything he believed. At the same time, he felt compelled to assuage the fear that was obviously growing steadily within her.

Believing his reticence was because he was revolted by her, Astraia started to cry, terrified by the thought her inability to excite him was going to get her children killed.

"Stop," Kastle demanded sharply. His face and body flooded with heat and he could feel her wriggling below him. "I can't control…"

"Please, please…" she squealed in panic as tears dripped down face to the pillow below her. She thought… Yes, she was sure of it now. The squeak of the loose floorboard in the entryway was proof that someone had entered her house. "They'll never believe we're married otherwise..."

Chapter 5

Unknown to the couple laying in the bed, a war was being waged around them, as well as throughout the rest of the house. A deathly cold had seeped in through the walls, as dozens of inky, black, shapeless clouds spilled through the windows and doors.

Met by three angelic figures with warrior builds, garbed in white attire of varying styles, the demons instantly coalesced into the dark shapes of men. Their once beautiful eyes, now red for the evil within them, gleamed with menace. Swords appeared in their hands as if they'd grown from the base of their arms. Clasping them tightly, the demons began fighting ferociously to aid their leaders who were already in the bedroom.

In the bedroom, four dark figures parried with the angel called Woreash, as another demon knelt over the bed, whispering in Kastle's ear, as well as Astraia's. Sensing the damage the demon called Fallen was creating, Woreash howled in frustration as he attempted to fend off Veranke and Zalman; two of the devil's favored minions.

Whirling about as he sensed another sudden presence behind him, he was relieved to see Maleeka appear with sword already drawn.

"About time you showed," Woreash practically shouted as Maleeka struck a killing blow to the demon now exploding before them, its black cloudy essence fizzling to the floor, disappearing into it.

"I couldn't exactly let you have all the fun, now could I?" Maleeka replied while charging Fallen. Nearly catching the demon on its side, it came up off the bed at the last minute. "Now, now, Fallen. You know full well you're not allowed to influence them in this."

"You've no place here." Fallen howled, distracted from his charge.

"Nor do you, either. We've been sent to prevent your meddling."

"And you know full well that we cannot allow this to happen! For we've been sent by..."

"Yes, yes we know. How is Luci' doing by the way?" Maleeka mocked, his blue eyes flashing with holy light.

Growling with unconcealed rage, the four remaining demons roared at the insult, igniting within them a feral desire to kill their adversaries.

"Must you incite their ire?" Woreash asked with not but a little hostility, glaring over at his friend while fending off a worthy jab to his gut from Veranke's lackey. Whirling around, Woreash bashed at two of the demon's blades, sending them to the far corner of the room in retreat.

"Yes, I must. As you can see it makes them much easier to defeat. They get sloppy." Maleeka said above the clang and clatter of the swords all the while grinning.

Snarling at Maleeka as a second sword appeared in Fallen's opposite hand, the demon, now thoroughly distracted from his original intent, met the angel in mid-air. Snatching at Maleeka's long braid, he attempted to cut it off but was thwarted by the angel's strong free hand grasping his wrist. Crying out in pain at the burning sensation he was experiencing at the contact, Fallen wrenched away from him, cradling his red inflamed wrist. At the same time, Maleeka deftly thrust behind him with his sword, killing the fourth demon as it attempted to sneak up on him.

Hearing Zalman roar with anger at losing yet another of his lackey's, Woreash grinned, while deflecting another of his tiresome attempts at cutting off his head.

"What's wrong, Zalman?" Woreash parried with Veranke. "Tired of losing your minions, are we?"

Growling darkly as he hissed, Zalman replied. "I actually liked that one!" The demon shouted as he seethed, then shrugged at Veranke's dark glare.

Zalman could tell his commander was not pleased with how things were going. Kobi Radford's henchman entered the house as they fought. Yet the humans in the bed below them were taking matters into their own hands. If the three men didn't get to them soon, then it would be too late to stop what the Lord had ordained would come to pass nearly fifteen years before.

Out of nowhere, a bright white light radiated down through the ceiling toward the bed. Halting abruptly in their fighting, the angels looked away and then soared up through the ceiling, knowing full well they could not be present any longer. The remaining demons turned toward the bed in dismay and then were suddenly punted from the room through the ceiling as an explosion of light appeared without warning.

Howling with pure rage at their defeat, Zalman, then Veranke, charged after Fallen, who had the good sense to disappear quite suddenly from view. Hovering in the sky above the house, Maleeka and Woreash peered down below them, using their ability to see through the ceiling of the living room, in order to watch the progression of the henchmen now moving through the kitchen.

A soft glow of light filling the bedroom obscured their ability to see inside as the men halted suddenly in the kitchen. The angelic warriors, for the most part, were holding their own in the living room but as they watched the ensuing battle, Woreash noticed two demons attempting to attach themselves to the men in the kitchen. Shooting down towards the house, he beckoned for Maleeka to follow.

"If they attach themselves to the humans, they will not survive the night," Woreash called out as he sped through the ceiling. Slicing his sword through the figure of the first man standing near the bedroom door, a loud screeching sound reverberated through the air as the demon within exploded out from the man's body and fizzled to pieces, which fell through the floor.

The body of the human barely flinched. His expression became confused and disoriented. The bright glow within the bedroom dissipated suddenly, and the room was left in shadows. Standing in the doorway of the bedroom, Radford's man stared into the room in confusion where the sounds of heavy breathing could be heard.

Catching the second demon as he attempted to jump into the other henchman, they battled him briefly. Realizing their numbers were dwindling fast, and that he was outnumbered, the demon fled through the window, escaping just as Woreash sliced through the air where he had just been.

Woreash and Maleeka turned towards the bedroom and watched anxiously as the two men entered the room. Knowing full well how this would likely play out,

Woreash attempted to urge the two men to leave but they wouldn't listen to reason. Hearing the woman's shaky voice as she tried to get Kastle's attention, the two angels exchanged uneasy glances and waited to see if they were needed.

"Dylan," Astraia could be heard whispering urgently, referring to Agent Kastle by her husband's name. "Somebody is watching from the doorway."

Nodding his approval at her quick thinking, Woreash listened intently from outside the bedroom door, while turning towards Maleeka. Distracted, he missed seeing one of the demons slither around toward Radford's man in the living room.

Regaining his composure quickly, Kastle's senses were once again on high alert. Remembering that Dylan had said he had a six-year-old daughter before he died, Kastle used that to his advantage.

"Sayleena, Honey! Not now! Go back to bed, baby…" Intentionally stopping short, he turned his head to look, pausing for effect. "What the…? Man, what are you doing in my house?" He roared.

Standing just inside the doorway of the bedroom, Kobi Radford's men stared in confusion, while the third could be heard pacing in the living room. The men held 50 caliber guns at their sides, which were barely visible from behind their legs. They seemed dumbfounded and at a loss for words until one finally moved towards the side of the bed and spoke as the second man came further into the bedroom.

"Wait a minute, you're married? This is your wife?" He pointed his gun at Astraia in disbelief, the silencer already in place. Wincing, she turned her head away, imagining all the reasons why he looked surprised. Fear and dread enveloped her at the sight of the gun so close to her head.

"That's right, and you just broke into the wrong house, buddy." Agent Kastle rolled off the bed, taking Astraia with him while flinging the blanket over her head. In one swift motion, he grabbed his gun in one hand, and the hunting knife he'd seen on the dresser in another, leaving her huddled on the floor behind the bed.

Surprised by Kastle's sudden movement, Astraia covered herself with the flannel shirt, and cowered on the floor near her nightstand, under the blanket. Unable to see what was happening, she shut her eyes anyway and cringed in terror at the sounds around her.

Rushing to her side, Maleeka hovered near the floor next to her as four large feathery wings sprouted instantly from his back. Whispering urgently in her ear to stay put and stay covered, the angel encased her with his wings for protection. The Lord had impressed upon him that it was not her time.

Distracted by the scene before them, Radford's men raised their guns a few seconds too late, their reaction times having been diminished.

Flinging the hunting knife across the room, Agent Kastle hit the man near the doorway square in the chest, causing the henchman to fall to the kitchen floor as his gun went off. The bullet shot wildly across the room and was deflected by Maleeka's giant wing. In the same fluid motion, Kastle raised the gun in his hand and shot the closer man, placing two rounds in him, one in the head, then chest. Kastle's actions had been so quick the henchman never had a chance to get a shot off, though he'd flung his gun-wielding hand up to shoot.

Moving around the bed to a better position, Kastle took his Sig Sauer P-239 up in both hands. The shot made little noise as his gun had a silencer, but the third man heard the faint whine nonetheless and ran to the bedroom doorway.

Alarmed to see black eyes staring out from the third henchman's face as he rushed towards the bedroom, his Glock at the ready, Woreash turned on the spot. Shoving his sword out in front of him, the blade went straight through the henchman's chest as he ran through the angel.

A keening wail erupted into the night air as the demon, now dangling from the sword, exploded in front of Woreash's shimmering eyes. Turning back around, Woreash watched as Kobi's last man barely had a chance to glance down and see his buddy on the floor before he was shot, both in the chest and head.

Agent Kastle never skipped a beat. Yanking the blanket off of Astraia, he took hold of her arm, instructing her to keep her eyes closed. He hastily dragged her up from the floor just as Maleeka disappeared abruptly, reappearing next to Woreash. She was shaking visibly but moved quickly in step with him as he directed her towards the door. Lifting her up over the bodies, he forced her head towards the living room, so she couldn't see the carnage on her bedroom and kitchen floor.

Shoulders falling as they gazed upon the men now lying dead on the floor, the angels' eyes glistened while they watched the spirits lift out from within their human bodies. Hovering above the now empty shells, like ghostly reflections of themselves, they waited for their judgment.

A tear trickled down Woreash's cheek as the Angel of Death appeared. Raising his head to the ceiling, he then shook his head, extending his arm below him, rather than above.

With a sudden fury, the demons from within the living room halted in their fight, sensing their presence was needed for a transfer. Deferring to the age-old rule of precedence, the angelic warriors sheathed their swords, bowed their heads towards Maleeka and Woreash and then disappeared.

Gnashing their jaws angrily at having to allow the angelic warriors to retreat, the demons coalesced back into their black wispy forms and soared together toward the bedroom. The chilly air seemed to flow with them as they passed by the humans, causing a faint, almost imperceptible shiver to run the length of the mortals' bodies as they moved into the kitchen. Latching onto the spirits, they dragged them down to the floor of the mobile home as the ghostly essences cried out with dread.

Turning their attention back to Kastle as he placed Astraia back on the floor in the kitchen, the angels looked on while she frantically attempted to button her shirt. Narrowing his gaze upon the couple, Maleeka made a noise of frustration and turned towards Woreash.

"We should hover. There will likely be stragglers." He showed clear signs of disapproval.

"Maleeka, wait..." Woreash said, but his friend disappeared abruptly from view. Shaking his head, he sighed heavily, knowing full well why Maleeka was so upset.

Chapter 6

Astraia could hear him speaking but didn't understand what Agent Kastle was saying. It sounded like he was speaking Spanish. She watched him with trepidation as he glanced from one side to another, while they stood next to the fridge in her kitchen.

Unable to see or sense the angelic presence nearby, they waited there, as Kastle held his gun at the ready, in case there were more. Noticing her attempting to glance back the way they came, he pulled her into him, turning her face to his chest.

Shaking his head, he whispered roughly, "You don't want to see that. It will scar you for life."

Astraia saw perspiration beading along his brow. Nodding, she huddled next to him in silence. Her heart was pounding in her chest like she'd never experienced before. She couldn't believe what she had convinced Agent Kastle to do to her as her husband lay dead somewhere. The guilt and shame of it all overwhelmed her. Horrified by what she'd done, she closed her eyes and turned her head away from him so he couldn't see her face.

Knowing full well what she was thinking, Kastle refused to allow her to berate herself over what happened. Cupping her face in one hand, he forced her to look back up at him.

"Don't," he whispered.

Shaking uncontrollably, Astraia stared blankly back at him.

Distracted, Kastle placed a hand against his ear, then spoke what Astraia thought might have been the words, 'all clear', but she wasn't sure. Having been married to a Mexican for over three years, she'd never learned much more than broken Spanish at best. Seeing him lower his weapon, he released his hold of her as he looked down at her.

"That never should have happened." Kastle's remorse was clear in his tone. He could see her face screw up painfully in distress.

"I'm sorry. I am so sorry."

He shushed her with his finger firmly pressed against her lips. "You misunderstand. *I* lost control, and *I'm* sorry. I am the one to blame for what happened."

Laughing almost hysterically, Astraia swiped at the tears threatening to cascade down her face. Mortified by her behavior, her eyes darted about anxiously, as her face flushed with heat. "How can you say that?" she wailed, becoming hysterical. "I'm a married woman, and I all but made you...."

"No, you are a widow now," Kastle interrupted her. "I know that may sound harsh, and I know everything that's happened is a lot to process but you should not experience guilt over what has, and will, transpire. No one would blame you for wanting to protect your children in every way possible." He spoke gently, though his words confused her. Looking at her intently, he went on. "What you did distracted those men and helped me keep you alive." Resting a hand on her hip, his gaze roamed over her in appreciation. "You're alive. That's all that matters right now."

Astraia shivered. She could see his eyes roaming over her. Refusing to look at him, she fidgeted, trying to ignore the direction of his gaze. When she finally did look back at him he was still staring at her. She attempted to fix the buttons again, only to realize that several buttonholes had been ripped.

Shaking, she imagined what Dylan would think of her if he could see her now. He would probably call her a whore. Sniffling miserably, she realized she must be. After all, she'd just begged a man she didn't know to make love to her. Guilt washed over her anew, and she was very aware of Agent Kastle next to her.

Blushing, Astraia's eyes darted away. She tensed in distress at the sight of Agent Henley stepping into the kitchen. Beams of moonlight hit him in the face, making his features and goatee easier to see. She didn't recall seeing which direction he'd come from. Had he been in one of her children's bedrooms the whole time?

"It seems you were right, after all, Agent Kastle." Henley stood with his hands in his pockets. It was clear he could see their state of undress for his eyes roamed her bare legs.

"About what?" Kastle asked, realizing he needed to redress quickly.

"About bringing that SUV back. This would have been a lot less believable initially had there only been one car in the drive."

"Yeah, would have been." He nodded, moving back to the bedroom to find his pants and t-shirt. "Turn away, Astraia. Don't look."

Making sure her gaze was toward the living room, he turned on the light and found them on the floor. The black jeans were easily accessible, but his shirt had gotten caught under one of the bodies, and it was now a bloody mess.

Groaning in frustration, he stepped quickly back into his jeans and shoes, leaving the shirt behind. Grabbing a towel from the bathroom, he wiped the blood from his chest, face, and hands with vigor. Noticing that his fingers were trembling, he shook it off, sequestering his emotions to be able to complete the job. Though he'd been well trained for such actions, the blood still bothered him. He always had to remind himself that he was saving far more lives than the ones he took. Yet, it was still never easy to take a life.

Turning towards Henley, his eyes narrowed darkly as he spoke, his tone carefully controlled. "It shouldn't have been this close in the first place. What happened to those extra few minutes you were supposed to buy us?"

Henley shrugged. "It all worked out in the end." Swiveling his head from side to side, he moved around the kitchen and back into the bedroom, passing by Astraia. He took in the state of the bed, and then looked at Kastle suspiciously.

"So, you got this, do you?" Agent Henley spoke coldly as he glared.

"In your absence, the situation warranted a more believable scenario." His response was evasive. He stood squaring his shoulders, with hands on hips. Staring Henley down, Kastle didn't look away until the other man had first. He wasn't about to embarrass Astraia by telling him she'd initiated it. No, he'd take the heat for this.

Shaking his head in disgust, Henley glanced back toward her, but she couldn't bear to meet his gaze.

"Mrs. O'Kahner, do you need any medical attention?" He asked her quietly.

She watched Kastle tense at the implication he was making. "No, I ... I'm fine." She stuttered awkwardly, feeling much like a teenager who had been caught in the act with her boyfriend. The man was making her very anxious. She didn't like the way he was looking at her.

"Then it's time to go." Henley walked back over the bodies as if they weren't even there. He headed back out of the bedroom into the kitchen. Standing with his back to her, she could see him raking his hands across his face. Then, with long strides, he walked down the hallway towards her boy's bedroom as a Hispanic man came in through the front door.

"We gonna do this already?" The man carried what appeared to be a small body bag in his arms. He followed Henley down the hall.

Astraia moved to the center of the kitchen as both men walked down the hall. Cautiously watching them, she wondered what they thought they were doing.

"We must be quick," she heard Kastle say behind her. She could see Henley and the other man carrying the curiously still forms of Saruman and Storman down the hall toward them. Her heart leaped to her throat and she gasped as they turned instead and disappeared through the front door.

"What are they doing?"

"Taking them to the vehicle." Kastle's voice was calm. He avoided her gaze as he walked away, heading towards her daughter's bedroom.

"I'll get your daughter. You have one minute to grab any personal items they might require." He turned then, realizing she had not been following. "Astraia, it's going to be okay. But we must hurry."

The situation seemed so surreal. She'd just been intimate with a stranger and now she was supposed to pack up their lives in sixty seconds. Silently praying that the Lord would be able to forgive her, she grabbed her boys' duffel bag from her desk, dumped the contents of her purse in it, and threw in the last of the nighttime pull-ups from the bookshelf in the living room. She tossed their coats in a pile near the door and ran down the end of the hall to the boys' room to get their little blankets and favorite stuffed toys they couldn't sleep without.

After grabbing Storman's items, she reached for Saruman's on his bed and saw the body of a little boy. Gasping in surprise, she stepped on one of her boys' toy cars and fell to the floor on the same leg she'd injured that morning. Pain shot up through her leg to her hip, and she sobbed in distress as she stared at the body.

From where she lay on the floor, she could see through the boys' bedroom doorway. She glanced down the hall and saw Agent Kastle coming out of her daughter's room, carrying Sayleena in his arms. She knew she was running out of time, so she crawled on her knees and reached in their dresser drawers, grabbing underwear, socks, and a couple changes of clothes for both boys.

Limping back down the hall to Sayleena's room, she had just shoved her little blanket and stuffed chocolate bunny into the bag when Henley popped his head in through the bedroom doorway, startling her. Her heart leaped in her chest. Walking past her, he dumped the still form of a little girl onto her daughter's bed and rolled the body bag it had been in under his arm.

"Let's go." His tone brusque, he stepped aside, waiting to follow her out. Astraia's heart leaped from her chest to her throat. She stared down at the little girl with similar hair to her daughter's, wondering at how and why her life had been taken from her. That could have been Sayleena, she thought, as her eyes grew wide, and she began breathing heavily. Forcing her eyes away as bile rose from her belly into her esophagus, she tried to drive the image out of her mind. God, please don't let that child, or any of the others, to have suffered.

Forcing her thoughts back to the task at hand, she tore the drawer to her daughter's dresser out. Grabbing the same essentials, she shoved them down into the bag. Astraia's fingers were shaking so badly, she could barely get the bag zipped. Henley reached down and zipped it for her. As the agent attempted to guide her out of the room, he placed his hand on her shoulder. She shrugged him off as if he'd burned her.

She could almost feel his eyes on her as she walked the short distance down the hall.

Standing at the front door, Kastle watched her progression down the hall while he held the coats she'd left there. Her face was stricken white and her pupils appeared to be dilating.

"I figured you'd have gone back for some jeans." Kastle nodded towards her bare legs.

Glancing nervously through the kitchen towards her bedroom, Astraia could see the still shapes of the bodies on the floor and began to tremble noticeably. Shaking her head, she stuttered, "I can't g… go back in there."

Reaching out for the bag, he took it from her and handed it to Henley, who sighed in disgust as he took it. "I'm sorry, of course," Kastle said, sounding chagrined. "I'll grab a pair of jeans for her and help deal with the rest. Why don't you take her on out, Henley?" Turning on his heal, Kastle walked back towards her bedroom.

Agent Henley walked her out of her house for the last time, looking as though he wanted to say something, but seemed to think better of it. He directed her to the black Honda Pilot parked at the end of the drive. The third agent she had yet to meet was now lifting what appeared to be another body bag from the ground. She could see him better in the moonlight and noticed this time that he had a shortly cropped mustache and goatee with brown hair and chocolate brown eyes.

Handing her the duffel bag, Henley silently motioned for her to get into the vehicle then walked away toward the house.

"I'm Agent Ricardo Pegueros, *Señorita*. Your *niños* are already safely strapped into the back section of seats." The man smiled as he gestured with his head for her to get into the second row.

Eyeing the interior, she asked suddenly in a whisper. "And where will Agent Henley be sitting?"

"Likely shotgun. Unless you'd rather him next to you," Pegueros finished with a grin.

"No," she said, sharper than she intended. "This is fine."

Carefully climbing in, she pulled down hard on the bottom of her shirt. Astraia hoped it didn't ride up as she went. Scooting all the way over towards the driver's side, she watched Agent Kastle moving quickly down the drive, holding a pair of jeans in his hands.

"Get it inside fast, Pegueros. Henley's in a snit and is about to start the fire." Kastle spoke hastily, sounding cross. Tossing the jeans at her, he lifted the second body bag with ease, pulling it over his shoulder as though he were lifting a bag of feathers and ran ahead of Pegueros towards the house.

Hearing Pegueros erupt in expletives as he struggled a little with his burden, she looked on anxiously. They both disappeared inside the house. At the same time, Henley walked out and down the steps, humming as he pulled gloves from his hands and placed them in his pockets. She then saw him pull out a lighter and casually light a cigarette.

"Let's go, let's go," Henley called towards the house. He held the cigarette between two fingers while scowling angrily.

Seconds later both men emerged from her single-wide mobile home and ran the short length to the vehicle. Watching as though mesmerized, Astraia saw Henley flick the cigarette toward the house, setting it on fire as it landed just inside the door. Flames burst out from the doorway and quickly enveloped the entryway along with the curtains hanging in the front window.

The look of horror was clearly etched on Astraia's face when Kastle hopped into the vehicle next to her. His mere presence made the sports utility vehicle seem visibly smaller. Reaching out, he patted her leg in a reassuring manner.

"You were never going back again anyways. There's nothing in there that cannot be replaced." He told her gently as he watched her deep blue eyes moisten with unshed tears. Her pupils had returned to normal but he was still concerned she might go into shock.

Seeking a distraction from the fire and the smoke now coming from what used to be her home, Astraia turned to check on her children. Relieved to see they had all slept through the whole ordeal without disturbance or waking, she wondered at that but assumed they were just exhausted.

"You should put those on." Kastle nodded towards the jeans still clutched in her hands near her lap.

Shaking her head up and down, Astraia slid her bare feet into the pant legs and wriggled her legs into them. Glancing in his direction, she saw him turn quickly away. Becoming self-conscious, she slid the jeans on. Zipping and buttoning her pants closed, she watched him peer back over at her, his eyes twinkling, as he chuckled. Looking away, heat suffused her face.

"Sure, now you're shy," Kastle said with humor.

Glancing back at him quickly, she noticed him smiling at her. She gave a timid grin back, took a deep breath, and shifted uncomfortably in her seat, leaning her head against the window. Her leg ached as she sat there anxiously twiddling at the small cross dangling from a chain at her neck while waiting for what came next.

Reaching around her, Kastle grabbed at her seatbelt, pulling it tight around her and latched her in. The action had forced a closeness they hadn't had since her bedroom. Their eyes met briefly before he sat back in the seat and buckled himself in.

Astraia stared out the window, looking up at the night sky. She noticed the full moon was out and shining brightly. Agent Pegueros hastily got into the driver's seat, while Agent Henley sat in front.

They took off.

She couldn't help but notice the tension between Agents Kastle and Henley as they drove along and had a strong feeling she was the reason for it. After a while, Astraia noticed that Henley had been texting for some time on his phone. He seemed agitated. Thinking she would ask what was happening, she was working up the courage to speak only to be stilled by Agent Kastle's large warm hand on her knee. Looking over at him, he shook his head as though he'd been reading her mind and knew what she was about to ask.

She watched as he glanced quickly over at Henley. His eyes narrowed. If Astraia didn't know better, she would have thought he seemed angry about something Henley had just said. But no one had said a word since Pegueros's discussion with Henley about teaching his son Tae Kwon Do. And that was easily fifteen minutes ago.

The unease in the vehicle seemed to increase exponentially the further they went. Even Pegueros could be seen glancing back and forth between Agents Henley and Kastle as if trying to assess the best way to diffuse a ticking time bomb. Unsettled by this, Astraia couldn't help but think there had already been enough drama in one night.

Turning from Astraia, Kastle focused his attention on Henley's back. He couldn't see his face but could tell regardless that the man was in quite a foul mood.

Kastle didn't want to know any more of the thoughts running through his pea-sized brain. But, for whatever the reason, the information was being given to him by the angel that was always with him. Learning what Henley's intentions were, Kastle grimaced in aggravation at the man's sheer stupidity.

From the moment Agent Henley had seen Astraia's bed sheets, he had been plotting and contriving the best way to lock him up, thinking he could do so without Kastle anticipating the move. The thought was laughable really, considering Agent Kastle's experience, expertise, and his ability.

Having worked with Agent Henley before, Kastle hadn't much cared for some of his tactics, nor his cocky attitude. Regardless of what his own personal feelings were, where Henley was concerned, he had to admit that the man was at least right about one thing. Agent Kastle had used poor judgment with Astraia, and he knew it.

Misconduct with their charges was not acceptable in his line of work. His job was to protect her and her children and keep them safe. Not take advantage of her. Whether she had tempted him or not, he should have had the fortitude to stop things before they had gone too far.

Glancing over at the woman next to him, he watched her curiously while she gazed out the window at the night sky. She appeared to be much calmer now. She did seem nervous about the level of tension in the vehicle. Interestingly, Astraia did not seem to care for Henley any more than Kastle did.

On several occasions, Kastle caught her casting furtive looks over at Henley, as if ever watchful. He could tell Astraia was lost in thought as to her situation, wondering where she was going and worrying about her children's response to the loss of their father. Curiously, she seemed to be only a little distressed over losing her husband. He wondered at that but chose not to probe further for now.

Breathing heavily as he looked away, Kastle turned his attention back to the man in front of him. Agent Henley was wrong about the most important aspect of what had happened. He had not actually forced himself on Astraia as he seemed to believe. The encounter had, in truth, been consensual.

Kastle was not about to correct him on this point, for he did not want this to become public knowledge, as it seemed to distress her a great deal. Her thoughts betrayed her, allowing him to be made aware of the guilt and embarrassment she was experiencing over encouraging him as she had.

Sitting quietly, Agent Kastle prepared himself to accept the inevitable consequences, waiting patiently for their arrival at the safe house.

Chapter 7

Battle-worn, the angels soared above the vehicle as it sped along the road below them. Swords unsheathed, they held them close, prepared for another foray if necessary. As they glanced furtively around, they investigated every shadow. After a thorough inspection of their surroundings, they nodded towards each other and made a beeline for the vehicle below them.

Touching down upon the sports utility vehicles rooftop, Woreash gestured for Maleeka to join him as the vehicle continued to move forward. Determined to see the enclosed passengers safely to their next destination, Maleeka's feet landed softly, spinning in place to face Woreash. Scowling at his friend, he turned on him. Lashing out angrily, he slashed his sword through the air.

"It should have never happened this way!"

"Maleeka, calm yourself," Woreash ordered, his tone unruffled.

"I will not. It was always meant to start with an act of love." His blue eyes flashed angrily and a lump formed in his throat.

"And you think it didn't?" he retorted just as angrily. "Is it not an expression of love to sacrifice of ourselves for those we love?"

Maleeka's aggressive stance wavered. He stared back at his friend, eyes softening, as he stared down at the roof of the vehicle. Averting his gaze to the skies above, he closed his eyes to the darkness below, seeking peace from the heavens. Eventually, looking back at Woreash, they stood facing each other. The vehicle continued to speed along.

"Do you think it was enough?" Maleeka asked, his curiosity getting the better of him.

"Yes, I do," Woreash grinned and laughed. "Did you hear Veranke howling in rage, as Fallen fled her room, trying to get away from him?" The sight of the demon's anger and subsequent punishment for their failure had been almost exhilarating to watch. "I do believe stopping him was Fallen's responsibility."

Smiling back at him almost crossly, Maleeka sheathed his sword and sat upon the roof. Looking up at Woreash, he motioned for him to do the same.

"This is one time I'd say; we can be thankful for mankind's lack of will."

"More accurately a Blackthorne man's lack of will, for they do seem to have trouble in this area," Woreash replied thoughtfully. "Though, I'm sure God would not see it that way. I imagine the circumstances which resulted in their union filled Him with great sadness."

Nodding in agreement, the messengers sat in companionable silence for a time, scanning the skies for their adversaries. They knew the woman's relocation might spare her from the dangers of man. But it would not spare her from the demons who sought to hinder God's will. They could find her whenever they wished.

"Their absence disturbs me. I'd have thought they'd be chasing her." Maleeka stated, deep in thought.

Shrugging, Woreash laid his sword in his lap, choosing instead to be ready if necessary.

"I can only presume they believe it's too late for her. Likely, they are regrouping, and moving on to the next one."

"Then we need to get to her, and quickly," Maleeka said urgently. One was thought to be already in place, but being the last of the first three, she was not their biggest concern now. But the second one was still unknown to them and needed to be found.

"Have patience, Maleeka." Woreash lifted his sword and crossed his legs. Sitting more comfortably in a relaxed state, he closed his eyes. He listened carefully to his surroundings, maintaining his vigilance.

"Patience! Are you kidding me?"

"Maleeka, we must see this one through. There is more at stake here with this one than just the prophecy. Their safety must take precedence right now."

Sighing heavily, Maleeka glanced around them, tensing as a car passed by. Woreash was right, of course, but that didn't dissuade the urgency he was feeling.

Sensing the woman's distress within, Maleeka chose instead to begin concentrating on the passengers, willing them to see reason.

- - -

An hour later, they arrived at what appeared to be a small office building. Astraia had no idea where they were and was too uneasy to ask. By the time they'd arrived, the tension inside the vehicle had become almost tangible.

At one point, not long before they had stopped, Agent Henley picked up his phone once more and began texting again. Shortly after, she heard Agent Kastle chuckle derisively next to her, and speak for the first time since they left her house.

"It would take more than that, Henley," Kastle said, getting a rise out of him.

Turning around in his seat, Henley faced Kastle head on. "Something you want to say to me, Agent Kastle?" he inquired, placing emphasis on the word 'agent.' Henley cocked his eyebrows as if daring him to speak.

"No. But I have a sense you've got a lot you want to say to me," he responded calmly as he leaned forward, getting right up into Henley's face.

Astraia could see the unease in Agent Henley's expression, as he'd turned back around, shrugging his shoulders. "There's nothing to say. What's done is done," he'd stated simply, finishing his last text. He placed the phone back into his pocket.

Glancing ahead of her, Astraia noticed Agent Pegueros looking back at her through the rearview mirror. He stared at her momentarily as if looking for a clue to the other two agents' behavior. Smiling slowly, he started chuckling but stopped when Henley glared over at him.

"What's going on?" Astraia asked tentatively. "Is there something I should know about?"

Henley wouldn't look at her. He stared straight ahead. "All you need to know is that you and your children are under my protection."

Kastle burst out laughing.

Confused, Astraia queried him in alarm. "But I thought Agent's Kastle and Pegueros…"

Interrupting her, Kastle placed his large hand on her knee. Leaning towards her, he spoke quietly.

"It's best to stay out of it, Astraia." Winking, he went on. "No worries. Your husband over there will take care of everything," he'd said loudly, giving Henley a pointed look.

Agent Henley just snorted in disgust.

"That's not funny." She snapped, gaining the attention of everyone in the vehicle.

Kastle glanced over at her in surprise. The angelic guide at his side made it obvious to him that the prospect of being protected by Agent Henley terrified her. Even without the angel's assistance, he could see in her expression it was true.

Knowing full well the other two men thought she was upset over the loss of her husband, Kastle turned to her and said aloud, "I'm so sorry. That was an extremely cruel thing to say under the circumstances."

Her breathing had become irregular, and he would bet if he had a stethoscope, it would tell him her heart rate had increased. Leaning over, he took her hand in his and squeezed gently.

"It's going to be okay." Kastle mouthed softly, realizing how distressed she was as her eyes brimmed with tears. He wished he could wipe away the fearful look on her face but knew that any consoling attempt he might make would be misconstrued by Agent Henley.

Astraia looked over at Pegueros self-consciously. He didn't seem to be laughing, or to be amused at all anymore. It was as though he had figured something out that she hadn't. He appeared agitated.

Seeing that they were waiting to be let into a gated parking lot near the vacant building, Astraia noted the light change on the gate monitor as the arm rose to allow them entry. They pulled in and parked near an elevator.

Proceeding to exit the vehicle, Agent Pegueros spoke. "This is our stop."

Unbuckling, Astraia reached down to grab the bag from the floor where it had been dropped. Stepping tentatively on her right leg, she got out of the vehicle and looked back at her kids. She couldn't help but be surprised at how well they were still sleeping.

Noticing the expression on her face, Pegueros got out. He came around to her door and placed his hand on her shoulder for reassurance. "They're going to be fine." She jumped at his touch. "No worries, they'll sleep really well for a while."

She watched as Pegueros disconnected the seat belt on Storman's seat and pulled him from the SUV.

"Let's get them inside shall we?" Pegueros gave her a reassuring smile. "We can lay them down where they'll be more comfortable when waking up."

Agent Kastle had just kicked the last door shut on the vehicle, when he shifted Sayleena in his arms, looking down at her.

"Your daughter is very beautiful. She reminds me of you." Kastle smiled and walked towards the elevator.

"She is very beautiful," Astraia agreed dully. "That means she looks nothing like me." Walking slightly ahead of them, she limped as she went. She did not see Agent Kastle stop suddenly, and then resume his progression behind her after a brief pause. His expression appeared troubled by her words.

The closer Astraia came to the elevator, the more she slowed down, allowing for Agent Pegueros to go in first. As they all piled into the elevator, she found herself reflecting in confusion on the agent's statement. Agent

Pegueros had been awful sure they would sleep well for a while longer, and they hadn't made a sound during the entire drive. It made her wonder if they had done something to the children.

The elevator doors opened on the third floor. They exited into what appeared to be a large living room, with a small kitchen off to her right in one corner. The place was set up in an open concept, where the room divisions were made obvious only by furnishings. It looked somewhat like a penthouse only with homier plush furniture pieces.

There were multiple doors on either side of the large room, where she assumed offices or bedrooms might have been set up. Two large couches were positioned a few feet away from the windows where they placed her children, situating them so they were more comfortable.

"Agent Pegueros," Astraia started, having built up the nerve to ask Ricardo about his comment.

"Ricardo, please," he requested, interrupting her. "It sounds like people are addressing my grandpa when they call me that."

"Ricardo," she said instead, acknowledging his request. "Why are you so sure they will sleep so well?"

Before Ricardo could explain, Agent Henley turned toward her and spoke instead.

"I gave them each a tranquilizer," he said nonchalantly, causing Astraia to look at him in alarm.

Her eyes flared angrily. Turning on Henley, she shrieked at him. "You did what?"

"Mrs. O'Kahner, calm down. There is no need to get worked up over this."

"Calm down? You dosed my children with tranquilizers. You didn't tell me or ask my permission! And stop calling me Mrs. O'Kahner!"

"Now you listen to me," Agent Henley responded with as much vehemence as she had. "I don't have to tell you anything, nor do I need your permission to put someone down to keep them calm in transit." He stepped away from her son on the couch.

"Was it really necessary to use tranquilizers on them? They're only kids and I was there. I could have kept them calm." Astraia became plaintive, her voice softening.

"I did what I felt was warranted," Henley said. Pulling out his phone, he punched something into it. "Besides, you weren't available to keep them calm, now were you?" He looked at her pointedly.

"What are you talking about? I was there the whole time."

"You were not always available."

Astraia watched uneasily while four men entered the room from the side doors.

At the sight of the men entering the room, Kastle tensed. He made sure Sayleena was properly situated before standing and moving to the center of the room.

"When was I not...?"

Henley didn't let her finish. "Mrs. O'Kahner, I sedated your children when I realized we wouldn't get out of the house in time. I'll admit it's not normal procedure to do things this way, but it turns out it was a good thing I did. I can't imagine you'd want them overhearing you being raped by the same man who was sworn to protect you."

"I... What?" Astraia was dumbstruck. "What on earth are you talking about?" Her face flamed.

From the middle of the room, she could hear Agent Kastle sigh heavily. He rolled his eyes, giving in to the inevitable by sticking his hands out in front of him. The four men advanced on him. Two had their hands on their

78

guns and were poised in a cautious stance, while one proceeded to place handcuffs on his wrists.

"Wait, what are you doing?" Astraia asked in alarm. "Franc, what are they doing?" Her familiar usage of Agent Kastle's first name sounded improper even to her own ears.

Kastle looked at her. For the first time, she heard the words he spoke to her earlier that evening when he said she didn't know what she was asking of him.

"I expect they are arresting me."

"Arresting you...for what exactly?"

"For raping you," he responded in a matter-of-fact way, as though this sort of thing happened to him every day. Turning away from her, he directed his attention to the man next to him. "Alderman, how's the wife doing?" Kastle spoke calmly to the man who had just handcuffed him.

"Doing quite well actually, the baby is starting to sleep more," Agent Alderman said in answer, and then cast a look of disapproval at Kastle. "I would have never pegged you for the sort to do something like this, Kastle."

"Yes, well..." He hung his head, looking almost as guilty as he felt.

Astraia was shell-shocked. She couldn't believe what she was hearing and seeing. Agent Franclin Kastle was allowing himself to be arrested for something he hadn't done.

Chapter 8

"No! Wait!"

Aghast by what was happening, Astraia ran around the chair towards them. Stopped by one of the other agents before she could get close to Kastle, she glanced back and forth between Agents Henley and Kastle in confusion.

"Listen to me. He didn't do anything wrong." Astraia looked over at Agent Henley almost pleadingly who was still standing near her son Saruman. "He didn't do anything wrong."

Staring at her, Henley walked toward Kastle and stood in front of him. "Agent Franclin Kastle, did you, or did you not have sexual relations with this woman tonight?" He asked directly.

"I did, yes," he admitted honestly, his face and tone were void of emotion, though his eyes hinted at the regret he was experiencing at the mere memory.

Agent Henley turned towards Astraia as if challenging her to argue the point. "Mrs. O'Kahner, are you telling me you're actually going to defend this man, who admits to forcing himself on you while under duress."

"That's not what he said. That's not what he did," she said angrily. Agent Henley was twisting Agent Kastle's words, making the situation out to be something it wasn't. It was making her angry.

"He just admitted to it." Henley glared at Astraia, his temper clearly getting the better of him.

Looking at him with both fear and disgust, she threw the bag and coats down on the floor in frustration. "No, you asked the wrong question, and you're making assumptions."

"Are you now telling me that he's lying? That he didn't, in fact, rape you?" He stared her down, a look of disbelief on his face.

"Yes. And yes," she said pointedly, each time punctuating her response by jabbing her finger in the air. By now, everyone was staring at her. She was getting confused.

"So, now you're saying..."

But Astraia had had enough and cut him off before he could finish. "No, I mean yes. I mean..." waving her hands in the air, she cried out in frustration as her face turned red. "You're such an idiot," she cried, making the mistake of allowing her temper to get the better of her. Her head felt like it was about to explode. Tears threatened at the corner of her eyes where she experienced sharp pain. She dropped to the ottoman next to her, favoring her leg in the process.

"Astraia, don't," she heard Kastle say quietly. He eyed her with concern.

"He didn't do anything wrong!" She looked around at all the men in the room as they stared down at her.

Astraia was feeling as though the room were beginning to spin. Her head lolled slightly to the left as if she were about to drop. Closing her eyes, she squeezed them tight for a moment. When she opened them, the room appeared different to her, and there was a feeling of unreality to it.

"He didn't do anything wrong," she repeated more quietly, tucking her head into her hands shamefully. "It was all me, all my fault."

This time, Agent Henley sat down next to her on the couch and reached out, touching Astraia's hand. She flinched almost violently away from him. Putting his hands together in frustration, Henley looked at her, searching her face as she seemed to cower there next to him.

"It's never the woman's fault when she's been forced," he said gently.

"I know the difference between being raped and giving consent. I'm not stupid," she said heatedly, cutting him off while shaking her head. "He didn't force me to do anything. It was all me. I made...I made him," she finally finished in distress, swallowing hard in embarrassment.

Startled by her admission, the men stared at her in dismay. Speaking up, Agent Alderman glanced furtively at Kastle who was becoming more and more agitated by the direction the conversation was taking. "Mrs. O'Kahner," he started, but saw her wince.

"I get the feeling she does not like her married name much." Agent Kastle offered, trying to be helpful as he'd just been given that knowledge quite unexpectedly.

Nodding understanding, Agent Alderman went on. "I don't mean to make you uncomfortable, Astraia, but I need you to be very clear here. Such an accusation like what Agent Henley is making is not only career ending but could prevent Agent Kastle from ever seeing the light of day. Can you tell us what exactly happened?"

Astraia took a deep breath and looked up at Agent Alderman.

"He didn't want to, and I don't really blame him," she said softly. She turned away from Agent Alderman towards Agent Henley. "Agent Kastle tried to warn me. But I didn't understand. Franc, I'm sorry, I didn't know you could get in so much trouble."

She sniffled suddenly and tried to clear her throat as she stared at her feet. Taking a deep breath, she proceeded to explain.

"I encouraged Agent Kastle to be intimate with me because I was scared and afraid for my children. I didn't think those men would believe that we were a married couple otherwise, because..." pausing, Astraia glanced sheepishly over at Kastle, her face flooding with heat. "Because he looks like a Greek god on steroids. Frankly, I'm anything but a goddess," she finished with a nervous laugh, as her hands shook in front of her.

The pain Kastle saw in her eyes nearly brought him to his knees. If he'd had any trouble at getting a sense at what she was thinking before, there was no doubt in his mind, he was being given her thoughts freely now. It was as though they were flowing directly into his mind.

"But in my defense, those men still didn't believe it. You remember?" Astraia asked Kastle pointedly, as Agent Alderman inhaled sharply. "That man said, 'wait, you mean you're married? *This* is your wife?'" She mimicked Radford's gunman, who had questioned them after they had been caught.

Kastle gaped at her incredulously as Astraia turned away from them, shrugging awkwardly. "He said it had been a long time since he'd been with a woman, so I encouraged him by..." Her speech faltered, her face flaming brighter. "Let's just say, I encouraged him and leave it at that," she said finally, too embarrassed to go into detail.

Hanging her head in shame and misery at what she was admitting, Astraia couldn't look at any of them. She stared once again at the floor.

"Agent Kastle, how long exactly has it been?" Henley inquired quietly while staring at the woman next to him, appearing disturbed.

Astraia heard what sounded like metal clanking together but didn't bother to look and see what was happening.

Sighing heavily, Kastle kicked at the couch and avoided his gaze. "That's personal," he answered gruffly, looking away. "But if you must know it has been over three years." He knew full well they wouldn't believe him if he told the truth, for it had been a great deal longer than that.

"Just let it go, Henley." Agent Alderman said as he eyed Kastle wearily, suspecting the man might have more scruples than what he often admitted to.

Shrugging it off, Henley decided to do just that. Standing abruptly, he noted the woman next to him shrank from him. Before walking back to the chair, Henley's gaze fell on her. He seemed puzzled for a moment, then on a whim decided to walk back around towards her to test a theory.

Astraia wasn't looking at him. As he neared her, she seemed to sense his presence. As Henley reached across her on the pretense of picking up the magazine on the end table, she gasped and jumped away from him, nearly falling off the ottoman.

Henley glanced over at Kastle and the others to see if they'd noticed the behavior as well. It seemed they had picked up on it also, for they appeared to be just as puzzled. Shrugging it off, Henley headed towards one of the adjacent doors, ready to be done with this assignment.

"Maybe next time, don't wait so long." Agent Alderman said, taking the cuffs from Kastle who had somehow managed to already remove them on his own.

Hearing footsteps receding in other directions, Astraia did not know which way they were going. She had chosen to close her eyes to avoid their gazes.

Hunched up on the ottoman, she pulled her legs up to her chest and wrapped her arms around them. In that moment, she was glad her children had been asleep through all of it. She didn't know what she would have done if they'd been awake for her humiliation and could see her like this now.

Astraia didn't know how long it had been before she realized there was still someone in the room. Almost afraid to see who, she peered over her knees to see Agent Kastle watching her quietly as if waiting for her to say something.

"I'm sorry," she finally said. "Agent Kastle, I'm so sorry, I had no idea. And, I'm not normally so wanton." Her voice rose in distress.

"Astraia," he said simply, speaking her name in such a soothing tone it made her want to sink into him. But he was too far away.

"I didn't stick around for an apology," Kastle said gently. "You don't owe me anything." He strode over to her then and bent down next to her so he could speak with her at eye level. "I know you think it's your fault..."

"It *is* my fault." Her eyes were wide now and wet from her tears. Very aware of him so close to her, she shivered slightly. "I was like Eve, tempting Adam with the apple in the Garden of Eden."

Kastle just shook his head and pressed his fingers against her lips, chuckling internally at her analogy.

"No," he said simply. "Besides, from what I understand, it might not have been an apple at all. And we could debate the merits of whose fault it was all night, but what it boils down to for them, is whether it was consensual," Kastle stated kindly. "Which I think we both well know that it was. Though I daresay, I don't think the fault lies solely with you." Shaking his head, this time, he went on. "They may be willing to forgive and forget my transgression but I know when it really comes right down to it, I made an inappropriate choice in the heat of the moment."

She looked at him doubtfully then.

Chuckling softly, Kastle smiled grimly. "Whether I lost control or not, I still made a choice to give into it. I relinquished my willpower for the sake of much-desired release. And you were so frightened, Astraia. It seemed prudent, at the time, to try and dispel some of that fear, if I could, which means there is fault on my end, regardless of your actions." He looked at her intently.

Astraia's hands trembled. Covering her face in mortification, she cried openly. The humiliation and shame were more than she could bear. Unwanted images from her past began popping up in her head as they did so often when she'd become upset.

She felt Agent Kastle reach around her and wrap her in an embrace with his strong bare arms. Tapping the tranquilizer, he had been given by Henley against her left shoulder, he watched as she passed out almost instantaneously. He held her momentarily in his arms while smoothing her hair away from her face. Lifting her from the ottoman, he placed her gently on the third couch, draping a blanket over her for warmth.

Kastle imagined, she had endured enough for one night and was going to need some uninterrupted rest. He watched them all for a little while, pacing back and forth between their respective couches. Then, though tired himself, he knelt before Astraia's still form and began to pray.

God, it's been a rough couple of days and I've sinned again, Lord. I took the lives of three men tonight and in the heat of the moment, sinned with this woman as well.

Resting his head against his clasped and shaking hands, Kastle's face contorted in agony. He finally allowed himself to experience what he was feeling. Breathing heavily, he struggled with his internal battle.

I'm so tired, Lord. You know when I began this path it was with the intent to utilize my gift in a way that would allow me to protect those who could not do so for themselves. And I wanted to rid our world of such people as Kobi Radford; men who knowingly and intentionally capitalize upon the suffering of innocent people.

Whether the men I killed were deserving of the end they came to is for you to determine. I know one day I must sit in judgment over this. Know only, Lord, that if I'd seen another way to end this tonight, I would have gladly taken it. Good or bad, they were still your children. I pray one day you may be able to forgive me for taking their lives and the lives of so many others.

Where this woman before me is concerned, Lord…

Cringing inwardly, his body shook with sorrow and a tear escaped from the corner of his eye. Shaking his head vigorously, he bowed it lower over her, resting his forehead against her shoulder.

I'm so sorry, God. Her husband asked me with his dying breath to save her and his children. I know, through him, that you sent me to protect her. Instead, I took advantage of her in the worst way and during a time of loss at that.

Groaning aloud, he shook his head again in frustration and pain. He stood abruptly and opened his eyes. Staring down at Astraia as she slept peacefully on the couch, Kastle inhaled sharply at the memory of how good it had felt to be with her. Clenching his jaw, his hands balled into fists at his sides. He attempted to ward off the carnal thoughts he was now having of her.

"How can I possibly ask for your forgiveness, God, when I cannot even forgive myself?" Kastle asked aloud. Kicking at the couch violently, he turned suddenly and walked away.

Chapter 9

Astraia was extremely disoriented when she finally woke up. She didn't recognize where she was. It took a few minutes to adjust her eyes well enough to see. She wasn't sure where her glasses had gone to.

And that's when it hit her.

In her haste to pack the children up, she'd left them behind.

Wanting to kick herself for her own stupidity, she sat up slowly and looked around the room. She could see fine without them but she was going to have trouble reading. Watching television for any length of time would give her headaches as well.

No longer in the living room, Astraia realized she had been moved to a bedroom and tucked into the bed she was now sitting in. Rubbing at her eyes, Astraia yawned. It occurred to her, with a start, that she had no idea where her kids were.

Throwing the blankets off in a panic, she crawled out of the bed, managing to get tangled up in the sheets. Her legs felt weak and unsteady once she'd finally become untangled. She lost her balance, falling to the floor, crying out in surprise at the pain she experienced in her right leg. She was a bit dazed and trying to push up to a sitting position when Agent Kastle flung open the bedroom door to find her sprawled on the floor.

"Are you all right?" He knelt on the floor next to her. She could hear sounds in another room of children playing happily while watching cartoons on a television.

"I fell." She peered up at him awkwardly.

Kastle looked good in daylight, extraordinarily handsome even with his unshaven face as he gazed down at her with the deep brown eyes. Still finding the eye color change a bit disconcerting, Astraia couldn't help but think he was every bit as attractive as the first moment she'd seen him in the grocery aisle.

He had put on a light blue t-shirt since she'd last seen him the night before and was now wearing blue jeans. Astraia hadn't realized she'd been staring at him until she heard him chuckling

"My mother used to say that if you look that hard at someone, you'll eventually find the window to their soul. Course, then she'd laugh, and ask if the person had stink-sap stuck to their face." He helped her up from the floor.

"What a funny thing to say after such a nice expression. She sounds like a really neat lady."

Astraia sat against the bed for a moment, then placed her feet back on the floor and gingerly added more pressure as she stood, testing her ability to stand without falling.

"She was." There was a note of sadness in his voice.

"I'm sorry. I take it she passed away."

"Yes, but that was over twenty years ago."

"A loss is a loss. It still hurts, especially when you love them a great deal."

His expression changed. He backed away as though attempting to distance himself from her.

"If you're all right, Ms. Thatcher, I know three people who are anxious to see you." Kastle put his hands in his pockets and walked towards the door. Turning about, he stayed there as if waiting for her to follow.

"Of course, yes." Feeling a bit stung by his formality, she noticed he chose to use her maiden name when speaking with her. It was better than her married name. Glancing around, she noticed a door that might lead to a bathroom on the other side of the room.

"I could use a restroom first." She blushed.

"I'll wait." Kastle nodded toward the bathroom.

While seeing to necessities, Astraia wondered how long her children had been awake and, for that matter, how long she'd been out. As she washed her hands, she noticed there were bags under her eyes, and her hair was a mess. Since she didn't have a comb, she ran her fingers through her hair, attempting to give some semblance of order to it. Deciding it was a hopeless cause, she gave up and stepped out of the bathroom into the bedroom where Kastle was still waiting near the doorway.

"What time is it, anyway?" She noticed the sunlight trying to peek through the shades.

"It's just after nine. You slept a little longer than we anticipated." Kastle tilted his head towards her children in the living room.

"I'm sorry! Have they been awake long?" she wondered aloud as she walked through the doorway, stepping lightly with her right foot, causing her to limp as she went.

"They've only been awake about an hour. Agent Pegueros set up the television so they could watch cartoons. The kids had breakfast already. They've been asking about you."

Astraia stood just outside the doorway and watched them. They were clearly glued to the cartoons on the television and, therefore, oblivious to her presence. Placing her hand on her heart, she heaved a great sigh of relief and called out to them.

"Good morning!"

"Mommy!" All three screamed at once. They raced across the room in their pajamas. Laughing with delight, they bowled her over. She fell to the floor again, only this time on her bottom. Astraia embraced them all in a gigantic hug and then proceeded to kiss and hug each one in turn.

"We're having a picnic in the living room, Mommy, come join us," Sayleena cried out, smiling brightly.

"Mommy! Mommy!" Saruman was exuberant, waving at her as he pointed at his bowl. "Look! Cookies for breakfast!"

"Uncle Ricardo gave them to us." Storman nodded happily.

"Your Uncle Ricardo did, did he?" Astraia emphasized 'Uncle' humorously. She looked in his direction, raising her eyebrows at him. Her expression changed suddenly, though, and she seemed to fidget where she stood.

"Yup, they are so yummy. You should try some," Storman said while lifting a piece of the cookie crisp cereal up at her.

Agent Pegueros was sitting at a table across the room reading a newspaper and drinking coffee. He peered over at her and grimaced, clearing his throat.

"Wasn't sure what they liked and, well, you know, I figured kids and cookies go together, right?"

"Yes, obviously," she said in a snappish manner. Realizing she was being unfairly harsh she softened her tone. "But we usually use cookie crisp cereal as a snack food at our house. Too many sugary foods, too early in the morning have the tendency to make them hyper and peter out early."

Pegueros's eyes became huge. He glanced towards the kids, watching them as they chased each other around the room. Grimacing again while folding his newspaper, Agent Pegueros laid it on the table.

"I'll have to remember that. Sorry."

Astraia shrugged. "No biggie, you didn't know. Though I'm betting you made friends for life," she chuckled, glancing their way as she heard Storman shriek over the sounds of Rescue Bots coming on the television. "Besides, I should have been up for them when they woke."

Noticing a pot sitting on a table and extra mugs, she slowly limped over, desperate for a cup. Fidgeting nervously with her shirt, she tried to keep it closed.

"Is there more coffee?" She asked almost shyly, sensing Agent Kastle come up behind her. Astraia could feel the hairs on the back of her neck stand on end, as well as goose bumps on her arms.

"Breakfast too if you're interested," Pegueros replied, shaking his newspaper.

She nodded, her belly rumbling at the notion. Figuring her need for caffeine and food outweighed any discomfort she was feeling being near him, she poured herself a cup and slid carefully into a chair on the opposite side of the table.

"Sugar?" Pegueros offered, handing it across the table.

Shaking her head, she took a sip. "I much prefer honey."

"Are you serious?" He looked up at Kastle and laughed out loud at his partner's raised eyebrow.

"I know, I get that a lot." She sighed. "Waitresses are annoyed by me."

Walking over to a cupboard on the wall, Kastle reached up to the top shelf and pulled down a bottle of honey, carrying it over to her.

"My private stash," he said. Sitting down next to her, he poured himself a cup. Tilting the bottle into his mug, he then took Astraia's cup from her and added some to hers. Stirring it in, he handed it back.

Taking a sip, she smiled appreciatively. "That's perfect, thank you," she said, seeing him shift his head in acknowledgement.

"I noticed you're limping," Kastle commented as he looked over at the children sitting on the couch. They seemed content for the moment to watch Rescue Bots quietly.

"It's nothing, just bruised really." She shrugged it off.

"I can look at it if you like," he offered, stretching his arm toward the small buffet table. Kastle placed a platter of muffins and fruit next to her.

"No," she said rather sharper than she'd meant to. Seeing his wounded expression, she took a deep breath. "I just don't want to be a bother any more than I already have been." Looking down at the platter in embarrassment, she suddenly didn't feel very hungry, so she pushed it away.

"It's no bother, and you should eat something." Kastle pushed the platter back in her direction. Seeing the distressed look on her face, he let it go for the time being. "Maybe, if it's still bothering you later."

"Okay," Astraia conceded weakly and reached out for a banana. "I'll just have a piece of fruit."

Just then, Saruman ran up to her and yanked on her shirt, popping several of the buttons open. Whispering loudly, he reached for the banana that she'd just been peeling.

"Mommy, can I have a banana?" Glad for the distraction, she broke a piece off and handed it to him. At the same time, Storman hopped over calling, "Nanner, nanner!"

As she broke another piece off, she glanced wearily over to the couch and saw Sayleena watching her.

"Suppose you want some too?" Astraia asked, shaking the remainder of the banana in the air. Sayleena giggled and ran over, taking the last of the fruit from her mother. Astraia laid the banana peel on the table, unsure of where the trash can was located.

"Wow," she heard Pegueros say aloud as he'd watched it all transpire. "You know, there aren't any more bananas," he stated, not understanding why Kastle was suddenly turning crimson.

Astraia rolled her eyes. "I know. That's typical. You have kids?" she asked conversationally, taking another sip of coffee. Even to her, she sounded as though she were forcing civility.

Pegueros smiled and reached for his wallet, pulling pictures out for her to view.

"Here we go," she heard Kastle say next to her, as he grabbed a blueberry muffin, trying desperately to avoid peering at the buttons that had popped on her shirt.

"Hush, you," Pegueros said as he laid pictures out in front of her. "That's my son, Javier. He's three months old," he said proudly, beaming from ear-to-ear.

"He's beautiful." Astraia looked confused.

"Beautiful..." Kastle murmured absent-mindedly. He was having trouble staying focused on the conversation at hand, as memories of the night before flashed through his mind. Physically shaking it off, he said a silent prayer, asking God to strengthen his willpower. He couldn't afford to be distracted.

"But last night, I thought you said you were teaching him Tai Kwon Do?" Astraia asked.

Kastle snorted, nearly spilling his coffee. Laughing out loud, he grinned over at his partner, grateful to Astraia for the distraction. "How exactly does that work again, Pegueros?" He asked, glad for a reason to look away from her.

Pequeros ignored Kastle, shooting him a dirty look. "I practice regularly while he watches me. *Niño's* learn by example, after all."

Smiling weakly, Astraia turned towards Kastle. "Do you have kids?" She asked curiously, grabbing a muffin from the platter.

From the look he gave her, she wished she hadn't asked.

"No," he said shortly. He got up and walked away. Taking quick strides, he exited through one of the doors on the opposite side of the room. He had to get her a new shirt promptly, or he'd never be able to think straight.

"If it's any consolation, I think it's a sore subject for him for some reason," Pegueros offered when he noticed her bemused expression. "That being said, the implication you make by the mere question makes him out to be a *mal vado*."

"How so?" she asked, recalling vaguely that '*mal vado*' meant bad guy or bad boy in Spanish. She was startled by Ricardo's assessment.

"Because, if he has kids, then he could be married, and if he's married, then he just cheated on his wife last night," he finished while stuffing the last of a lemon poppy seed muffin in his mouth and taking a large swig of coffee.

"I didn't mean anything by it."

"Of course you didn't." Reaching over, he patted her arm.

Her reaction was automatic. She jerked away suddenly, slid off her chair, and falling to the floor. Agent Pegueros looked down at her, stunned at first, then extended an arm to help her off the floor.

"N…No, I'm okay. Thank you," she stuttered, eyeing his hands with something akin to trepidation.

"Let me help you." Pegueros reached for her again. Swinging her arm around, she knocked his hands away just before they latched onto her arm.

"I said no," she said sharply. Startled, her children looked over at her in alarm.

Stepping back, Ricardo looked as though he'd been slapped. Drawing himself up to his full five height, he walked away.

"Agent Kastle will be back in shortly." He turned as he stopped in front of the same door Kastle had gone through. Astraia tensed visibly. "Wait to say anything about your husband just yet. He'll help you figure that out." And with that, he disappeared.

\- - -

Watching from the elevator entrance, Maleeka stood, resting his chin on the butt of his sword. He could see the woman struggling on the floor. His heart reached out to her, understanding the internal battle she was suffering.

Sensing so much turmoil within her, it was a wonder she hadn't gone crazy. Though she appeared tired, and in desperate need of rest and peace of mind, he could see now, more than before, why Woreash felt so strongly about her being the one. With everything she was going through now, and maybe because of what she had endured in the past, the woman had become strong. Even now he could see her pulling herself together to be able to be there for her children.

Acknowledging it was a good fit, he was about to pop into the other room when he felt Woreash's sudden appearance behind him. Turning to face him, he could already see the disapproval on his old friend's face.

"What could I possibly have done to warrant that look?"

"Maleeka, we've done what we came for. It is time to go," Woreash responded with more than just a little irritation.

"Woreash, you said yourself…"

"We found her," Woreash interrupted, as he shook his head.

Surprised, Maleeka blinked once, then sheathed his sword. "Then what in the world are we still doing here?" Maleeka responded, staring back at him. His tone was serious, though the mirth in his eyes gave him away.

"Come," Woreash grinned back at him. "We must set things in motion."

Glancing in the direction of the woman on the floor, then through the window of the other room, Maleeka peered back at his counterpart with concern.

Seeing the direction of his gaze, Woreash replied as he shrugged. "It's up to them now. They must figure the rest out themselves. A Guardian has been tasked. We shall see them again in time."

Acknowledging his words with a nod, Maleeka followed as Woreash led the way.

Chapter 10

Closing the door behind him, Pegueros folded his arms over his chest and glared over at the window paned wall.

"Good grief! Did you see that?" He said aloud, thankful the room was soundproof.

"Settle down." Kastle waived him off while trying to concentrate on what she was saying. One or the other of them had been watching Astraia and her family all morning long through the one-way mirrored window. The most recent scene, with Astraia and Ricardo, had drawn Agent Blackthorne's attention.

They watched together as Astraia, while still sitting on the floor, scooted over behind the couch where her children couldn't see and curled her legs up tight against herself. She cried into her hand quietly and could be heard murmuring softly.

"What is she saying?" Pegueros stared at her intently. "Cisteen? Is she saying, Cisteen ears?"

"No, fifteen." He took a deep breath, hastily determining how much information he should provide.

"She's saying 'you'd think after fifteen years it'd get better,'" he finished, then went on to add, "She's also saying something about a blue baseball cap."

Running his hands over his face in frustration, Kastle turned away, then turned back. Were he in closer proximity, he had a feeling he would be learning more from her. From this distance, all he could get were jumbled images but they were starting to make more sense. As he began putting them together, he was leery of providing Ricardo with too much information or he would start to wonder how he was coming up with it.

No one Franc worked with knew of his abilities. All they knew was that he tended to be extremely perceptive, and accurate in his assessment of people

When he was younger, his father had originally been concerned that he was reading minds. He sent him away, believing his ability was born of the devil, rather than from God. In the end, they learned he was being given information, or thoughts, from a secondary source, presumably one of the messengers, or angels, that his brother Breydon could see. The day his mother died, and he had returned home for the first time since he was three, Breydon had been able to confirm this. He indicated there was a messenger who appeared to be ever present at his side.

The gifts, in a sense, had been inherited from both sides of his parent's heritage, as both his mother and father had been blessed in similar ways. By extension, he along with all five of his siblings had been born with a gift or ability as it was often referred to by his father, of his own. Though at times beneficial in his work, it tended to be problematic in his personal life. It opened him up to all kinds of knowledge of people he'd just as soon not know, but for whatever the reason was deemed he needed to know.

Glancing over at Pegueros, he noted his partner was also rubbing his face in frustration. He could tell the man was annoyed. Pegueros had been hoping he wouldn't have to deal with this case for any length of time because he wanted to go home to his son.

Agent Pegueros turned suddenly towards Franc then glanced away. Walking towards the table, he reached for the coffee pot and poured himself a cup.

"You're watching the wrong subject, Kastle."

"I didn't mean to make you feel so uncomfortable." Kastle chuckled softly, turning back towards the window.

Astraia still sat on the floor hiding behind the couch. Her daughter, Sayleena, not seeing where she was, called out for her.

"It's okay, baby girl," he heard Astraia choke out. "I'm here, Honey, I just need a minute." Her voice was strained, and her eyes were red from crying.

"You okay, Momma?" Sayleena asked, appearing worried.

"Yes, Baby. I'm okay." Moving her legs, so she sat Indian style, she placed her hands on the floor for support. Tilting her head back, her eyelids fluttered slightly, and she heaved a deep sigh. Then, having finally gotten control of her breathing, Astraia opened her eyes wide and pushed up off the floor. Wiping the tears from her face, she turned and looked at her kids.

"She seems to at least have some control over it," Pegueros said as sipped his coffee.

"No, I'm not sure she does," Kastle replied. If his sister, Megorah were here, he imagined she would be getting a pretty strong emotional read on her. As such, she wasn't, and he didn't have that ability.

"What makes you say that?" Pegueros asked, glancing over at him.

Kastle pointed towards the window. "She was wobbling as she came up off the floor. I'm betting she's still dizzy, and she's sensitive to sound right now."

Seeing Pegueros's raised eyebrows, he pursed his lips in irritation. "Just look at her face. And look, now her eyes are closed and her hand is at her ear. See? I'd say both light and sound sensitive right now."

What he didn't tell Pegueros was that, at that very moment, she was practically screaming inside her head. Astraia was doing an impressive job of attempting to tamp the symptoms down. But she was struggling with it more than usual, from what he gathered, which worried him.

Agent Pegueros put his cup down and peered closer. Sighing heavily, he sat down in the chair next to Kastle and picked up his mug again, taking a big gulp of coffee.

"Hate it when you're right."

"She's suffering from Post-Traumatic Stress Disorder," Kastle assessed, sipping at his coffee.

"I thought PTSD was what guys got coming back from war?" Ricardo looked at his partner in confusion.

"You don't have to go to war to suffer from PTSD. Any number of things can happen to you to cause it." He rubbed his chin as he watched Astraia with her children. "It can result from various forms of traumatic experiences, such as seeing action in war, an act of God, an accident..."

Pegueros interrupted, "I remember now; being attacked, assaulted, or losing a family member."

"Or rape," Kastle looked meaningfully at Pegueros. They exchanged looks.

"That's kind of what I was thinking too. You think last night?" Pegueros asked, peering quickly over at his partner while attempting to gauge the reaction to his question.

Kastle shook his head. "No, that was consensual. It has nothing to do with it. Although, in hindsight," he said tilting his head thoughtfully. "That might not have helped any, as it was a highly charged, highly dangerous situation that warranted the intimacy." Pausing, he shook his head and went on, "No, she was just talking about a fifteen-year period. I'd say this is an old case, from back then, maybe even with a possible assault attached to it."

"I did her background check, but don't recall seeing anything about a rape or assault case anywhere. Parking ticket and a couple speeding tickets but otherwise, she seemed clean." By now Pegueros was watching her through the window again. "Maybe it's a sealed case. You know? Something that happened before she turned eighteen."

"Good thought, but it doesn't jive with this fifteen-year period she's talking about."

"Why not?" Pegueros countered.

Smiling almost smugly, Kastle answered his question with another question. "What's her birth date?"

Pegueros looked down at the pile of papers scattered all over the table. Leafing through it, he found her stats. "April 21 of 1977. Right, *treinta y seis*, she's thirty-six years old. That wouldn't jive." Cringing slightly, he went on, "Lousy timing. Birthday's in two days."

"Dead husband and fleeing for one's life, does rather put a damper on the celebratory feeling, I'd wager," Kastle added dryly. "Take another look at her background and go a little deeper. There's got to be something back there. I'd like to know how bad she is. If it's a severe enough case she might need help. We should take that into consideration when we decide where to relocate her." He looked over at Pegueros. "Is she on any medication? Cause if she's suffering from side effects of PTSD or medication withdrawal, she might have been given a prescription by a psychiatrist. In which case, she's going to need meds."

"If she were taking meds, I'd have thought she would have said something. It's the first thing these people panic about, right?"

"You have a fair point there, but let's check to be sure. She might be too embarrassed to say anything."

"Man, I really don't care if she's got PTSD or not. That's her problem. Let's just get her placed and get this over with. I wanna be home in a month. I miss my *niño* and…"

"Enough," Kastle said crossly. "We're going to do right by her."

"Look, man. I get you made a promise to her husband, but that's on you, not me. I made no such promise. And this wasn't my screw up, to begin with." Pegueros sounded just as cross.

Breathing deeply Agent Kastle attempted to gain control of his anger while staring his partner down. "You never answered my question."

"Again, there was nothing in the background check."

"You did medicals on the kids, and the mother?"

"Yes," he started to say something then shook his head again, looking over at Agent Kastle. "Wait… no, I pulled it on the kids because of the possible need for tranquilizers, but never did on the mother."

"We need to pull her medicals. I want to know everything."

Ricardo made a face and walked away toward his laptop to put in the request.

"The kids are asking about their father," Agent Kastle said as he glanced towards the living room.

Kastle quickly grabbed his folder and placed it under one arm. Balancing his coffee, he headed towards the door. "We better get in there. Pegueros?"

"Yeah?"

"Take off the baseball cap, and hand me that shirt over there."

Pegueros reached up, took the cap off and tossed it on the table. Grabbing up Kastle's shirt lying across the chair next to him, he groaned outwardly at the loss of the view, then followed behind his partner's glaring countenance.

Kastle rapped on the door before entering the living space and headed straight for the table, setting his file and coffee mug down. Accepting the shirt from Pegueros, he eyed him knowingly.

"Morning kiddos. Mind if I borrow your momma for a bit?" Kastle asked the children. They squealed in delight at seeing him. Suddenly, they burst out in a chorus of 'We are the Champion,' surprising Astraia.

"I was the first one in here this morning when they started waking up." He smiled openly. "I explained about everything and then entertained them for a bit until my partner was able to get back with breakfast and the box for the television."

"What did you tell them?"

He noted her increasing anxiety level. "Come. Let's talk for a bit and I'll go over everything." He waved her over to the table. "And do me a favor. Put this on, please."

"Why?" She gave him a suspicious look but took the shirt from him.

He frowned over at his partner. "Just trust me."

Peering down at the shirt falling open before her very eyes, she gasped and turned away as she frantically threw the one he gave her over her head. Yanking the oversized shirt down as far as it would go; she turned back, her face having turned three shades of red. Seeing Agent Kastle gesturing for her to sit at the table, she looked at himself consciously but did as he asked, sitting in a chair near him.

Folding his hands together in front of him, Kastle sat for a moment just looking at her before speaking.

"I want to express my condolences where your husband, is concerned. I'm truly sorry he found his way in the middle of this and was killed. We make it a practice to avoid casualties at all cost where civilians are concerned, but sometimes we cannot control all the variables."

"Thank you, Agent Kastle, but what exactly is it that we've found ourselves in the middle of? Why would someone want to come after us? And why…?"

"Why would they care about you and your children, is what you're asking?" he finished for her.

"Exactly. How did he get in the middle of this anyway? Was there a shoot-out at Walmart or something? Is that how he died? Was he shot by accident?"

Kastle cut her off, a bit perplexed by her questions. "Walmart? No, I'm sorry I'm not at liberty to discuss the details of an ongoing investigation."

"Not at liberty?" Astraia looked at him incredulously. "You come into my home. You tell me he's dead because he got - what - in your way? Then you tell me I must leave everything behind, taking my kids away from everything they know and love, burning down my house in the process. You couldn't even get us out in time before these men show up. So, then I…" She stopped abruptly, unable to continue or to look at him for that matter. Her face suffused with color once again, and she suddenly became very hot.

Observing her discomfort at the near reference of her encounter with him, Kastle decided to ignore it for the time being. Moving on to the heart of her main issue, he continued.

"Ms. Thatcher, I wish I could tell you everything you want to know. What you deserve to know. But telling how he died, would lead to a whole lot of other questions and answers, of which I am not at liberty to disclose right now." Leaning forward in his chair, Kastle reached intentionally for her to gauge her reaction. He was expecting she'd pull back suddenly or gasp at his touch. She didn't. Instead, she accepted his hand almost eagerly. "The less you know, the better off you are."

Sitting back once more, he twiddled his pen in his fingers and tilted his head towards Agent Pegueros, as if sending out a silent message. His partner, who had been standing watching the children while listening in, turned towards the table and moved up behind her. He knew what Kastle was up to, without even being told. The man wanted to know if her flight response was indicative to all men, or just those who reminded her of her attacker. Astraia's expression became increasingly distressed as Pegueros came up behind her. It was clear she'd heard him.

"Ms. Thatcher," Pegueros said quietly as he reached out and took hold of her shoulder. He felt her tense in his hand. "I know it may be small consolation, but I *can* tell you he died an honorable death. We believe he was trying to help us."

Astraia felt Agent Pegueros's hands on her shoulders. She cringed inwardly. Her body jerked in her chair, her stomach churned painfully, and bile rose in her throat. She struggled to choke it down, making a kind of gagging sound in her throat.

Pegueros glanced back up in time, to see his partner curiously watching the exchange.

"Look, I'm trying to figure out the best way to tell my children that their dad is gone," Astraia whispered, still tasting the bile in her mouth. "You're not exactly giving me a lot to go with here. Maybe they don't ask the questions now. 'What happened' and 'why' and 'how did he die?' But one day they will. When that day comes, what am I supposed to tell them?"

Pegueros released his grasp on her shoulders then, and she breathed an obvious sigh of relief.

"Ms. Thatcher…" Kastle started, but she interrupted.

"Why are you calling me by my maiden name?"

"You gave us the impression that you did not care to be called Mrs. O'Kahner." He noticed her wince. "We thought your maiden name might be more likeable. Am I to assume you do not like your maiden name as well?"

"I'm not going to lie. I hate my married name." She rolled her eyes. "I've hated it from the moment Dylan told me what his last name was but calling me Ms. Thatcher will confuse my children. Just call me by my first name – Astraia."

"If you wish. If I may ask… What is it about your married name you do not like? Is it the name or the man behind it?"

Surprised by his line of questioning, she looked at him for a moment, without speaking. Then, taking a deep breath, she finally responded.

"Why would you ask that?"

"Forgive me. You've showed signs of grief and loss initially, but now you seem more concerned about what to tell your children and how it will affect them than you do about losing your husband," he said frankly, hoping he wasn't trivializing her loss.

Taking another deep breath, she leaned forward and rested her head on the table. After a moment, she giggled almost derisively and raised her head enough to look the agent square in the face.

"The name is more the issue, not the man. That being said the man himself was no prince either." Seeing their eyebrows rise in surprise, she went on. "Truth be told, I lost my husband a long time ago. Or maybe I never had him," she said thoughtfully.

Reticent of speaking ill of her deceased husband, Astraia explained that she grieved at the loss of him for her children. They would grow up without a father in the home. Tactfully describing the lack of relationship her husband had with his children, and her, she went into more detail.

"Dylan either went to work or played games on his PS2. Nothing else. The man suffered from Post-Traumatic Stress Disorder as the result of his service in the 82nd Airborne, or so he claimed. That was always his excuse for closing himself up in his games."

Struggling to maintain control as he listened, Kastle was disturbed to hear how minimal Dylan's contact had been with his family. Learning the man frequently complained of having to work, and about the kids getting in his way while playing games, he seethed inwardly. Such men never seemed to understand the true blessing they had, and he had a hard time understanding why.

Astraia rubbed her eyes wearily. "I sometimes wonder why he bothered tricking me into marrying him in the first place." Glancing over at her children, she noticed they were playing in the cushions of the couches, making forts. She smiled.

"He tricked you?" Pegueros asked.

"Yes." She winced, realizing she'd said too much. "I really don't want to talk about that." Unknown to her husband, Astraia had figured out shortly after they were married that Dylan thought she was the daughter of a wealthy man. It hurt to think he might have married her with an ulterior motive, but he'd stayed when they found out she was pregnant with Sayleena. Wanting a father for her child, she had let the matter go, hoping things would work out okay.

Kastle decided not to push her on the matter. "Did he take medication for his PTSD?"

She shook her head. "He'd tried some after he got out of service, but they didn't work, so, he self-medicated with excessive amounts of coffee."

"Did you?" Kastle asked, taking a chance.

"Did I what?"

"Take medicine ... for PTSD?" he asked tentatively.

"Why would I do that?" She failed to meet his gaze.

"He's just trying to get an idea of medical history and your relationship with Dylan," Pegueros said quickly, brushing the question off for now. Clearly, she did not wish to talk about that, either.

"Dylan and I, we'd been fighting for a couple weeks now," she began, telling them about the circumstances behind their argument. "The kids were doing so much better with me home." She sighed heavily. "But Dylan didn't care. He wanted me to work so we could afford all the stuff he wanted. Am I broken up by his death? Yes and no. He was my husband. Though I loved him, I was no longer in love with him because this is just the last in a series of promises he has broken," she said, lost in thought.

Confused, Kastle reached over and took her hand in his again. "What promise did he break?"

"He said things were going to change. That I wouldn't have to work so much anymore. After over six years, he finally realized I had been doing more than my fair share, and that I was worn out. It was like he'd had an epiphany or something. But then he goes and gets himself killed," she said irritably, realizing as she spoke how horrible her words sounded, even to her own ears.

"His life was taken from him. The man didn't have a choice in the matter 'cause someone else chose for him." Agent Pegueros sounded annoyed.

"Where was it that he died last night?" she asked suspiciously, suddenly knowing somehow that her late husband might have been the cause of the danger they'd been placed in.

"You know we can't..." Kastle started, but Astraia interrupted once again.

"Just tell me this." Her eyes darted back and forth. Thoughts began popping in her head. "When he left our house, it was to go pick up champagne and cake from Wal-Mart, and then come straight home. If that's all he was doing, then how, between less than a mile from our house to the store and back, could he have possibly found himself in the middle of whatever this is, if that's all he was doing?" She looked at them pointedly then and received no answer.

Agent Pegueros cleared his throat uncomfortably and Astraia glanced his way.

"See, there... That tells me right there my husband didn't just go to Wal-Mart. For all I know, he didn't even make it there." She spoke angrily. "What I do know is he had me waiting at home for him expectantly, and he never showed."

Sitting back in her chair, Astraia's mind was on overdrive. Recalling that Dylan had left at eight thirty, and the agents hadn't shown until after midnight, it made her wonder what her husband had been up to last night. It was only a fifteen-minute round trip.

"What was he doing?" she asked Kastle finally. Her eyes darted towards him, clearly in confusion. "Where was he that I'm not to know about, and wouldn't have otherwise found out about, had he not gotten killed last night?"

Astraia turned on Pegueros, somehow suddenly knowing that Dylan had been the cause of his own death. "You say he died with honor. That he was trying to help. I'm betting he got himself killed out of guilt because he was somewhere he wasn't supposed to be in the first place and it blew up in his face."

She got up then and paced the floor, clearly agitated, then looked over at her kids. Astraia knew it was time to tell her children about their dad, but she didn't know what to say. She didn't even know how to begin. Her chest heaved with anxiety, and she found herself holding her stomach, as it had become quite queasy.

"Kastle is really good with kids, Astraia. Surprisingly so," Pegueros said, ignoring the look he got from him at the statement. "He can help you tell them in a way that will preserve the memory they have of him. If you want him to, that is."

Nodding, Astraia hobbled over to the table then and steadied herself by placing her hand on it and leaning against it. She was still limping, which concerned Kastle.

"Will you help me?" she asked, almost pleading. Distressed at the task, her face had paled suddenly as if she were struggling with a bout of nausea.

"Of course," Kastle nodded. "But first, sit down. You look like you're about to fall."

Astraia came around and took a seat next to Kastle, surprising them both. It was as though she gained strength by being near him.

"I have some questions for you first, that will help me determine the best way to tell them. You've already answered many I had about the family environment and their relationship with him." Agent Kastle said, scanning his notes. "Right now, I'm going to ask about the kids themselves. And then, we'll tell them together."

Chapter 11

Agent Kastle's ability to be able to handle children was impressive, as far as Astraia was concerned. He was so much better than she was with them. She envied him for it. The way he'd sat with her kids, and explained how daddy wouldn't be coming home anymore, had even made her feel better about his passing.

She had become so angry with Dylan during her conversation with Agents' Kastle and Pegueros, that Astraia was afraid she would speak ill of him with them. And it was clear to her now that Dylan had, in fact, managed to get himself killed. Both agents' reactions led her to believe that he never made it to the store. Her husband had gone somewhere else instead.

Sitting holding her kids as they quietly spoke of their daddy and the things they would miss, Astraia sighed wearily. Interestingly, they seemed to remember him doing things that he'd never actually done with them. They were making up tall tales about him playing games with them and reading them stories.

Kastle warned they might do this, and not to discourage them. It was their way of dealing with the fact that Dylan would never be able to do all the things they always hoped he would. After a while, they lost interest and asked to watch more cartoons. Soon they were wrapped around each other, resting on the couch, watching Strawberry Shortcake quietly. The giddy, excited mood from earlier was replaced with silence, born of the sadness they were experiencing at their loss.

Agent Pegueros had wanted to go over more information with her but Astraia had been developing a headache. He deferred to her need to lay her head down for a bit and rest. The men excused themselves to their office. They watched her from the window, as she settled in next to her kids and placed her arm up over her forehead.

Drawing the shade over the window to give her some privacy for a while, they grabbed drinks from the mini fridge under the desk and sat down at the table.

"It would seem that you're the only one she does not feel threatened by so far." Pegueros looked at Kastle quizzically. "I wonder why? I would have thought, out of the two of us, she'd be more intimidated by your sheer size." He'd said it more for himself than anyone else.

"I wouldn't want to speculate." Kastle knew full well the reasons why. It didn't take much for him to figure out why she was so comfortable around him.

"Please, speculate away. You seem to be quite good at it." Pegueros began leafing through information on Astraia O'Kahner.

Reaching for a dry erase pen, Kastle grabbed the large whiteboard from the floor and propped it on the table. He then proceeded to write three names on the board next to each other: Henley, Alderman, and Pegueros.

"In the end, I think she has singular reasons for feeling threatened by each one. Interestingly, she seemed to have the most problem with Agent Henley. I think it's because he's the same build, height, weight and has maybe even a similar personality. You know, cocky."

"Right," Pegueros said, nodding his head. "Which is why she'd have an issue with Agent Alderman because aside from the attitude, he's the same build and everything."

"You, on the other hand, are a similar height, but different build and coloring because you're Hispanic rather than black like Henley or white like Alderman. With you, I think the issue is primarily because of your knowledge of Tae Kwon Do. And I don't think she liked your baseball cap much. Add it all together, and we gain a better picture of the person who likely attacked her."

"Awe man, who cares? Let's just get this done." Pegueros banged on the table in exasperation.

"You were the one who asked me to speculate on the matter." Kastle dropped the whiteboard on the table. "I get it, Pegueros, you want to go home. You're not the only one."

Pegueros looked at him in surprise. "You? Man, you always seemed like a lifer to me," he finished as he popped the cap off his soda.

"We all have our breaking points. This one was mine." Kastle sat back in his chair. Noticing Pegueros giving him an odd look, he sighed. "I've lost people on the job before. It goes with the territory. But this one..." his voice trailed off as he stared off into space.

"You're taking this too hard. This Dylan guy doesn't even sound like much of a loss anyway," Pegueros said, tapping on the table with his pen.

"Any human casualty is a loss," Kastle said gruffly as he frowned over at Pegueros. "Regardless of whether he was a lying snake or not, he tried to do right by her in the end. He took a bullet for me, and he made me promise I'd make sure she was taken care of."

"I remember; I was there. Dylan said, and I quote, 'Astraia takes care of everyone but herself. She cannot do it alone. She deserves better than me. She deserves the real thing.'" Pegueros finished, chugging down half his soda. "What do you suppose he meant by that? You know, 'deserves the real thing.'"

Kastle shrugged and shook his head. "Who knows?"

"It didn't sit right with me either, him doing what he did. He was clearly looking for trouble that night. It almost seemed to me like he was intending to put himself in harm's way or something."

"I get what's done is done, and all that matters right now is getting her safely relocated, but I can't help but wonder..." Kastle pondered the situation.

"*Que?*"

"Whether he realized how truly close he came to getting his family killed. All for the chance of what? What was he really trying to accomplish?"

"Personally, I still don't get how he found us there at that bar and knew who we were? How did he know what was going down?"

"I think we just got our answer on that score." Kastle sat up suddenly and began tapping keys on his laptop. "She said he was 82nd Airborne. That he suffered from PTSD after getting out. When we did our search on him initially, what did we find?"

Pegueros snorted. "That he was already dead."

"Exactly, when his military record popped, it showed he'd only been in for two years with Army. It didn't show anything about being in Airborne."

Pegueros's face lit with comprehension. "Before he died, he said he'd been a sniper and was a jumpmaster. That requires a minimum of five hundred jumps to attain. The timeline for that wouldn't jive with only a two-year span. Why would he already be showing he was deceased unless he was trying to disappear at one point?"

"Exactly, which means…"

"He was in for more than two years," Pegueros interrupted. "Dylan may have been one of us, undercover special ops."

"This wasn't planned, either. He's had training, so he probably figured it out days ago but initially didn't intend to intercede until his and Astraia's fight the other night." His excitement mounting, Kastle was starting to get a better picture as to what may have happened.

"Remember what she said in there? She said, 'It was like he'd had an epiphany.' I think it's because he did." Kastle threw his arms out wide for effect.

Pegueros got up and paced the small room. "Right. She said it herself, this guy was lazy. Why fix their life himself, when he can get someone else to fix it for them? Think about it, a fresh start, new location, new names, a line of credit, and a new home. Man, this guy wasn't stupid! He was crazy smart, with an emphasis on the crazy. He intentionally put himself in the line of sight, as a witness to Kobi Radford's drug dealings, so Homeland Security would swoop in to save the day. And he'd look like a hero to his wife. But killing Kobi's brother, Lionel, was an accident."

"The problem was he'd been out long enough that he was rusty, hence the mistake. Killer shot, literally, but he didn't realize who he was shooting until it was too late." Kastle rubbed his brow irritably. "Then he got himself mortally wounded, and he knew it, too. He'd already dropped his checkbook, which had their home address on it. He couldn't move to go back and get it, which left Astraia and their kids vulnerable unless he gave us a reason to go save them."

Disgusted, Franc threw the dry erase marker down on the table and stood, running his hands across his face in agitation.

"He screwed up again," he declared heatedly. "Only worse because he put them all in danger. I mean of all the bad guys out there to choose, he had to go after Kobi Radford."

"You aren't kidding, that guy's organization is vast. If we thought Kobi was pissed about his former sister-in-law and her kids disappearing on them, then just imagine what he's going to be like now that Lionel is dead."

"Disappearing, eh? Huh, and here I was told they were dead." One eyebrow quirked up knowingly at his partners blunder. Seeing him squirm he shook his head an let it go. "Either way, finding a safe place for Astraia and her kids now, is going to be next to impossible." Kastle shook his head in exasperation. "Kobi isn't going to just let this go. That was his little brother that Astraia's husband killed. He's liable to figure out that they aren't dead, even with everything we did to prevent that, and he's bound to come after them again. And instead of starting over with her, she has to start over all alone with three kids."

Pegueros stopped pacing and looked his partner straight in the eye. "In the end, defeating the whole purpose of Dylan's plan, which was…"

"To keep his promise, that things were going to change and she'd never have to work again," Kastle interjected, running his hands through his hair. Astraia didn't deserve what had happened to her, what had been done to her. He now understood better why Dylan had said what he had when he died.

"Man, this lady got screwed ... literally," Pegueros said tactlessly. Seeing the look on Kastle's face he shrugged. "I call it like I see it."

Shaking his head, Kastle flung his hands up in the air in defeat. "What can I say, when you're right, you're right. But look..." He picked up the whiteboard, even as the guilt of what he'd done to her that night washed over him again. "This guy, Dylan. I think we can safely say he was one of ours. At one point, he could have been one of us, for all we know, meaning CIA. Whether he was still in it or not, his job had once been to protect and serve people, not throw them in the line of fire. To do this to his own family..." He shook his head in disgust. "What he did was unconscionable."

Pegueros walked over to the one-way window and opened the shades so he could see. They both watched her with the kids for a while. At one point, she'd been playing with them on the floor but after a bit, she called a timeout. Standing, she limped over to one of the couches and sat down, holding her leg with one hand and rubbing her eyes with the other.

It was obvious that Astraia was tired. Tired and worried. She had a right to be. Their lives were in danger, for Kobi Radford wasn't the kind of man who would end his vendetta with Dylan's death. No, Kobi was the sort who would hunt down and kill the man's brother, mother, wife, children, and their dog for good measure, if they had one. And all just to prove the point: that he was all-powerful, and that he could get to anyone, anywhere.

Kastle watched her. The wall he'd built up around his heart began to crumble. Her life had been torn apart and she was now different for it. He could already see the change occurring, and the toll it was taking on her, which worried him.

She had a giving, loving nature about her that had been obvious to him, even as he'd watched her in the check-out aisle at the grocery store. And he had been amazed at how far she had been willing to go in order to protect the ones she loved, which had only added to his growing opinion of her.

Sighing next to him, Pegueros shook his head. "Man, it's just not right."

"You know what I wonder?" Kastle asked as a nagging thought wriggled to the forefront of his mind. Having moved away from the window, he began tapping at his laptop again.

"*¿Que?* What's up?" Pegueros inquired, distracted now.

"Was Dylan really the real Dylan O'Kahner? There's a death certificate here, after all."

Deep in thought, Pegueros didn't reply right away. "I get it. You're thinking maybe this guy was like you and me. He wanted to disappear, so he took up the identification of a dead man?" Pegueros whistled through his teeth and pondered this new possibility.

"I think we should figure out for sure before Kobi does. There may be more people out there we don't know about that this might affect. We'll need to find out all she might know about her husband." Kastle lifted a sheet of paper from the table. "Per Agent Henley, we've already got some people put on her parents and brother, just to make sure Kobi doesn't go after them to get to her."

Pegueros sighed heavily and raised his face towards the ceiling. "*Oy, Dios!*" he proclaimed. "This is a mess. You know, I'd say let's just dump her and move on, but even I'm starting to get a bad feeling on this one."

Kastle met Pegueros's direct gaze, knowing full well how badly the man wanted to be a dad to his son, without the worries of backlash from his time in service. With the O'Kahner's being the direct focus of Kobi Radford's wrath and vengeance, they both knew that if the family's relocation wasn't handled just right, there most certainly could be.

"Let's make a deal. We'll get her set up and we'll do it right. If anyone is deserving, she is. Wouldn't you say?" Kastle pointed to the window. "But when this is all over...." he said, leaving the words to hang in the air.

Shifting uncomfortably, Pegueros knew full well what Kastle was implying, but didn't answer right away. Then, without saying a word, he nodded his head in silent agreement. After the job was done, for all their sakes, they would all disappear.

Kicking at the floor as he became thoughtful, Pegueros finally replied. "The sad part here is that you're right. I mean, apparently, she got shafted a long time ago, too. From the sounds of it, all this bad luck started fifteen years ago."

Kastle nodded, stretching out his hand. Taking Pegueros's hand in his, they shook on it. As he pulled his arm back, he noticed the newspaper on the table was dated April 19, 2015. Seeing the date, he realized it seemed important to him somehow. And then it came to him; it was the same day his wife Elizabeth died exactly fifteen years before.

Chapter 12

They had determined through a rather extensive debate that they had their work cut out for them. In the end, the main goal was to find a safe place to relocate Astraia and her children and to order up some new identification for her and her kids. They knew the names and story wouldn't be an issue. What could be problematic was finding a location where no one knew her, was related to her or had an association with Kobi Radford's organization. Finding an area within the United States that Kobi Radford hadn't left his mark and didn't have any of Astraia's relatives or former associations was proving to be problematic.

Pegueros set up a map of the United States in the kitchen the next day and began marking off all of Radford's well-known territory. Later on that day, Kastle enlisted Astraia's help in placing push pins at cities and states she would need to avoid because of her family.

Before long, the map was a veritable color-coded mess of areas they would need to avoid. Five more days went by. They were still working on eliminating cities and states. Astraia's graduating class had apparently spread themselves throughout the states in many of the, thus far, 'safe locations,' which began eliminating even more of the country.

During this time, it had been necessary for Kastle to spend more time with Astraia and her kids, to prepare them all for the changes to come. They were now on day six. He was having a lot of difficulty keeping his mind on the tasks at hand. He kept reverting back to the night he'd been intimate with her, and Kastle couldn't get it out of his head.

It didn't help any when yesterday morning he'd gone in to wake her and discovered she'd been sleeping without clothes. Not being much of a morning person, she couldn't seem to wake in the mornings without an alarm. So, when she didn't get up when he knocked on her door, Kastle, thinking to be funny, tried to encourage her by throwing her blankets off.

Not only did it serve to wake her up, but it prompted a much-needed trip to the store for some pajamas, undergarments, clothes, an alarm clock and a Bible, upon her request. Kastle had been pleasantly surprised, and pleased, at her desire to have her Bible replaced, though he noted Pegueros's annoyance at the request. Having never shopped with three children, it made for a rather eventful morning. Both Kastle and Pegueros required the rest of the day to recover from it, much to Astraia's amusement.

Normally adept at re-training his thoughts upon the matter at hand, Kastle was finding it difficult to think about pretty much anything else but her. Even before that morning, he'd been replaying the events of that night over and over again in his mind. He knew it was common for men to think about women in that way a lot, his brother Breydon being a prime example. But never had he had such difficulty as what he was having now. He knew there were two reasons why.

Part of it was because Kastle was finding he liked her a lot, the more he got to know her. The other reason was that, as a Blackthorne, each child had been gifted with not only a special ability but for some reason, an extremely heightened desire for intimacy compared to most people.

Kastle had never understood why God had allowed them to be born this way. The Bible always spoke of the importance of morality, fidelity and abstinence unless you were married. These laws had been ingrained in them from a very young age by their father. He had always tried to live by them as best he could. But when that overwhelming need wasn't satisfied, it made them more than just grouchy or irritable, as in the case of most people. It made them extremely aggressive, and at times, even dangerous if they couldn't find an outlet. It was a highly embarrassing state to be in. Particularly considering the environment in which they had been raised; a Christian household.

Kastle shifted restlessly as he stood against the wall, staring at Astraia as she put puzzles together with her kids. She'd chosen to wear the new navy-blue long sleeve t-shirt today; with the dark faded jeans, she'd picked up the day before. The t-shirt had six snaps starting at the collar and ending just below her chest. Only two of the snaps were undone, but his imagination was on overdrive.

"If I didn't know better, I'd say you were drooling over the pizzas I got in my hand," Pegueros said as he dropped three boxes on the table.

"I don't know what you're talking about." Kastle spun around and grabbed a box without looking. Desperate for something to do with his hands, he opened the pizza box, picked up a slice and took a bite. His reaction was instantaneous. Face contorting in a grotesque fashion he reached for a napkin, spitting the contents of his mouth into it, managing to get the attention of everyone in the room.

"Yuck! What *was* that?" Kastle said, gagging on the taste left in his mouth while searching for his soda. He could hear Pegueros laughing uproariously next to him.

"That would be mine," he replied, as he walked over to the table and took the offending pizza box away. "Ham, pineapple, sardines and jalapenos." Pegueros sniffed the box in appreciation.

Both Kastle and Astraia made faces at him as they watched him inhale an entire slice in three bites.

Turning his attention back to Kastle, Pegueros reached out and slapped him on the shoulder.

"What has gotten into you, Man? You've been stomping around here for the last couple of days, all grouchy and irritable. And every time I look at you, you're looking at her," he whispered, pointing towards Astraia.

It just so happened, that at that moment, she had chosen to stretch her arms up over her head, and then back around her back. The action caused her shirt to draw tight against her. Kastle's mouth dropped and he could feel an uncomfortable ache below his waist. Groaning softly, he looked away quickly, at the same time asking the Lord to give him strength.

"Did you just say what I think you said?" He barely heard Pegueros speak as he dropped the pizza back onto his paper plate.

"Wait, what?" Kastle asked stupidly.

"Snap out of it, Man. Are you hearing what your own mouth is saying? Better not let her or her kids hear you say that." Pegueros grinned.

Bemused, Kastle asked, "Why? What?"

After repeating for Kastle's ears what he'd said, without clearly thinking, Pegueros watched with a wide-mouthed grin as heat suffused Kastle's face at the inappropriate comment.

Standing up suddenly, Kastle started walking away. Not having realized he spoke out loud, it had become obvious to him that he had to get away from Astraia for a while. Her proximity was giving him ideas he knew he shouldn't even be entertaining in his head.

"Hey! Where are you going?" Pegueros hollered after him.

"Up." Kastle pointed towards the ceiling. A little walk on the roof in the fresh night air might do him some good.

- - -

Astraia was preparing the children for bed when Kastle finally returned. Grateful for the additional reprieve before needing to be in her presence again, Kastle took a moment to eat some cold pizza. After wolfing down his last slice, he guzzled half his bottle of root beer, while ignoring the look he was getting from his partner.

"Here's everything you asked me for earlier today." Pegueros handed Kastle the information he'd need to go over with her. "And I'm turning in for the night." His brows rose in a silent question.

"Right," Kastle said while spreading the papers on the table. He waited for Astraia to return from putting the children to bed. Kastle tried to concentrate on the words on the pages. Instead, he found himself listening intently to her sweet voice coming from the kid's bedroom, singing 'Jesus Loves Me' and 'Twinkle, Twinkle Little Star.' He was impressed at how well she could sing.

Sitting back in his chair, he could hear her singing another song about butterflies. He wasn't familiar with it but it was just as beautiful. By the time she'd returned to the living room, it was to find him sitting at the kitchen table, with his head back and his eyes closed as if asleep. Thinking he might have dozed off while waiting, Astraia attempted to tiptoe across the room to her bedroom.

"It's okay, Astraia. I'm awake," Kastle said slowly in a soft, smooth voice that made her shiver. He looked at her then, with his dark brown eyes, and she found she missed the amazing crystal-clear blue eyes she'd seen the first time she met him. Wondering why he'd been wearing the blue contacts in the first place, she asked him about them.

"Why do you ask?"

"They were so unusual, striking even. I liked them," she admitted, blushing.

"What? You don't like my brown eyes?" he teased, grinning back at her.

"No it's not that, it's just ... they don't seem to suit you as well, I guess." Seeing him staring at her intently, she realized she must have blundered somehow. "I'm sorry. I suppose brown is your natural color."

Eyeing her curiously, Kastle sat watching her for a moment. Getting up, he walked over to her and took her by the hand, with the intention of dragging her over to the table so they could get started. Feeling the soft skin of her hand in his, he realized this simple gesture had been his first mistake, as well as his undoing.

Groaning at the contact, he reached out to her without thinking and took her in his arms. Cupping the back of her head in one hand, he leaned forward and enveloped her mouth with his, as he angled his head. The kiss started out soft and sweet, but his insatiable need for more was becoming overpowering. Using as much restraint as he could, Kastle was determined to leave this at just that, a kiss… or two.

Breathless, Astraia whimpered softly next to him. She had spent the day asking for God's strength and forgiveness. Praying now for restraint and the willpower to keep what was happening from turning into something else, she took a deep breath. She knew full well this was one of the reasons why such intimacy was meant to be between two people who were married. Because once you had a taste of what it could be like, it was that much harder to restrain one's self.

Sensing her uncertainty, Kastle inhaled deeply, willing himself to slow down as he internally spoke with God. Asking the Lord to give him the fortitude to abstain from taking things further, he lifted her from the floor. Swinging her into his arms with ease, she gave a startled cry of surprise as he carried her to the couch, placing her in a reclining position on the cushions. Kneeling next to her, he wrapped his arms around her, nipping at her bottom lip, ending the kiss as he sighed against her.

Pulling away from her slightly, to give them both a chance to breathe, Kastle was surprised by his reaction to her and realized she was breathing just as heavily as he was.

Inhaling sharply as he stared down at her, he could see her lips were damp from his. Her eyes mere slits as she stared back at him, mirroring his internal battle. Wanting so much more than just to hold her, he realized he couldn't do that to her again, especially not right now. He was responsible for keeping her safe, and that, above all else, had to take precedence.

"Feeling a bit overwhelmed, are you?" he asked in a ragged breath, with as much mischief as he could muster.

Seeing her nod, he sighed heavily and set back on his heels near the couch.

She looked at him then, with an odd kind of expression, and he wondered if he'd gone too far. Instead, she surprised him. "At times, it's as though you can read my mind. But that's not possible, is it?" Her words left an awkward silence in the air. Kastle chose not to respond, not wanting to lie to her, and yet, not able to tell the truth.

"No one can read minds," he said instead, for truthfully no human to his knowledge could.

"Of course, I'm sorry," she said quickly, not wanting to lose the moment with him, yet knowing it had likely already been lost.

Astraia knew that allowing the kisses had been wrong, especially after just having lost her husband. Yet she couldn't deny her attraction to him. From the first moment, she'd seen him in the store, she had felt drawn to him, and the guilt she experienced over that was strong.

"I'm embarrassed to admit this, but I've wanted you to do that all day long," she said honestly, as she lay before him on the couch.

Sighing heavily, Kastle pulled her to him, curling her into his arms as he leaned back against the cushions.

"I don't want to take advantage of you, Astraia. You've suffered a great loss and I know I shouldn't be messing with you so soon after Dylan's death. It's just ... I like you a lot more than I know I should under the circumstances. Yet, I have this insatiable need..."

"I know," Astraia whispered quietly, thinking she fully understood what he was talking about, as she ran her fingertips surreptitiously against his jawline.

"Oh, no." His eyes twinkled. "You really don't."

Astraia tried to speak, but he stilled her words by placing his fingers on her lips, hushing anything else she might say.

Knowing he couldn't go any further than what he already had, he refrained from kissing her again. Trailing his fingers up her neck and along her cheekbones, he moaned softly as he buried his head in her neck.

Giggling, she held him to her by laying her hand at the base of his neck. Playing with his collar, she inhaled the scent of him, wanting desperately to ask for more but knowing she shouldn't and couldn't. Her children were in the bedrooms right next to them. Were they to wake and see them together like this, it would be very confusing for them.

"Kastle." A random thought occurred to her. "Had it really been over three years since you'd last..."

Tensing next to her as she floundered for words, he grimaced into her shoulder. Raising his head to meet her gaze, he decided it wouldn't hurt anything, to be honest with her.

"It had been much longer than that," he answered finally, trying to sound nonchalant. "Over eight years or so."

Surprised, Astraia wasn't sure she believed him at first. Noticing the look in his eyes, she realized he was telling the truth.

"Why? The way you look, you could have anyone you wanted. I'd think women would be lining up in droves."

"I've dated, and I won't deny that I've had numerous offers," Kastle answered cautiously, knowing she was unaware of his faith. "But, I was raised to respect women, and to believe that such intimacy should be confined to the marriage bed."

"Does that mean eight years ago you were married?" Astraia asked curiously.

Choosing not to answer the question, he avoided it by making a statement instead. "I am human, Astraia. Though I strive to overcome temptation, at times, even I fall now and again."

"So, you weren't married when…"

"No," he said abruptly, sounding frustrated.

Sensing it was a sore subject, she opted instead to drop it, not wanting to upset him further and alienate him.

Eyes narrowing to slits, he scowled at the memory. "When I was active, the need was insatiable." He spoke without warning, not sure why he'd said it.

"Meaning daily?" she teased, as her eyes twinkled and she grinned. She had been surprised by his honesty with her over the subject.

"No, nothing like that," he said truthfully, his gaze boring into hers. "It was a great deal more frequent than that."

Chapter 13

Seeing the look of pure shock on her face, Kastle couldn't help but laugh out loud. "I take it you weren't accustomed to that much activity?"

"Truthfully?" she asked, looking at him now more seriously. Worry lines furrowed her brow. He realized she was self-conscious about discussing her late husband with him.

"Truth is always best," he said gently as he nodded. "It's okay, Astraia. Dylan was your husband after all. You were bound to have been intimate with him or you would never have had children."

Her facial expression changed then. Kastle realized he'd hit a nerve somehow but he couldn't put his finger on what it was. He gathered her thoughts were apparently shifting back and forth too quickly to be able to learn anything.

Sighing heavily, while twirling tips of her wavy blonde hair in her fingers, she responded. "At best, it was infrequent," she said simply, the desire to change the subject very apparent. Then she looked over at him, her mind racing again. "I've been wondering, do you mind if I ask a personal question?"

Kastle laughed again, the sound warm and rich. "I've just asked you about the frequency of intimacy with your recently departed husband and you're wondering if I mind if you ask a personal question." They looked at each other, grinning at the irony.

"I was just wondering what your heritage was," Astraia said a little nervously as if she thought the question might bother him. His unusual features and skin tone almost led her to believe there might be Native American Indian in him.

Curious as to why she wanted to know and a little anxious, he sequestered his emotions. Leaving his expression blank, he answered her with a question of his own.

"What do you think it is?"

"I don't know that I'd want to try to guess."

"Why not?"

"What if I guess wrong? I wouldn't want to offend you or hurt your feelings somehow. Some people are sensitive about their background."

Smiling at her thoughtfulness, Kastle reached out absent-mindedly, and ran his hand along her side again, enjoying the feel of her in his hands.

"In that case, we'll just leave it to the imagination, shall we?" He hoped she would let well enough alone. Explaining his background might open a line of questioning he wasn't prepared to answer. Deciding it was time to change the subject entirely, he took one of her hands in his.

"I need to tell you something," he said more seriously.

"What's up?" She sensed that Kastle was not inclined towards opening up to her about such things. Content with the notion of being curled up next to him instead, she rested her head against his shoulder.

"We're having a lot of difficulty finding a safe location for you and the kids."

He could feel her hand start to jerk away, but he held them firm. Seeing her facial expression change suddenly, from bright, inquisitive eyes, to ones shadowed with sadness and fear, he cringed inwardly at having to mention this to her.

"We're not any closer to making a decision about where to relocate you."

"I see. Is there nowhere safe for us?" she asked quietly, her voice shaking a little as she spoke.

"No, that's not what I'm saying. We'll figure it out. I'm merely trying to warn you that this may take some time."

"How much time are we talking, a few more days or a week?"

"In cases like yours, sometimes it can take as much as a couple months."

"A couple months? Kastle!"

"I'm not saying it's going to take that long. All I'm trying to tell you is that you might want to make yourself comfortable here. We're going to be isolated from the rest of the world for a while."

"I see."

Taking a deep breath, Kastle prepared himself for the request he wanted to make of her while fiddling nervously with the fabric of her shirt between his fingers.

"Because of that, there's something I may need your help with. That is if you're willing. Keep in mind, you're not obligated in any way, for any reason. But it might be easier on all of us if you were willing."

"What is it?" she asked, realizing he was embarrassed by something but anxious to discuss it.

"Here's the thing, as previously mentioned I tend to have a problem with intimacy," he said bluntly, watching as her eyes grew big. "Over the years, I've found I can force myself to abstain for long periods of time. But once I've been active again, I experience this rather insatiable desire for some time thereafter." He could see, and hear, her struggling to force down a giggle. Running his hands across his face, he looked away uncomfortably.

"What exactly are you trying to ask me?" Her eyes twinkled with humor, and yet, she was a little anxious at what he might be getting at.

"Would you have a problem if I joined you every morning in your room until we've managed to relocate you?"

She stared at him in surprise, and then cocked an eyebrow. "Did you say every morning?"

"Yes." Kastle held his breath. He waited impatiently for her response, all the while hoping she'd say yes.

Pulling back from him a little, Astraia looked at him, as if she was seeing him for the first time. "You're not asking to join me because you have an ulterior motive, you're asking for entirely different reasons altogether, aren't you?"

Smiling, his eyes brightened with mischief. "Yes, but only if you're willing to suffer my presence and think you can handle it."

"I'd sure try," she replied while giggling. When he smiled at her like that, it was like getting hit with a soft punch and her heart rate would escalate. Sobering quickly, she glanced back at him. Not accustomed to sharing her morning ritual with anyone, including her own husband

Dylan, she was becoming a little uncomfortable with the request.

"I'll be honest with you. I've never been the sort of person to … share my mornings with anyone. I was raised with Christian values but I'm a very private person where such things are concerned." She looked at him anxiously, expecting him to react in a disdainful manner.

Kastle did the last thing she would have expected. Leaning up, he wrapped his arms around her and smiled.

"It's nice to see there are others like me with a similar problem." He stared at her seriously.

Gazing at him with a curious expression, her eyebrows rose as she spoke. "And what problem would that be exactly?" she asked, a little puzzled by his statement. Astraia wondered suddenly if she might have misunderstood what he was asking of her.

"A secret and insatiable desire for a relationship."

Confused, Astraia flushed, becoming increasingly embarrassed by her previous behavior. Glancing around herself frantically, she struggled to think, realizing he must believe her to be desperate for his attention because of the way she'd acted with him. Kicking herself for giving in to temptation, she sat there feeling wretched.

"Don't get me wrong, Kastle, I'm sure any decent woman would jump at the chance to… see you regularly like that, it's just I have reservations about…"

Sighing heavily, Kastle interrupted. "I shouldn't have asked you that. It was unfair of me." He wished they could drop the subject.

"It's my fault, isn't it?" There was a look of guilt in her eyes. Astraia suspected she knew why he wanted to share in her morning ritual. "-That you're in this state. I mean, you never would have kissed me just now if I hadn't provoked you that night into…"

"Don't," he said crossly, not wanting to get into this debate again. Sitting up suddenly, he turned away from her. "I don't want pity from you. You have my word; I won't bother you again." He stood then, as she gasped in surprise and anger.

"Wait just a minute!" she said, not sure which part she was more upset about: the part where he was brushing her off or the part where he was making her feel unwanted. "You know what, that's okay, I get it. You must think if I'm that easy, then I'm willing to do just about anything with you, right?"

Kastle walked over and stood in front of her, shocked at her words. Worse, he was being conveyed the images and thoughts currently running through her mind. Thoughts filled with pain and hurt, reverberating over and over in her head, about only needing the right parts.

"That's not what I meant." Bewildered by the sudden turn the conversation was taking he stared openly.

"Really? A man like you would normally never give me a second glance. I should be grateful you're willing to...."

"Do not finish that," Kastle said sharply. "A man like me? You mean a Greek god on steroids," he said with heat, watching her nod. "Because you're no goddess, right?"

"Right." Astraia agreed, surprised he'd thrown her own words back at her and yet feeling inferior, nonetheless. "I figured that's what you thought." She swallowed hard, the hurt aching in her chest as her eyes threatened to brim with tears.

Kastle saw then it was like he'd punched her in the heart. The look on her face made his gut clench. She sobbed, trying hard to mask her tumultuous feelings.

Disgusted by the woman's view of herself, Kastle couldn't help but respond in kind. "You know nothing of what I think, or you would never say such a thing. Why do you do that anyway? Why do you think so horribly of yourself, that you'd make such a statement in the first place?"

She sat quietly in front of him. Her head was bent, staring down her front. "To answer that, all you need to do is just look at me," she said softly, tearing up.

He gazed over her full-figured shape and glanced back into her eyes. "Honey, as far as I'm concerned, I see nothing that would warrant such a statement."

She sighed in frustration, seeming almost weary of the conversation. "I'm not stupid. I know…"

"You know nothing." He realized where she intended to go with this. "You know what some man told you, what, fifteen years ago, about how all it takes is having the right parts?" He finished in disgust and then watched her pale noticeably.

"Kastle," she started quietly, her voice almost a whisper as her lips trembled. "When you've been told something as often as I have, from as many people as I have, for as many years as I have, it makes it really hard to believe that anything else could be true."

Taken aback, he simply stared at her, appearing thunderstruck. Her damaged spirit appeared as a gaping wound before him, making it very apparent that someone or something had inflicted this on her intentionally, and it hurt him to his core to see her in such pain. Picking her up from the couch, he stood there, embracing her as she dangled in his arms. Running his hands through her long hair, he shushed her gently as he heard her choke back a sob, trying desperately to keep from crying.

"What happened to you?" he asked her, genuinely concerned. "Who did this to you?"

Kastle saw it then, an image from her mind of a man's face, placed there by the angel at his side. Then another image was imprinted upon him, of the same white male, about five feet eleven, weighing 210 pounds. He was wearing a navy-blue baseball cap, and Nike running suit. As the image moved, as if in slow motion, Kastle could see the man practicing Tae Kwon Doe on another man of African American descent whom he couldn't get a clear image of. The picture in his head showed the white man having just broken the other man's hand.

No wonder she'd been so afraid of Henley. Her attacker and Jericho Henley could practically be brothers. They obviously weren't the same man for the attacker was a white man, not black American like Henley. But they both did have decidedly similar features and a goatee.

- - -

Waking the next morning earlier than normal, Astraia yawned wearily as she crawled out from under her warm blankets. Staring back at the bed longingly, she slowly made her way to the restroom, then returned in short order. Grabbing the book and pad of paper from her nightstand, she crept from her room, tiptoeing across the living room to Kastle's bedroom.

Taking a deep breath, she gingerly opened the door, then closed it quickly behind her. Padding towards the bed, she leaned over Kastle and was about to tap him on his bare shoulder, when he surprised her by speaking unexpectedly.

"What is it, Astraia?" He groaned into his pillow.

"How did you know I was here, and that it was me?" she asked in surprise.

"You're very noisy and I could smell your shampoo the moment you walked in the door," he said, rolling over onto his back. Sighing up at her, he placed an arm over his face to shield his eyes. "What do you want?" He sounded testy already.

Cocking an eyebrow at him, she waved the items in her hand before his face. "You were the one who wanted to join me every morning, right?" she responded irritably.

Peering out at her from under his arm, Kastle cocked his head to one side. He realized she was holding in her hands the Bible she'd asked him to get for her.

"Really? I thought you said…"

"Obviously, I changed my mind, or I wouldn't be here."

"Okay. But we can't do it here," he said anxiously, sounding relieved as he sat up in bed. His blanket dropped, showing he wasn't wearing a shirt. Realizing he'd have to get dressed before he could do anything, Kastle shifted self-consciously in the bed.

"Why not?" She glanced furtively away.

"I'm much more likely to maul you in here," he responded honestly while rubbing at his eyes. The contacts he left in the night before were becoming dry. "We'll go to your room."

"In that case, wouldn't the living room be more prudent?" She rolled her eyes, her insides warming at the notion of being mauled by him.

"No," he said promptly.

"But … there's no bed there."

"I'm aware of that, but Pegueros might see us."

"Are you serious?" Seeing the look on his face, she stared at him incredulously. Was it possible he was a closet Christian? "You've got to be kidding me. Are you telling me you're embarrassed for him to find out you do morning devotions, or that you believe in God?"

"It's not like that," he said irritably.

"Really?" She was unconvinced.

"It's complicated, all right? Can we just go to your room already?" He was becoming extremely frustrated. In the past, he had made the mistake of allowing his partners to become aware of his faith. In every instance, the men he worked with would question his ability to do his job because of it. Knowing full well where it might lead if Pegueros found out, he preferred not to do this publicly.

"Fine," she said while continuing to stand where she was. "Well, what are you waiting for?"

"For you to leave," he said in exasperation. "I'm not wearing any pants."

Her eyes suddenly widened in understanding. "Oh!" She then turned abruptly, banging her face against the door in her haste.

Kastle couldn't help but smother a laugh as he watched her pelt from his room and cross the living room to her bedroom door, disappearing behind it.

Moments later, he joined her in her room, having dressed in jeans and a white t-shirt. He was carrying two mugs of hot coffee with him. Handing one off to Astraia, she thanked him, then sipped at the honey sweetened brew in appreciation.

"What made you change your mind?" Kastle asked, curious by her unexpected change of heart. He could see a red mark on her nose from where she bumped into his door. It made him grin.

"Not many men put themselves out there like you did last night," Astraia said hastily. "It occurred to me, with what you do for a living, that your needs should take precedence over my selfish desire for privacy."

Touched by her consideration, Kastle walked self-consciously towards her. Gesturing at the bed, he watched as she nodded her ascent. Sitting down next to her, he placed his Bible on his lap.

Noticing that the cover of his book was badly worn, and the pages seemed bent and crinkled from heavy use, Astraia stared up at him, her interest piqued.

"That has seen some use," she commented, pointing towards the Bible in his lap.

"So it would seem." Speaking mildly, he adjusted his seat on the bed, so he could turn and face her.

"It says a lot about you."

"What it says is that I sin a lot as the result of my line of work," he replied, his lips thinning as he became agitated. Normally, such discussions didn't bother him. But for some reason, he was suddenly uncomfortable with her knowing what he did for a living. He grimaced. "Where would you like to start?"

"I thought, under the circumstances, we should cover the merits of overcoming temptation." She fidgeted next to him. Watching as his lips twitched, it eventually curved into an endearing half smile. "First Corinthians 10:13 seemed like a good place to start maybe."

"As you wish." He found her choice extremely amusing, and yet at the same time, highly appropriate in his case. This passage had been exactly what he was hoping for. He was more familiar with the passage than he cared to admit. "As I recall, it covers how every test that we experience, is the kind that normally comes to us, and that God will not allow us to be tested beyond our power to remain firm. It also goes on to say, that at the time we are put to the test, he will give us the strength to endure it, and so provide us with a way out."

"Yes, I believe that is where I fell short that night." Her gaze drifted shyly away from him.

"How so?" He was curious to know where she was going with this.

"I failed to see that God had already presented me with an out." Shame filled her words, as she sat fiddling with the pages of her Bible. "You had been sent to protect me. I allowed fear to rule me. As a result, through his test of temptation, I was blind to see…"

Cutting her off gently, Kastle shook his head. "I think you might be a little confused. I got the feeling temptation wasn't the issue for you that night. Your issue was fear."

"I don't understand."

"The verse is much more fitting for my situation for I was the one being tested or tempted in this case, and I failed to rise above it," he countered. "I do believe God sent me there to protect you that night. You're right about that. But, you were so full of fear and self-deprecation, that you were blinded from seeing that I could, and would, protect you, and that such intimate actions weren't necessary."

Brushing her long hair away from her face, she peered up at him, her eyes shifting uneasily as she stuttered.

"I see, and after such a long time… I'm so sorry. Can you ever forgive me?"

"Forgiving you isn't necessary as far as I'm concerned. I do understand where the fear was coming from. But if it makes you feel better, I do." His gaze was warm upon hers. "But can you forgive me?" He hoped to get to the heart of his reasons for wanting to speak with her in this way. Maybe then, they could both finally heal. "I placed you in an extremely compromising position that night. I used some uncharacteristically poor judgment and am still unclear as to why," he said, looking just as confused as she felt.

"Of course, you were just trying to protect me."

His conscience getting the better of him, Kastle winced openly. "I was trying to protect you, yes. But if I were, to be honest with myself and you, I had been having inappropriate thoughts about you much of that day and I knew you were married. The situation could have been just as easily resolved with my clothes on, as opposed to off."

"Let me get this straight. You were actually coveting me?" She asked in surprise. Seeing him nod uncomfortably, she stared in bewilderment, feeling almost flattered. Regaining her composure, she stared down at her Bible, then over at him, feeling lost and inexperienced.

"I'm fairly new at this, within the last year or so. Most of the time I really don't know what I'm doing," she explained with a nervous chuckle. "Would you mind taking the lead?"

Giving another of his half smiles, Kastle suggested, "Why don't we start with a prayer for direction first, and go from there?" Seeing her nod, he proceeded. After he prayed, it came to him he knew where to start for the them both.

Chapter 14

"We may have to start looking further north."

Looking at the board in frustration, Kastle shook his head. It had been two weeks since he had learned the face of Astraia's attacker. He was having trouble concentrating on the task at hand for the similarities between Henley and the man who hurt her were wearing on him. All he wanted to do was find the man who had hurt her and tear him apart. Instead, he was staring at hundreds of pushpins on a map.

Kicking at a chair angrily, he caught Pegueros looking at him in surprise.

"You need to take her in her room and go at it for a while?" Pegueros asked boldly while munching on a pretzel.

Kastle stared at him in astonishment. "What did you just say?"

"I can watch the kids for you," he offered, grinning as he grabbed another pretzel.

The look on Kastle's face made Pegueros a little nervous, but he laughed out loud anyway, drawing Astraia's attention. Distracted by her daughter begging for another game, she returned to the task of catching a fish with her game pole.

"Close your mouth, Kastle," Pegueros said while smiling. "Honestly, did you think I wasn't gonna figure out something was going on between the two of you?"

"It's not what you think."

"Right, and I'm a ballerina."

"What tipped you off?" Kastle sighed, turning back to the board, not paying much attention to it.

"Sayleena came running in my room one night almost two weeks ago and said you were attacking her mommy." Kastle spun around, looking at him in horror. "When I went to investigate with her, I heard, and then saw the two of you on the couch. I made my own deductions, of course."

Head in his hands, Kastle moaned, "Don't tell me she saw."

"Yeah, but she's little, so she didn't understand what was going on. That's why she came and got me. So, I put her back to bed after the two of you disappeared and assured her that you weren't attacking her mommy. Told her the two of you were just playing and she needn't worry, 'because that's the kind of noises mommies make when they're happy."

Agent Kastle sat suddenly in the chair next to Pegueros nearly missing the seat. "I'm going to have to tell Astraia about that now, and she won't be happy about it."

"Don't go and do something stupid. Sayleena is fine. She just thinks you were playing a game. As for me?" Pegueros made a motion across his lips as if closing a zipper. "My lips are sealed. I know nothing." He raised his brows and smiled knowingly.

Kastle cast a furtive glance over at Astraia, to make sure she couldn't hear what was being said. He bowed his head in thought for a moment. Knowing honesty was always best, he couldn't help wondering if, in this case, silence might be the best course. Peering over at Pegueros, he saw he was waiting for a response.

Giving a half smile, he shrugged finally and said. "I'd sure appreciate it if you kept quiet about that night. She's real sensitive about how it might look."

Shrugging, Pegueros rolled his eyes as if in exasperation. "I wondered if it was just that night. You've been too grouchy the past week and a half for it to be otherwise," he said as he stuck another push pin in.

"I'm telling you for the last time, it wasn't what you think. We just kissed."

"Whatever you say. As for it looking bad... people always seem to hold those who were raised in a church to higher standards because of the values they're taught. Which is as it should be, because if, for example, you're going to call yourself a Christian, you should sure behave like one, right? That's why I've been surprised by how you've been acting with her."

Glancing over at his partner curiously, Kastle gave him a questioning look. Seeing him tap a finger against his forehead, the man grinned back at him.

"I know you're a Christian or, at the very least, of similar faith. You think you're the only one that can put two and two together?" Pegueros asked, glancing down at the list in his hand. "Besides, I accidentally overheard you praying for forgiveness for having to kill those men that night when we first arrived here."

149

Exchanging an uneasy glance with him, Kastle became introspective. More and more, he was beginning to realize he had to get out of his line of work and out from under the CIA's radar. If Pegueros was picking up on such things, how long would it be before he figured out what he was truly capable of?

"Here's the thing everyone always seems to forget, though," he heard Pegueros continue, as he leaned forward conspiratorially. "A person of faith is just as human as anyone else. They have the same feelings and the same temptations. Just because they might fall now and again, doesn't mean they're bad people."

Leaning back, Kastle eyed the other agent with a renewed appreciation. Knowing the man was an admitted atheist, he found his perspective on Christianity very interesting. "And this is coming from a man who claims no faith."

"Just because I don't believe there's a God doesn't mean there couldn't be one. I've studied enough about it in my youth to know the basic rules," Pegueros replied as he shrugged. "Mind you, I still think Christians and Catholics are loony to believe what they do. But I'm not so set in my lack of belief I can't admit that I might be wrong."

"So, you're not saying you think it's right, you're just saying…"

"I'm saying, what you're doing with her, you know, sleeping with her out of wedlock, it's a sin by your faith's standards."

"I'm not sleeping with her!" Kastle snapped angrily, his voice rising.

"All right, all right. I believe you." Pegueros raised his arms in front of him as though for protection. "So you're not sleeping with her. Regardless, for arguments sake, if you were, you should try not to mess with her, if you can.

But if you do, you better experience guilt over it and ask for your God's forgiveness. If you don't, then you become no different than a man who murders without compunction in His eyes. That is, of course, if there is a God."

"Trust me, there is a God."

"So you say."

Deep in thought, he peered over at his partner almost guiltily. He knew all of this, of course, as he'd been taught it by his father at an early age. But to be reminded of it by a self-proclaimed atheist, of all people, was more than a little disconcerting.

Cocking one eyebrow, Pegueros asked suddenly, "Why didn't you sleep with her that night anyway? Did she tell you no or something?"

"What do you say we just drop it, okay?" He really didn't want to get into this discussion with him.

Pegueros put his hands up in front of him once again, "No problema. It's dropped. But..."

"Here we go," he interrupted, becoming disgusted.

"No, now just a minute. You listen." Casting a furtive glance over at Astraia, he looked back at Kastle with a serious expression on his face. "I wasn't quite sure what was going on. Honestly, I suspected you weren't messing with her. I would have thought your aggressiveness would be dissipating, rather than increasing, if you were," Pegueros said as he began eyeing her openly.

Scowling over at his partner, Kastle couldn't exactly argue the point, for he knew it was true. Groaning softly into his hand in irritation, he looked back up at Pegueros to realize he was still talking.

"She's been looking awful tired over there like she could use a good night's rest. So it made me wonder if you were keeping her up after all," he finished with genuine concern.

Glancing over at her, Kastle couldn't help but agree. "When I went in to get her up this morning, I overheard her getting sick in the bathroom. She's not feeling good today. I'm afraid she might have the flu."

"Vomiting, eh? You sure it's the flu?"

"I don't know. Could be food poisoning, I suppose." He gave Pegueros a foul look. The way the man cooked on the nights when it was his turn, food poisoning was a possibility.

Glaring back at him, Pegueros harrumphed in disgust at the implication. Reaching for another list from the table, he watched in pure amazement as Kastle snatched it out of his hand and growled at him. The man was getting impossible to talk to, let alone be around.

"Besides, what else could it be?" Kastle practically snarled, while adding another push pin to the board.

"Who's that?" Pegueros pointed to the board where he had stuck the pin.

"Audrey Rabiel, a member of her graduating class," he said with a frown. "That takes care of Colorado." He sighed heavily.

"Wow, her class is spread out!" Pegueros turned from the board to face Kastle. "Man, she's throwing up." He looked at Kastle meaningfully. "She could be pregnant."

Kastle tensed, but promptly answered, "She's not pregnant."

"How can you be so sure?"

"I'm sure, all right. It's not possible." He added another push pin to the board, eliminating yet another state.

"From my experience, anything is possible," Pegueros said. "Wait a minute, did you just eliminate Tennessee?"

Kastle took a deep breath. "Yup." He yawned and stretched, "She can't be pregnant because I found out after my ex-wife died that I can't have kids." He tried to sound matter-of-fact about it.

Genuinely confused, his partner scratched his head while watching him with a curious look on his face. Seeing his expression, Kastle elaborated.

"She'd aborted my baby right before dying in a car accident. Or at least, I thought it was mine at the time. Found out afterward that it was her dead boyfriend's, and that it could have never been mine in the first place." He shrugged it off as though it were no big deal.

Pegueros winced. "Ouch." Shocked at his admission, he paused for a moment in what he was doing. "I'm sorry, Man. That's too bad, though, 'because you'd a been a good dad I bet."

"You think so?" Kastle asked, sounding only mildly interested, as he was going through another list.

"You're really good with hers." Pegueros waved his hand towards Astraia.

Kastle looked up then, in time to see Saruman starting his Batman toy into a nosedive, smashing it into the fishing game, causing a bunch of the fish to pop out.

Chuckling while he smiled, he shook his head and said, "She's got some great kids."

Pegueros crossed his arms and stood still facing his partner. He took a deep breath. "Kastle," he said sharply, trying to get his attention.

Turning, Agent Kastle just looked at the man. "What, Pegueros? You got a bug up your butt? Just speak your mind already."

"She could still be pregnant," Pegueros said, staring at him intently. "She *was* married after all."

Kastle just looked at him, not saying a word. Truthfully, this hadn't occurred to him and it should have. Sighing heavily, he turned back towards Astraia and the kids, watching them almost longingly.

Pegueros waited patiently until he finally responded.

"Yeah, all right." He got up from his seat. "I need a break from this. I'm heading into town for a bit. Text me with anything else we need."

- - -

The next morning, Kastle woke for the third time. He was having trouble sleeping. Deciding it was time to finally get up, even though Astraia was likely still asleep, he crawled out of bed and grabbed a pair of jeans from his bag. After stepping into them, he zipped them up and walked, shirtless, into the living room.

Tensing suddenly as he neared the television, Kastle glanced toward Astraia's bedroom, instinct sending a warning as the hairs on his arms rose ominously. He waited, hardly daring to breathe while trying to figure out what it was that was bothering him. A sense of urgency knotted his gut. He finally moved with caution towards her room. Only a few steps away from Astraia's bedroom door, Kastle could hear what sounded like retching sounds coming from her room. Opening the door, he peered in to see Astraia still lying in bed. The second he saw her, he knew something was wrong.

Flinging the door open, he was across the room and on her bed in three strides. The sudden jarring motion of the bed as he landed next to her didn't seem to faze or wake her.

Bent over on her side, she appeared to be seizing as though she were throwing up. Eyes clenched tightly, her body jerked. Her legs and arms went limp, and her head lolled back with her eyelashes flickering. Her current behavior was more than a little reminiscent of the kind of fit his sister, Megorah, would have sometimes when she would foreshadow an event in her dreams. Kastle had only ever witnessed his sister do it once. He couldn't be sure if that was what was happening or not.

He called out to her in concern. Wrapping his arms around her, he lifted her up from the bed. Her head drooped to one side as he set her in his lap, cradling her head against his chest. Suddenly, her eyes opened wide and her pupils dilated.

Staring unexpectedly up into Kastle's eyes, Astraia inhaled deeply at the feeling of Deja Vue she was experiencing. When she attempted to exhale, she fought against overwhelming nausea she was experiencing. Scrambling desperately from his grasp, she nearly fell to the floor while trying to run in a panic for the bathroom. Barely making it in time, she knelt before the toilet and threw up.

Feeling suddenly chilled, as though she'd stepped out of a heated room into a winter storm, Astraia was grateful to feel Kastle's warm chest lean against her back as he flushed the toilet for her. Handing her a tissue, she gladly accepted it with trembling hands.

"Are you all right?" He asked gently. The tone of his voice was clearly worried.

Shaking her head in confusion, she leaned into him, desperate for heat. She felt his strong arms wrap around her, enveloping her as though a human heater.

Kastle could feel Astraia shiver next to him. She was cold and her skin felt almost clammy to the touch. Perspiration beaded across her forehead, and her lips trembled against his skin.

"Don't let go," he heard her whisper hoarsely. "Please, whatever you do, don't let go. You're so warm," she said desperately, still clinging to him.

"I won't. I've got you, Honey," he assured her, adjusting her so he could better cradle her in his arms. Worry lines appeared on his brow as Kastle asked, "What's going on? What happened just then?"

Astraia shook her head, "I don't know. I just don't know." The skin around her eyes were lined with worry and confusion. "It was like I was dreaming." Speaking quietly, she was unsure of how much she wanted to tell him. The experience had been unsettling. "It was so bizarre. I felt like I was awake, but somehow I knew I was dreaming."

"What were you dreaming about?" he asked uneasily.

"This," she replied simply, staring up at him with her deep blue eyes. "I was dreaming about this exact moment, right now, as well as a moment ago when I got sick. I know, it probably sounds crazy." Her voice trailed off. Astraia's eyes were beginning to droop, as though she were suddenly overwhelmed with exhaustion.

"Has this ever happened before?" Staring down at her, Kastle was becoming increasingly uneasy. What she was talking about almost sounded like she had foreshadowed an event. He had never met anyone who could do that before, aside from his sister and mother.

"Yes." Her response came quickly. "It's been happening every night for the past week and a half or so. But, it's the first time it's been so... so real," she answered while struggling to keep from falling asleep.

Kastle held her for a long time, rocking her gently as she plastered herself against his chest. It wasn't long before she closed her eyes again. By then, he could hear the restless sounds of children playing in their room. Not wanting them to see him with Astraia in the bedroom, he lifted her and carried her into the living room with him, so she wouldn't be alone when she woke.

Situating her on the couch furthest from the television, he covered her with a blanket and placed another pillow behind her head. Pushing up off the floor, he stood, then saw his partner coming out of his room. Kastle assumed he must have appeared distressed, because Pegueros stopped in his tracks, and queried him promptly.

"What's up?" He started to walk towards him. Waving him back, he headed around the chair and into the dining area.

"I'm not sure exactly," he replied, glancing back to make sure she was still okay. "I went in to check on her this morning and found her in the middle of some kind of fit."

"Fit? Wait, you mean like a seizure or something?" he asked in surprise.

"It wasn't like your normal seizure."

"So, she wasn't having convulsions?"

"No, she looked like she was going to be sick, but she was still sleeping." Kastle shook his head. Deciding he didn't want to go into any more detail, he left it at that.

Pegueros set a couple of coffee mugs on the counter and pulled the sugar tin from the cupboard. Pouring a cup of coffee for them both he handed one to Kastle and added sugar to the other.

"It almost sounds like she just had a bad dream maybe," Pegueros said, shrugging it off nonchalantly. "I'm sure it's probably nothing."

Sunlight was now peeking through the drawn blinds of the windows. The coffee smelled good and the honey Kastle had just poured into his mug tasted, oh, so sweet.

He rolled his shoulders and attempted to shake off the unsettling vibes, from the events of the morning.

"Maybe. You're probably right." He took a sip of the coffee. He could feel the hot liquid as it slid down into his belly, warming him from the inside out.

An hour later Astraia woke to the sounds of cartoons and children playing on the furniture. She sat up suddenly, gasping as though in distress. Looking wide-eyed into the kitchen, she saw both Kastle and Pegueros watching her. Standing quickly, she bent over, grabbing at her belly and dashed for her bedroom, praying she'd make it to the bathroom in time.

Moments later, Kastle found her leaning over the toilet seat, having just thrown up again. Bending down next to her, he rubbed her back gently as he laid the brown paper bag he had next to her on the floor. Placing a washcloth on her forehead first to cool her off, he then ran it down across her cheeks and over her mouth. He looked at her, concern evident in his eyes, and a weary expression on his handsome drawn face.

"What's in the bag?" she asked weakly, relieved her stomach was starting to settle.

"Something I think you need to take."

Taking the bag in her hand, she could feel a box inside. She reached in to pull it out. "You mean like medicine?" Taking the item out, she stared down at the early pregnancy test, and moaned softly.

Thinking she was distressed by the possibility of being pregnant, Kastle reached out and patted her hand. "It's okay Astraia, it's best we find out now, so we can make sure you get what you need."

She giggled then, surprising him. "You think I'm pregnant? With your baby?" She smiled, a pleasant change from the distressed state from but moments before.

"No," Kastle said firmly, his gaze colliding with hers as he shook his head. "I don't think it's mine because I can't have kids."

She giggled again, and it turned into a hysterical laugh. "Oh, it's worse. You think I'm pregnant with Dylan's baby."

Confused by her curious behavior, he sat back on his heels and looked at her. For the life of him, he couldn't glean anything from her this morning. It was making him crazy.

"Astraia," he started, but she reached out and placed her hand across his lips.

Shaking her head, she spoke. "Kastle, I'm not pregnant. I can't get pregnant anymore. I had a tubal ligation after my boys were born. I had no intention of having any more children by that man.

Chapter 15

Ten days later, Astraia was still getting sick.

She awoke that morning for the third time to another one of the dreams that left her cold and exhausted. Only this time, she dreamed Kastle was waking her from a nap and telling her to pack everything up because they were leaving within the hour.

The night before, she could have sworn she had woken and gone in to check on her children in their bedroom. Then, she woke up in her bed, realizing she was about to do what she had dreamed.

Sitting at the table over the lunch hour, she attempted to eat a small bowl of chicken noodle soup and a chicken sandwich as she pondered on what was happening to her. She'd managed to eat only half of the soup and half of the sandwich but was getting full already.

Seeing her struggling, Kastle encouraged her to eat more. "If you can't eat the sandwich, maybe try eating the soup."

Shaking her head while holding her belly, she hunched in her chair. "I just can't, I'm getting too full. The sandwich is good though. I'll save the rest for maybe a snack this afternoon." Astraia smiled weakly back at him. She felt bad because somehow she just knew he had gone through a lot of effort to fix something light for her that was homemade. There were remains of a roasted chicken on the stove, and her sandwich had consisted of carved chicken, rather than sandwich meat.

Kastle frowned, putting his dish down in the sink.

"Hey kids, tell you what. If you're done, I'll have Uncle Pegueros get you each a fruit pop for dessert."

Squealing in delight, Sayleena, Saruman and Storman dropped their utensils, jumped from their chairs and attacked their honorary uncle as he headed towards the fridge.

Grabbing the box from the freezer, he quickly handed out their treat and herded them into the living room to enjoy it there. Turning on the television for them, he was back in time to see his partner standing at the table in front of Astraia.

"We need to get her to a doctor," Kastle said to Pegueros, looking down at Astraia with concern.

"We're of the same mind," Pegueros said upon taking a real good look at her. He noted her drawn face and tired eyes. She also appeared to have lost a fair amount of weight.

Glancing back and forth between the two men, Astraia sighed in exasperation. "Guys, I'm fine, really. It's just a bug I'm working through … I'm sure of it."

Kastle pulled a chair up next to her and looked her in the eye. His expression was stern. Worry lines furrowed his brow. "Astraia, whatever this is, it's not just a bug and I think you know it. You've lost weight, you're barely eating, and what you do eat you can't keep down. Then there are the dreams you're having."

Pegueros came up next to them and gazed down at her as well. "You've been getting sick for over a week now. That's too long, even for stomach flu. It could be food poisoning if other people were getting sick. But no one is. Astraia, we're gonna get you to a doctor. That's final."

Kastle and his partner exchanged worried looks before Pegueros walked away towards the office.

Trying to find a way to change the subject, Astraia spoke of the kids. "Did you know that Sayleena likes to crawl in bed with her brothers at night?"

Shaking his head, he asked curiously, "No, how did you find out? Did Sayleena tell you she did that?"

"No, she didn't, she... I think maybe... Somehow I just know she does it. Like last night, she started off in her bed, but after Pegueros read them their story and tucked them in, she waited for him to leave, then got up and crawled into their bed. It's really quite sweet, don't you think?" She smiled easily once again.

Baffled by what she said, Kastle asked, "Somehow you just know?" He watched her nod. His eyes shifted suddenly towards the one-way window uneasily. The way she was talking almost sounded like his father's ability to simply know things without knowing why.

Astraia was confused. "I don't know, I guess... Well, it must have been a dream, I guess. That's right. I had to have dreamed it."

- - -

Casting a furtive glance toward the scene in front of him, the Guardian eyed the woman with concern. Knowing the importance of the situation he lifted his head to the ceiling above and, in an instant, found himself on the roof of the building. Having cast a call to the winds, he waited patiently for their arrival.

Moments later, he felt a presence nearby. Turning towards them, he reached his well-muscled arm out in greeting. Clasping his hand just below the first angel's elbow, Woreash returned the gesture, and they shook arms in the age-old friendly greeting.

"Maleeka, Woreash." He nodded towards each of them in acknowledgment. "It's good to see you both." Standing a full foot taller than them, with a warrior's build, he was barefoot, clad only in loose tan pants. Peering down at them, he rested his hand on the hilt of his sword out of habit.

"You have news, Rokon?" Maleeka asked, greeting the Guardian.

Rokon nodded his head for effect. "There are symptoms."

"Already?" Woreash asked in alarm. "What are you seeing?"

"She dreams of events as she sleeps before they happen, which means she has the gift of 'Foresight'. I also was witness to several instances of being aware of things she shouldn't be, while other angels were present, which means she has...."

"The gift of 'Knowing' as well. Yes, of course!"

Exchanging glances, Woreash and Maleeka smiled in excitement. If things went as expected, she should be experiencing another symptom soon. And they suspected they knew which one it would be.

"Hold your excitement just yet." Resting his hands on each of their shoulders, the Guardian eyed them intently, gaining their attention. "This appears to be taking a huge toll on her. She becomes exhausted after each experience, and she has been getting sick a lot. Additionally, he does not seem to understand what is happening to her."

"How daft can he possibly be?" Maleeka said irritably. "And why is it taking such a toll on her? These gifts are meant as a blessing. She should not be experiencing distress."

"Maleeka, they all still believe it's impossible, and for that reason, we knew this might happen." Woreash said. "Even with the journals for reference, the human mind often cannot associate history with present events. And as for the exhaustion and nausea, she is, after all, human. Some of these abilities might be alarming for them initially, as they have never been experienced or seen, for that matter, for several hundred years."

"He needs to take her home. Are they any closer to that conclusion?" Maleeka asked the Guardian. Seeing him shake his head, Maleeka sighed in frustration.

"I know you're busy with other matters, but I think they could use counsel for they want to take her to a local doctor," Rokon said.

Alarmed by this news, Woreash threw a thoughtful glance below him. If they did not get them home soon, it could complicate matters for her. Clearly, she needed to be tended to by his sister, Crisalya, and her husband, Royce, but he had yet to determine that. Woreash also knew God would want them bound by man's law. He was already aware they had not accomplished this task yet. And again, it had to be their decision.

"Thank you for your protection. We'll take it from here."

"Are you sure? I can stay longer if need be."

"Why? Have there been demons present?" Maleeka inquired.

"Of course. Their interests, at present, seem to be the same as ours; to watch, to learn. They became very agitated when the gift of 'Knowing' presented itself."

"Yes, I imagine they did," Maleeka said, his face downcast and brooding. No longer in God's favor, the demons would be envious of such a gift which allowed a human knowledge which can only be bestowed by the Lord's grace alone. The angels that fell to Lucifer's side had lost God's favor, as well as the ability to 'Know' when they became demons.

"There has been no move against them otherwise?" Woreash asked, to confirm his own suspicions. Shaking his head, both Woreash and Maleeka smiled up at the Guardian with hope in their eyes. Seeing their expression, Rokon leaned back and chuckled.

"I take it things are going well."

"The other has already arrived. For now, we'll switch."

Nodding in understanding, Rokon reached out and clasped his hands about the old angel's head. Reading Woreash's thoughts, he took the information he needed, and then promptly disappeared.

- - -

Sunday, May 17, 2015
2:17pm EST
Near Jacksonville, Florida

A few hours later, Kastle and Pegueros met up during the children's naptime in the office. They sat at the table with a pile of lists they'd been working on while munching on snacks. Pegueros had just polished off a small bag of chips, as he watched his partner grab the last cracker from the pack he'd been eating from. Piling it high with cheese and turkey as he had with every other one, he popped it in his mouth.

"I've never seen anyone eat like you," Pegueros said while eyeing him in disbelief. "With the exception of maybe one other man I worked with once."

Kastle looked over at him, his brow furrowing in annoyance. His excessive eating habits were nothing compared to his brother, Drinian, who was several inches bigger all the way around and had no more fat on him than he had.

"Being as big as I am, I already need more nourishment than most. But add to it an extremely high metabolism...."

"And sex drive," Pegueros muttered under his breath.

"-And I tend to inhale twice as much food as most." Standing, Kastle stretched and reached for the bottle of strawberry kiwi juice in the fridge. "By the way, I heard that. We haven't been sleeping together. You know that full well. Stop insinuating that we are."

Pegueros sniggered. "Atheist, remember?"

"It's got nothing to do with religion and everything to do with showing a woman respect," Kastle countered angrily while scowling at Pegueros.

"Fair point," Pegueros said finally. Then, his expression turned serious. "What are we going to do about her?" he asked, clearly referring to Astraia's odd illness. "At the rate she's going, she's bound to get dehydrated too."

Kastle shook his head. "No, not dehydrated. You haven't been paying enough attention, have you? She's drinking plenty of water and juice since she stopped drinking the coffee she thought was causing her vomiting."

"I noticed you still go in to get her up in the mornings. Sometimes you're in there with her awhile before you leave," he observed while opening another bottle of soda.

"Been watching have you? Little pervert."

Pegueros laughed, "I don't need to watch to sense how much of a pain you're getting to be. You look like you're about ready to clobber someone."

"I just might," Kastle snapped.

Shrugging it off, the man merely grinned. "Besides, I mention it simply because I noticed something."

Kastle glanced over at him, waiting expectantly. "What is it already?" He snarled angrily; his patience nonexistent.

"She doesn't seem as lethargic or tired on the mornings when you spend time with her before bringing her out." Pegueros shrugged back into his jacket. "If you're not messing with her, then what are you doing with her those mornings anyway?"

"Praying," Kastle said abruptly, making a grunting sound. He appeared momentarily thoughtful.

"Really?" Pegueros both sounded and looked surprised.

"You know," Kastle eyed his partner grudgingly. "I think you're right."

"Then don't give her space and keep praying. I'm not saying there's anything to it but she seems weaker and more tired on days when you don't."

Pegueros watched his partner pace the room. He seemed more agitated than usual, and he hadn't bothered shaving in a couple days. It didn't take a rocket scientist to figure out that Agent Kastle was not only sweet on the O'Kahner woman but really worried about her too. Seeing him stop suddenly, he noted the man was standing with an odd expression on his face, as though he were looking past Pegueros instead of at him.

"I know what I've got to do." Kastle stared at his partner. "Pack your bag, Pegueros. You're going home."

Surprised at what he thought was a sudden change of subject, Pegueros sat up straight in his chair. "*Que Pasa?* What's up?" he asked repetitively, having to correct himself for reverting to Spanish. It was an old habit he had when he would get caught off guard or wasn't thinking."

"Follow me a minute. Let me show you something."

Confused, Pegueros stood, and they walked out into the kitchen towards the map. Kastle stopped in front of it, putting his hands out in front of him.

"What's the only state that doesn't have anyone in it?" he asked Pegueros.

"They all have someone in it," Pegueros said in exasperation.

"Exactly." Looking at the board, Kastle began yanking out push pins haphazardly and placing them back in the box.

"Man, what are you doing? We've spent forever trying to find a safe place for her."

"That's my point. There isn't anywhere safe for her and the kids alone. It's time to clean up and move. Go home, Pegueros. I'll take it from here."

Pegueros looked at Agent Kastle then. He narrowed his eyes. "What exactly are you planning?"

Kastle just stared at him then, as if waiting for him to come to some sort of conclusion.

After a moment, Pegueros realized where he was likely going with this. He let loose with multiple expletives, as there was no point at internalizing it because he had a pretty good idea what his partner intended to do.

Kastle watched his partner sit suddenly, resting his elbows on the table. Cupping his face in his hands, he shook his head in disgust for not seeing this coming sooner.

"Where's the safest and the best place for her to be right now, and where could I take her that's just about as safe as Camp David?"

"I don't know, where?" Pegueros asked, laughing humorlessly. He already knew full well what Kastle's answer would be.

"That's for me to know and for you...?"

"To never know. Yeah, yeah, I got it." Pegueros swore loudly again. Staring at Agent Kastle for a mere second, he then began pulling push pins from the board.

"Do me a favor and clear out the office and your room before you go," Kastle said. They were quickly eliminating all the pins from the map.

"Got it. Need help with the kids?" Pegueros removed the last push pin. Once done he began clearing the papers from the table.

"No. But you should tell them goodbye within the hour," Kastle stated while starting to shred papers.

Pegueros's head whipped around. He stared at Kastle with a mixture of alarm and awe across his face. Meeting his steely gaze, he began shaking his head in dismay.

"Whoa. You mean to tell me you can move all four of them before dinner time?"

Kastle glanced back at his partner. He continued to shred papers, barely cocking his brow at the effort. "Yup," he responded while continuing at his task. "I'll finish up here. Go clear out the office first."

Not saying a word, Pegueros saluted Kastle, turned, and walked toward the office. Reaching for the handle on the door, he heard his partners cell phone ring behind him.

Turning back, he overheard Kastle chuckle, as he peered down at his phone, then watched as he answered.

"I should have known I'd hear from you. How do you do that anyway?" He heard his partner ask the person on the other end of the phone. Figuring the call was personal Pegueros disappeared behind the office door.

Watching his partner warily as he left, Kastle continued the conversation with the party on the other end of the phone. Laughing at their response, he had to admit to himself that it was good to hear his voice. He would have eventually had to call him soon anyways. This just saved him the trouble.

"Where am I sending the boat?" Rafe Blackthorne said from the other end.

"County port near Jacksonville. You pick and let me know," Kastle said quietly, making sure his face was turned away from the one-way window. Emptying the shredder bin into the trash, he began mutilating more papers.

"I'll take care of it. Text you on secure in five."

"Right. Oh, and Watcher," Kastle began, realizing he should probably mention how many would be joining him.

"Just bring them home, Franclin," Rafe said crisply, interrupting him. "We'll figure it out from here. I have four add-ons. Is that correct?"

Surprised, Kastle couldn't help but wonder at his father's accuracy, and at how he knew. Figuring he'd get his answers soon enough, he thought it best not to go into it over the phone. Besides, brevity was always best in these cases. The only thing left was to tell Astraia what had been decided.

Chapter 16

Sunday, May 17, 2015 - 3:25pm EST
Safe house near Jacksonville, Florida

When Kastle woke Astraia from her nap, she was surprised to hear him tell her to pack up her things right away. Having an overwhelming feeling that she had experienced this moment once before, she realized it was because she'd dreamed about it the night before. A little unsettled by the realization, she had some difficulty shrugging it off.

After pooling together what few items she had, Astraia realized she didn't have a bag to put them in. Her children's backpack was overflowing. In the end, Kastle had taken her things for her, as well as a few for the kids.

Grabbing a trash bag, he placed her clothes, toiletries and the remainder of her kids' stuff inside it and drew the red plastic ties together. Watching as he placed both bags near the door, she stared at their belongings with a mixture of sadness and regret on her face. Seeing her expression, he tried to reassure her.

"I know it looks grim right now, but you'll have all brand-new things and a nice big place to call your home real soon."

Astraia couldn't figure out why he was acting the way he was. He sounded almost irritated with her as he spoke and had also been getting increasingly irritable over the past several days. More so then usual anyway.

"It's not that. I can replace their beds, the couch, and a kitchen table. I don't need new things or a big home for that matter. I never have. I'm used to second-hand clothes, and a large home would be too much to clean, what with three children and a job." She sat down, resting her head on the table.

"Then why the face?" He sat down next to her. Laying his hand on her back he began massaging her shoulder blades.

Sighing, Astraia spoke quietly. "I can never replace the quilt my grandmother painstakingly sewed for me before she died, nor the kids baby pictures. And the children will likely never remember what their father looked like. They won't have a picture of him to reference."

Relieved by her response, Kastle bowed his head in understanding. Grateful that she didn't appear to be the superficial sort, who was only concerned with worldly possessions, he ran his hand through her hair. Unconsciously, he bent forward and kissed her on the head. Realizing how familiar he was being with her, he stood abruptly and stepped away from her.

"I believe Pegueros has already said his goodbyes." Kastle thought it best to change subjects for the time being. He was already experiencing some guilt for what was about to happen.

"I have." Pegueros stepped out of the office. He was holding two large duffel bags. "All's clear. Double and triple checked. Here's hoping I never see any of you ever again," he declared emphatically while smiling. Eager to be on his way, Pegueros headed toward the elevator door.

"Pegueros, wait," Astraia called. Standing faster than she'd intended to, she became very dizzy, requiring Kastle's help to steady her. Seeing Pegueros turn and glance back behind him, she was thankful when he stopped and waited for her. Stumbling over to him, she surprised both men when she reached out and gave him a big hug.

"I'm ever so grateful to you for helping me and my family. Thank you for doing what you do. Not everyone is made for such things," she said gratefully as she smiled. "I gather you're a non-believer from what Kastle has said, but I wanted you to know I'll be praying for your safety and happiness anyways."

Cocking his head to one side, Pegueros looked at her with annoyance. "I don't need or want you to pray for me. I do just fine on my own," he responded, sounding more than a little irritated.

"See, that's where you're wrong. You may not want my prayers and you may not believe you need them. But I believe you do, and because of that, I intend to pray for you regardless."

"What's a man to say to that?" Pegueros dropped one of his bags to scratch his head.

Grinning, Kastle shrugged. "Just roll with it."

"Tell you what, if you want to pray, that's your choice cause you're gonna do what you're gonna do, right?" Seeing her nod Pegueros continued. "And I'm gonna do what I do and that's my job. We'll just leave it at that. Sound fair?"

"Sounds fair enough." Astraia smiled brightly.

Grabbing up the duffel bag he dropped, Pegueros took a long hard look at the woman before him. Then, glancing over at Kastle, he paused before stepping onto the elevator.

"You're a real nice lady, Astraia, regardless of being a church lady and all." Hearing the elevator doors open, he stepped in and dropped his bags on the floor. "And you know, I never noticed it before, but you got yourself a glow about you there, *Señorita*. Make sure you take good care of her now, Kastle. And the kids too, you hear?"

Nodding towards Pegueros as the elevator doors closed, Kastle couldn't dispel the feeling that it wasn't the last time he'd see that man. Attempting to shake off the unsettling notion, he called for the children while grabbing up his own bag.

"All right everyone, it's time to go!"

"Where are we headed anyways?" Astraia asked, her curiosity getting the better of her. They'd been holed up inside the safe house for so long that she was rather anxious about leaving.

Glancing around the living room and kitchen as Sayleena and Storman came running from their room, Kastle shook his head. Seeing Saruman following not far behind them, he hit the button for the elevator.

"Not here." He thumped the wall with the palm of his hand loudly. "You never know what bugs might be left behind."

Looking at Kastle in surprise as the elevator arrived and opened, she watched as he held the door for the kids and tossed their bags inside.

"You honestly don't think that Pegueros..."

Noting Kastle's tight-lipped expression, Astraia closed her mouth. Her face went white. Stepping into the elevator after her kids, she couldn't help but get the feeling she was missing something important. She hated having to follow Kastle blindly, but couldn't help but think that to be on her own with her children would be an even worse situation than the one she was in.

Were she to be completely honest, she hadn't made the habit of praying a whole lot over the last several years. She said prayers over her children every night, of course. She would also often pray along with the pastor at her church during services, or during morning devotions. But she hadn't prayed for her own needs or for others, as much as she realized lately that she probably should. Nonetheless, she found herself saying a silent prayer for God's protection as they were heading down in the elevator. Peering up at Kastle afterward, she noticed he'd been watching her.

"Kastle, what's going on?" she asked nervously. She was holding tightly to Storman and Saruman's hands, afraid to let go. "Why is Pegueros taking off without us? I thought you both were supposed to be relocating us."

"Soon, Astraia. I'll tell you everything soon but not just yet." Kastle eyed her uneasily. "Prepare for your mind to be blown."

- - -

Hub Airport near Jacksonville, Florida
Departure time 4:17pm EST

It occurred to Astraia, as they drove along in silence, that they must be traveling by plane somewhere when she saw the signs for a small airport along the way. Turning towards Agent Kastle, she opened her mouth to inquire only to be halted by a stern look from him.

"Not right now," he said aloud while checking his GPS, then the text on his phone again. "We'll talk later."

Sighing in frustration, she wrapped her arms across her belly and leaned back in her seat. Sensing her distressed movements next to him, Kastle glanced over at her. Noting the way she was sitting, he became alarmed.

"Do I need to pull over? Are you going to be sick?"

"No, I just... I'm anxious." She was becoming extremely emotional and had no idea why. Shaking her hands in front of her, she felt tears spring to her eyes. "I'm sorry. I don't know what's wrong with me. It's just this not knowing. It's really getting to me, and I can't...." Unable to finish what she was saying; she simply shook her head and shifted uncomfortably in her seat. Breathing deeply, she turned her head toward the window in discomfort, her face turning red.

Eyeing her with concern, he peered quickly through the rear-view mirror to make sure the children were all right. Seeing them intent upon the movie he'd put in for them to keep them quiet, he reached across and lay his hand on her belly.

"It's okay, Astraia. See, we're almost at our destination." Kastle pointed toward the sign for a small county airport. Stopping at the light, he waited for the signal allowing him to turn in near the hangar he wanted. Pulling up near the hangar, Astraia could see an Embraer Linear 1000 jetliner parked nearby.

Turning back toward Kastle in surprise, her eyes widened. She pointed towards the luxury jet liner. "Are you serious?" She sounded incredulous. Seeing him nod, she mouthed the word, 'wow', eliciting a chuckle from Kastle.

Calling back to the children, Kastle turned off the engine. Pivoting in his seat, he gave them a bright smile.

"Now kids, do you remember the game?" He watched them giggle in delight. "Who's gonna win?"

"Me!" All three called out in excitement, forcing a smile even to Astraia's face. Recalling Kastle's instruction to the children about the game of silence he wanted to play with them, she couldn't help but giggle herself. He'd explained about it on the way down in the elevator. It hadn't made much sense to her until now.

Getting out of the vehicle, Sayleena, Storman, and Saruman all piled out, quick as a wink, while giggling and whispering to each other.

"Remember. Quietly, and don't say a thing," Kastle whispered. He saw the children's eyes widen at the sight of the plane.

At the exact same moment Astraia was closing the door of the vehicle she was hit suddenly with the thought that Storman was about to cry out unexpectedly. Whipping around, she clasped her hand across his mouth as Kastle was whispering. Grabbing him up, she carried him away from the vehicle as he exclaimed loudly into her hand.

"We get to fly in a plane! Oh, my gosh! A plane, a plane!"

Fortunately, with her hand clasped across his mouth, her son's words came out muffled and hard to hear. Now several paces away from the vehicle she turned towards him apologetically.

Standing near the back of the sport utility vehicle, hastily pulling the bags from its end, Kastle stood looking back at her. At first, he appeared surprised for some reason. Then, his head dropped as he shook it. Glancing back up at her, he smacked his forehead and then chuckled. Grabbing the kid's duffle bags and his as he closed the back end of the vehicle, he urged them toward the plane.

"Come on kids, let's go! Who is gonna beat me?" Kastle began jogging quickly towards the Blackthorne family luxury jet liner. Racing along beside him, Saruman was determined to try and win. His long blonde bangs blew back over his head as he pelted across the pavement, his little legs pumping along madly as he grinned from ear-to-ear.

Astraia jogged along as quickly as she could while carrying Storman haphazardly in her arms. She could hear him laughing with elation at the thought of riding in an airplane for the first time in his life. Reaching the steps of the plane, Astraia set him down so he could race up them on his own.

"Oh, my gosh! Oh, my gosh! I can't believe it! A plane! A plane!" Storman cried out while running up the steps. The other two children had already made their way up the stairs and disappeared inside the jet.

"I'm so sorry." Astraia paused near the steps, breathing heavily from exertion. "I realize now the game was so they wouldn't say anything about the plane when we arrived. You were afraid of bugs in the vehicle, weren't you?"

"Yes, but you did great. You caught him in time and got him far enough away." He stared down at her with an odd expression on his face, then urged her up the steps. "How did you know he was going to do that?"

"I don't know. I mean, he loves planes. Well, you know that." She glanced back at him as she took the stairs slowly, feeling a bit dizzy. "But it was like it came to me out of nowhere. I don't know how else to describe it. Women's intuition I guess."

Stepping inside the plane, she glanced around, taking in the sight before her. The interior of the jet was bright and exquisitely furnished. There were luxurious fabrics on the furnishings along with plush cushions and pillows. The cream-colored velvet fabric, highlighted with light and dark blue accents, added to the rich look. One side of the plane had a sofa couch along the length which was clearly designed for comfort. On the other side of the jet, there were large cushy reclining chairs as well as a table.

Astraia stepped further into the plane to allow Kastle to walk in behind her. Watching her children as they bounced on the couch and proceeded to investigate every inch of the luxury jetliner, she heard Kastle pull the door shut behind him.

Touching an intercom pad on the wall, she heard him speak into it briefly.

"How long, Mitchell?"

"Been topped off and ready for takeoff for a while now, Sir."

"Mitchell, when did you arrive?" Kastle asked.

"Forty minutes ago, Sir," the voice responded. Chuckling, Kastle shook his head, listening to Mitchell continue. "Air traffic and wind speeds are favoring us today. Currently showing clear skies ahead. Arrival time in Kalispell in five hours." The masculine voice said through the intercom. Peering over at Kastle, she saw him glance at his watch.

"It's about a quarter after four now, by Jacksonville time, which means we'll arrive home by quarter after seven." He spoke as he frowned. "That'll be after the kids' bedtime, but it'll still be light out." He walked lazily towards the table and set the two bags on the floor. "Why don't you go ahead and have a seat? We'll be taking off any second now."

Glancing around her, she opted to sit in one of the reclining chairs near the table instead of the couch. Swiveling the chair, she depressed the lever which allowed the footrest to rise. Sensing his unexpected presence above her, she peered up at him in time to see him leaning down toward her. Bumping the lever back down, Kastle spoke close to her ear as her feet dropped suddenly.

"Seats must be in upright position for takeoff," he said quietly. His deep voice sent shivers up and down her spine. "Once we're airborne I'll check the galley. I'll bet Dad had food put in there for dinner."

"Did you say your *dad* put food in the galley?" Astraia watched him settle the children in seats.

"Just for the moment you stay put. You can get up as soon as we're in the air," he told them sternly.

To Astraia's amazement, they all listened, even Saruman who was the most difficult of her sons. Smiling sadly, she realized how much her children were going to miss Kastle. Striding back toward her and the table, he settled himself in the chair across from her. The jet began taxiing down the runway. Watching her boy's expressions, she listened to their excited squeals with delight. Moments later they were finally in the air.

Realizing much to his chagrin that he couldn't wait any longer to tell Astraia the truth, Kastle turned to her reluctantly. Exchanging looks, he saw her take a deep breath as though preparing for the worst. Brows raising, he reached down and took a pouch from his bag. Opening it up he pulled out its contents and proceeded to remove the colored lenses from his eyes.

Astraia watched the man across from her remove his contacts. Gasping softly as he placed each color contact back into its case, she stared at him momentarily in stunned silence. Looking back at her were the beautiful,

180

crystal clear blue eyes she'd seen the first day they'd met at the store.

"But I thought... I thought you said you were wearing colored contacts that day," she said when she finally gained her voice.

"I did say that. I'm sorry. The truth is I use the brown ones to cover my real eyes."

"But why cover up such a unique feature? They're amazing!"

"Thank you. But that's part of the problem. They are unique. In my line of work, that could signal me out in more ways than one."

"I guess that makes sense."

"Plus, it helps cover up my true identity, which is one of the most important reasons for wearing them."

"I don't understand, what do you mean?" Astraia became uneasy at the way he was looking at her.

Sighing heavily, he explained. "You were right to disbelieve me when I told you who I was. I am not Franclin Kastle. I assumed the name when I joined the armed service and then the CIA." He proceeded to put his contact case away and placed drops in his eyes. Blinking, he looked directly at her. "My real name is Dante Blackthorne, and my home is in Kalispell, Montana with my father on our horse ranch."

Chapter 17

Astraia's mouth dropped in shock and dismay. There was silence between them, though her children's voices could be heard exclaiming at the view from the windows. Hand against her belly, she took a shaky breath, becoming quite anxious and very angry.

Glancing around her almost fearfully, she eyed the man before her with trepidation. What had she done? Had her faith in him, and his willingness to protect her children been misplaced? Trying desperately not to panic, she swallowed hard, her heart pounding so loud, she was certain he'd hear it. Attempting to control her escalating hysteria, Astraia took a deep breath.

"Your name is Dante Blackthorne, and you live in Montana," she repeated, her voice rising as she spoke.

"Yes."

"On a horse ranch with your dad," she continued, her panic obvious but unavoidable.

"Yes, listen to me, Astraia." Dante's tone was soothing, as though trying to console a wounded bird bent on taking flight.

Standing abruptly, she eyed him wearily. "You lied to me, Kastle. What's going on?"

He interrupted her. "Dante. My name is Dante. It's very important that, from here on out, you use that name. You're not the only one changing names at this point." Reaching out to her, he took her trembling hands in his and guided her back to the table.

"Changing names! Are you saying you're reverting to your given name?"

"Fifteen years ago, I made a decision to make a rather drastic change in my life and enter the army. My father did not approve of it initially, but after a time recognized it was necessary."

"Why was it necessary?"

Shoulders slumping, he sat back in his chair, his expression pensive. "I'm not sure I'm ready yet to explain why. My reasons were personal. What I can tell you, is that my father insisted if I was going to do this, then I needed to enlist under an assumed name."

"But why?" she inquired, clearly confused and appearing very hurt by his subterfuge. Her anger was almost a tangible thing, as the tension ratcheted up another level inside the plane. They'd spent so much time together in the morning, doing their devotions, and repenting for the poor decision they had made together. Now she was finding out he wasn't who he said he was. Was his devotion to God a lie as well?

"There were a couple different reasons. I'm only at liberty to tell you about one right now." Reaching behind him, he rubbed at his neck as he spoke. "My father knew that with my size, strength, intelligence and abilities, that

I had the potential for special operations level of service. He also knew if I made it that far, and chose to go that route, that one day I would tire of it and want out."

Staring at the man before her, she realized somehow she just knew where he was going with this. "Would it be safe to assume that it would be awfully difficult to find your way out of such an organization? If you're good at what you do, that is?" She sounded more than a little irritated. "And that by enlisting with an assumed name, it would allow you to disappear without anyone being the wiser?"

Eyeing her with something akin to admiration, Dante leaned back again in his chair. "Very intuitive, and yes, that's exactly it. He anticipated I might one day find the need to disappear suddenly." Tapping at the corner of one eye with his finger, he smiled. "By changing my eye color, while in service, it would make me less...."

"Conspicuous?" Seeing him nod, she took a shaky breath, and then glanced at her children. Worry lines creased her brow as she tried to understand what was going on.

"What exactly is happening right now? Where are we going? Where is Kalispell exactly?" she asked in quick succession, her brow furrowing in confusion. Astraia was sure she'd never heard of the place before, and yet, somehow it seemed familiar to her.

"In answer to all three of your questions, you are coming back home with me to Kalispell, Montana. My father sent the jet to come get us."

Startled, Astraia glanced around her, then back at Dante. "What do you mean by I'm coming back home with you?"

Peering at her as though uncomfortable now, he stood suddenly, choosing to evade her question for the moment.

To that point in their conversation, the children had kept themselves busy investigating their new surroundings. Having become bored with its newness, they were now climbing onto the couch and jumping off it, pretending they were airplanes preparing for take-off.

"How about we get into that while we eat? I'm going to check the galley to see if there is any dinner." Pointing towards one wall as he spoke, he walked away. "Why don't you have Sayleena and the boys pick a movie from that cabinet?"

Finding a collection of animated Ironman episodes, the kids quickly agreed upon that. Glancing around her, Astraia realized she had no idea where the television, or for that matter, DVD player was. Calling out to Kastle, she used the wrong name and found she had to correct herself.

"Dante, where are the DVD player and television?"

"Sorry." Dante came back and grabbed a remote from the table. Pushing a button on the remote, a large flat screen television rose from the stand next to the table, eliciting excited cries from the children. Grinning, he took the case from her, their fingers touching briefly, drawing their eyes to each other. Bending forward, he then placed the first disc into the slot on the side of the stand.

"I'll say it," Astraia commented rather dryly while attempting to shake off the thrilling sensation of the contact of their mere fingertips. "That is pretty cool." She gained herself a wink from the man next to her, of whom she clearly knew nothing about.

Finding personal pepperoni pizzas and fresh fruit cups in the galley, Dante settled the children in front of the screen on the floor, as they watched Ironman. Busying himself by grabbing the garden salads and several pizzas, along with drinks for himself and Astraia, he set them on the table. Adding blue cheese dressing to his salad, he dug into it first, then indicated for her to sit down across from him. Taking a deep breath, he proceeded to explain to her the plan and how he had decided upon it.

"Here's what's going to happen. I've already told you you're coming home with me to Montana. What I haven't told you is that you'll be doing so as my fiancée and that I will be adopting your children once we're married." He took a deep breath then, as he watched the play of emotions crossing Astraia's face.

Stunned, she stared back at him, her hand still holding a slice of pizza in mid-air. Already feeling blindsided by his new identity, she recalled his last comment to her on the elevator. She had not anticipated truly having her mind blown away as he had said.

Setting the food down in front of her, Astraia stared down at it in confusion. Unable to understand why he thought anyone would ever think she was his fiancée, let alone his wife, she became quite agitated.

"First, not to poke holes in your plan there, but how exactly do you intend to accomplish that, without having access to the CIA, Kastle? Oh, for heaven sake, Dante. Don't we need documents, like birth certificates and marriage licenses?"

Dante interrupted her train of thought. "That would be easy enough to get without the aid of the CIA. In either event, my father, Rafe Blackthorne, will be able to help with that as I received my new identity from him. He's capable of handling such things since he used to be CIA at one point."

He hated having to be dishonest with her about his father's service history. But as Rafe's status was not his secret to divulge, he knew he had to maintain discretion where that was concerned, regardless of how he might feel about her.

"How legal is this going to be?"

Shrugging, he took a large bite of his salad. "It's complicated. I cannot explain to you how exactly he will do it because to do so would divulge a family secret which is not mine to share. That being said, it will be legal." Seeing her look of disbelief, he spread his arms in a plaintive fashion. "It's the same process used when a person goes into witness protection and assumes a new identity." Cringing inwardly, Dante realized he might have alluded to the truth of the matter too much.

Appearing thoughtful, she toyed with her salad then glanced up at him. "But then wouldn't that mean that your father...."

"Best not to think about it too much, Astraia." The wheels were clearly spinning in her head. He could tell she was coming close to figuring out the truth about his dad. "I suspect we will be hearing from him shortly. It is entirely possible he will have your new identities for me by then, which will help facilitate the transition for the children, by giving us a few hours to work with them before arriving."

Nodding, she twiddled with her hair anxiously as she listened. She'd anticipated her children would have to eventually take on new names, but the reality of it was finally setting in. It broke her heart to know, that for the rest of their lives and hers, they would be perpetuating a lie, for they would never be able, to be honest about who they truly were. She'd been wrestling with that knowledge ever since the night the man next to her had removed her from her home, and she had asked God for his guidance and wisdom as to how best to handle it with them.

"When we arrive at the house, my family will be there to greet me, as I haven't been back in about five years. I'll announce then that we'll be getting married, and that I intend to adopt your children."

Leaning forward in his seat, he placed his salad back in front of him on the table as he ate. His pale, almost translucent shimmering eyes mesmerized her as he talked, his voice denoting a calm he wasn't quite feeling himself.

"My brother, Breydon, is a lawyer, so he'll be able to handle the adoption papers for us." Setting his fork down, Dante reached back, placing his hands behind his head self-consciously, and stretched as he watched her. "I should warn you... They will be expecting a wedding ceremony rather quickly." His heart rate escalated at the notion.

"How soon?"

"I'd say by Saturday." Trying to gauge her reaction to what he'd said so far, Dante eyed her anxiously. She looked as though her head was literally spinning in circles, like a globe being spun on its axis, and he couldn't help but feel guilty for being responsible for that.

Heart in her throat, Astraia placed her hands in her lap. Her eyes darted frantically back and forth, as her world seemed to be closing in on her for the second time in less than a month. The prospect of being married to him sent little shivers of excitement up and down her spine, and yet, she couldn't help experience guilt over the fact it was happening so soon after Dylan had died.

"How are you doing with this so far?" he asked after giving her a moment to process what he'd said.

Dumbfounded, she tucked a tendril of hair behind her ear with a shaky hand. "Honestly, I just don't know quite what to make of all this," she said anxiously.

Dante was confused by her reaction at first. He had been having a lot of trouble lately at being able to glean information from her and was having similar difficulty now. Assuming it was because of the tension between them, and his inability to be able to concentrate in her presence, it hadn't bothered him until that moment. Normally, he didn't have difficulty ciphering information from people, apart from the occasional fellow undercover operative.

After a moment of silence, it occurred to him how it all might be sounding, so he reached out to her.

"Astraia?" He coaxed her gently.

"I guess I'm just trying to figure out why you're doing this," she said abruptly. "My understanding was that you and Pegueros were trying to find a new location, where just the kids and I would settle," she said quietly, trying hard to keep the kids from overhearing. "It was never originally in the plan, was it? For one of you to stay with me, that is." She was unable to tell him her real reasons for her sudden anxiety.

"No, you're right. Standard procedure would have been to relocate you elsewhere and on your own. We never place ourselves, or another fellow agent, in a permanent position with a charge. But in this case, this situation is a bit of an exception," he said calmly, hoping she would soon come to some sort of understanding. "In the end, this serves both our purposes."

"How exactly does this serve us both?" She eyed him suspiciously. "And why is our situation so different?"

"In answer to your last question first, it's different because of who is after you," Dante spoke in an undertone, to keep the children from overhearing and becoming distressed. "I do not wish to alarm you, but Kobi Radford's drug organization is vast. You're better off being placed somewhere as a whole family unit, rather than as a single mom with three kids."

"Because that's what they're looking for, a single mom with three kids and not…"

"A married woman," Dante finished for her. "And with you having health issues right now, I would feel much better knowing you weren't alone, and that you had some help." He glanced meaningfully over at Saruman and Storman, who were currently giggling on the floor. The boys were amazing and fun but at the same time quite a handful, what with being the same age.

Touched, and a little overwhelmed by his obvious concern for her and her children, she took a deep breath, trying hard to think clearly. Her head was buzzing with everything new that she'd learned.

"I think I understand, but…."

Sensing her resistance to his plan, he stopped her. "This way, not only do you and your children gain new identities, but you're doubly hidden by way of the marriage and the adoption," he explained, tapping off the reasons on his fingers. "And I can get you the medical attention you need immediately, because my youngest sister Crisalya is a nurse, and my other sister Megorah married a doctor. A bonus to this is that my sister-in-law Lylia is a teacher."

"What's the advantage in that?"

"My brother's wife home schools most of the children in our family," he said offhandedly by way of explanation. "As Sayleena, Saruman and Storman get used to their new last names there will be less chance of unwanted flags being raised with her than there would be in a public-school system." As almost an afterthought, he added, "And for added protection, on the off chance someone would come looking, my father's house is as impregnable as Camp David. Plus, my twin brother, Dartanian, is the Sheriff of Breckenridge County."

"Wait, did you say twin?" She did a double take. "As in, identical twin?" Seeing him nod, her eyes grew wide.

Grinning back at her, he chuckled. "We get that reaction a lot."

Trying to keep up but realizing she'd nearly missed something significant, she paused with her fork twirling in her salad. "Let's back up a minute here. You said something about the kids getting used to their new last names. Won't their first names change as well?" Astraia inquired, her confusion mounting. Every movie or television show she'd ever seen perpetuated the idea that people's names changed in situations like these.

"That's a common misconception among most of the public. If they were older, say, teenagers, it would be necessary, but they're young. Besides, it's much easier to work with the last name change, as opposed to a first name. It's too confusing for them otherwise."

"But won't these people who are looking for us be able to find them with…"

"He won't be looking for *them*." He interrupted abruptly, wanting to make sure she fully understood the situation. "Kobi Radford will be looking for *you*. That's why you must become a completely new person," he said emphatically. He pointed towards her with his fork. Then, finishing off the last of his salad, he moved on to his pizza, groaning when he took his first bite, as gooey mozzarella cheese and sauce oozed over his hand and dripped onto his napkin. Realizing it had come from his favorite restaurant in Kalispell, he was grateful that his father had stocked the plane with his favorite meal.

Astraia swallowed hard, having finally come to a full understanding of the precarious position she was in. She stared back up at him thoughtfully, both marveling, and envying, his ability to enjoy his food.

"I don't understand. What exactly are you getting out of this? You said this serves both our purposes, but it seems to me as though this is awfully one-sided."

"Do you not want to be married to me?" Dante asked out of the blue, interrupting her.

She blushed self-consciously. Fidgeting in her seat, she looked down at her dinner as though incapable of considering eating at that moment. Glancing back up at him, she could see he was clearly waiting for an answer.

"It's not that I wouldn't want to be married to you, Kastle..."

"Dante."

"What?"

"My name is Dante."

"Right," she replied, becoming flustered. "I can't even get your name right... Dante. And you want me to marry you?" she asked, eyeing him closely.

Noticing his uncomfortable posture at her question, Astraia inhaled sharply and carefully chose her next words. "Do you really want to be married to me?"

"Right now, it's not about what we want. It's about what needs to happen to fix..."

"No. Listen to me, Dante," Astraia said abruptly, gaining his attention. "I may flounder in my faith sometimes, and I may not be as well-read where the Bible is concerned as you, but I am pretty sure that God's plan for the sanctity of marriage wasn't for it to become a band-aid to fix things."

Chapter 18

Aggravated by her statement, Dante ran his hands across his face as he stared back at her self-consciously. "I'm well versed on what God's plan is for marriage," he finally said, sounding cross.

"Enlighten me then, because what you're suggesting seems to fall under the premise of being a band-aid fix."

"Genesis 2:24 tells us that a man leaves his father and mother and is united with his wife, and they become one. He created it for two people to come together in love."

"Exactly my point," Astraia said loudly, causing her daughter to turn and look over at them. Nodding her head towards her, as though to say everything was okay, she realized she needed to get her emotions under control.

"What, Astraia? What is your point?" Dante asked in a heated whisper, becoming more and more agitated by the moment. Typically, a master at schooling his emotions, he found himself struggling to maintain that control with her. It was making him crazy.

"You don't love me, Dante," she said angrily, finding it difficult to keep from crying while causing the man across from her to appear startled. She didn't understand why she was becoming so upset, but she could feel her heart aching in her chest.

"You don't love me," she repeated more softly, her lips quivering as she spoke. "And you're asking me… No, you're not even asking me. You're telling me that we're getting married. It's almost as though you're saying I have no choice in the matter."

"You have a choice," he said after a long moment. The unease created by the topic at hand was evident in both their faces.

They sat for a time, staring at each other. Several more minutes passed before he noticed her expression had become crestfallen. Glancing away, she wiped at tears forming in her eyes.

"What is it? Why do you cry?"

"I was married when we were together. I'm having difficulty getting past the fact that I cheated on my husband," she proclaimed softly in distress. The statement, though seemingly off subject, hadn't come out of nowhere. The discussion of another marriage had been a reminder of what had happened between them.

Shaking his head, Dante sighed heavily as he spoke, regret clear in his posture and tone.

"First Corinthians 7:39 says, 'A married woman is not free as long as her husband lives, but if her husband dies then she is free to be married to any man she wishes. But only if he is a Christian.' In God's eyes, you were released from that marriage the moment your husband died. Dylan had already passed on by then, making you free to be remarried. If you wish, that is," he said as he paused, then watched her expression carefully. "Aside from allowing your fear to take over, the only other sin you committed that night was not being married before we were intimate."

Seeing the wounded expression on her face, he grimaced, for the last thing he wanted to do was hurt her. She'd been through so much already. "Please don't be upset."

Shaking her head, Astraia couldn't hold back the tear that trickled down her cheek. "No, you're absolutely right. If I hadn't begged you and tempted you...."

"We both know full well that I am not entirely blameless in what happened either." Dante tried hard not to become cross with her at her insistence to carry the weight of their guilt for their actions. "It's one of the reasons why I have chosen this path with you." Seeing the perplexed look on her face, he proceeded to explain. "Do you remember the Exodus chapter we covered a couple days ago?"

"It was chapter twenty-two as I recall."

"I'm referencing verse sixteen, where it states that if a man seduces a woman who is not engaged, he must marry her." The statement had been blunt. He watched her blink.

"But... Dante, the verse also states the woman in question is a virgin, and I've been married. It also says the man must pay the bride price for the woman. Who do you intend to pay? Me or my father?" Her eyes sparkled and her voice was filled with humor.

"I'm trying to do the right thing by you. I feel more responsible for you than I would any other charge for the simple fact that we've been intimate." He appeared annoyed with her.

"Are you sure you're not trying to make the verse fit the situation, rather than reading it as it was meant to be read?"

He frowned at her.

Wiping at her eyes with trembling hands, she shook her head in distress as a sudden thought popped into her head. Staring back at him in dismay, she nearly choked back a sob.

"Do I really have a choice in the matter? What happens to me and my children if I were to say no to this plan of yours?"

Dante shifted uncomfortably in his seat. He glanced away, trying to think quickly. It had never occurred to him that she might not go along with his plan. At the time, it had seemed the most prudent course, to relocate and place her somewhere so she could be safe and get the medical attention she needed.

"You always have a choice. And if I've given you the impression that I'm trying to bully you into something you're not ready for then I apologize. That was not my intent. I am merely trying to protect you and those beautiful children of yours." He glanced over at her kids on the floor, a look of longing carved into his handsome features. "I couldn't bear to see anything happen to them. I've become quite fond of them, and you, for that matter."

Getting up from his seat, he came around to her side and knelt next to her. Taking her hands in his, he kissed her knuckles gently, then stared up into her glistening blue eyes, the clarity of their color a stark contrast to her smooth, pale white skin.

"That said, I would urge you to consider this as an option."

"What other option do I have?" Her voice sounded dull even to her own ears.

Hurt that she seemed so against the idea of marrying him, Dante exhaled as he pondered other possibilities.

"I can still take you to Kalispell and place you in a home there near the ranch if you'd prefer. But I am leery of doing that, as I wouldn't be able to watch over you from there as easily. My time would be split between the two locations, and it wouldn't be anywhere near as secure as my ranch home."

Appearing thoughtful, Dante continued. "You could still get the medical attention you need, but you would be a single mom on your own with three children. A lot of women manage just fine. My sister-in-law, Hialey, was a single mom for a while until she met my brother, Breydon. And it shouldn't be too difficult to get you work somewhere. But..." His voice trailed off. He saw the look of distress on her face at the prospect of being a working mother again without help. The fear in her eyes was obvious.

"What you're proposing is for us to get married." Astraia weighed her options in her head, hating the fact that she was having to potentially choose between a loveless marriage or being a single mother trying to make it on her own. "So that you can see to our protection, and at the same time, take care of us?"

"Yes, Honey, I can take care of you and your children." Dante trailed his fingers along her cheek, his eagerness evident in his expression, as well as his touch. "I have the means to do it. If you were to marry me, live with me at the ranch, you would never have to worry about anything, because I can see to all your needs. I can get you the help you need for whatever is wrong, and you would have help. You wouldn't have to do this alone." He hoped that he had finally reached her.

Closing her eyes, Astraia yearned longingly for what he spoke of. Security, a real father for her children who believed in God, and the hopes of a loving husband, who would truly care for her as she always dreamed. Anticipating that these hopes would likely be dashed, she opened her eyes as the familiar sensation of hopelessness filled her anew.

"What do you get out of this? What advantage is there for you?" She searched his face for answers which he was clearly reticent to give.

Sighing in exasperation, he debated quickly on how much to tell her. "I would gain a beautiful wife and three adorable children. I've always wanted to be a father," he admitted finally, figuring starting with such an admission might soften her resistance. "And by finally returning home, I'd be able to keep the promise I made to my father about taking over the ranch for him."

"Is that what you want?" she inquired, concerned that he was being pressured into a life he might not want. "To take over your father's business?"

Smiling, Dante's face lit up at the notion of spending his days on the ranch, tending to the horses and breeding stock. Sighing almost contentedly at the prospect of finally being able to do that, he stared back at her happily, then suddenly his face fell. Leaning back on his heels he realized that he was imagining it with her at his side, and yet, he couldn't fathom doing it without her for some reason. Unsure of what that meant he stared back at her curiously.

"I want that very much," he said finally then prompted. "What are your misgivings? Do you think you would not be happy with me?"

"You're an extremely attractive man, Dante." She showed clear signs of distress. Tears welled in her eyes. Wiping at the corner of her eye anxiously, she continued quickly. "I cannot imagine your family seeing us as a couple because of that. And it just seems like I'm getting more out of this than you. So, what real purpose does a marriage between us have for you aside from giving you a chance to be a father?" She noted his exasperation with her but was unable to help it. She wanted and needed answers. She just couldn't follow him blindly in this. "I take marriage very seriously."

"As do I and the rest of my family, my father in particular. My mother may have been of Mandan Indian descent, but we were raised to believe in God and the laws He has placed before us, including where marriage and family are concerned." Dante leaned forward again and took her hands into his. "It's why they will expect us to marry quickly if you were to stay at the ranch, for it would be unseemly otherwise, especially with you having children."

"And this would be a permanent solution, I take it?"

"Yes, and it's important to me that you understand what that means." He grimaced, realizing he was going to have to tell her. "In answer to what purpose, this serves for me…" He shifted uncomfortably before her, knowing he needed to be very careful. "You saw me as Dante Blackthorne in the store that day, without my contacts. I am not at liberty right now to get into why this is so significant. But the fact that you saw me as Dante that day, rather than as Kastle could become highly problematic for me and my family, were you placed in witness protection. By coming with me, by marrying me, you'd be protecting me and by extension my family in a similar way as I would be protecting you."

"I see," Astraia said weakly. Her brow furrowed for she didn't really understand. She sensed he was keeping something from her.

Seeing her confusion, Dante stood. Running his hands across his face, he stretched, then took her gently by the shoulders. Brushing her hair away from her face with the soft pad of his fingertips, he cupped her cheek tenderly in his hand and bent toward her.

"As for my family, you should know that I believe they will not only like you very much but be very pleased with the match." He caressed her hand, his tone gentle. "Any concern I might have with this is more for your potential discomfort among them than anything."

"Why?" This time, she looked at him in surprise. Then she rubbed at her eyes, clearly showing signs of exhaustion. For some reason, she didn't seem to have a whole lot of energy for anything lately.

"Because, other than my father, they will not know the truth about how we met and why I am coming home with you. They will get whatever story we come up with. And you and I will need to live together as husband and wife once we are wed. For example, as a married couple, it would be expected for us to share my bedroom and by extension my bed."

Inhaling deeply at his words, Astraia froze in her seat as their gazes collided. Glancing away, her face flooded with heat. She suddenly became overwhelmed at the notion of being intimate with him again, only this time as his wife. The vivid reminder of their first experience flashed before her eyes. She realized the idea appealed to her more than it probably should.

Dante moved around behind her back, having noticed how tense she'd become. He ran his hands through her hair, moving it aside, and began rubbing her shoulders gently with his strong fingers. If he didn't know better, he would have thought she felt more fragile in his hands than before.

Astraia moaned in appreciation. "I see," she said again. Only this time she just sounded defeated. She reveled in the feel of his hands upon her.

Too tired to debate any further, Astraia hunched her shoulders as he manipulated the muscles in her back. "I suppose my only concern would be for the kids."

Nodding his head in understanding, he glanced down at her. "You're concerned about how they will respond with all of this, and how well they will remember the story." He could feel her head bobbing up and down in agreement in front of him.

Cringing at the thought of having to lie to his family where she and her kids were concerned, Dante prayed for guidance and a solution that would keep him from having to be quite so dishonest with them. He knew it would be much safer for everyone involved if they didn't know who she was. And yet, Dante wanted them to know the strong, courageous woman he had grown so fond of in the past four weeks.

"They've been uprooted from their home and taken away from their friends. They've also been told their dad is dead and that he's not coming back." She glanced up at him as she whispered. The worry for her children was evident in her eyes, and he was pleased to see she had such a strong love for them.

"Now, suddenly, they're going to be told that mommy is getting married and, by the way, here's your new daddy!" She placed a hand upon her head. "Let's not forget the part where they're told they have new last names, and that they can't ever tell anyone their old one or talk about their old life. At the same time, we're not able to tell them why everything is changing, because it's either too classified or too scary for them to know."

"These are all legitimate concerns. But we'll figure this out together, Honey, I promise. I know you're worried about them and frankly, I am too." Dante's voice soothed her as he spoke. He continued to massage the sore muscles in her neck, causing her to feel drowsy.

"What I do know, from experience, is that children can often be a lot more resilient than we give them credit for. Personally, I've been impressed with how they've been doing so far."

"I suppose so." She struggled to keep her eyes open.

Kneeling before her once more, Dante took her hands into his. Bowing his head before her in contemplation, he then looked her straight in the eye.

"I'm going to do this the right way this time. I know you're scared, Astraia, and I can tell you're very tired. I won't force something on you that you don't want." Pausing, he thought quickly, choosing his words carefully. "I like you, Astraia, and I get the feeling that you feel similarly about me." He searched her face. Seeing her weak smile as she tilted her head self-consciously, Dante grinned, knowing full well he'd hit dead on.

"I get the feeling, if we give this some time, we might have what we both are looking for. But to do that, we need to…"

"Get married first, then date?" She chuckled.

Resting his head in her lap, he groaned, then looked back up at her in distress. "You deserve so much better than this. You deserve time to be able to grieve for your loss. You deserve to be courted and to be romanced."

She was touched by his words and knew that he was right even as her eyes drooped wearily. Seeing him adjust his position so that one knee was bent and another was on the floor, she realized what he was about to do.

"Astraia O'Kahner, will you marry me? Will you allow me to adopt your children and raise them as though they were my own?" He met her gaze.

Inhaling a troubled breath, Astraia didn't answer at first. Then, after a moment, with her heart in her eyes, she nodded, saying a silent prayer that she was doing the right thing for her, for Dante, and for her children.

"Yes, I will marry you, Dante Blackthorne. And yes." A tiny glimmer of hope was lit within her that one day he might love her as God had intended.

Pleased and relieved at her response more so than he could have imagined, Dante leaned forward and brushed his lips against hers tenderly. Wanting more, and yet, knowing it would be inappropriate in front of the children giggling next to him, he pulled away as a soft smile lit up his face.

Taking a deep breath, she opened her eyes wide and trembled at the contact of his warm lips against hers. Seeing the tired look in her eyes, and feeling her body growing limp next to him, he decided it was time she lay down for a while.

Pulling her chair out, Dante lifted her up into his arms. She clung to him weakly. Astraia made no objection to his movements as he carried her over to the couch and laid her on it. Grabbing one of the blankets they kept on the plane, he wrapped her loosely in it.

He heard her softly say, "I'm so sorry, I'm just so tired. Why am I so tired, Kastle?"

"It's Dante now. Remember? Just rest for a little bit. I'll take care of the children. And I'll wake you when my father calls. There is still much I need to go over with you."

Grabbing his food from the table, he took up a place on the floor next to the children in order to watch their shows with them. Glancing behind him, he watched her for a moment as she lay sleeping peacefully, her long blonde hair curling around her face and down her shoulders to her waist. Her heart shaped face carried such fine features. As she slept, the worry lines that normally furrowed her brow disappeared. Though she appeared a bit more tired in the last several days, she was really quite pretty.

Dante turned his attention back to the show and the children, after glancing down at his watch. He was hoping to hear from his dad soon, so he'd have as much time as possible to work with the children before landing. It was imperative that he worked quickly with them on getting their names and stories straight.

Chapter 19

Rafe Blackthorne had at one time held a position within the CIA, but was no longer involved with them, or so he'd told most of his children. He had managed to maintain contacts through various branches of the government, which was how Dante knew his dad could keep tabs on him while he'd been in service.

When Rafe's father, Rathbourne Blackthorne, had established the Blackthorne family horse ranch in his father's formative years, he had added various security measures to protect the house and grounds.

Once Rafe had taken over the ranch in his early twenties, he had the forethought to update the vast property lines, as well as the stables and house, with the best of security as he became aware of new technology through his work. This made bringing Astraia and her children to the Blackthorne Horse Ranch an ideal situation in Dante's mind.

After talking with his father, though, Dante could tell that Rafe was not entirely pleased with his decision. Once he'd met the children through the video phone, his displeasure seemed to dissipate measurably. Astraia was unable to meet him at the time, as she'd been asleep for the duration of the call, and he'd had difficulty rousing her.

Seeing her sleeping form on the couch through his desk monitor at the ranch, Rafe had seemed disturbed by her appearance for some reason. Taking his father off the video phone, Dante had continued the conversation in private, while the kids continued to watch cartoons quietly.

Listening while his dad inquired as to her health, Dante explained that he had some concerns, but wanted to wait until he arrived to get into it.

Learning that everyone was already assembled at the house for the summer months, Dante was both relieved and anxious. Their presence would allow for Astraia to receive medical attention sooner than anticipated. But it did give Dante cause to realize that he needed to be teaching Astraia about his family. Peering over at her as she slept, he hated the notion of having to wake her since she'd seemed so tired. But he decided it might become necessary rather soon.

In the end, Dante did not have to make that decision. Waking within a half hour of falling asleep as the result of turbulence, Astraia had sat up quite suddenly in alarm. It had taken her a moment to recall where she was, and why they were on the plane. Looking dazed, and still quite tired, Dante could hear her stomach rumbling from where he sat. Smiling, he'd gotten up and reheated her food for her, so she could finish eating while they talked.

The flight into Kalispell was going to take longer than anticipated due to unexpected weather issues they'd run into as they flew. May rainstorms caused them to be diverted. They were going to wind up landing later in the evening than anticipated. The extra time was going to give Dante a chance to give Astraia a run down on his family.

"There were six of you?" Astraia asked almost incredulously. "And of those six your mom had a set of triplets and a set of twins?"

Dante nodded, showing her the family tree he'd drawn out to try and help her. "Technically two sets of twins as my brother Dartanian and I are identical, but we were born at the same time Drinian was, making us triplets."

"Wow, and I have a hard-enough time with three!"

"Originally, it was thought there were only five Blackthorne children. My brothers and sisters did not know I existed until I turned eighteen and was graduating high school, which is why most of the people in town do not know me. I'd returned home to say goodbye to my mother since she was dying of cancer," he explained, knowing his family would expect him to at least tell her this part.

Astraia gave him a funny look. "I don't understand. Why wouldn't they know about you? I thought you just said you were one of a set of triplets. The eldest of three, I think you said."

Dante stared across the table at her with the realization that this was the part where he had to be extra careful what he said. Being one of six children with such gifts as they had, they'd made a pact, years before, that they did not share the secret with anyone unless all the siblings agreed the person being told could be trusted. This meant he had to choose his words carefully, to keep from telling her too much, and to avoid having to lie.

"When I was little, about three years old, there was an incident one day while we were all out playing near the river. I caused an accident without meaning to. It almost got my brother, Drinian, killed. It's also how I got the scar on my temple." He waited for her reaction. She sat calmly listening, but didn't appear horrified by what he was saying, so he went on.

"My parents were concerned that I might need special attention, so they sent me away to distant family we had on the reservation in North Dakota on my mother's side. They never told the rest of my siblings, as they came along, about me. My brothers were so young; they just thought a friend of theirs had moved away."

"Let me get this straight. Your brothers and sisters didn't find out about you until you were eighteen years old and your mother was dying, all because of some accident that happened when you were three?" She shook her head. "There are holes in your story, Dante. Something doesn't fit. What kind of special attention could an Indian relative of yours give you that your Indian mother couldn't? Why send you so far away, for so long, and not tell anyone? You were only three when it happened. A child that age has no comprehension of consequences and shouldn't be held accountable for their actions. The parent should."

Dante breathed in uneasily and then exhaled. Glancing out the window of the jet, he thought quickly, trying to come up with an explanation that might make sense for now. If the angelic guide of his would only cooperate, and pass her thoughts on to him more readily, then it might make explaining things that much easier. But unfortunately, either the angel was refusing to aid him for some reason, or she'd become a blank slate to them both. He wasn't getting anything from her at all anymore, which had never happened before. And he was starting to see how hard it must be for normal people to communicate.

Turning back towards her, he saw she'd been watching him.

"Astraia, the thing is…"

"It's okay." She patted his arm. Tentatively reaching for his hand, Astraia took it in hers, investigating his palm as though she was trying to read it. "Dylan used to do that. He'd be telling me some story from when he was in the service and he'd realize too late he'd told me too much. He wouldn't catch on until I'd ask him a question he couldn't answer." Glancing up at him, she sighed, and then peered back down at his hand again. "When it would happen, he would respond by saying, 'I can't tell you, but it's not because I don't want to, it's because I'm not able to'."

For a moment, Dante was quiet. "He told you that?"

Nodding, she went on, "Just tell me this much. Am I right to assume that there is more to this story, but that by telling me you'd be breaking a promise, or oath, or something to someone else? Or maybe putting someone in danger?"

"Yes, but I can't…"

Astraia shook her head and waved him off. "When, and if, you're able to tell me the whole story, I know you'll tell me. Until then, I'll just have to accept whatever you're able to give me for now."

Dante had been so surprised and pleased at Astraia's reaction that they'd sat in his stunned silence for a while. By the time he'd thought to continue their conversation, she'd fallen asleep on him.

- - -

Kalispell, Montana
Arrival Time - 7:47pm MDT
9:47pm Jacksonville time

Astraia woke as the plane was landing at Weaver Airport near Kalispell. Looking out the window, it was odd for her to see daylight, for if she were currently in Jacksonville, Florida, the sun would have already set. She knew they had arrived later than Dante had hoped and that he was both frustrated with her and worried about her because she hadn't been able to stay awake.

They lost a couple hours in transit, so the children were tired and cranky. The excitement of the plane ride had clearly worn off several hours before. For that reason, Dante opted to drive straight to the ranch, rather than attempting any sightseeing on the way.

By the time they arrived, Storman was in desperate need of a bathroom, since he hadn't bothered to use the restroom on the plane as he'd been instructed to do. Pulling into the long driveway instead of parking near the garage, Dante decided instead to pull up to the front of the house due to the urgent need. As he glanced over at Astraia, he was about to speak, when he heard her gasp.

"Kastle! You said you lived on a horse ranch with your dad!" She sounded horrified.

"Yes, why?" He glanced back at the house and unhooked Storman from his seat. "And remember, it's Dante now," he continued uneasily.

Astraia sat in the passenger seat, unable to move. "Dante, this isn't a ranch house. This is a mansion." Extremely distressed, she gaped openly at the house. From the seat behind her, she could hear Sayleena and Saruman exclaiming in awe at the home and their surroundings.

"Mama, is this where we're going to live?" She heard Sayleena ask at her ear as she'd unhooked from her seat. Dropping the book, she'd been reading on the floor of the vehicle, her daughter exclaimed in delight as her eyes lit up. "It's my dream home, mama!"

Astraia couldn't answer. She just stared at the house in disbelief. Dante had said he'd be able to take care of them, but she'd had no idea how well off his family must be. The house wasn't overly stated, by any means, but it was very large, housing multiple rooms, too many for her to count, and there was a patio porch that extended all around the front of the house towards the back.

A little worried at her reaction to his home, Dante couldn't stop and ask her about it. Storman had jumped out of the vehicle and was at a dead run for the front of the house.

Dante took off after him, scooping him up as he heard the boy holler, "I gotta pee!"

They tore into the house, barely missing his brother, Drinian, as he ran the boy to the first-floor restroom around the banister, near the front living room.

Drinian could be heard bursting out laughing as they'd sped by him, while hollering, "Mihapmak!" At the top of his lungs in greeting.

Sayleena and Saruman weren't far behind, as they ran up the steps of the porch, and slowed as they got near the front door. Drinian motioned them to come on in, so they did, giggling excitedly as they went, all the while staring up at the massive man in awe. Being even larger than his brother, and taller by a couple inches, the children stared openly at him as they stood transfixed in the entryway. Moments later, Dante returned with Storman in tow.

"Whew! That was close." Dante leaned up against the banister, appearing relieved.

Drinian smiled. "So I gathered." His matching crystal blue eyes sparkled with uncharacteristic amusement.

The French doors of the kitchen burst open to reveal most of the rest of the household pouring out to greet Dante after so many years away. He was met with much laughter and smiles as he introduced the children to his family.

"This beautiful little girl is Sayleena Jordan," Dante said proudly, starting with Astraia's little girl. He noted Breydon's head shoot up and look at him in alarm.

"And these very rambunctious boys are Saruman and Storman Jordan." He placed his hands on the boys' shoulders. Dante saw Breydon glance over at him and give him an odd look.

"Their last name is Jordan, you say?" Breydon asked.

Knowing Breydon would be able to tell this was a lie, as his gift was to be able to discern truth from people, Dante tried to catch him with a look before he spoke.

"You're such a..." Breydon faltered when he noticed Dante shaking his head vigorously at him. He tried to cover up last minute. "...likeable young man, now aren't you?" He finished, catching Dartanian's attention as well as Royce's. Pursing his lips in annoyance, Breydon could see Dante mouth the words "later." His brother was lying, and it irritated him. He was tempted to confront him on it but had the feeling that now wasn't a good time for that.

The first to greet the children was Dante's youngest sister, Crisalya; the baby of the family. Blessed with a slender medium build, she was several inches taller than her older sister, Megorah.

"Hi, Sayleena!" Crisalya greeted her brightly. She bent down to greet the girl. Her medium-length, black hair swung around her shoulders, framing her face. The same clear blue eyes shone brightly, and the little girl stared at them as though transfixed. "You look to be about Katie's age."

"Who's Katie?" Sayleena asked inquisitively while staring in rapt attention at Megorah's long, black hair in awe. Reaching out to touch it initially, she drew back shyly instead.

"Katie is my eight-year-old daughter." Megorah looked down at Sayleena. The same pale, shimmering eyes watched the little girl intently. She pulled her waist length, long black hair over her shoulders.

"I'm six. I'm in kindergarten," she said excitedly. "Is Katie in kindergarten too?" Sayleena asked, her curiosity at a possible new friend evident.

"No, she's in second grade actually," Megorah replied, her eyes widening as she glanced over at Crisalya in surprise.

"My goodness, Sayleena! You are tall for your age," Crisalya said, realizing that the little girl was likely to outgrow Megorah's five-foot, three-inch frame by the time she was in sixth grade.

"I know. I get it from my dad. Momma says I'm going to be taller than her one day. I can't wait till I can look down on her," Sayleena said brightly, making everyone laugh.

"I take it she's pretty short?" Dartanian asked her.

Sayleena turned towards Dartanian's voice and her eyes flew open wide. "You look just like daddy Kastle...uh...Dante!" she corrected herself as she exclaimed.

Eyes narrowing on his brother, Dartanian knelt down next to her and said, "You know, I get that a lot. But you know what?" he spoke conspiratorially to her then.

"What?"

"I'm better looking," he responded seriously.

Sayleena cried out in delight, laughing as she held her hand over her mouth. Turning towards Dante, she giggled.

"He said he's better looking than you and you look the same!"

Everyone laughed then and began introducing themselves.

"Where is the fiancée? Are you hiding her somewhere?" Dartanian asked as Saruman crawled up on his lap, surprising him.

"Wait, where is she?" Puzzled, Dante turned towards the front door. "She didn't come in?" Nearing the front door, he heard retching sounds coming from the porch.

"What is it, Dante?" Megorah called out, sensing Dante's sudden unease, as well as the woman's distress just outside the house.

"Uh, oh!" He sprinted through the door, across the porch, and down the steps. Finding Astraia hovering in the grass at the bottom of the steps near a bush, he could tell she was getting sick again. Bending down next to her, he placed his hand on her back for comfort.

"Alaina, Honey," Dante said, using Astraia's new name. Sensing his family had come out onto the porch, he inquired with concern. "What happened?"

"I'm sorry. I'm so sorry." She covered her mouth self-consciously and looked up at him. "I was trying to make it to the house."

"You know what, it's okay," Dante reassured her with a smile. "Better than on the porch, right?" Helping her up off the ground, Dante steadied her as she appeared to be dizzy.

The moment Alaina lifted her gaze up to the porch and saw Dante's family standing there watching her, she stepped back anxiously. Flustered by the impression she must be making at getting sick in his father's front yard, she became very distressed. Feeling suddenly dizzy, she nearly fainted next to Dante.

Catching her before she fell, Dante stared down at her in alarm. "Whoa, Alaina, what's wrong?" He could feel her limp body struggling to stand next to him. Her legs had suddenly buckled and he felt like he was going to lose her again, so he opted instead to pick her up to carry her inside.

Dante's brothers and sisters had crowded through the door to try and see what had happened. Drinian, Breydon, Dartanian and Crisalya stood staring at the woman in their brother's arms in surprise. Attempting to push past everyone so she could see, Megorah had just found her way around them in time to watch Dante carry a pretty woman with long blonde hair toward the front door.

"Megorah, get Chase," Dartanian said next to her, not realizing she had stepped around him already to get a better look. Meg's eyes enlarged at the sight of her.

"Oh, my! That poor thing appears to be in a lot of distress." Megorah said aloud, without thinking. "She seems a bit scared too."

"What's going on?" Dr. Chase Ryans asked his wife, having just come out onto the porch. Stepping out of Dante's way so he could enter the house, he noticed his brother-in-law was carrying a woman who appeared to be only partially conscious.

"What's happening, Dante? Did she faint?" Dr. Chase Ryans asked, following behind him.

Still carrying her, Dante strode into the front living room and laid her on the couch. Glancing over at Alaina's children, who'd been watching in alarm, he smiled at them reassuringly.

"Mama's just tired, guys. Remember how sleepy she was on the plane? Why don't you go with Aunt Lylia and Uncle Dartanian into the kitchen?" he continued, indicating his sister-in-law and brother. "You can meet some of your cousins before bed, okay?"

"Okay, daddy Kastle..."

"No, it's daddy Dante." Sayleena hissed, interrupting her brother Saruman. "Remember the game. And mama's Alaina and all our last names are now Jordan," she continued, pointing to each of them in turn. Nodding at their sister, they smiled then giggled and followed a very confused Lylia into the kitchen.

Watching them go, Dante didn't miss the suspicious look his twin brother gave him before he closed the kitchen door.

Turning towards his brother-in-law after they left, he said finally, "I don't know, Chase. Frankly, she's why I came home. I'd hoped I'd have a chance to explain. She's never actually fainted before, just gotten sick." Dante was clearly distressed.

"How long has this been going on?" Dante heard Rafe ask sharply as he stepped further into the room. Having seen his son arrive home from the display in his hidden room next to his bedroom, he had witnessed what was going on with great concern. His father stood now in the entry way, taking in the scene.

"About ten...maybe twelve days now. When she gets sick, it's usually only in the morning," Dante explained. He noticed her coming to on the twin sofa he'd laid her on. "Not in the evenings like this. She can't seem to keep anything down. She's tired and weak all the time and I've noticed she's been losing weight."

"How much weight?" Chase inquired, sounding concerned.

Shaking his head, Dante responded quickly as he watched her sit up. "Unsure exactly but it's enough to be noticeable."

Blinking several times, Alaina glanced toward Dante in confusion. "What happened? How did I...?"

"You fainted, Alaina." Dante placed emphasis on her name as he stared at her, hoping she wasn't too disoriented to remember her new name.

Inhaling deeply, her face flushed in embarrassment. "I am so sorry...Dante." She sounded a bit formal. The way she spoke, for whatever the reason, made Rafe smirk as his eyes began to twinkle. "Wow, what a way to make an impression on your family! How humiliating!"

"Not at all," Megorah said graciously. "Dante just explained you've been having some issues." She exchanged knowing looks with her sister, Crisalya. Cocking their eyebrows at each other, both women found themselves staring back at Dante, looking almost annoyed.

"Alaina, is it?" Chase asked as he extended his hand. Seeing her nod, he smiled at her in a reassuring manner. "I'm Dr. Chase Ryans, Megorah's husband. If you'd like, in the morning you can come by my clinic with Dante, and we can get you checked out."

"Yes, that would probably be a good idea." Alaina sounded both grateful and relieved. "Course, it might just be the jet lag from the long flight. I'm not used to flying and we're a few hours ahead of you guys. And the kids are getting quite cranky, as it's past their bedtime," Alaina continued, not realizing she was rambling.

"Is it now? Where did you hail from?" Breydon's wife Hialey asked curiously.

"The east coast," Dante responded quickly before Alaina could. Deciding it was time to get the kids and Alaina off to bed for the night, he explained they were all very tired from the trip. He hadn't had the chance to run through much with her on the plane and didn't want her having to answer too many questions just yet.

Evading their queries for the moment, he made sure Alaina was all right. Showing Alaina to the kitchen so they could round up her children, he was about to head upstairs with them when Dartanian stopped her suddenly. Reaching out, he took her right arm in his hand and pulled it toward him to get a closer look.

Eying the bend in her arm, he looked up at her suspiciously, "Are those track marks on your arm?"

Surprised initially by him grabbing at her arm, she'd stared at Dartanian at first in alarm. After hearing his question, she chuckled softly as she smiled. Shaking her head, she tried to explain.

"No, well, I suppose in a way they are. I donated plasma quite regularly. Twice a week, for the past five years." She yawned while trying to politely cover her mouth.

"Why would you do that for such a long time?" Crisalya asked, clearly perplexed.

Shrugging, Alaina pulled her arm away self-consciously. "Because I love my children," she responded sadly, staring down at her arm. "And because I understand that by doing so, it helped others. So, it benefited everyone in the long run." Rubbing at the spot on her arm rather absent-mindedly, she moved to turn back toward the stairs. "It was nice meeting all of you. I'm sorry if I gave such a poor initial impression. Hopefully, I can rectify that in the morning." Heading back toward the stairs, she noticed Dante stood watching her.

Following Dante up the stairs, he showed her and her children to their rooms near the front of the house. Alaina set to work getting the children settled in, while Dante ran to the vehicle to get their bags. Bringing them back up to the children's rooms, Alaina managed to get them all in their pajamas and had them brush their teeth.

Figuring they could do baths in the morning, she read them a story and sang them all songs, before tucking them into bed. Realizing she couldn't find their little blankets and stuffed chocolate bunnies in their duffel bag, Alaina recalled Dante had placed them in the trash bag with her clothes. Not seeing the bag anywhere, she gave her children kisses and hugs, promising to bring them up when she found the bag.

Remembering Dante said he'd be in the kitchen, Alaina headed back that way. Getting mixed up, she found herself walking down, then up steps again as she crossed the landing to the opposite side of the house. As she walked, she could see down into the vast entryway and when she looked up she could see the chandelier that hung from the ceiling. Overwhelmed by the sheer grandeur of the house, she was feeling a bit out of sorts by the time she found the stairs which led down into the kitchen.

Seeing Alaina step down into the kitchen from the stairwell, Dante was relieved at the interruption. His siblings had been harassing him about what Alaina had meant by her response to her regular plasma donations. He couldn't come up with a good answer as he was still quite rattled by her episode occurring during waking hours. Avoiding yet another question, he took a drink from his soda and then called out to her.

"What's up Alaina?" He appeared drawn and irritable. Not intending to sound so annoyed, he noticed her step back as though afraid to interrupt him. "No, really. What is it?" he asked again, softening his tone. His shoulders fell in defeat.

"Do you know where the kid's little blankets and stuffed chocolate bunnies were put? They need them to sleep with," Alaina asked softly, her tone apologetic.

"Should be in the duffel bag."

"No, I checked. Remember? You put them in with the things in my bag," she said, trying to jog his memory. "Do you happen to know where my bag is?"

Stopping suddenly near the fridge, Dante peered down at his root beer bottle. He grimaced. Refusing to look at Alaina, he began kicking himself inwardly as he clenched his hand around the bottle. It occurred to him that he knew exactly where the bag had been left.

"What did the bag look like? If it's still in the vehicle, I can get it for you." Breydon said.

"It was just a white trash bag." Alaina stared at Dante. An uneasy sensation filled the pit of her belly as she watched the careful play of emotions cross his face.

"You packed your clothes in trash bags?" Lylia asked in surprise.

Glancing towards the beautiful, golden blonde bombshell, Alaina noted the look of dismay on her face. Annoyed by her reaction, she sighed.

"One trash bag, actually, and I don't have a suitcase anymore."

"Why?" Hialey asked.

"They burned in the fire." She was becoming more and more distressed by Dante's lack of response to her question. "Dante, I really need those little blankets and bunnies. They don't sleep well without them when in a new environment, especially Saruman. You know he's prone to night frights."

"Did you say your son is prone to night frights?" Rafe turned towards her in alarm.

"Yes, he gets them regularly." Alaina yawned, attempting to cover her mouth again. "Singing 'Jesus Loves Me' is the only thing that calms him down. But, if he has his security blanket and bunny it helps."

Rafe had been standing near the patio doors listening to the conversation and knew already that Dante had screwed up big time. But hearing this bit of news had him glaring at his son in reproach, wondering how Dante could have possibly thought bringing a child with such an issue into their home would be healthy for him.

Exchanging looks with his father, Dante proceeded to stare at the ceiling to avoid her gaze. Aware that everyone was now staring at him over the exchange, he rolled his shoulders to dispel the tension.

"Uh, Alaina..." He groaned, an expletive escaping his mouth. He finally looked over at her, guilt written clearly across his face. Seeing her go pale, he realized she figured out what had happened.

"Please don't tell me that bag got left behind." Alaina shook in distress.

Placing his soda bottle on the long counter, Dante leaned up against it. He seethed inwardly. Thinking back to when he packed the trash bag with her things and the kid's stuff, he tried desperately to remember if anything of real significance got left behind that could lead to her. Determining quickly that there wasn't, he finally looked back up at her.

"I'm sorry, Alaina. I really am. I promise we'll go out and replace them in the morning, first thing. You can borrow a T-shirt from my dresser until then."

Wincing outwardly at the loss of the only items that meant anything to her children, she clenched her jaw angrily. In her anger, his comment about the T-shirt didn't register initially. Glaring at him without saying a word, she turned to head back up the stairs then whipped around suddenly. Gasping, she stared back at him in horror.

"Franc! You have me staying in your bedroom in your father's house and I have no clothes. Oh, frell!"

Clamping both hands across her mouth at her mistake, she whirled around in embarrassment and raced up the stairs.

Chapter 20

Watching as she disappeared up the stairwell, Dante bowed his head and leaned against the counter for support. Smacking his hand hard against the counter, he swore again as he scowled, winning himself an angry glare from his father.

"Did she just say what I think she said?" Breydon asked, his eyes twinkling with humor as he gazed over at Royce.

Giving each other a high five, Royce responded in kind, "I feel a Farscape marathon coming on."

While Royce and Breydon were enjoying the notion of another Farscape groupie in the house, they still managed to catch the byplay between Rafe and Dante.

Peering over at his father, Dante watched as the man seethed. Walking towards him, Rafe stopped at the fridge and grabbed an ice-cold root beer from within. Knocking the cap off, Rafe took a long drink as he eyed his son with contempt.

"You know it's a real wonder you made it as long as you did," Rafe said in disgust. He walked away toward the patio. Staring out the French doors, he then turned on his son. "And what were you thinking bringing that boy here? Those night frights of his are liable to get ten times worse in this house. You know that!"

At the same time his twin brother, Dartanian, got up from his chair and walked over to him. Bending down he looked him dead in the eye.

"So, who's Franc?" he asked. His brother stared back at him, looking clearly annoyed. A muscle twitched in his jaw. "What did you do, Dante?" They both stood looking back at each other as if they were in the middle of a stand-off. "Is this work? Did you bring your work home with you?" He gestured toward the stairwell where Alaina had disappeared.

Not saying a word, Dante's muscles flexed in his arms. His gaze never left his brother's face. Eyes narrowing, he picked up his soda, took a final swig, and tossed it in the recycling bin. Grabbing another root beer from the fridge, he could feel everyone's eyes upon him.

Getting up from his seat near the partition wall, Breydon walked around the table and stood near the counter. Placing his hand on one of the bar stools he began spinning the seat, then glanced back and forth between his father and Dante.

"You're lying, and I want to know why." Breydon challenged his brother while continuing to spin the seat.

"Just let it go, Breydon, it's for the best." Dante cracked his jaw with his hand, refusing to answer his brother, hoping all the while he'd drop it, but knowing he likely wouldn't.

"What's he lying about?" Dartanian and Hialey asked in unison. Heads turning towards each other, they grinned in unison as well.

"Breydon..." Dante warned.

Eying his brother as he spoke, Breydon responded, "Their last name is not Jordon, her name is not Alaina, and he apparently has been going by Franc for quite some time now."

The muscles in Dante's face twitched angrily. He gave his brother a deadly glare. Scowling in frustration, he tossed his now empty root beer bottle in the recycling bin, next to the last one he'd pitched there.

Turning towards his father, Breydon expelled an exasperated sigh. "I can't believe this! Dad, are you really going to stand there and tell me you're okay with this?" Breydon asked, his voice getting louder as he spoke. He was clearly aggravated.

Rafe chuckled humorlessly. "Regardless of whether I'm okay with it or not, what's done is done. They're already here. They will be married by Saturday night," Rafe said emphatically, his tone brooking no quarrel. "So a decision needs to be made. Do we tell her or not?" He eyed each one of his children.

Peering around the kitchen at his sisters, brothers, and their spouses, Breydon nodded toward each one in turn. They all knew what Rafe was referring to; the family secret.

"What do you all say? Do we tell her?" Breydon asked.

The silence in the kitchen was deafening, as everyone exchanged glances, not wanting to be the first to say, yeah, or nay. Becoming exasperated with the silence, Dante banged his hand on the counter, eliciting several startled yelps from the ladies.

"No," Dartanian finally said out of the blue.

"Are we really going to do this, Dart?" Dante got right up into his brother's face. "This is payback, isn't it? Because of Lylia." He gestured towards Dartanian's wife. Dante had known he was going to have difficulty getting his twin brother's vote because he'd been against allowing Lylia to know of their secret years before.

"My vote has nothing to do with my wife," Dartanian ground out.

He eyed his brother in disbelief. "Then why? Give me one good solid reason why?"

"We have no real assurance of the permanence of this situation," Dartanian said vehemently. "Your return home is sudden, and you've arrived with a supposed fiancée and children, who it would seem, have come by way of your last job. For all we know, you might take her back to wherever it is she comes from two months from now."

Chuckling derisively, Dante glared at him. "Trust me, it's permanent," he said with such finality it stunned even Rafe.

"But how do *we* know that?" Megorah asked, stepping between her two brothers. It had become clear to everyone what wasn't being said. That the woman and children Dante had brought home were not who they said they were.

"You have my assurance. That's all you need," Dante said.

"I can appreciate your feelings on the matter," Chase began carefully. "But not even you can guarantee us..."

"Yes, I can," Dante said coldly. He placed his new soda on the counter while glaring at Chase. He wasn't sure why, but he'd become awfully thirsty and suddenly very tired as well.

"I'd like to hear how you think you can guarantee it," Dartanian said in a mocking tone.

"Because there is nowhere else safe for her. They have nowhere else to go." Dante growled, his temper flaring.

Seeing the dark look in his son's eye, Rafe gestured for Megorah and his other sons to back away from him. Walking cautiously toward him, Rafe eyed his son warily.

"Dante, when was the last time you prayed?" Rafe asked curiously.

Dante smiled blandly, though it did not reach his eyes.

"You don't understand. I *have* been praying, and with Alaina at that." Dante said in frustration, his voice sounding strangled. "We've been doing devotions together for the past several weeks. As for Alaina..."

"Just let him tell her, Dartanian!" Lylia spat out angrily, her gaze shifting between her husband and brother-in-law. "Don't put that poor woman through what I went through."

"Lylia, it's not just Dartanian's decision to make. It's not only up to him. The rest of us have just as much say." Crisalya's eyes narrowed upon Lylia, not liking that the woman seemed to think she had the final say.

"No, you're right. You all get to decide her fate," Lylia said scornfully. Her bright blue eyes pierced into each one of the Blackthorne's causing all but Rafe to glance away with discomfort. "Yet, I can't help but get the feeling that this Alaina..."

"If that's really her name," Breydon scoffed.

"Is it Alaina? You called her Straya, or something like that, earlier in the living room." Drinian said, flicking his bottle cap across the table, hitting Hialey in the arm.

"Oops, sorry."

Dante took a long hard look at his brother and could tell instantly that Drinian was still struggling with his social skills.

"No, he called her Astraia." Royce said.

"It's more of a pet name, really," Dante said half-heartedly. The fact that he'd slipped up and called her by her real name aggravated him a great deal.

"That's an unusual pet name. Where'd you come up with that?" Lylia asked, reaching up toward her husband.

Dartanian stooped, smiling as he kissed her gently and caressed her waist. Settling into a chair beside her, he leaned forward and pulled his wife to him.

"It's Greek," Rafe said suddenly, knowing Dante wouldn't be able to explain that. "According to Greek lore, Astraia was the virgin Goddess of Justice. During the golden age, she lived on earth among men, whom she would bless," he paused then, tilting his head towards Dante, a thoughtful expression on his face. "She was driven away by lawlessness," he explained, giving Dante a meaningful look. "Her father, Zeus, eventually placed her amongst the stars as the constellation Virgo." Leaning against the patio door, he tapped his root beer bottle against his leg.

"That man never ceases to amaze me," Breydon said while gesturing towards his father. They watched Rafe as he leaned his head against the patio door and rubbed at his brow.

"Constellation of stars," Megorah could be heard mumbling distractedly. "Little Star. Mom would have named her Little Star."

"It's a very interesting pet name," Rafe said in a caustic manner, ignoring his daughter's musings. "Or would you say it was more of a nickname, Dante? Given to her as a child, maybe?"

"Did I say pet name? I meant nickname. Couldn't say where exactly she got it from, but I'm sure it doesn't really matter," he countered irritably.

Seeing they'd gotten completely off subject, Lylia rolled her eyes while sighing heavily in exasperation. The attempt at verbal subterfuge was clearly unnecessary at this point. Everyone knew the woman's name wasn't really Alaina. Tapping her stiletto heels on the kitchen tile in irritation, she leaned forward in her chair.

"Regardless, this; Alaina person seems to already have been through enough, from the sounds of it. She's arrived here with three little kids, a duffel bag and no clothes of her own. What little she had was being carried in a trash bag that got left behind in their clear haste to get here." Lylia eyed Dante first, then her carefully manicured nails.

"She's donating plasma, probably to be able to, what, feed her kids, and apparently lost everything she owned in a fire. Not to mention she's throwing up and fainting, and she doesn't know why." Lylia paused and stared around the room. "This woman is clearly scared, and in need of rest. Now, I don't know what exactly she's been through, Dante, and I don't need to know, but I'm betting it's quite a lot if she's come by way of your work. Am I right?" She asked on a softer note. Seeing him nod in the affirmative, she tapped her neatly manicured hand on the table. "My vote's yes. Are the rest of you really going to put her through even more?"

"Lylia, who's to say it wouldn't be worse for her to know, under those circumstances," Hialey said, legitimately concerned that it might be. In the back of her mind, she also couldn't help but think they knew nothing about this woman. She was anxious for someone she didn't know to be aware of what her husband could do.

"Trust me. I know from experience, it's worse to find out *after* the fact." Lylia sulked, while slouching against her chair. "There's a feeling of betrayal that's really hard to get past."

Rafe eyed Lylia warily, not for the first time wondering whether she'd ever fully forgiven Dartanian. His son hadn't been able to tell Lylia about the family secret until after they were married because of the pact the siblings had made. He had everyone's consent but Dante's to share it. But his brother had been off saving the world so he hadn't been able to get his consent. And when he had arrived home, by pure happenstance within a couple weeks after their wedding, Dante had said no, insisting he needed time to properly read her. The ensuing fight had been inevitable.

"Don't make her wait until after the wedding like I had to," Lylia said in a plaintive fashion as seven years of hurt could clearly be seen in her deep blue eyes. "Besides, it won't take long, with her living in this house, for her to figure out there is something different about the Blackthorne family."

"I have the impression it might not matter one way or the other whether she was to find out before or after the wedding Saturday." Royce stared at his brother-in-law curiously. "Dante, does she even have a choice in the matter here?"

"I told *her* she did but the truth of the matter is ... she doesn't have much of one," Dante sighed. "Obviously, I can't force her, but..." Within minutes of being home, he could feel how truly drained he was. Devoid of all energy, it felt as though much of his life had been sucked out of him. Dark circles were showing under his eyes that hadn't been there before and his stance was no longer as though ready for a fight.

"You make it sound like, whether we tell her our secret now or not, she has no choice as to whether she marries you or not." Hialey glanced between Royce and Dante. Watching as her brother-in-law cracked his jaw uncomfortably once again, her eyes widened in surprise, and she peered over at Lylia cautiously. "Dante, are you really saying she'll have to marry you no matter what?"

"It's important to me that you all know she has already agreed." He chose to evade the question. Seeing Hialey wasn't going to let it go, he became exasperated. "No one can force anyone to do anything. We make our own choices. That said, it would be in all our best interests for the two of us to marry."

"But why?" Crisalya sounded abhorred by the notion that a woman would have no say in the matter of marriage.

With a pained look, Dante glanced around the room, while avoiding everyone's gaze. "Because, in a decidedly sick and twisted turn of fate, she saw me as Dante Blackthorne prior to the incident which brought her here." Pausing briefly to allow the condemning news to sink in, he continued. "You know what that means," he said, nodding toward his father.

Wincing, Rafe scowled and nodded back. "She can't go into witness protection."

Without even having to tell him the circumstances which led to their arrival, Rafe knew the danger this placed all of them in if Alaina had fallen into the hands of government placed protection. His son had been smart to bring her here with him. Were the big brass ever to discover what Dante could do, and he'd tried to disappear, they would have pulled all of his son's charges in for questioning. That would have included Alaina since he had been one of her handlers.

The fact that she'd seen him without the contacts would have eventually gotten out, and they would have begun searching for large men with similar features and unusual blue eyes. In the end, it would have inevitably led the CIA back to his identical twin brother, Dartanian, rather than Dante, and thereby the rest of the family. The fact that she had inadvertently found herself wrapped up in the middle of something that had forced Homeland Security to step in so soon after having seen him was more than a little disconcerting.

"When did this happen?" Rafe asked his son sharply. "Specifically, what was the time frame between you meeting her and then having to...."

"Same day," Dante said, startling his father. "I saw her when grocery shopping that morning, and then that night I found myself in her house."

"Without telling details in front of everyone, can you tell me how she was involved in this?" Rafe asked anxiously of his son.

"She wasn't. Her husband was." Dante's voice cracked as he spoke. "She's an innocent," he explained, his eyes reddening noticeably. "But I'm afraid it's not the only reason."

"Explain," Rafe said crisply. He could not only see but feel the turmoil within his son coming off him in waves.

"Because, to save her, I had to take her as though she was my wife," he admitted finally. His face reddened, unable to meet his father's gaze. Hearing Megorah inhale sharply, he cringed as she began to cry softly.

The kitchen was quiet for a moment, as several family members exchanged looks. After a time, Dante finally continued.

"Regardless of what might accidentally fall from her lips from here on out, what occurred between us was my fault and mine alone," he said with a quiet urgency, his voice straining as he spoke. "I take full responsibility for what happened."

"You got tired, didn't you?" Rafe asked knowingly. He could see the toll serving in undercover operations had taken on him.

"No, it's not that at all," Dante insisted weakly.

"Have you ever taken the colored contacts out in public before?" Rafe scoffed, sounding disgusted.

"No."

"Then you got tired," Rafe said firmly. "You were tired and wanted out. You wouldn't have left the colored contacts out otherwise."

Turning abruptly at his father's words, Dante's face twisted with rage. Slamming his open hand against the fridge door, he reeled back, hitting it repeatedly as he roared, startling everyone in the room. Stopping abruptly, he flung himself against the fridge door, causing it to rock on its casters. Sliding down the face of the fridge, he began to sob as he neared the floor. Landing heavily, he bent over, resting his head against the cool surface of the now thoroughly dented fridge door.

Watching his son, in clear distress over the circumstance which had brought Alaina to them, Rafe worried that he might be losing his faith. Closing his eyes, he could sense a need within his son for penance and absolution.

"Boys," Rafe said quietly as he stared at his son, now prone on the floor. Tears threatened at the corners of his eyes. It pained him to see his son so tortured, and he hated that Dante had been placed in the position where he'd had to do the things he had.

"I got him, Dad," Drinian said, his expression serious. He dragged his brother up off the floor.

Coming around the counter, Breydon waited as Dartanian took hold of Dante under his other arm. Hefting him up, they practically carried him from the kitchen. Breydon followed after them.

"We know what to do. Where do you want us?" Breydon asked. They all paused near the hallway.

"Downstairs library," Rafe said in answer. "There'll be more room."

"He died because of me." Dante could be heard to say, his vast chest heaving as he cried. His expression was wracked with guilt. "Because of me!"

"Who died, son?" Rafe stepped closer to Dante in order to hear him better.

"Their father. Her husband took a bullet meant for me," he croaked. His bloodshot eyes sparkled with unshed tears. Exchanging glances over his head, Drinian and Dartanian both whistled softly at the news. Rafe peered over at Breydon and could see by his startled nod that what Dante was saying was true.

"Mind if we join, Rafe?" Royce asked as he and Chase sidled up next to the rest of the men.

"By all means, the more the better."

Rounding the kitchen corner, the men disappeared down the hall, heading towards the library. Rafe stared after them with a heavy heart. He'd known fifteen years before after Elizabeth had died, that Dante's faith would suffer many setbacks. He had not realized to the extent he would suffer for it, until now.

"Guess now isn't a good time to tell him," Crisalya said dryly, as she sat in her kitchen chair, sulking. Playing with a spoon she lifted and dropped it in a rhythmic fashion, allowing it to bang on the table

"Tell him what?" Rafe asked.

Sighing heavily, Megorah wiped her tears away. She sniffed and sat straighter in the chair she'd taken near her sister.

"He would have had to buy her new clothes anyway," Megorah looked up at her father. Her black lashes, wet from crying, accentuated the crystal blue eyes that mirrored her fathers.

"Why?" Rafe looked back and forth between his daughters while trying to keep up.

"Because she's pregnant." Crisalya glanced furtively toward Lylia to gauge her reaction to the news. "Going and getting checked out by Chase tomorrow will simply be a formality because I already know that's what's wrong with her."

"You know this because of her symptoms? Or do you know this simply because you know it, by way of your gift?" Rafe cocked his brow with interest, wanting to be sure that what she was saying wasn't just supposition.

"I just know it." Standing, she grabbed the teapot from the stove and began filling it with water from the sink. Suddenly craving Earl Grey tea, as she always did after being given such knowledge, she went to the cupboard and pulled an assortment from the cabinet for everyone.

Hearing the news about Alaina's impending pregnancy, Lylia stood as well. Intentionally keeping her expression blank, she turned towards Rafe and spoke. "We'll get the kids to bed. They're all in the playroom. Shall the rest of us ladies all meet in the front living room, then?" She asked quietly.

"Yup, I'll be there, my Bible holstered to my hip." Hialey headed toward the hallway. "You want to grab a spiced Chai for me, Cris?" She called as she disappeared down the hall to get her boys off to bed.

"Already on it," Crisalya called back.

"At least one good thing came from this," Megorah said aloud. Both Rafe and Lylia disappeared down the hall, going in opposite directions.

"What's that?" Crisalya asked, reaching for the Raspberry Tea that Lylia liked.

"Dante seems to be home for good now. If that's true, we no longer need to worry so much about where he is, what he's doing, or even if he's still alive," Megorah said in answer.

"Yes, so it would seem." Crisalya turned towards her sister. "But at what cost, Meg? You saw him just now. He's suffering and he's in pain emotionally, spiritually. The things he's had to do to help people like the woman sleeping upstairs…"

"I know, Cris. I don't like it any more than you." Megorah grabbed teacups from the hallway. "But dad was right about what he said all those years ago. Somebody must protect our people, our nation. We cannot exclude ourselves from serving, simply based upon our faith."

"And why not? Why should my brother, a Christian man, suffer through this? Meg, every five years he's come home in this condition. And this time, it's worse! You can see it, can't you?" She exclaimed angrily, tears welling in her eyes.

Nodding sadly as her heart ached, Megorah turned to her sister, "I not only see it, Cris. I *feel* it." Tears spilled from her eyes. Banging at her chest with her fingertips, she began to cry. "*I feel it right here*. You know that. It's overwhelming."

"Then why were you okay with it?" Crisalya asked plaintively. She rubbed her sisters back, hoping to calm her. Concerned over her sister's emotional state, she decided to grab Chamomile tea for her, to help ease her tension. Megorah's ability to sense other people's emotions was clearly taking a toll on her tonight.

"Because it's not right, okay? It's not right to expect non-Christians to serve and die for *us* if we are not willing to serve and die for *them*," Megorah explained. "How can we honestly say we love everyone if we aren't willing to do that for them? They have just as much right to live in freedom as we do."

Crisalya stared at her sister and pondered what she was saying. She hadn't ever thought about it in those terms before. Unable to find fault in her reasoning, she stayed silent, knowing there wasn't anything more to be said on the subject. Dante had served his time and he was home now. That was all that mattered. If this Alaina had helped somehow in finally bringing him home for good, however inadvertently, Crisalya was, and would be, grateful to her for that.

Chapter 21

An hour later everyone had found their way back to the kitchen. The women had completed their Bible study for the night, while the men finally emerged from the library after having sat in prayer over Dante.

Feeling much calmer than he had before, and embarrassed for his earlier violent behavior, Dante considered disappearing for the night. Instead, he opted to take a seat with his family at the kitchen table near the patio; being in their presence after coming home from a tough job always seemed to help him decompress.

Watching them as they got settled with their drinks and snacks for the night, Dante sat in silence, enjoying the sound of their camaraderie. During the few years, he had lived at the house after his mom had died, it had become a nightly ritual for his family after having evening Bible studies and prayer. It seemed they were picking up where they'd left off. Or at least, he was just getting back into the swing of things.

As he munched on his Sun Chips, he noticed his father stood near the patio doors staring out at the night sky, hands in his pockets. Rafe had aged a bit since the last time he saw him, but he still appeared strong and healthy. A small amount of his hair had turned a distinguishing salt and pepper color near his ears. His build seemed to have diminished only a little in stature, though he was still as tall and almost as big as Dante could remember him to be.

With a weary sigh, Dante accepted the strawberry kiwi juice his twin offered and screwed the top off. After taking a drink, he set it on the table and glanced around at his brothers, sisters, and their spouses. Most of them had just come back downstairs from checking on their children. He had just come from checking on Alaina's kids himself. Children of which, Dante realized with renewed excitement, he'd soon be calling his own.

Running his hands through his hair, he tilted back in his chair, recalling how he'd checked in on Alaina as well. Curled up in his California king size bed, she had looked so small and fragile laying there. The t-shirt she'd chosen from his dresser drawer dwarfed her, making her appear that much smaller. Leaning down, he'd kissed her on the cheek after pulling the blankets back up over her sleeping form.

Shaking off the image of her sleeping in his bedroom, his mind returned to the general noise and hubbub of the kitchen. Allowing the chair legs to drop heavily on the floor, he grabbed up his drink and took another swig, while avoiding his family's gazes.

"What else are you gonna tell us about them?" Breydon's wife Hialey asked as she plopped down on her husband's knee. Quickly engulfed by his arms, he began tickling her mercilessly.

"Babe, give the man a chance to speak." Breydon continued to pester her until she finally cried 'mercy.'

"What?" Hialey giggled, pushing her husband away. Sitting upright on his lap, she gave him an impish grin. Looking around at everyone, she spoke defensively. "Someone has to get him talking again because so far he's not saying anything."

Dante chuckled softly when Breydon gave her a quelling look. He recalled the last time he'd been home, that Hialey had an open, no-nonsense kind of personality, which tended to shock people. He also remembered well, the couple's inability to keep their hands off each other.

"No, it's okay, Breydon. She's right." Dante came to her defense. "This whole situation is complicated. I'm not sure where to start. There's only so much you can know, and frankly, you all know more already then you really should."

Rafe turned toward him, a knowing look in his eye. "I think it's obvious to everyone what the situation is with her. Maybe you should just start with the stuff you *can* tell us, rather than making us ask questions you know you can't answer."

Wincing at his father's directness, he noted everyone looked from him to his father then back again. "Alaina said it best on the plane. There are aspects of our relationship or story that we won't be able to explain. When and if we're able to tell you, we will. Until then, I'm hoping you all can accept whatever we can give you, for now."

The room was quiet; the silence being broken only by the sound of the freezer motor kicking on. Rafe adjusting one of the bar stools and sat down, looking over at Dante with a thought expression.

"She said that, did she?"

"For the most part."

Rafe nodded his head slightly, a half-smile playing on his lips. "Would it be safe to say she was referencing another situation when she said it? Possibly, I don't know... *your* own story?"

He laughed out loud. "Is there nothing lost on you, Dad?"

"Not much." Rafe grinned mischievously. His son didn't need to know he had eyes and ears everywhere, in more ways than one.

Grinning back, he gave his father a suspicious look. "I was trying to tell her about us on the plane, without really telling her about us." He pointed to each of his siblings in turn. As he glanced around the room, he observed the looks of understanding from each of them.

Dartanian peered cautiously over at his brother, "So, what exactly can you tell us? Because it sounds like you haven't known her for long yourself."

"I haven't, though I won't specify a timeframe. There is much about her and the children I am still learning myself. I can tell you that her kids have a fondness for vanilla flavored steamed cows at night before bed and that Alaina likes honey in her coffee." he grinned sheepishly at them.

"Seriously?" Royce asked. Seeing his brother-in-law nod, he continued, "Man, what are the odds?"

"A billion to one, I'd say," Hialey quipped, winning herself a few stares. Eyeing them right back, she defended her numbers, as Breydon tried to hush her. "How many people do *you* know that put honey in their coffee? I'd never even heard of it until I met *him*." Hialey pointed at Dante.

"Seriously, though, as far as all of you are concerned, her name is Alaina Jordan and she is my fiancée. She has three children; Sayleena, Saruman, and Storman from a previous marriage, all of which I will be adopting once we're married on Saturday." He noticed Breydon raising his eyebrows. "Yeah, Brey, gonna need your help with that, if you're willing." Seeing him give an affirming nod, Dante continued. "There will be times when both she, and the kids, will say things that don't match with what they've previously told you. It's extremely important that you not make a big deal about it. Merely correct them." Taking a deep breath, he went on. "And I need to know when they slip, especially the kids, Lylia. In fact, I was hoping that you would…"

"Home school them? No problem. It makes more sense to do it that way, under the circumstances, anyway. I'll work with them," Lylia said between mouthfuls of popcorn. "It's gonna get really confusing for them, though, because if you think about it, what with the impending adoption, they're changing their name twice.

Grateful for his sister-in-law's understanding, Dante couldn't help but wonder if he might have been wrong about his misgivings he'd had of her years back. Appearing thoughtful as he eyed her, he shook his bag of Sun Chips, and then tossed the bag on the table.

"I'm not going to sit here and give you some half-baked story. Nor will I answer questions regarding their past. The less you all know the better. Trust me."

"Just tell us this. You, being home with her now, does that mean you are home for good?" Megorah asked breaking the tension and his train of thought.

All Dante had to do was look at her and she knew the answer. She smiled brightly then and lifted her glass of juice in the air. "Big brother has come home for good. Mihapmak!" Megorah raised her glass. Everyone else did as well, and let out a loud, "Mihapmak!"

Rafe rolled his eyes. They were using the word incorrectly, as 'mihapmak' was meant more as a friendly greeting. He understood why they chose to use it to welcome him home, nonetheless.

"In the end, that's all that matters," Crisalya said meaningfully, as their respective bottles and glasses hit the table. "I think we can all agree; we can now breathe a sigh of relief."

Dartanian dropped his empty mango juice bottle on the table. "We're all glad you're home. As far as I'm concerned, if this Alaina helped bring you back, then that's all I need to know." Patting his brother on the shoulder good-naturedly, their heated discussion from mere hours before had been shrugged off as inconsequential.

"That being said, I think it's time we discuss what they need from us." Chase glanced over at Dante. "I'm assuming you wouldn't be bringing them here if you felt they could get help elsewhere. And when I say they, I mean more specifically Alaina."

Dante chuckled. Good old Dr. Chase Ryans had been clearly flummoxed by Alaina's behavior and was looking to do some fixing.

"My thought when I made the decision to bring her here initially, was that she needed some medical attention. But now, I don't know what to think." He shook his head in frustration. "I'm starting to wonder if there's something else going on here."

"There's not," Crisalya said flatly. She turned and eyed Rafe. "Can I tell him now?" Seeing her father nod, she trained her gaze on Dante. "She's pregnant."

Chuckling softly once again, Dante played with his juice bottle. "No, Crisalya, she's really not." His nonchalant, knowing response received several raised brows.

"Yes, she is, Dante. She's pregnant," Megorah piped in urgently.

"My partner and I thought that initially, too. She was married before, after all. I even went out and bought her a test. But she's not pregnant."

"Did the test come back negative?" Chase stared at Dante intently.

"No, she never took the test."

"Then how can you know for sure?" Crisalya inquired, looking confused.

"Alaina had a tubal ligation done after her boys were born," Dante explained while eyeing Lylia cautiously. Seeing her bang her soda on the table in disgust, he became irritated. "I'm sorry, Lylia. I know hearing that probably upsets you, but you have to understand your situations are entirely different. You may want more children, but she didn't. From what I gather she was very unhappy with her spouse and did not want more children with him for that reason." Pausing, Dante turned away from Lylia's angry stare. "Plus she did not come from money like you did, so that was a big concern as well."

"That doesn't make any sense. I was so sure," Crisalya mumbled. Exchanging confused glances with Megorah, she leaned forward in her chair deep in thought. Being a nurse, and the Healer of the family, she was very good with herbs and teas, as well as discerning what often ailed people by simply looking at them.

"It doesn't mean she couldn't still be pregnant," Chase said suddenly, leaning forward in his chair as well. "I hate to say it, but it's still a possibility."

"Oh, no!" Lylia whispered. Her widened eyes filled with tears. "You're thinking a tubal pregnancy."

Dartanian turned his wife towards him and wrapped her in his arms where she huddled there. The subject of pregnancies was a sensitive issue around Lylia as she'd had such a hard time getting pregnant with Kayla. Since the Blackthorne men couldn't have children of their own they'd reverted to a sperm bank in order to be able to have Kayla and she'd had several miscarriages before one finally took.

Chase nodded. "It's possible. These symptoms: nausea, fatigue, fainting - even losing weight. They are all symptomatic of a pregnancy in its early stages, but they could be indicative of other health issues as well."

"Most of you saw what happened, right?" Dante asked, glancing around the table. Seeing them all nod he went on. "This is the first time she's ever fainted after getting sick. Usually, she just gets really weak and tired afterward. But here's the thing..." Shifting in his chair he leaned forward. "And this, in the end, is why I brought her home. Alaina's been having dreams too."

"What do you mean by dreams?" Rafe asked.

"Dreams like the kind Meg gets on occasion," Dante said, pointing towards her, gaining everyone's attention.

"Are you serious?" Breydon gaped at his brother.

Nodding, Dante explained about the morning he'd walked into her bedroom to find her acting like she was retching in her sleep.

"When Alaina woke she couldn't get to the bathroom fast enough. I initially thought she was just having night-frights - possible symptoms of Post-Traumatic Stress Disorder." He eyed Megorah then in order to gauge her reaction. Chase observed the exchange and tensed noticeably.

"You think she has PTSD?" asked Dartanian.

"No, he thinks she's suffering from RRPTSD," Royce said quietly. Everyone turned and looked at him, including his wife Crisalya. "Rape-related," he continued off-handedly with a shrug. Royce had been silent until that moment, as was usually his habit. Glancing over at Dante, he grabbed another handful of peanuts from his bowl and asked, "Am I right?"

"Yes, though she hasn't actually said anything happened." Dante was a little uncomfortable with discussing this part with them as he felt he was somehow breaking her confidence. Only he didn't know how to help her without telling them.

"I don't understand. Did she tell you something happened to her?" Megorah asked, watching him shake his head in the negative. "Then how are you coming to this conclusion?"

"Within the first day, I met her she'd referenced an incident that happened fifteen years ago. Additionally, I asked her once who had hurt her and received the image of the man in my head. I know what her attacker looks like and I have a pretty good idea what he did to her."

"Wait a minute. The angel at your side, he's giving you her thoughts?" Megorah asked rather sharply, sitting up straight.

"No," Dante sighed. "Not anymore anyway."

"You're saying, at one point you were able to discern her thoughts, but now you can't?" Dartanian asked. "When did this happen? What changed?"

The room seemed to be buzzing with energy and everyone sat forward intently waiting for an answer. Sensing that there was something significant about this detail he asked a question of his own.

"Megorah, when you saw her after the attack, I overheard you tell Dad that Alaina was a shield. What is a shield? What does that mean?"

"A shield is someone who has been given the ability to protect themselves from a person trying to use their ability, or gift, on them in a negative way," she explained. "I cannot sense her emotions and I won't be able to unless she allows me. Thing is, she might not even realize she's doing it. I've found, on the rare occasion I've come across a person who is a shield, that they typically have no idea of what they are capable of."

"But you said she was distressed and scared, Honey. If you can't discern her emotional state, then how did you know that?" Chase asked. He reached around her and patted her gently on her side. Her slight frame was dwarfed by his size, though his build was not as large as the Blackthorne men.

"Anyone can read an expression. That's all I was doing." Megorah peeked up at her husband. "I wasn't actually sensing her emotions, just looking with my eyes."

"Did any of you get anything off her?" Dante peered around at everyone. Seeing his family shaking their heads in the negative, he sighed in frustration.

"Obviously, I'm not getting anything from her," Crisalya pouted.

"Not necessarily true," Dr. Chase Ryans said. "But we'll know for sure one way or another tomorrow morning."

Observing Dante's scowling countenance, Rafe noted his son's expression change to a thoughtful one. "What is it, Dante?" he asked.

Pursing his lips, he shook his head. "Earlier today, she told me she discovered her daughter liked to crawl into her brother's bed and sleep with them. When I asked her if she'd seen her do it, she said she hadn't. That somehow she just knew it. I didn't think much of it at the time because she just played it off as though she'd dreamed it. But what if...?"

"She really just somehow knew it?" Rafe asked, eyebrows raised.

"Is it possible?" Dante stared at his father then around the room. "Could she be presenting with abilities?"

"Anything is possible." Drinian shrugged while leaning back in his chair, appearing bored with the subject.

"What 'Man of few Words' means, is that to think we're the only ones in the world with such abilities would be rather presumptuous of us," Megorah said dryly, rolling her eyes. "That said, I've never really heard of someone presenting with such gifts as an adult unless…"

"Unless…" Dante prompted. His sister had drifted off in thought.

"Unless they experienced a traumatic situation," Rafe answered for her. "Did she see her husband die?"

"No, that happened elsewhere. But she was present during…" Pausing, he tried to come up with a good way to explain what she'd been through, without telling them what happened.

"Was she present during a violent encounter perhaps?" Rafe asked carefully.

"Yes."

"So, we have a woman presenting with possibly two different abilities, after experiencing a traumatic event," Chase repeated more to himself than anyone else. Somewhat befuddled by the picture he was getting off the woman's situation, Dr. Ryans became introspective.

"That still doesn't explain her other symptoms unless there is more than one issue here," Royce commented. "Cris, what do you think? Could Alaina possibly have a medical issue and is presenting with abilities all at the same time?"

"It's possible," Crisalya answered slowly, sounding more than a little unconvinced. "But with two different abilities?" She looked to her father for direction.

"It's not impossible for a person to be blessed with more than one gift," Rafe responded. "If you really think about it, all of you have more than one."

"How do you figure?" Dartanian asked as his wife Lylia stared at him anxiously.

"Your predominant gifts are the ones that are most prevalent to you. Dartanian's to discern the good from the bad, Breydon to discern truth from lies, Crisalya to discern what ails people, Megorah to discern a person's emotional state and so on. But you all have some measure of the gift to 'know,' which comes from me, rather than your mother." Rafe snatched up the bag of Sun Chips with a rueful grin at Dante's irritated expression over his theft. "I've noticed you all, at some point or another, coming to conclusions you might not otherwise, because of it."

"Somehow, I just knew he was going to steal my chips," Dante mocked as those around him chuckled.

"Were you intimate with her before or after the traumatic event?" Drinian drawled unexpectedly. Leaning back in his chair, he had his head tilted back against the wall with his forearms resting on the chair's armrest. He pondered the quandary Alaina was in. It occurred to him, in that moment, the shadows' behavior towards her and what was going on at the time was rather curious. Dozens of the demons had appeared suddenly as he'd arrived on the porch. They'd hissed at Alaina angrily as though she'd done something to upset them.

"What does that matter anyway?" Breydon asked crossly.

Dante swiveled in his chair, looking at Drinian in surprise at his improper question.

Shrugging, Drinian replied, "Just trying to get a clear picture."

"Before," Dante finally answered. Staring at his brother, he lifted his drink to his lips. "And just be sure you're not getting too clear of a picture there, Drin." His gaze narrowed upon Drinian's drawn face.

Eyes still closed, Drinian gave him a toothy grin. "Why? Afraid of a little brotherly competition?"

"Knock it off, Drin," Dante said darkly.

"She *is* kind of pretty and they were awful interested in her." Drinian mumbled as though oblivious to his brother. "Why were they so interested in her?" He said under his breath.

"Why was who interested in whom?" Breydon asked in confusion as Royce and Rafe stared intently at Drinian.

"Wait a minute. You mean the shadows were interested in Alaina?" It finally registered to Dante what his brother must mean.

"Yup," was all he said in response while yawning.

"Drinian, how exactly were they interested in her?" Rafe asked pointedly.

Scowling as he scratched his head, Drinian appeared thoughtful. "Acted like they were trying to get inside her," he answered finally, shocking everyone into silence.

Chapter 22

For the first time in fifteen years, Dante was actually afraid. Drinian's revelation had cut him to the core. Standing suddenly, he knocked over his chair and nearly dropped his Strawberry Kiwi Juice bottle on the floor. He began pacing the room in agitation as he glanced over at his brother at the table.

Drinian, apparently ambivalent to his brother's plight, had begun flicking another bottle cap across the table. This time, Breydon caught it before it hit Hialey and gave him a dirty look.

"What does that mean?" Dante ran his hands through his hair in distress. Drinian looked him in the eye for the first time since arriving back in the kitchen. He could see the dark circles under his eyes. It was obvious that it was getting harder and harder for his brother to cope with seeing and hearing the demons around him. Being the third of the triplets born, he'd been gifted with an ability that was more of a curse than a gift.

"Don't know. Don't really care." Drinian shrugged.

Dante rounded on him. Tossing the empty bottle in the recycling bin near the fridge, he turned suddenly and smacked his hands on the kitchen table with great force. The resounding thud startled most at the table, yet Drinian just sighed and rolled his eyes as though completely immune to Dante's anger.

"Attempting to split the table, like you did dad's desk fifteen years ago, will not earn you my attention anymore so then it would if Dart were to draw his gun on me," Drinian said, giving his brother a disinterested look. He was completely unaffected by his brother's anger.

"What do you mean by, 'they were trying to get inside her?' Can you tell me that at least?" Dante asked pleadingly, his voice softening as he said it. "How were the demons acting towards her exactly?"

"They were dive-bombing her," Drinian replied as though it were no big deal. Everyone looked at him, stunned at both his response, and the callousness through which he'd given it.

"Drin!" Megorah hollered at him in disgust for she could sense the fear building within Dante as he stood looking at Drinian in horror.

"I'm being serious," Drinian said mildly, looking around at her. "There were dozens of them present. They just swarmed up high in the sky and began taking turns at diving towards her." Closing his eyes, he tilted his head to the side. He was visibly tiring, whether, from the shadows that tormented him or the late hour, Megorah was not sure. Reaching his arm up high, he flattened his hand and sent it fingers first into a nosedive for the floor, making zooming noises all the while.

Dante growled then deep in his throat. Drinian had always been difficult but his utter lack of feeling was hard to take at times. He honestly didn't know how his brothers and sisters had coped with it as they grew up with him.

"Drin, stop it. You're upsetting your brother." This time, it was Rafe that spoke up, hoping to avoid a fight at this late hour. "Tell him what he needs to know."

"I can only tell him what the shadows choose to show and tell me. We all know how honest they can be."

"You haven't been talking to them, have you?" Rafe asked, giving his son a dubious look.

Staring back at his dad, Drinian sighed with resignation. "Of course not, Father," he replied as though humoring him. "They merely talk to me, and I hear them regardless of whether I want to or not."

"Are they talking to you now?" Breydon narrowed his gaze and glanced around the room. There were times when his brother was present that he could swear he could almost sense their dark presence. It usually meant they were in great numbers. He'd learned over the years to be more cautious around Drinian when he sensed it, and he had the feeling his sister could tell as well. At the moment he wasn't feeling anything, but he got the impression from the way the man was acting that something was whispering in his ear.

Drinian glanced meaningfully towards Breydon then, and said, "The shadows pester me incessantly. Don't the divine beings always bother *you*?" He swatted his hand in a backhanded motion near his left ear.

"Not always, they give me space when I need it." Breydon wrapped his arms around Hialey as she shivered next to him. Pulling off his flannel shirt, he wrapped it around her bare shoulders. She smiled up at him gratefully.

"Really?" Drinian asked. "How fortunate for you because the shadows rarely ever leave me alone." He sighed heavily, clearly weary and in need of rest.

"Why didn't you say something about this before?" Rafe stared at his son looking cross.

"Not but two days ago you told me to keep what the demons were doing to myself," Drinian reminded his dad with a scowled.

Exasperated Rafe said, "That's because you were telling everyone how the shadows were making inappropriate and lewd gestures towards Lylia while you were laughing. It was upsetting her."

Shrugging, Drinian countered on a sigh. "Doesn't matter anymore anyway," he said, sounding morose.

"Explain yourself," Rafe demanded.

"They just rebounded right off of her. It was quite comical really." Drinian chuckled at the memory. Flinging his hand back up in the air, he pointed it once again towards the ground. Sending his hand into another nosedive, he halted it mid-way. "Boom!" he bellowed loudly, as his hand stopped, popping back as though hitting a brick wall.

"Never seen them do that before. Rebound so fast that is. It was pretty funny. Zalman was clearly furious over it, too." Smirking, Drinian glanced around the room and sighed. The rest of his family didn't seem to have his sense of humor.

"But what does that mean?" Lylia asked Rafe anxiously. "I thought you said they could get into anyone."

"They can, make no mistake. They could get into even you if they really wanted to, Lylia." Drinian said. She cringed openly.

"Knock it off," Dartanian growled, pulling his wife to him protectively. "A demon can only get inside a believer if they let them in. It means, for some reason, she is either strong in faith or being protected by an angel. Breydon, did you see anything?"

Shaking his head, Breydon responded, "The only angel present at the time that I saw was the one who's always attached to Dante. And I can't always see him."

"Unless..." Drinian could be heard to say, drawing everyone's attention once again. He appeared deep in thought as he sat up abruptly. The expression on his face changed instantly to excitement. He turned suddenly towards his sister. "Meg, is it possible?" His eyebrows rose and his body tensed. She looked back at her brother, pausing mid-sip as she stared in confusion.

"Think, Meg, think." Drinian urged in exasperation. "None of us are able to discern anything from her right now. The three of us turned forty and Dante was intimate with her. Alaina is tired, nauseous, losing weight, fainting and presenting with possible abilities; which could mean..."

"Oh, my gosh! Of course," she exclaimed without warning. Eyes darting towards Dante, they both stared at him in shock.

"What?" Dante asked, becoming irritated.

"A Blackthorne pregnancy," Megorah said suddenly, startling everyone. "It would explain why we couldn't discern anything from her, and why you were able to at one point, Dante. She's not a shield at all."

Blinking at them stupidly, Dante shook his head. "We've already covered that. She can't get pregnant anymore, remember?"

"Dante, he's right. Drinian *is* right!" Megorah cried excitedly. "Miracles happen every day and you *are* forty years old this year. Wasn't there something in one of mom's journals about a change occurring when three turned forty?" She directed the inquiry towards her father first, then Drinian. You all already had your fortieth birthday this year." Jumping up from her chair then, she put her glass on the table.

"I'd have to look back over mom's journals." Drinian tried hard to keep his expression neutral. At the same time, his insides had ignited with a hope which he hadn't experienced for years.

"Dad, don't you remember?" Megorah asked. "In one of mom's books, there was something about an Indian story from about 200 years ago. I'm trying to remember. It's been so long since I've read it. It started by having something to do with three gifted brothers with similar abilities as Dart, Dante, and Drin. One of them had been given a second chance at children when he'd turned forty."

Rafe appeared thoughtful for a moment. "I believe you're right, Meg. We should look into it." The possibility that one of his sons might actually have the chance at children of their own lit a spark of hope in his eyes.

Sputtering in denial, Dante reeled back in his chair. "No. No, it's not possible, we were all tested and she had a tubal ligation procedure."

"Dante, that procedure, though highly effective, still isn't one hundred percent guaranteed." Chase insisted, attempting to get his brother-in-law to understand the potential danger Alaina might be in. "I don't want to give false hope but Meg could be on to something here. Being as I'm in a field where unexplained healings occur every day, I have to admit there have been cases where a woman's tube has grown back of its own volition, after being cut or burned off. It is rare, but anything is possible where God is concerned, you know that."

"I'll pull the journals out tonight." Rafe tossed the empty chip bag in the trash. "Either way, there may be something in them that could help Alaina. That is, if this is in fact what we're thinking it is."

"Good, you guys do that. I'm going to drink myself to sleep." Drinian stood up and reached for the four remaining bottles of the six-pack he'd brought. His father didn't allow beer in the house, so he usually brought his own stash with him, but always had to take the remaining bottles home. Grabbing them up, he started to head for the patio door.

"Drin," Rafe called out, stopping him in his tracks. Taking a deep breath, he spoke to his son softly, "Why don't you stay here for the night, rather than going back to the cabin? It's a long trek and it's late...."

"Can't. Must away." Shaking his head he walked out the door, not bothering to say good night.

"And good night to you too," Breydon mumbled under his breath.

"You know why he doesn't say that," Lylia said quietly.

"I have no clue, enlighten me."

"Because for him ... it never is." Lylia peered out the patio door. She could barely see him now as he cut a swift path across the lawn towards the trail. "Forty years of seeing demons. It's got to be driving him mad. No wonder he drinks." Lylia shook her head worriedly as Dartanian hugged her close.

- - -

Drinian walked towards the path, jostling his beer bottles in his arm. His mind raced wildly. The moment his feet touched the path where he knew he could no longer be seen from the house, he started a dead run for the cabin. His feet crunched softly in the grass as he picked up speed. He could sense the shadows soaring along beside him. By the time he'd reached the cabin, he was breathing heavily from his run. A run that had taken him only fifteen minutes, what would have normally taken at least twenty.

Skidding to a halt at the door, leaving a muddy stretch of grass in his wake, he yanked it open. Flinging the bottles on the couch, not caring that one had missed, smashing against the wall, he threw himself at his bookcase. Pulling the old box from the top shelf, he dug through the handful of journals within it, finding the one he was looking for with a shaking hand.

Drinian stumbled then, falling to the floor in a heap, barely missing the footstool. Shaking as he reached for the lamp on the nearby stand, he turned it on and sat there, just staring at the book in his hand. He glanced up then, seeing that the shadows were cowering in the corners of the room a little more so than what they usually do. Drinian stood then, his towering frame even larger than his twin brothers, seemingly filling the cabin. Holding the book out in front of him, he turned in a circle where he stood.

"Is it possible?" He spoke aloud, knowing they could hear him as they began spilling from the walls and out of the corners of the cabin from all directions. They danced eerily around Drinian as he held the book, becoming more and more frantic in their movements. The black shadowy forms rolled and writhed, as they each made attempts at sliding through the worn pages. One finally slid through it slowly, making a popping noise upon coming out of the other side

"Could it be, Lord?" Drinian searched the ceiling anxiously, his excitement mounting. "Is it happening now?

Is she the one?" He asked the room at large. Hope began to build within him for the first time since the night his mother had died. The night she'd told him of the prophecy she had made that might one day end his torment and of the two-hundred-year-old tale.

The shadow that had slid through the book began bobbing up and down in place. As Drinian watched, it began growing in size, forming into the shape of a faceless man. Rarely having ever seen them in their truest form, he was grateful only to ever see them as oily faceless black substances. Their real form was terrifying to witness.

"Yeeesssssss," it hissed as it floated before him. The cold emanating from the figure chilled him to the bone.

Drinian stood there, his eyes wide with excitement. Then suddenly they narrowed as he looked back at the demon before him. He knew full well from experience that the shadows often lied. Yet, they often spoke truth. It had been a constant struggle for him over the years, determining the truth from the lies. Drinian often wondered why his brother Breydon had been given that gift when it would have much better served him. The question now was whether it was speaking the truth.

"Tell me truthfully," he roared, knowing full well there was still no guarantee he'd get an honest answer. He didn't have any real power over them after all. Therefore, could not force them to do as he told. But he did know, that for some reason, the sound of his voice when he became loud or belligerent tended to make them shrink away as though in agony. For this reason, they would often respond simply to avoid his rage.

The shadowy form floated silently for a moment, and then finally answered.

"She is the one," the voice whispered eerily. The demon's head appeared to bob up and down. "She will bring you peace. You must take her as your own."

He looked at the dark figure in anger. His ghostly pale blue eyes flashed violently. "Are you telling me I have to make love to my brother's fiancée?" His voice shook with outrage and dismay and he clung to the book in disgust.

"Noooooo!" The demon hissed back at him angrily. "You must take her as your *wife*." It jeered, placing significant emphasis on the fact that she had to be his wife first.

Stunned, Drinian fell to his knees in horror. The shadow dissipated into its original form and joined the rest of the heckling demons. They converged on him.

He cried out in anguish, falling forward over the book, heaving sobs of despair at the injustice of it all. Tears spilled from his eyes and he wept bitterly.

"It'll never happen," he said through sobs. "I could never do that and he'll never let that happen." Even as Drinian wept, he knew there was still a possibility that what it had said wasn't true. Bowing low, he deferred his head to the floor as he began to pray.

"God, have mercy on me! What did I do to deserve this? Have I not lived by your word, your law? Please tell me this isn't true. Tell me there is another way, that you have another plan. How much longer must I bear this burden? Shall I die with it, Lord? Is that my destiny? If that's the case then please let me die quickly. I can no longer bear to see them, to hear them. I am not strong like your son Jesus, who died on the cross."

Aware that he should have started with a prayer in the first place, Drinian banged on the floor in frustration. With the demons ever present, it often stripped him of his common sense. He knew he wasn't to speak to the shadows directly by asking or even answering a question.

His father had ingrained it in him early on when they first discovered what was happening. But at times, their presence was felt stronger than God's and that alienating feeling was confusing for him.

Closing his eyes wearily, he crawled across the floor to the couch. Grabbing up one of the unbroken bottles, he cradled it against his chest as a shadow slithered across his blurred vision.

Drink.

He wanted to drink it all away.

Drinian knew it was wrong, but it was the only thing, it seemed at times, that helped dull his tortured senses. Shaking his head, he allowed the bottle to slide from his hand to the floor. Cracking as it hit the ground, the liquid within seeped out into a puddle around him, as the smell of alcohol invaded his senses.

Wiping at the tears on his face, he decided in the end that he didn't want to drink tonight. Instead, he allowed himself to wallow in misery, as he sought out the solace of the woods surrounding his home. Maybe he could find some peace there.

- - -

Back at the Blackthorne ranch house, the woman now called Alaina turned in her sleep. The ethereal form of an angel, with blue eyes and dark hair, slid through the wall and floated towards the bed. He stood watch as Dante entered the room quietly, grabbed pajama bottoms from his dresser drawer, and then left again. Following closely behind him down the stairs, Maleeka was pleased to see Dante taking propriety very serious in his father's house.

Changing in the downstairs bathroom, he then crawled onto the couch, dragging a plaid flannel blanket with him. He lay there a moment, staring up at the ceiling, and then sighed heavily. The man was clearly distressed over what he had learned and was struggling with it a great deal.

The angel hovered nearby, gazing at the man before him, then floated to his side and knelt down next to him. Leaning into him, he whispered in his ear.

"Keep to your plan, Dante and marry her on Saturday." Maleeka urged him. "She needs you."

The man moved, turning towards the back of the couch so the light from the windows wouldn't disturb him. Closing his eyes, he waited for sleep to take him.

Maleeka looked at him, hoping that he had heard him. It was moments like these that he wished the Lord allowed them to have more influence over their charge's decisions. Seeing him lying alone on the couch, his expression softened. Maleeka floated there, watching as Dante's breathing changed. He sensed he'd fallen asleep.

Worry lines creased Maleeka's face when he heard Drinian's cries in the distance.

"What have we done to them?" Maleeka asked God quietly.

Another angel materialized through the wall then and Maleeka could see it was Woreash. He floated towards him, taking up a position next to him.

"Evening, Maleeka," the elderly messenger said in greeting. His wise gray eyes peered over at him searchingly.

Turning towards the elderly angel, Maleeka gestured towards the man on the couch.

"What have we done? Are we sure mankind is ready for what is to come, Woreash? Are we sure they are prepared for the responsibility of these gifts?"

"Our Father is sure, and that's all that matters."

Woreash looked at his friend, then down at the sleeping form on the couch. Sighing heavily, he took Maleeka's arm in his hand and guided him away from the couch towards the hallway.

"Come, you know full well we should not be here." They both disappeared, and then re-appeared suddenly in the bedroom Alaina slept in.

"But Woreash, how…?"

"Shush, Maleeka," he said, pointing towards the woman as she slept soundly. "It is time for her to know. But He says we must wait until the moon is high in the sky."

Maleeka's eyes sparkled brightly and his face lit with laughter.

"I love our Lord's sense of humor," he chuckled. The notion that the placement of the moon made any difference whatsoever was almost ludicrous.

"We shall meet here again and we will tell her what she needs to know." Woreash looked suddenly at Alaina. In an instant, he disappeared and then reappeared next to her near the bed. Resting his age-worn hand near her forehead, he closed his eyes and waited patiently.

Floating over next to Woreash, Maleeka looked back and forth between the two of them. "What is it?"

Turning and looking at Maleeka, he opened his gray eyes, and they shone brightly with delight. "I see she may already know. Come away now," he smiled, guiding his counterpart from the bedroom. "We shall commune with her when it is time."

They disappeared through the bedroom wall and flew quickly up through the ceiling. Four gray and white feathered wings erupted suddenly from each of their backs as they soared up and outward into the night sky. A bright golden light exploded around them, encasing them in pure white light, as though encircling them in a giant golden orb. Sighing as though in relief, they both spread their massive wings while hovering above the house, suspended in mid-air. Without warning, the angels shot across the dark sky in search of the cabin in the woods. It was time to help keep the demons at bay, so Drinian could play his part.

Chapter 23

Alaina awoke suddenly and sat up in bed. Her eyes were wide as she glanced around the bedroom. Heart pumping in a steady rhythmic fashion in her chest, she took an easy breath, allowing her body to relax further. Perspiration dripped from her forehead, clinging to strands of her hair as they stuck to her face and neck. Turning, she saw the empty space next to her in bed, and she trembled anxiously.

Pulling her legs up towards her chest, she sat holding herself tight. First, she stared down at the bed, then, off into space. Tears threatened at the corners of her eyes as she rested her head on her knees momentarily. Overwhelmed by what she'd just experienced, seen, and heard, Alaina cried softly. Not in fear or trepidation but with joy. Truly hoping that it had been real and not just a dream, she smiled softly at the notion as she wiped away a tear.

She didn't know what time it was, or for how long she'd been crying, but what she did know was she couldn't seem to stop, and that she felt a strong urge that she was meant to be somewhere else. Crawling out of the bed, she moved quietly towards the bedroom door, opened it, and left the room. Still unfamiliar with her surroundings, she became disoriented and didn't know exactly which way to go. Sensing her anxiety level was increasing because of getting lost in such a vast house, she turned to her right and crept along the long hallway. She stumbled a little, picking up the pace as she walked faster and faster down the hall.

Finding a set of stairs, she gingerly took the first step down, testing her wobbling legs as she went. At first, Alaina started slowly, but then she ran down the steps, stumbling on the bottom two before her bare feet hit the cold tiled floor of the kitchen. Running the length of the kitchen, her feet slapping noisily against the tiles, she grabbed hold of the French style patio doors and tried to open them unsuccessfully. Disengaging the manual lock, she pushed both of the glass doors open, and pelted out of the kitchen, onto the patio, then out on the lawn.

The cool night air whipped around her face and down her back, spreading goose bumps all over her body, but she didn't care. Her breathing had become extremely erratic as she'd found her way out of the house, and the chance to breathe in the fresh, crisp, clean mountain air was heavenly. Taking a deep breath, she inhaled, as though she were desperate for oxygen. Her reaction was instantaneous for her whole being seemed to come alive.

Spreading her arms out wide, Alaina felt the oversized t-shirt she wore flapping in the wind. It was only then that she realized she was still running. She stopped suddenly, turning in a wide circle, taking in the view as the cool night air lapped up under her arms, swirling and whirling up through to the night sky.

The lawn was vast and had swing sets and a playground of sorts tastefully set up at one end. As Alaina took it all in, she realized she'd seen it all before but from a different vantage point; the sky, and it was gorgeous out tonight.

Realizing the magnitude of what her dream meant, Alaina looked up and saw the full moon shining high above her. She stared at it, in awe at the knowledge, that what she'd seen and experienced had not been just a dream as she'd feared, but real. Taking comfort in the fact that she truly was not going crazy as she originally thought she was, Alaina's anxiety began to abate a little.

The initial confusion and unease she had experienced in her dreams could not be completely dissuaded, however. So she cried on, unaware of the tears streaming down her face in waves, as both joy and sorrow wrenched at her heart. The blessing which had been bestowed upon her and the task she had been given was more than she thought she could handle. For some reason, God believed otherwise, and she could not fathom why.

How was it that she, Alaina, could possibly be so important to these people of whom she had just met and knew so little? Yet, it was clear now to her that she was. Laying her hand on her belly, she allowed it to rest there while she contemplated the gravity of her situation. Thirty days before her only concern was of her own children. Now, having made the choice to accept the gifts God had placed within her for the duration, she had the chance to affect many lives in a positive way, including two men desperate to be free of the torture which plagued them.

"*Lord,*" she whispered reverently, falling to her knees. Placing her hands on her heart, she spoke a prayer of gratitude.

"I am no one, Lord, but one of millions. Of all the good, virtuous women on this earth you could have chosen, you chose me. In the book of Luke in the Bible, the angel told Mary not to be afraid for God had been gracious to her. Your messenger, Woreash, told me the same, not to be afraid. Somehow you found favor in me, as you did with Mary, the mother of Jesus.

I shall not question why, or even how; we both know this shouldn't be able to happen. And yet, here you have healed my body, so this may be. Though I may not carry your son as the virgin Mary did, I shall cherish the child you have given me: this miracle within me. I know not your grand plan Lord, only what Woreash and Maleeka shared with me. But I say to you Lord, as Mary did to the angel in Luke 1:38, that I am your servant Lord, may it happen to me as you have said. Amen."

Feeling humbled and wholly unworthy of the charge she'd been given, a sense of peace filled her. She stared out at the beauty before her in the sky. It was as though it had been placed there, in order to signify the beginning of something new and wonderful.

Lord, it's so beautiful. Thank you for this rainbow in the sky. It's just what I needed. You alone know what I need when I need it, she thought as curtains of pale green and white wisps of lights danced in the air above her and over the mountain peaks. It created an extremely beautiful effect.

Having never witnessed the Northern Lights before, Alaina was in awe of the sight and found peace in the wonder God had created in the sky, as well as the miracle that he had placed within her.

- - -

Dante awoke slowly, rolling from his side onto his back. He could tell the sun was just starting to rise, as there was a faint light peeking in through the curtains of the living room window. Stretching his arms out wide, he reveled in the soft cushions of the couch. Feeling a slight chill, he pulled the soft flannel blanket up over his shoulders as he rolled onto his other side. Resting there languorously for a time, he opted to enjoy the moment. It had been a long time since he'd been home. An instant later, his eyes shot open, as he sensed something wasn't right in the house.

Throwing off his blanket, his first thought was for the children and Alaina. Running up the front steps, Dante could feel the unease build within him as he popped his head into Sayleena's room first. Seeing her sleeping peacefully, he moved on down the short hall to Saruman and Storman's room. He was about to peer into their room when he noticed the door to his bedroom was wide open. In a few quick strides, he'd entered his room only to find that his bed was empty.

Where was Alaina?

Dante gazed around the room, and then checked the bathroom next, thinking she might be in there if she'd gotten sick. Not finding her, he ran to the balcony and flung open the doors, frantically looking across the front of the house and down towards the garages.

Seeing no movement, he ran back into his bedroom, grabbing one of his shirts from the closet as he went. Not bothering to put it on, he carried it with him as he turned left and walked down the hall toward the front of the house. Leaning over the banister, he glanced into the front room but didn't see her there either. Starting to get concerned, he called out down the stairs, thinking she might be in the restroom under the stairs for some reason.

"Alaina?" When no response came, Dante turned around and headed towards the boy's bedroom, thinking she might be in with Saruman if he'd had a night fright.

Cautiously opening the bedroom door, he glanced in to see if she was with Saruman and Storman. Not seeing her there, he closed their door and went down to the next room, checking in on Sayleena again, hoping he'd simply missed seeing her. But still, she wasn't there either. Confused and starting to get a little alarmed, Dante ran down the length of the hallway. As he took the steps there three at a time, he called out her name again.

"Alaina?"

Still no response.

Jumping down the last four steps, he hit the tiled floor and glanced into the kitchen. Where was she, he thought? It was barely even sunrise. She couldn't have gone too far.

Dante searched the main floor of the house, checking both of the living rooms, the study, the library, the movie room and the children's school room, as well as the playroom and the laundry room.

Alaina was nowhere to be seen.

Now in full panic mode, he ran back through the house shouting her name.

"Alaina! Where are you?"

He was about to step into the kitchen, when Dartanian came out from the stairwell, nearly knocking him over.

"Dante, what is it? What's happening?" he asked as Breydon and Chase followed close behind, buttoning their shirts in their haste as they went.

"We could hear you shouting from our room," Chase said as Megorah rushed down the stairwell. She had just finished tying her house robe and was attempting to braid her long hair as she went.

"I can't find her. I can't find her anywhere." Dante said, clearly panicking, which was highly unusual for him.

Dartanian looked surprised but began to ask if he'd checked the rest of the house.

"You don't understand, Dart." Dante interrupted. "I have checked everywhere in this house aside from your rooms. Astraia..." Shaking his head he corrected himself. "Alaina that is..."

"Oh, give it up Dante," Megorah said sharply.

"Alaina is not in the house. I've checked everywhere."

"Then we start checking outside the house." Dartanian headed towards the doors that led into the front living room as his cell phone rang at his belt. Rolling his eyes upon seeing who it was he went to answer it. "What now?" He growled in frustration.

By then, the noise had attracted the rest of the members of the house. Royce and Crisalya, as well as Hialey and Lylia, had found their way into the kitchen in varying sorts of disarray. Though Royce and Crisalya had taken the time to throw clothes on, Hialey was still in her night shirt, and Lylia was wearing a thin slinky nightgown and robe.

"Wait a minute. What?" They could hear Dartanian saying into his cell phone. "Dad, are you serious?" He glanced over at Dante in alarm. "I'll tell him." Turning off his phone, he raked his hands across his face.

"What is it?" Dante came around the counter towards him.

"You're not going to believe this, but Dad said, if you're looking for your fiancée, you should look outside the kitchen patio."

"Wait, what? How did he...?" Confused, Dante rushed towards the patio and opened the doors easily, without having to unlock them. Several of the women gasped in surprise as the house was always locked down once the last person went to bed at night.

"How did she get out without setting off the alarm?" Royce questioned, peering over at Breydon and Dartanian.

Shaking their heads, everyone watched as Dante stood completely still in the patio doorway, looking out over the lawn.

"What is it? Is she okay?" Hialey walked towards him while placing fluffy blue and green house slippers on her feet as she went.

"I don't know," he said, sounding worried. "She's just sitting there." Taking a deep breath, he stepped out onto the porch and started walking the length of the lawn to where she sat in the grass.

She didn't appear to be hurt or to have been harmed in any way. She was still wearing the white T-shirt she'd borrowed from him the night before but nothing else. Her feet were shoeless and her legs were bare. She looked like she'd just crawled straight out of bed and come outside.

Alaina's long wavy blonde hair blew gently out behind her and around her face, which was tilted up towards the sky. She sat there still and quiet gazing out on the horizon. At one point, as he walked towards her, he noticed her eyes closed for a moment and then opened again. The closer he got, he could see that she'd been crying at one point but didn't appear to be any longer.

"Alaina? Honey, what are you doing out here?" Dante inquired when he finally was close enough for her to hear. She didn't answer him at first but then she called out to him.

"It's beautiful isn't it?" she asked, nodding towards the sunrise.

He hadn't noticed it before as he'd been intent on finding her. Peering in the direction of the sunrise, he observed the golden light that was peaking up over the looming mountains in the distance.

"Yes, I suppose it is." He took a moment to appreciate the view he so often took for granted. It never occurred to him that seeing this could be significant to her.

Standing over her quietly for a moment, he gave it the respect it deserved. Then, glancing down at her, he started to speak. "Astraia…"

"Don't you mean Alaina?" she asked softly.

Dante sighed, "Yes, although I don't know that there's much point to it. I keep calling you the wrong name." There was a slow, sad smile that spread across her lips. He wondered at it but couldn't tell what she was thinking at all.

"You'll have to work on that." She sounded tired.

"Astraia."

"Alaina you mean."

Annoyed now he continued, "Alaina, how long have you been out here?" he asked, noting a blue tinge to her skin.

"I don't know for sure." She spoke in an airy manner as though time was insignificant. "But I suppose, if I had to guess, I'd say since somewhere around midnight," she said, startling him.

"You've been out here since midnight?" he asked in surprise. "You must be freezing! You shouldn't have been out here all night alone, it's not safe," he insisted as he glanced at his hands, looking for the shirt he'd had.

Finding the shirt missing, he realized he must have left it somewhere in the house during his search. Looking back towards the house, he saw his family, walking out onto the kitchen patio.

"Why?" She turned to look at him for the first time. "I thought you said I was safe here?"

"The ranch is a fortress from *human* predators. But there are still dangerous animals that roam these mountains. They don't often come down this way but they have been known to on occasion." Dante noticed her eyes were wide open, and they seemed to shine with a bright light as she looked up at him.

"You never said anything about that." She said softly.

He reached out and touched her cool skin. "You're chilled. We need to get you in the house." There was urgency in his voice now, and she sensed he was distressed. She conceded to walking, by allowing him to help her up and beginning a slow stride back to the patio with him.

"You needn't worry so much. God was with me. Besides, if it helps I don't think I was alone the whole time."

Dante turned towards her with a questioning look as they walked.

"What do you mean?" he asked.

"Your brother was watching from the trees at one point." She nodded towards a path on the other side of the yard.

"My brother?"

"Yes, the big one. I believe he's the youngest, right? Drinian?"

"Uh, yes. How did you know?"

"They torture him you know, the demons? If something isn't done soon, they will kill him."

Her statement came so suddenly, so abruptly, that he wasn't sure at first he'd heard her right. Dante stopped in his tracks, turning her towards him.

"Wait just a minute. How do you know that?" He asked, looking cross, noting they were halfway back to the patio. His father, who had joined them, was watching Alaina intently. She continued walking slightly ahead of him.

"You should have told me, Dante," Alaina said quietly. She turned her head to look back at him. "This, all of it... It would have been so much less alarming for me. But I do understand why you didn't."

He looked at her face then, really looked at it hard, and realized something there had changed. He couldn't put his finger on what though. It was almost as though she had come to some sort of understanding and had made peace with it. Catching up with her, he took a hold of her arm and coaxed her to turn and look at him. They were at the edge of the patio now, within earshot of his family.

"What exactly is it you think you know?" Dante asked, his gut clenching with unease. If she had figured it out somehow, it would not go over well with his family. He didn't have their permission for her to know yet.

"It's okay, Dante. I don't think they will really be angry with us. I couldn't help but know about them."

Startled at her uncanny ability to sense what he was thinking, Dante fidgeted uncomfortably. He now understood how unnerving it must be to the others when he could discern what they were thinking so easily.

"Yes, you're right. They don't like it when you do that. Especially Chase, he considers it a violation of his privacy," Alaina said, in a matter of fact way. She glanced over at the doctor, causing Chase to look at her in surprise.

Dante was incredulous. "What?"

"Don't you think you should introduce me to them all properly? I know I saw them last night but we didn't really get a chance to formally meet." Confused by the sudden change of subject and her statement, Dante just stood there for a moment.

"Of course, I just thought you'd be wearing pants when you met them."

"I wasn't wearing any when I met you. I suppose, this time, at least I can say I had a shirt on."

Chapter 24

Dante was stunned. He couldn't believe Alaina had just said that aloud. Glancing over at his father, he could see his angry stare, as Rafe looked with reproach at his son. Hanging his head in embarrassment, he almost missed his brothers' expressions as they looked at him, flabbergasted. He couldn't even bring himself to peer over at his sisters.

"Dante Bilius Blackthorne," he could hear Rafe bark as he stood facing his son.

"In my defense, she *was* wearing clothes the first time I saw her at the grocery store," Dante defended himself while straightening to his full height and meeting his father's steely gaze head on. Forty years old and the man still had the ability to intimidate him on occasion.

"The first time we met, I suppose, yes, but…" Alaina stopped suddenly, realizing that she'd done something wrong. "Oh, dear. Dante, I'm so sorry," she apologized, noting the horrified expressions of some of his family, although Breydon's eyes were bulging with mirth. "I didn't realize until now how important it is to your family.

Of course, I should have known." She turned towards Rafe, sounding chagrined. "Mr. Blackthorne, I'm terribly sorry. I did not realize the importance you had impressed upon your sons to have respect for women until now. I'm not allowed to speak of how we met, so I cannot explain the circumstances, but you should know that your son has always been a gentleman with me." Embarrassment suffused her cheeks with color. "I can tell you, that out of fear I acted in an inappropriate manner, which tested his willpower beyond measure." She peered around at the others plaintively, as though asking for forgiveness through her eyes.

"I already told them what I did. You don't have to do this." Dante spoke urgently.

"No. I need to explain or they won't really understand." She looked at her hands as though ashamed. "The thing is, I wouldn't be in the condition I am presently if it were not for my own actions." She looked back over at Dante as though trying to send him a message. "But you must to understand, when a mother fears for her children, she'll do literally anything to protect them." Alaina's voice shook, and she choked back a sob as her eyes began to tear up. Looking away from everyone, her shaking hands went to her mouth as she glanced up at the sky now painted with shades of pink, gold and blue. "Of that, at least, I think you might be able to appreciate the most, Drinian."

The group was startled by her statement for they had not seen him join them. Drinian was walking towards his family on the lawn and stood behind Alaina where she could not have seen him.

Megorah's eyes flew open wide at the realization that Alaina had known he was there before anyone else did. She walked towards her slowly. Alaina stared directly back at her, continuing to speak.

"The angels are the ones who make the shadows go away, though."

Drinian stepped around Rafe and Dante, then around Alaina's side, in order to stand in front of her.

"-So that you can sleep," she finished softly as he stared at her, not saying a word. "But you already know that, don't you?"

His expression never wavered as he stood watching her. Alaina could hear the stunned gasps and words of shock from others. She could also see a look of awe on both Megorah and Breydon's face as well.

Turning towards Breydon, she spoke with him directly, knowing full well she needed to help him understand what he was seeing first.

"I did not see them in the sense that you're thinking, Breydon. I know that's what you believe right now, but I didn't and can't. You're the only one who can actually see and speak with the angels, all except two of them that is."

Dante stared at her in confusion, unsure as to what exactly what was happening but Rafe looked upon her as though slowly starting to figure something out.

"Then how? Explain to me how you know of them." Breydon stepped forward, blinking at her in confusion. "And how did you know that I should be able to see them in the first place?" He glared at his brother then blinked again crossly as he shook his head and banged at his left ear with his left hand. It was as though he was seeing and hearing double for there were two identical angels standing near Alaina and Dante. Their voices echoed as they spoke their truths, causing a ringing in his ear.

Alaina shook her head then. "Dante didn't break the vow you all made," she said at first, trying to reassure everyone. "But I did communicate with two angels last night and they were able to pass the news on to me." She looked meaningfully at Megorah, knowing she would figure it out soon, if not already.

"That's how I know. I know Megorah can discern a person's emotional state, and that Crisalya can often discern what ails a person. She can help or even heal them sometimes with teas and herbs. I know Dartanian can discern the good and bad in people, and that Drinian can see demons or shadows, as he calls them." She peered at the enormous man before her and shivered slightly, though not for the reasons many of the others were likely now thinking. "I know you can see messengers of God and discern when someone speaks the truth, Breydon, and I know…" She paused then, looking around at Dante once more. "I know you can discern a person's thoughts, Dante, although you cannot sense mine right now, can you?"

He stared back at her in stunned silence. Moving towards her, Dante pushed his brother out of the way. Standing before her, he searched her face intently. He wasn't being given anything from her.

"You're right, I can't. I don't understand. How is it you know all this?" He searched her face once more. His voice was dangerously low and laced with barely repressed anger. "Because I never told you. Are you claiming that you know because a couple of angels told you?"

Alaina trembled; anxiety clear in her eyes.

"I was sleeping. The angels came to me while I was sleeping."

The instant the words were out of her mouth, he grabbed hold of her arms and lifted her up so they were face to face.

"In a dream, Alaina?" Dante asked, his voice full of cynicism. "You will tell me the truth," he growled, staring her down. His crystal-clear blue eyes flashed with anger.

"Dante, I think she's actually telling the truth," Breydon spoke in her defense.

"And I think *you* need to recheck that ability of yours," Dante scoffed.

"Why is that so hard for you to believe, when your own mother and sister have had prophetic dreams?" Shaking her head sadly, Alaina's face twisted in distress. "I knew you would never believe me. I told them you wouldn't." The tears that had been building welled in her eyes. She shook in his gentle but firm grasp, her arms starting to ache from the pressure. "But Breydon knows I'm telling the truth, don't you? And Megorah, you know too don't you?" She turned her head to look at her, while her feet dangled in the air.

Megorah stood completely still with her hands covering her face. She appeared shell-shocked, her translucent blue eyes, so like her brothers, lit up with light and laughter as she squealed and ran over to them.

"Put her down," she urged. "Put her down, you're hurting her, and I daresay, scaring her as well." She grabbed hold of her brother's arm and pulled on it to get him to let Alaina go.

Dante looked back and forth between the two women while setting Alaina down. His voice softened a little as he spoke gruffly. "I want answers. I want to know what's going on."

Megorah took hold of Alaina and wrapped her in her arms. Laughing and crying out joyously as though she were greeting a long-lost friend.

"You are right, Little Star! Dante will not believe until he sees. Many of them won't." Megorah continued to hug Alaina.

Alaina just stood there, unsure of how to respond to Megorah's reaction. She peered out at the rest of Dante's family, seeing the many faces in various states of confusion and understanding. She was having difficulty focusing on any one individual until she sensed Drinian nearby. Pulling away from Megorah, she turned to him.

"You knew, didn't you? How?" The instant she asked, she received a sudden picture of an old, worn and faded book in her head. "A journal of sorts? And then you pieced it together?"

Drinian nodded his head in answer and smiled brightly. He turned towards Dante. "Now I care," he said firmly, passing by Alaina as he spoke. Eyes twinkling uncharacteristically, he walked into the house with a bounce in his step. He appeared much less irritable than what was his norm, which was picked up by his brother-in-law, Royce who was giving him a curious look.

Megorah watched him go. "So that's where it went? He had the journal all this time and never said anything. I wonder why?"

"Megorah, I think you know the answer to that." Rafe had stayed quiet throughout the exchange, watching everyone closely, wanting to make sure he didn't miss anything. Something was definitely up, and he looked at Alaina with renewed hope. Rafe had a suspicion what it might be, especially by Meg's response to her.

"Mr. Blackthorne, by all means, get your hopes up. For, as I understand it, the next year will provide many a shock for you." Alaina took hold of Dante's hand tentatively. "I want to tell you. You deserve to know but I need to go to the hospital, or at the very least, Dr. Ryans's clinic to be sure first. That is, if he has there what I need in order to prove it to you because you will not believe until you see. Even I am struggling with believing, and I'm the one experiencing it." She smiled half-heartedly as she spoke. "And you'll be able to discern my thoughts again … after we're married."

"Chase's clinic. He'll be able to do it there," Megorah said emphatically.

"What exactly am I supposed to do there?" Chase had a strong suspicion he already knew what Alaina needed. "Meg, you're thinking along the same lines as you were last night, aren't you?"

Beaming, without saying a word, Megorah patted his hand as she led Alaina towards the house. "Now, let's get this girl inside. She has been out in this cold for too long. Run upstairs, Little Star, and put some pants on," she urged Alaina. "Bring your kids down and we'll get everyone fed. Royce, do you think you can wrangle up some breakfast for everyone?"

"Yeah, I can do that. You're thinking to keep it simple this morning, right Meg? Cause you're in a hurry?" Royce followed her through the patio doors, Crisalya trailing behind them. "But you want Alaina to have eggs, fruit and milk with maybe some wheat toast also?" He'd figured it out as he watched Alaina walk back to the house with Dante. Grinning from ear-to-ear, he smiled knowingly over at Crisalya as Meg responded in the affirmative.

Crisalya stopped dead in her tracks.

"No way! Really?" She cried out, having figured out what Megorah and Royce were on about. Meg grinned and shook her head, making a zipping motion across her lips. She then proceeded to dole out directions for the morning's breakfast as she gathered items from the pantry.

- - -

Once breakfast was over, the children went with Lylia and Crisalya to the playroom, where they were delighted to discover all the wonders of living at the Blackthorne estate. Most of the family did not live on the premises at all times, but when family events occurred, they all came and stayed at the house together. Since most of the kids took their schooling from Lylia unless they were in Junior High, like Megorah's eldest, it made daytime childcare extremely convenient. This suited Dante just fine since it meant Alaina's children wouldn't have to be placed in public school just yet.

Dante and Alaina hadn't spoken since their exchange on the patio. Having picked up on all the signs, like everyone else, Dante suspected he already knew what was going on. Struggling with the possibility that he might actually be a father soon, and overwhelmed at the notion, he missed seeing Alaina's attempt to come sit near him as he stood to leave. Oblivious to her hurt expression, he left to eat on the patio with his brothers. There he sat, deep in thought, while his brothers exchanged curious stares.

Lord, is it truly possible? Could she really be pregnant with my child, he prayed anxiously. *Please don't give me false hope. You know how much I've wanted children. If it is your will then let it be, God. Let it be.*

Inside the kitchen, Alaina anxiously watched him while attempting to eat her breakfast. She knew he hadn't intentionally meant to snub her but had felt hurt by it, nonetheless. Staring down at her half-eaten plate in distress, she fidgeted in her seat.

"Don't mind him," Hialey said while trying to put her at ease by telling bad jokes. But Alaina's sense of humor was not working today. She was getting a headache from all of the unexpected information that kept appearing in her head.

"It's overwhelming, isn't it?" Drinian asked at one point, looking at her with sympathy as she nodded her head. "It's one of the reasons mom and dad sent him away. It can be dangerous, you know?"

"How so?" she asked, trying to concentrate on what he was saying.

"When you can discern a person's thoughts you could easily manipulate them if you were so inclined," Drinian said.

"I would never!" Alaina exclaimed as he got up and walked away, putting his dishes in the sink. Alone at the table, she peered down at her hands in her lap.

"Ready to go?" Megorah asked, coming into the kitchen from the front room. "Chase has the vehicle pulled around the front."

Alaina bobbed her head up and down slowly and stood, wobbling on her legs. Her nerves were getting the better of her. Having already given all her kids hugs and kisses when they went to the playroom, she walked out of the kitchen into the front room and headed for the front door as Dante followed at her heel.

It didn't take long for them to arrive at the clinic since it was only fifteen minutes away. By the time they had Alaina set up in a room and on the exam table, she felt like she was going to be sick, and then did. Megorah had been kind enough to foresee this and made sure a trash can was nearby.

"Okay then," Chase said without preamble while walking in the room with his stethoscope in hand. "Anticipating the need, I called ahead to make sure the ultrasound room was open, and that Ms. Maylore would be available first thing."

"Thank you," Alaina said gratefully.

"We really are thinking she's pregnant then?" Dante sounded hopeful.

"Yes. I'm pregnant, I'm sure of it."

"You said you couldn't have kids."

"I'm not supposed to be able to anymore," Alaina said urgently. "I did have a tubal ligation. Which is why I didn't think I was pregnant until now."

"Just to clarify, what makes you think you are now?" Chase asked while checking her blood pressure. "If what you say is true, then it's much more likely a tubal pregnancy, which could be very dangerous for you. It may be why you are experiencing some of these symptoms you're having."

Alaina didn't say anything at first, and then finally she spoke. "Because he told me."

"Who told you?" Both men asked in unison, suspecting they already knew the answer.

Covering her eyes as Chase placed his hands on her belly, she took a deep breath and replied. "The messengers." She peered out under her arm, looking at both men in turn. "One called himself Maleeka, and the other angel was called Woreash. They told me of your abilities and said to not be afraid of what I was experiencing because I am with child."

Both men looked at her with stunned expressions.

"I know how this sounds. I do. It sounds crazy, but…"

"Alaina," Dante began. "I can't have children."

"I know, neither can I, yet here I am," Alaina spoke in a small voice. She was angry and hurt that he seemed so unwilling to believe her, but she knew why and understood why. It just didn't make it any easier. "I need that ultrasound, Chase. He needs to see. I think we both do."

"That's in another room so we'll need to move you," Dr. Chase Ryans said while helping her to sit up.

She stood, her knees trembling for the faint feeling she was experiencing. The room around her seemed to spin as she struggled to maintain consciousness.

"Whoa there, I got you." Dante caught her as she fell, picking her up in his arms. He could see she appeared a bit disoriented and grew concerned. "Which way, Chase? Tell me where to go."

"Down the hall. At the end to the left." Chase led him toward the ultrasound room.

Placing Alaina on the examining bed when they arrived, Dante tried to make her comfortable while they waited for the technician to show.

"Good morning, Dr. Ryans." Rachel greeted them when she came out of her office mere moments later. "I understand we have a special case this morning. Family is it?"

"Yes, my brother-in-law, Dante and his..."

"Wife, of course. I'm Rachel Maylore," she said by way of introduction, extending her hand towards Dante, then Alaina.

Leaving her assumption as just that, an assumption, Chase felt somewhat guilty for not correcting the technician's error. "Her symptoms would imply a pregnancy but she had a tubal ligation several years back."

"Hence the hasty appointment," Rachel responded in understanding, knowing what that might mean. "Let's see what's going on."

Placing gel on a pad, Rachel lifted Alaina's gown. She instructed Dante to lay a warm blanket down over her, to cover what he could. Rubbing the pad low across her belly, she began searching to see what she could find. Appearing thoughtful, Rachel glided it slowly across her again. "If it is a tubal pregnancy, Mr. Blackthorne, then she'll need surgery." Stopping suddenly, she stared in surprise at the screen.

"What is it?" Dr. Ryans watched with concern as the technician gaped at the screen.

"You say she had a tubal ligation how many years ago?"

"After my twin boys were born," Alaina responded. "They are four now, will be five in October."

The technician was quiet for quite some time. She moved the pad across Alaina's belly, pausing multiple times, and then moving it back over certain areas again.

After a while, Dante could no longer take the silence and gestured towards Chase, hoping for some glimmer of news.

"What's the prognosis there, Rachel? What are you thinking?" Chase asked, realizing as he spoke that she appeared to be adding numbers and measurements into the keyboard as she worked.

"I've heard of a few cases before, but I've never actually seen..." Rachel said looking over at Dr. Ryans, then Dante, before peering down at Alaina. "It would seem you are definitely pregnant, with a viable pregnancy at that. Would you like me to show them to you?"

"What?" All three of them exclaimed in unison.

"Did you say them?" Dante inquired, staring in shock down at Alaina.

"Oh, yes. See here." She turned the monitor so they all could see. "This one here is baby A." Adjusting the pad on Alaina's belly, she applied a few keystrokes. "And over here is baby B. They appear to be sharing the same sac," Rachel continued.

"Twins!" Chase exclaimed, gaping openly at Dante, who in turn was running his hands through his hair in astonishment.

Alaina stared up at the monitor, in shock at seeing the two specks on the screen, which couldn't be more than a quarter of an inch in length. Hearing the technician tapping away at the keyboard, she could feel her adjust the pad on her abdomen to a lower position.

"Now here," Rachel continued to explain. "This one here is in its own sac alone. That one is baby C," she finished. "You are having triplets."

Chapter 25

Alaina shot up from the exam bed in a panic, displacing the towel that had been laid over her. The angels, Maleeka and Woreash, had said nothing about three babies.

"Triplets," she squeaked out.

The unexpected motion dazed her, causing her to black out. Sinking back to the exam bed, she would have fallen off had the technician not caught her before she fell.

Too startled by the news to react, Dante's chest heaved as he stared first at the monitor screen, then back down at Alaina who was being laid back down on the bed by the technician. Breathing heavily, his eyes bulged as he staggered and nearly fell himself.

Recovering from the shock quickly, Chase managed to catch Dante by the elbow and assisted him to a nearby chair.

"Chase, how accurate...?" Dante croaked. "How accurate are these ultrasounds?"

"They can be fairly accurate, especially when done within a month of conception," Rachel responded instead.

She adjusted the blanket and continued to work at gaining the remaining information she needed. "Which is right about where she is at right now. According to this, she appears to be about four weeks, two days. But it is possible to be as many as four days and anywhere up to two weeks off. When she has her next ultrasound done, it might give you a better picture of…"

The technician's voice became an echo in Dante's ears as blood rushed to his head. If Alaina wasn't already presenting with abilities indicative of a Blackthorne pregnancy, the fact that she was thirty days pregnant was proof that the babies were his. A mixture of joy and panic seized him at the knowledge he was definitely going to be a father, of triplets.

Meeting his brother-in-law's gaze, which seemed to mirror his own stunned expression, Dante's face slowly spread into a wide grin. Laughing out loud, he sprang up from his chair.

"Where's Meg? I have to tell her!"

"What about, Alaina?" Chase smiled, seeing Rachel shake her head good-naturedly as she beamed. Clearly, she was just as excited about the discovery as the rest of them were.

"Right! I can't leave Alaina," Dante declared, clapping his hands together eagerly.

"Sure you can. She'll be fine for a moment. I'll get you guys if she wakes," Rachel said with a smile.

"Right then!" Dante gestured toward the woman in appreciation. Dashing from the room, he could hear Chase call after him, saying that his sister was in the waiting room. Sprinting down the hallway, he almost knocked over a nurse as he neared the door to the waiting room. Flinging it open exuberantly, he charged through it, startling several people on the other side. Seeing his sister stand abruptly at the sight of him, he stared back at her, the shock still not having worn off yet.

"She's not pregnant with a baby," he said louder than he intended, watching her face fall instantly at the news. "But she is pregnant with three babies!"

It took a moment for the news to register before she finally understood what he was saying. Squealing in delight, her eyes lit up and she danced where she stood.

Within a few strides, Dante reached his sister and grabbed her up by the waist, swinging her tiny figure about as they laughed together.

A pregnant woman sitting nearby gazed at the two before her, then over at Dr. Ryans, who was standing in the doorway of the waiting room.

"That ain't catchy is it?" The woman patted her swollen belly protectively looking a bit distressed.

Shaking his head as he chuckled, Chase replied with a sigh, "No Josie Mae. Not usually unless there's history in the family."

"Thank the Lord Almighty!" Josie Mae responded while heaving a relieved sigh. "I'm too fat with one. Couldn't imagine havin' three in me."

- - -

Dante was holding Alaina in the examination room when she finally awoke. She seemed to struggle with the notion of waking as she burrowed into his chest for comfort. Snuggling into his shoulder, Alaina didn't look at him for the longest time. He ran his hands through her hair and down her back, trying to calm her while murmuring softly that things were going to be all right.

Still in her examination gown, Alaina struggled to calm down next to him. She had been prepared for a single pregnancy, but the shock of finding out she was having three was overwhelming her. Recalling what she'd gone through when she was pregnant with her twin boys, she shivered lightly. Mistaking the motion for being chilled, Dante pulled the blanket up around her shoulders, covering her completely.

She knew they were waiting for results from her blood test, and the official reading of the ultrasound, having been told as such by Dante when she awoke. Chase had explained to him while she was still out that normally it would take longer to get results back from the ultrasound, but he'd requested a rush under the circumstances. So now they were just waiting for confirmation.

They heard a knock on the door, and then a second later both Dr. Chase Ryans and the technician who handled the ultrasound entered. She introduced herself to Alaina again and placed copies of the ultrasound pictures in her hands.

"Nice to see you awake again," Rachel said, smiling brightly. "You're the first set of naturally conceived triplets we've had in this area in a long time." Rachel pulled out her copy of an ultrasound picture and showed it to Alaina. "You weren't alert when I completed it, so I thought you might like to see it again. The copies I gave you are yours to show family."

"So there is definitely a set of twins and then a third baby?" Dante inquired, glancing at the woman then Chase. Seeing them nod he took a deep breath then asked, "And you said she is around thirty days, right?"

"Yes. So you are only about a month along, Alaina." This time, it was Chase who responded, giving his brother-in-law a meaningful look as he did so. Dante stood suddenly, placing Alaina on the exam table.

"Can you guys give us a few minutes, please?" He waited to hear the door shut behind them before speaking. "Astraia…" Dante started.

"You have to start calling me Alaina. Why is that so difficult for you?" She asked him.

"I don't know. I guess you don't seem like an Alaina to me," he said in exasperation. "The angels you spoke with, Maleeka and Woreash, did they tell you that you were expecting triplets?"

"No. They just said I was with child. They never said it would be three babies."

Worried more than ever about Alaina's safety, Dante paced the room in agitation. Thinking quickly, he turned towards her and took her hands in his.

"I know you said you would marry me but…"

"Have you changed your mind?" Alaina gasped. "Do you not want to get married?"

"Yes! Yes of course I do, now more than ever. Not that I didn't want to so much before, it's just…"

"I know. They'll need both of us. I cannot do this alone, Dante. I just won't. Not with what I'm experiencing. How do you do it? How do you cope with these abilities?"

Appearing thoughtful, his face filled with humor. She watched him stare at the pictures of their babies as he trailed his fingers across each child, one at a time.

"Are you happy?" She asked tentatively.

"I'm overjoyed. You?" He beamed.

"Terrified."

"Why?"

"Have you ever birthed three babies?" Her voice rising as she spoke.

Appearing chagrined he responded, "Well … no."

"I had twins and even I still have no comprehension of what's to come. And the diapers... so many diapers. I went through twenty-four a day when I had my twins."

Startled, he eyed her in dismay. "Twenty-four?"

Nodding, Alaina replied, "Sayleena wasn't out of diapers yet and hadn't quite progressed to pull-ups."

"Wow! I need to buy stock in Pampers or Huggies or something," he joked as he paced.

"Or a warehouse full of them anyway. And the formula!"

"Formula? You'll breastfeed won't you?" He halted before her.

"Are you kidding me? I only have two," Alaina exclaimed, gesturing towards her chest while giving him an exasperated look. "Where do you expect I'm going to put the third?"

"Right, formula. Going to need stock in that too," he grinned.

"Three cribs, three bouncers, three swings, three of everything. Oh ... my ... gosh!" She began to hyperventilate.

"It's overwhelming, I know. But my mother and father did this so we can too." Stepping closer to her, he placed a hand on her waist and another at the back of her neck. Dante stared into her eyes, his expression holding a gentleness she'd never seen there before.

"But what happens when this is all over?" The uncertainty of where she stood with him was clear in her eyes.

"First of all, as far as I'm concerned this, us, is a permanent arrangement. I'm not going anywhere and neither are you. I pray that God blesses our union and considers us husband and wife, in every way for the duration of our lives. The wedding Saturday is a necessary formality in order to signify to my family and God that my intentions toward you are real."

Lips trembling, Alaina stared back at him in delighted surprise.

"Does that sound all right to you?" he asked on a softer note.

"Yes." She smiled brightly. "I agree wholeheartedly."

Feeling an overwhelming and urgent need to kiss her, he bent down and brushed his lips gently against hers. Embracing her in his arms, he deepened the kiss, pulling away moments later in desperate need of air. Warmth flooded through him as he dipped closer, kissing her neck and throat. A sense of peace and contentment overcame him as he held her. Lifting his head so he could peer into her eyes, he searched them for any uncertainty she might be experiencing. Not seeing any, he continued.

"And second, regardless of what happens with the situation with Kobi Radford, and maybe even more so because of it, I'm not about to let you and any of our children out of my sight for one minute. I care for you all too much." His voice was filled with emotion. Kissing her forehead, Dante held her protectively in his arms.

Alaina laughed then as tears welled in her eyes. Seeing the pure joy in his glorious and shining pale blue eyes, she was happy to find that he was overjoyed with the news of his impending fatherhood.

"I'm going to be a daddy! Praise God!" He whooped loudly as Megorah and Chase knocked, then finally pushed through the exam room door together.

Megorah appeared taken aback by the initial onslaught of emotion spilling over from them. But the moment she looked at their faces and sensed their hearts beating at the same steady rhythm, she knew her brother had finally found his place at Alaina's side.

- - -

The news spread quickly once they managed to return home to the Blackthorne Horse Ranch. They took a slight detour on the way, at the insistence of Megorah, in order to pick up some much-needed clothes for Alaina. Once home, Dante called out to all edges of the house, receiving a reprimand from his father for doing so. But after telling his dad that he was about to be a grandfather again within the next seven to eight months, Rafe promptly thumped Dante on the back and congratulated him with a bear hug, while smiling warmly.

The whole family congregated in the kitchen, as glasses of ginger ale soda were tossed from one hand to the next. Dante had carried Alaina into the house, insisting that she shouldn't be walking in such a state and had set her down in a cushioned chair in the kitchen. Tucking a blanket around her legs, he was about to wrap another around her shoulders when she playfully chucked his hands away.

"I'm pregnant, not ill." She laughed as he tried to wrap it around her again.

"Get used to it, Little Star," Megorah said while passing Alaina a glass of ginger ale. "The Blackthorne men are notorious for pampering pregnant women." Her eyes sparkled with laughter.

Having heard the commotion from outside in the yard, Drinian had come inside to investigate what was happening, although he already had a pretty good idea. Overhearing the others speak of the impending baby, he realized no one had mentioned exactly how pregnant she really was.

"Have you told them the best part?" Drinian shouted so that everyone could hear him.

Seeing his brother's anxious expression, Dante realized Drinian had somehow suspected Alaina was expecting more than one child. He had apparently been waiting on pins and needles, to hear if his suspicions were true or not. Raising his glass in the air, as everyone but Chase and Megorah turned to look at him, he made the announcement.

"Drinian is right. Everyone, Alaina and I are having triplets."

Chapter 26

Alaina's face turned crimson red. His entire family became eerily silent, stunned by the announcement. Dante tossed the ultrasound pictures on the table and watched with delight as everyone grabbed for the pictures so they could see. The room was quiet for a moment when Royce finally spoke.

"Wow, Dante! That's amazing. Congratulations you guys!" He sounded genuinely happy for them.

"Three babies! I can barely manage the two kids I've got, and they came nearly two years apart." Hialey appeared shell-shocked and in need of sitting down.

"That means you're going to have six kids to raise - like mom and dad." Breydon spoke as though he were in awe. "You're going to need all the luck you can get."

"You're having *triplets*?" Lylia said angrily above the noise, her brow furrowed. "The two of you? I don't understand. Were you *trying* to have kids? I mean, were you taking something?" She stared at Alaina in confusion.

"No, it just happened. I shouldn't even be able to get pregnant." Alaina stopped suddenly when she saw Dante flinch next to her. Sensing something was wrong, she looked at him and noticed he was staring at Dartanian and Lylia earnestly. He seemed anxious at Lylia's response to the news.

Dartanian stepped towards Lylia as she spoke. "It just *happened*," Lylia said bitterly. "You two, who aren't even supposed to be able to have children, just *happened* to *accidentally* somehow wind up pregnant with *triplets*?" The room was quiet and Alaina clutched at her chair. Heat suffused her face again and spread throughout her body.

Placing his arm around Lylia's waist, Dartanian pulled her to him. "I think what Lylia is trying to say, is that although we're very happy you're expecting, it's just a little confusing. Please understand Alaina, we're not meaning anything untoward. And it would make sense that my brother would sire three what with there being a long history of triplets in the Blackthorne line. It's just ... we all," Dartanian paused, indicating his other three brothers, "...took a test many years back and were told we'd never have children. Lylia and I tried for several years before having to resort to other avenues." His eyes misted over as his wife looked away painfully.

"You know what? That's okay, Dartanian. If the angels hadn't come to me last night, then I would be questioning it as well," Alaina said.

Breydon peered at her closely and then nodded towards his father's questioning look.

"Course, they never said anything about triplets." She laughed nervously at Lylia's seething expression.

"Why? Why would God bless *you* with these babies? You and *Dante* ... *of all people*," Lylia hollered, winning herself a scowl from Dante. His jaw clenched.

"I of all people?" He growled.

"You weren't even married at the time," Lylia exclaimed angrily, shocking everyone at her boldness. Tears welled in her eyes. Shaking off her husband's consoling hands, she stamped her heeled feet on the kitchen tile. "No, don't touch me, Dart. After everything I went through, after so many years of trying... And God just gives them, not one but three babies? Why them? Why now?" Sobbing uncontrollably, Lylia wailed as she fled the room. "It's not fair! It's just not fair! I've done everything you asked of me, God! Why?"

An uncomfortable silence was left in her wake as most attempted to avoid eye contact. The celebratory mood of moments before was lost because of the outburst.

"Does this mean Alaina will present with another ability?" Hialey asked quietly, breaking the silence when understanding began to dawn on her.

"I suspect she already has." Rafe cleared his throat. "Would I be right?" He peered between his son and Alaina, while still holding his glass.

Dante replied, "It would seem she is experiencing my gift as well."

Glancing over at Dante, mouth agape, Hialey stared in awe. "Two of you in this house who can discern thoughts? *Oh, man*! I ain't ever getting away with *anything* anymore."

Chuckling, Dante wrapped an arm around Hialey's shoulder. "Something tells me, Hialey, you never got away with much anyway."

Scowling, she shoved at his arm playfully when several people started laughing. The tension of moments before gradually began to diminish.

"This is wonderful news." Crisalya smiled brightly as she spoke. "I guess I'm just wondering how it's even possible?" She exchanged nervous glances with her sister. "Somehow I knew you were expecting, but Lylia's not entirely wrong about what she said, regardless of how she said it."

"I don't have all the answers. I can only tell you what I have learned since I have been here." Alaina indicated the Blackthorne home. "Before I arrived here it was all very confusing. I was experiencing things ... seeing things that just didn't make sense." Pausing, she lay her hand across her belly and shifted uncomfortably in her chair. "I'm sorry. Crisalya please, do you know if you happen to have some – oh what did Woreash call it? – Lemon something... Oh, yes! Lemon Balm Tea?"

Frowning, Crisalya thought for a moment. "We haven't really kept that on hand in a while, but I believe we have some peppermint leaf tea or ginger root, which would serve a similar purpose."

"I could go for some of that peppermint leaf tea right now I think." Alaina attempted to stand but Dante promptly pulled her back in her chair.

"I'll make you some. You're feeling nauseous?" Crisalya asked. Seeing her nod, she went to work setting a pot of tea on the stove and headed to the herb pantry to locate the tea.

Alaina rolled her eyes at Dante. "I thought I was going crazy and I was afraid to say anything because I figured you'd have me committed if I did." Her hands trembled in his and she took a deep breath. "But then last night, when I fell asleep, I saw them and spoke with them."

"So you can't see them during the day, like Breydon can?" Drinian asked, seeking clarification.

"That's right," Alaina said appearing thoughtful. "It would seem seeing angels is not meant to be one our children's gifts. But sometimes I simply know when someone is going to say or do something, without knowing why. Like the other day, when I stopped Storman from exclaiming over the plane."

"That would be a form of 'Knowing' like what you can do, right dad?" Megorah inquired.

"Something similar anyway," Rafe acknowledged. "There are varying degrees of it, I would wager. Some more ... extreme than others." He'd paused, searching for the right words.

"Then there would be nights I'd go to bed and have what seemed like random dreams," Alaina went on. "But then, I'd wake up and either that morning, during the day or several days later, I'd experience exactly what I'd dreamed. Like yesterday, when you woke me from the nap in the afternoon and told me to pack up because we were leaving."

"You dreamed that?" Dante inquired in surprise.

"Oh, yes. I woke yesterday morning having had that dream. It's a little disconcerting when it happens really."

"Prophetic dreams of sorts?" Royce asked of the room at large. "Kind of like we were thinking last night?"

"So it would seem." Drinian stretched his legs, appearing agitated compared to that morning. He acted as though he wanted to be done with the conversation and on his way.

"I need to go check on Lylia," Dartanian said suddenly as he stood. "But before I go, I *am* curious. Am I understanding right? You say there were two angels you spoke with last night? From what I gather, they told you about us and of your impending birth. Is that correct?"

"While I was asleep the angels Maleeka and Woreash came to me. They explained about what was happening to me, and that the abilities I was experiencing had been blessed by God through the Blackthorne line," Alaina said.

"Did they say anything else?" Drinian asked.

"They told me I would experience a total of three separate abilities." On an afterthought, she murmured softly. "I guess, in their own way, they were trying to tell me I was expecting more than one child. They just didn't say it out right and I didn't fully understand."

"But how is it these two messengers communicate with you but not me? You said this morning at breakfast that I wouldn't be able to see them if they were present. Do you know why?" Breydon asked petulantly as though a child who wasn't getting his way.

"You really don't know, do you?" She glanced around the room at large.

"Don't know what? Clearly, there is something you need to tell us, a message of sorts," Megorah said earnestly. Her long black hair cascaded down her shoulders to her waist. She had been playing with her hair by taking her braid out as they talked.

Taking a deep breath, Alaina closed her eyes and recalled her experience from the night before. Keeping her eyes closed, she began to speak. "They said they are not allowed to speak to, or be seen by anyone outside of a dream, for the Lord won't allow it."

Startled, Megorah sat forward as did Breydon and Drinian. "Why on earth not? I see others. That *is* part of my gift after all. Why not these two specifically?" Breydon asked before Megorah could.

"They said that they are not like regular messengers or guardian angels. They are a different kind of angel and are not normally allowed to speak to humans except on rare occasions, as I did last night. I got the feeling they ranked higher somehow." Alaina said, as she opened her eyes and glanced across the table at Drinian. "If that makes any sense."

"A higher-ranking angel?" Rafe spoke up in alarm, his attention at full alert. "The Bible does speak of there being different types of angels. There are some even that sit at the throne of the Lord while others guard the Garden of Eden. I wonder why they are making themselves known to you and by extension us now."

"Because Lilyandhi made a terrible mistake." Alaina's expression changed then, and her hand flew to her mouth. She struggled desperately to maintain her composure.

"What mistake? What could mom have done?" This time, it was Dante that spoke but Alaina shushed him.

"Maleeka and Woreash said she didn't understand." Alaina looked back and forth between Breydon and Drinian. "Honestly, Drinian, she didn't know."

Drinian stood suddenly, his chair falling over, having gotten caught on his foot. His chest heaved and his fists clenched.

"Wait a minute, what's going on here?" Dante looked back and forth between Alaina and Drinian, trying to understand his brother's reaction. In that same moment, Megorah bent over in her chair as though overwhelmed with emotion.

"Your mother, Lilyandhi, was so scared when she went into delivery with the three of you. It was her first birth, and she was afraid. She didn't know that calling on an angel for guidance during your birth, Drinian, would be a problem. Maleeka thinks Lilyandhi had Dante first." Alaina covered her mouth briefly with a trembling hand.

"So we were right," Rafe said thoughtfully.

"As I said, Maleeka believes so, though he was very clear about the fact that God had not made it clear to them yet." Alaina smiled. Then, nodding towards Drinian, she began to cry. Tears streamed down her face, and she looked at the enormous haunted man who stood not far from her, struggling with his emotions. She knew he was finally realizing what had happened so long ago when he was born, and why he was now tormented with the shadows.

Taking a deep breath, she trembled as she continued, "Being able to see and communicate with angels and by extension, demons have rarely been gifted to mankind. When bequeathed, it was always meant to be and has always been before, a combined gift, for it is dangerous to man when separated, as you are now aware." She stretched her arms out in front of her, interlocking her fingers together. "According to Woreash, a woman carrying children with abilities must suppress the abilities meant for the child during childbirth, so that they may fall to the baby when born."

This time, Alaina peered over at Breydon, noticing he'd sat forward suddenly, clearly intent upon what she was saying now. Taking another shaky breath, she explained. "Breydon, you were never meant to have the gift to see angels. You were only ever meant to discern the truth."

Chapter 27

The look of shock on Breydon's face was a mixture of emotions, ranging from dismay and alarm to relief. Hialey reached over and laid her hand on his, attempting to comfort him. She leaned forward as well.

"It would have been fine if the angel Lilyandhi called on had gone away before you were born Drinian. But there were complications and the cord was found to be wrapped around your neck, so he stayed to ease your mother's anxiety. By doing so, your gift was ripped in half as you were born." Alaina pulled her hands apart then, signifying the separation of his ability. She had Rafe's full attention then. "The angel who caused the tear by tarrying at her side was cast out. When Lilyandhi became pregnant the second time around the partial gift fell to you Breydon, because you were the next in line to be born who could handle the gift."

"Which means Drinian was born last, not second," Crisalya interjected as Royce and Rafe could be seen shaking their heads.

"No. Alaina just said the next who could handle it. It could imply that, for some reason, to discern good and evil and to see angels is not safe to be combined for some reason," Royce explained.

"But why? I would have thought it more likely a bad combination for Dante's gift, rather than Dartanian's," Breydon said thoughtfully. "You know, because of the angel already ever present at his side?" Breydon queried while staring at Dante and Alaina intently.

"Is it there now?" Hialey asked curiously.

"Oh yes. There is one attached to Alaina now too."

"Really? What does he look like?" Alaina asked curiously.

"They normally show as a hazy bright ball of light and typically only take form when the message they are relaying bears significance to me, like earlier this morning, for example. It was like I was seeing double," Breydon said.

Hiccupping softly, Alaina was grateful to Crisalya, in that moment, for placing the cup of tea in front of her. Taking it up in her trembling hand, she lifted it to her mouth to sip at the hot herbal brew. Glancing up, she saw Drinian was staring at her with an odd sort of look on his face. He was breathing heavily while clenching and unclenching his fists.

"Woreash told me that God felt Lilyandhi should have known better," she continued, "...and he was angered by the angel in question, for the Lord knew the divine being knew better, which was why he was cast out of heaven."

"But that doesn't make any sense." Crisalya glanced down at Alaina as she hovered next to her side.

"She's right. I can see taking issue with the angel. After all, they are otherworldly beings, who have a clear connection with God. But mom … how was she supposed to know this would happen?" Dante asked.

Closing her eyes, Alaina said quietly, "Because it's happened before." Opening her eyes, she looked over at Megorah, then again at Drinian. "Hasn't it?"

Observing the exchange, both Dante and Dartanian said at the same time. "What is she talking about?"

"Do you know?" Dante asked next. It was frustrating to keep up, as it felt as though they were constantly two steps behind Megorah and Drinian.

Megorah spoke first. She'd closed her eyes and rested her head on the table in front of her. "Why didn't I see this before? Why didn't I see this coming?"

"What is it Megorah, just spit it out," Dartanian said in irritation.

"The journals," she moaned, as though what she said answered everything. "Mom's journals. One of them tells of a story from about 200 years ago. I mentioned about this last night. You have it, don't you Drinian? I've been looking for it and can't find it but you know where it is."

Drinian nodded his head. "Mom gave it to me when she died."

"I wonder why?" Crisalya asked curiously.

"In her own way, I believe she was trying to give me some hope, that one day it would all end. I gathered at the time she didn't realize how significant the story was." He paused, glancing towards his dad uneasily. Running his hands across his face and through his hair, he continued. "I don't think she knew exactly what she had done before she passed away, although I got the feeling when we last talked, that mom was starting to realize that she may have caused it somehow, for she asked me to forgive her. Then she asked me to help her pray for God's forgiveness as well."

"I take it you've read through this journal?" Dartanian asked his brother, wanting to stay on topic. Seeing him nod again, he sat back down in his chair in frustration. "Can you tell us roughly what this story is about, so we can all finally be on the same page?" His tone was irritable and he was clearly anxious to go check on his wife.

Drinian paced back and forth near the patio doors, then, moving towards the fridge he grabbed a root beer, popped the cap off on the counter and took a swig. Resigned to having to relay it, he began.

"It tells of a young Indian woman, who'd become pregnant by way of an Indian warrior, who'd been given a second chance at children shortly following his fortieth birthday. This was unusual, as most natives did not live that long for one reason or another. The woman showed signs of three different abilities, only not understanding the gifts they had, they called them something else. Reading minds..."

"Discerning thoughts," Breydon piped, glancing at Dante.

"Visions of future events," Drinian relayed.

"Prophetic dreams," Crisalya said quietly.

"And seeing shiny men with giant feathered wings, as well as evil shadows," Drinian finished. "Which, of course, we all know as seeing angels and demons." Glancing furtively over at Alaina he continued. "She was warned by an elder not to utilize the gifts recklessly, but she continued to do so anyways. She especially liked to call upon the shiny men, because she enjoyed looking at them and seeing their massive beautiful wings. Measures had to be taken to protect her during the days, and as she slept, but she would often disappear from her guardians, in hopes of calling upon and seeing the shiny men."

"Why were protective measures required?" Dartanian asked.

"Because she claimed the shadows kept trying to cause her harm." Everyone turned to look in alarm at Alaina.

"One day, as she was washing in the river, she went into labor. Running back to camp, the elder aided in her delivery, warning her not to use the gifts as she gave birth. She wanted to see the shiny men one last time, and so she called upon her favorite, urging him to come to her so she could see his glorious wings." Pausing in his story, Drinian glanced over at his father. "The angel in question is described as magnificent and cocky. He called himself Solmen."

"Are you kidding me?" Dartanian gaped.

"Is it possible, that this Solmen is actually the demon Zalman? The demon who tried to kill you when we were three?" Dante asked, having put the connection together at the same time as his brother.

"And fifteen years ago," Breydon reminded darkly, as he brooded over his juice bottle, having never forgotten the day Drinian had nearly shot both him and Dartanian by accident because of the shadows when his horse died.

"I thought I recalled hearing or seeing that name before," Rafe commented. "And frankly, that would make perfect sense. It would explain his animosity towards this family and his constant presence."

"So it would seem," Drinian said dryly. "From what mom wrote, the delivery went quickly. Triplets were uncommon back then, and there were complications. It is thought Solmen, arrived amidst a swarm of shadows as she was delivering her last child, for the skies were clear and sunny, yet a sudden chill permeated the air around them." Watching his father's expression as he winced,

Drinian could see that he already knew somehow, what that likely meant. Arriving when he did, and in the presence of demons, the angel Solmen had likely lost favor with the Lord, as did the angel which had been present at his son's birth and been cast out.

"The three babies were passed to a midwife, so they could receive nourishment. One child later developed mind reading or discerning thoughts, another developed the ability to see visions of future events or prophetic dreams. The third possessed only the ability to see shadows, which terrorized the child. The elders believed the gift to see shiny men had been ripped from her at birth because the mother had been selfish and utilized the gift as she was being born."

"*She*, you say? The child in question had been a girl. What happened to her?" Chase asked.

"The little girl mysteriously drowned at age three," Drinian responded, startling everyone, even his father.

"That *cannot* be a coincidence," Rafe said darkly. He stood abruptly and began to pace. Deep in thought, he wondered if there was some possible significance in the age. Drinian had nearly drowned at age three as well. And unknown to the rest of his children, Rafe's third brother had also died in the same way at the same age.

"I don't understand," Hialey said suddenly, shaking her head in confusion. "If God wants, say this child to have this gift, then why allow that power to be ripped from them?"

"First of all, you are presuming that these abilities are some kind of a special power Hialey, which is not so." Rafe corrected. "Only God has powers, in the sense, you're talking about. What my children are capable of is different for they have no more power within them than you do, Hialey. It's more like a tool He has blessed them with, I would imagine, so that they may be able to help those around them."

Completely flummoxed, Hialey stared at Rafe in utter confusion. "A tool? I don't get it. I always thought…"

"Hialey, the human brain is vastly underused," Chase responded, having a better understanding where Rafe was going, with what he was trying to say. "The minds of the Blackthorne children, for whatever the reason, have simply developed at a greater level comparatively than the rest of us."

"Yes, Chase is right. All mankind has the capacity for such gifts. Very few are blessed with the ability to develop and utilize their minds, to that end as they have." Rafe explained as he sat finally in his chair. "Speaking hypothetically, they each could develop one or more of their sibling's abilities, but it would seem they are only meant to have what they have been gifted with."

"Okay, I get that part now. I suppose it even makes a kind of sense." Hialey sounded as though she were losing her patience. "But I still don't get why God couldn't have just given the ability back to her. Then maybe…"

"He could have, Hialey. God is all powerful after all," Rafe interrupted. He stared down at his glass appearing agitated. Sighing heavily, he went on, "I believe it has something to do with free will. Lilyandhi made a choice to call on the angel, knowing that there was a risk involved in doing so. She told me once, that she believed God granted the abilities to the mother so that she might experience them during her pregnancy and know what her child will one day go through. Then, when it is time to give birth, she is to pass them on to the baby. It would seem that by choosing to use the gift, Lilyandhi held onto it, not fully understanding the potential consequences. I'm betting she thought, by utilizing only part of the gift…"

"That it would still pass on to Drinian," Crisalya finished, as she nodded in understanding.

Sighing in exasperation, Hialey sat back in her chair in a huff. "I still don't get..."

"Hialey, God didn't just give the ability back to Drinian because I'm betting what happened was meant to serve as a lesson." Royce interrupted, becoming exasperated. "I'm sorry Rafe, I don't mean to be harsh. But from the way it sounds, the stories in the journals Lilyandhi and her ancestors wrote, were meant to be guides to learn from. These journals were, to her father's tribe of that time, sort of like the Bible is to Christianity. God's word was written down for us in the Bible for a reason after all. We were meant to live by His words and laws and learn from the errors of those who preceded us. Christianity and God were unknown to Indian culture at that time. But there was still relevance in what they were experiencing and living, which was why the elders of the time likely began passing the stories along, and insisting they be written down when the ability to do so came about."

Impressed at Royce's grasp of the situation, Rafe concurred. "Yes, unfortunately, Lilyandhi allowed her fears to rule her that day. She failed to have faith that the Lord would see to it that everything would work out in the end," Rafe said, regret clear in his voice.

Hearing his words, Alaina tensed, glancing in discomfort next to her at Dante. He took her hand in his. She herself had allowed fear to rule her the night their children had been conceived. It almost felt like there was a link somehow. As if events were coming back around full circle. Sensing that Dante had made a similar connection she made a mental note to speak with him on it later.

"And since we didn't get it right once again, we're probably meant to learn from it, so it doesn't happen yet again," Rafe finished almost wearily while nodding down the table towards Alaina.

"But Alaina's experiencing a different ability."

"Maybe it's a gift yet to present itself?" Chase inquired thoughtfully.

"Anything *is* possible," Rafe said quietly, gazing with concern at Alaina.

"What did happen to the mother, Drin?" Anxiety was slowly building within Dante at the notion of Alaina possibly seeing the demons.

Drinian looked at his brother as though he were clueless. "There were complications, and as stated, the children were passed on to a midwife. The journal is non-specific but the implication is that she died." His gaze moved to Alaina then, and he stared at her as though transfixed.

"No!" Dante stood suddenly, shaking his head. "This cannot happen. I will not let it happen to my wife." His eyes were wild. He glanced around the room as though seeking answers from anywhere he could.

Staring down the table at his son, Rafe noted, with interest, his son's familiar usage of the term 'wife' where Alaina was concerned. Finding it interesting that Dante had gone from referencing her as a fiancée, to a wife, within a span of a few hours, he wondered briefly at what had transpired between the two of them at the clinic.

Alaina trembled in her chair; a tear trickling down her left cheek. She peered over at Dartanian who sat towards the end of the table looking back at her. Smiling weakly at him, she spoke quietly.

"Lylia should not envy me. I may have been blessed with these babies inside me. But I don't believe you would willingly care for her to accept the potential consequences of their birth. I don't know how to control these gifts I am experiencing." Feeling Dante's strong arms reach around her as he lifted her and pulled her into his lap, she nestled into him. "What will happen to them, Dante? Will you take care of all of my children, if I orphan them that day?"

"Don't talk that way. We'll figure this out. I'm not going to let anything happen to you," Dante assured her. He enveloped her in his arms and held her close. Sighing softly, he rested his head on her shoulder, smiling regardless of the fear he was experiencing over the thought of her possible loss.

Dartanian stared at his twin brother and Alaina from where he sat. It was quite clear to him that Alaina had become extremely important to his brother. He worried at what losing her during childbirth might do to him. Dante had already lost one wife. Could he survive the loss of another?

"I'm glad Lylia is not here for what I'm about to say," Dartanian began carefully while rubbing his hands together in agitation.

Sensing he knew why his son was glad his wife wasn't present, Rafe sighed and leaned back in his chair, clearly vexed by the turn the conversation was about to take. Setting his ginger-ale glass down, he stood and began pacing the room, deep in thought.

"I think maybe the two of you need to consider…"

"No!" Megorah said heatedly, glaring over at her brother. She knew full well what he was going to say. "Dartanian, I cannot believe that you, of all people, would even suggest such a thing."

"Wait what? Suggest what?" Hialey asked, at a loss for what was being unsaid.

"I realize it's a risk," Breydon added, ignoring his wife's confusion. "But if we can figure out a way to help her through the delivery, then maybe…"

"Then maybe what, Brey?" Dartanian asked, becoming cross. "This pregnancy is already taking its toll on her."

"But Dart. That was before she arrived," Crisalya countered. "She's here now and maybe we can help her."

"Help her how exactly?" Chase inquired, giving Crisalya a hard stare. "Do we even know how to help her?"

"Wait a minute. What are we talking about here?" Hialey piped in, having difficulty keeping up with the conversation. Staring at each one, in turn, her eyes suddenly widened in surprise. "Whoa, now wait just a minute. Are you serious, Dart? You can't possibly be thinking what I think you're suggesting here. They're babies!"

"Babies with gifts, Hialey," Royce countered, winning himself a heated look from his wife Crisalya. "Now just take it easy, Cris. I'm not saying they should. I'm stating a simple fact. These triplets will have abilities just like all of you. It's exciting to think of the possibilities, no doubt. They'd be the first out of our generation. But is it worth the risk to Alaina to carry them? She has three other children to consider, after all, who have already lost a father."

"What better way for her to see their father again," Drinian said suddenly, shocking everyone into silence. He shrugged nonchalantly. "She could spend eternity with him then."

"Drin, that's enough," Rafe hollered crossly.

Growling deep in his throat, Dante cursed loudly. Thrusting Alaina in his chair as he got up, he kicked the nearby chair out of his way and advanced on his brother. Chase and Breydon stood in an attempt to block him.

Glaring at Drinian, he tried to push past them. Dante could see nothing but red as he seethed angrily.

"Sit down, Dante," Rafe ordered sharply. "There will be no fighting in my house today…" Turning towards Drinian, he glared at his other son. "Regardless of the blatantly callous statements and inappropriate suggestions that have been made," Rafe finished, turning on Dartanian as well.

"She could lose her life." Dartanian response was heated. He squared his shoulders and stared down his father then directed his next question to his twin brother. "Are you willing to risk it?"

"Enough! Stop it." Alaina wiped at her eyes and directed her gaze at Dartanian. "Your unsaid suggestion is well meaning Dartanian, and I do truly appreciate your concern. But the decision to have them is mine, for I carry them."

Dante felt a mixture of elation and distress at her words, causing him to rethink his position on the matter. "I hate having to admit it, but he might be right, Alaina. Generally, as a whole, this family does not believe in, nor condone the taking of a baby's life. But I'll admit, I don't want to lose you over them," he proclaimed. He knelt down before her, his anger with his brothers dissipating a little as he took her hand in his. "And as much as I might want these children, maybe it's too much to ask."

Placing her hand on his lips, Alaina halted his speech. "First and foremost, I do not believe in abortion," she said emphatically, as Megorah, Crisalya, and Hialey all beamed at her. "Your mother survived the three of you. Who's to say I won't? Psalms chapter thirty-seven verse five tells us to give ourselves to the Lord. It tells us to trust in Him, and He will help us. So that is what I'm going to do, for I know, one way or another, He will take care of me. Second, God is the one who granted us this miracle in the first place. Who are we to mess with His grand design?" She asked, winning herself a decidedly curious stare from Rafe. "And third, I could not live with myself knowing that I had destroyed your brother's chances of one day being free of their torment."

Rafe stopped pacing. Walking briskly back toward the table, he inquired, "Alaina, what do you mean by this?"

"Maleeka and Woreash were given strict orders to correct the egregious wrong committed by the angel and Lilyandhi. They're words, not mine," Alaina said quickly, sensing that she might have offended several of the Blackthorne family members. "Something about an order to set things right that have been driven amiss by free will. It would seem this pregnancy is just one of the first in a series of events that would aid in fulfilling a prophecy of sorts." Alaina patted her belly and smiled up at Dante. "I gathered it went beyond correcting the wrong committed to Drinian and Breydon and ending their torment. Because Woreash was very clear, that God does not make mistakes, and that, what He ordains, will come to pass as He sees fit. Only man's will or choice, and angels who have been influenced can affect an outcome adversely."

"Wait a minute. Alaina you said, 'their torment.'" Megorah caught Drinian's and then Breydon's weary eye.

"Yes," she nodded. "Maleeka was very specific. Both he and Woreash stated that setting right these wrongs would end both their torment."

"Breydon?" Megorah turned to her brother then, and asked, "What tortures you so? And why have you never told us?"

"You know what? You don't need to know everything," Breydon said firmly. He pushed away from the table angrily and stood. Grabbing up his empty juice bottle, he turned to walk away, only to be stopped by Drinian.

"How can seeing angels possibly be a torment to you?" Drinian looked at Breydon, clearly perplexed.

Breydon gave Drinian a look but didn't say a word. Glaring, he spun around, threw his bottle in the recycling bin, and stalked away, leaving the kitchen without giving any kind of explanation.

Everyone turned their attention towards Hialey who stared miserably after her husband.

"Hialey, you know, don't you? If you do you need to tell us," Rafe urged, clearly not caring he was putting her on the spot.

Pursing her lips, Hialey looked away, wiping a tear from her eyes. She shook her head and stood, turning towards the kitchen door as if preparing to follow Breydon.

"Hialey," Megorah prompted but was met with an icy stare as Hialey spun on the spot.

"No!" She shouted. "You will not get the answers from me. I've asked him many times to share this with all of you. I've even gone so far as to beg him but he would never waver. Breydon has his reasons why he's never said anything. As his wife, I have to respect that." Hialey's almond colored eyes flashed and filled with tears. Placing her hands on her small hips, she squared her shoulders, as if ready for a fight. "And though I've wanted to tell you all many times, I couldn't, because he swore me to secrecy when we first married." Hialey whirled towards the kitchen doors and was about to leave the same way Breydon had, when she turned back suddenly, pointing her arm towards Alaina.

"And if you happen to know somehow because of these angels, then you better keep it to yourself. It's not your place to say. When and if he's ever ready, he'll tell them."

Chapter 28

What was meant to be a celebration of sorts had turned into something else entirely. Shortly after Hialey departed, Dartanian followed close behind, expressing his apologies as he went. Royce excused himself along with Crisalya into the pantry, since it was their turn for kitchen duty that night, and they wanted to get an early start on dinner. Although Alaina sensed, Royce might have recognized there was a need for everyone to take a breather.

Megorah and Chase followed Drinian out onto the patio, as they argued over her need to see the journal they had been discussing earlier. For reasons Drinian would not explain, he seemed reticent about allowing her access to it.

The only person left in the room was Rafe. He sat at the head of the table, holding his glass. Reclining in his chair, the head of the house stared at his knees deep in thought.

Dante watched as Alaina wiped tears from her eyes. "This is why we found you outside this morning, isn't it?"

Alaina nodded and took a deep breath. "I'm sorry about that. I didn't mean to worry you or upset anyone. I woke and was just so overwhelmed. It felt like the walls were closing in on me and I just had to get out."

"That's understandable, of course, considering the abundance of information you had just learned. But that being said, Alaina, how exactly did you get out?" Rafe asked. He set his glass on the table after taking a sip and leaned forward, clasping his hands in front of him.

"What do you mean?"

Dante turned towards her and answered for him, "Fifteen years ago Dad installed a state-of-the-art security system in the house and grounds. It extends the entire perimeter of the property, including the stables, barn, and even the foreman's house."

"I update the system every five years or so. The only thing it doesn't cover, as of right now, is the log cabin on the far side of the property that was previously used as a vacation home of sorts. Which, incidentally, has been recently rented."

"When did this happen?" Dante asked, sounding surprised.

"Yesterday. To a woman by the name of Veta Rohann," Rafe said mildly. "It seems our receptionist, Freedom Raines, rented it out while Megorah was out of the office for a while yesterday."

"Uh, oh." Dante groaned. Rolling his eyes heavenward, he rested his head on the table. "How bad did Freedom screw up this time?"

"Wait a minute. There's an actual person named Freedom Raines?" Alaina asked, her eyes twinkling with laughter.

"Can you believe it? It's for real. We went to school with her, even though she was a few years behind us – I think maybe in Meg's class. Her parents were 70's free spirit hippies or something." Dante turned towards his dad. "Has she been checked out then, or what?"

Rafe bobbed his head in annoyance, letting a short laugh out as he did so. "And it's worse than you might think. Freedom rented it for five hundred dollars a month, for an entire year lease."

Dante's head shot up from the table. "Are you kidding me?"

"Why, what's the matter with that?" Alaina asked in confusion.

"It normally rents for fifteen hundred a month." Seeing her eyes widen he explained. "By cabin we mean a luxurious, upscale, and well-maintained log home in mint condition. It's a vacation hot spot tourists which is near a pond at that. So in the spring and summer people will stay for the water and fishing. In the fall and winter, people will rent it for the trails."

"Wow! That's a pretty big screw up," Alaina agreed.

"Yup. I had Megorah contact Ms. Rohann this morning regarding her lease. She agreed to move without too much coaxing. I had the impression from Megorah the lady might have gotten spooked by something while she was there last night." Rafe gave Dante a meaningful look. "I've got Dartanian checking into it. Turns out she was on his radar anyway."

"Why?" Dante asked, perplexed by his father's look.

"She just came into town the night before. Apparently came in with a U-Haul, which was stolen while she was out getting coffee and stopping by the rental office."

Dante winced inwardly, as did Alaina. "That's some bad luck right off the bat."

"Worse luck then you might think," Rafe said, trying to gauge Dante's reaction. He noted his son gave him an odd look, as if sensing there was more to the story then what Rafe was telling them. Seeing his son's eyes narrow suspiciously, he quickly changed his thoughts to another subject, not wanting to alarm Alaina.

"Yes, I've got Megorah setting her up elsewhere more in her price range. I also told her to give the first month's rent free and only charge the pet deposit because of the inconvenience."

"That's awful kind of you." Alaina was a bit surprised at his generosity. She was finding herself liking Dante's family more and more as she got to know them. Though granted, she hadn't known them for more than a day. She did, however, sense she'd missed something in the exchange and wondered at it.

Rafe shrugged. "No need to make her troubles any more difficult. I understand she lost something of rather a significant sentiment to her. At any rate, we've kind of gotten off subject here."

"You're right, sorry. The thing is, Honey, the security system has been updated frequently over the years, as Dad said, in order to maintain the height of security. We lock the house down every night. You shouldn't have been able to get out without entering the code which you wouldn't have known." He pointed to the keypad on the opposite wall.

"I tried the door initially and it wouldn't budge. So, I just disengaged the lock and they opened."

Confused, Dante turned towards his father. "But wouldn't that have set the alarm off throughout the house?"

"It should have," Rafe said. "I'll have to look into it and right away, especially under your circumstances. I don't think we want to be taking any chances right now." Hearing children squabbling from the stairwell they all turned in that direction. "It would seem the kids are rousing from their quiet time and naps." Rafe grimaced.

Alaina laughed. "I'm sure my kids are probably wondering where I am and worrying."

"I don't know. They seemed quite fascinated by their new surroundings and extremely pleased with their new play area." Rafe chuckled. "Honestly, I'm not sure they even noticed you were gone."

Alaina harrumphed. "I'm feeling the love."

Both men laughed as they stood. "It is a pretty fun room. I wish we'd had it when we were growing up. Come, we'll go check on the kids, and I'll show you around your new home." Dante smiled as he helped her up.

"At least now I know it's going to the correct son." Rafe walked away towards the stairs near the pantry. Turning suddenly, he glanced at Dante and said in parting, "We will need to talk more. And by the way... Congratulations, to the both of you. This truly is wonderful news." Turning back around, Rafe left.

"What did he mean by that? Going to the right son?" Alaina asked curiously.

"There was some confusion years back as to who was born first." Dante directed her towards the stairs, explaining as they went. "Originally, it was thought that Dartanian had been born first, Drinian second, and I was last. So, when Dad was redoing his will about ten years ago, he was in debate as to who to leave the house to. He wanted it to go to the eldest which he thought was Dartanian at the time." They started up the stairs, hearing kids playing in the hallway above them.

"But Dart was interested in building his own place. He had already drawn up plans and was even staking out a piece of land for it. Dad offered it to Drinian since he thought he was next, but Drinian didn't seem all that interested either. He likes his cabin in the woods. As Drin put it, 'though I love the place and will always cherish the memories, I figure The Blackthorne Ranch house should go to the one who had the least chance to live in it.' And that is verbatim. I never forgot it. I was always grateful to him," Dante said as they'd stopped on the stairs briefly.

"I take it Rafe offered it to you?" Alaina asked cautiously. Seeing him nodding she responded, "I see. And what did you say?"

"I told him I would be more than happy to have it as my own one day. I didn't get the chance to grow up here like the rest of them did. I've only had the opportunity to live here for about seven years in total and then I went away again."

"So this is where we will be staying then, indefinitely?" She asked.

"Yes, I hope you like it as much as I do," Dante said sounding anxious. She could see that for some reason, it was really important to him.

Smiling brightly while putting on a brave face, she said, "I'm sure I will. What I've seen so far is very beautiful. A huge step up from where I was living before, really."

"Alaina? What's wrong?" Dante asked, sensing something was wrong.

"So why did you leave again?" She hoped he'd drop it. His expression changed then and he tensed noticeably. Apparently, it was just the right question to ask.

"Right, listen there are some things I need to tell you that I'm just not ready to get into right now. Can I trust that you won't probe me on this and allow me to explain in time?" He looked at her uncomfortably.

"Dante, my life is an open book to you. You know more about me then I do of you." She was becoming frustrated by his unwillingness to open up to her.

"I know. I realize this probably seems somewhat unfair." He ran his hands through his hair, as was his tendency when he was anxious. "I don't mean to be intentionally evasive."

She could tell he was struggling with some unseen turmoil. For the time being, she decided to let him off the hook. Seeing him sigh with relief, she realized he picked up on her response.

"Thank you, Little Star."

He kissed her softly, pulling her towards him in a brief embrace. Shivering slightly, she allowed him to guide her up the stairs towards the kids' rooms. Upon reaching the landing, Alaina was promptly attacked by all three of her children. They tackled her to the floor, giggling happily.

Chapter 29

Disturbing developments came to Alaina's attention over the next few days. It seemed the household was in the middle of a mystery where a certain woman was concerned. The name Veta Rohann was on everyone's minds by Friday morning. From what Alaina was able to decipher, something pretty bad had happened to her at the Blackthorne's family vacation cabin she had rented. Without being told, she had managed to ferret out enough of the details for the situation to be disturbing to even her.

As much as Alaina wished to be able to concentrate on unraveling this puzzle, she found herself distracted by a mystery of her own. Each morning she woke to a single black baccara rose on her pillow. Since Dante had the habit of waking before everyone else and tiptoeing into his room for clothes, she'd assumed that they had been from him. She had thought it was such a thoughtful and romantic gesture at first but when she went to thank him for the roses Friday morning at breakfast, she saw Drinian walk in from the patio.

She had been holding the rose in her hand as she leaned towards Dante when Drinian had caught her attention. Nodding his head towards her, she was startled to learn from her angelic guide that Drinian hoped she liked the roses. She wasn't sure which part bothered her the most. The fact that he was giving her roses behind Dante's back. Or the fact that he'd been in her bedroom as she lay sleeping, with nothing but a t-shirt on in her bed.

Alaina's face had reddened in embarrassment and she'd glanced at Dante in alarm. Moving towards the stove, she filled her plate with scrambled eggs, bacon and fruit. She decided she needed to try and determine why her future brother-in-law would be giving her roses. So, she opted to sit across from him at the table on the patio under the guise that she wanted to sit next to Megorah. Anxious at the looks he was giving her, she tried to concentrate on her breakfast. Placing the rose on the table next to her plate, she looked up at him and gave him a questioning look.

Drinian appeared uncomfortable at first. Then he began conversing with Megorah on a topic related to one of his mother's journals. At first, Alaina didn't realize the correlation between her and what was being discussed, but it became clearer as they talked.

"I noticed you managed to read through most of that journal I gave you last night," Drinian commented as he eyed Alaina.

Seeing him watching her so closely, it occurred to her that he wanted her to hear about what Megorah had been reading.

"Actually, yes!" Megorah licked the frosting off her lips from her cinnamon roll.

Alaina stared at the woman, feeling slightly jealous as Meg took another bite of her roll. She'd been trying to lay off eating so many sweets now that she knew for sure she was expecting.

"It made for very interesting reading. I couldn't put it down until I finished it," Megorah wiped at her mouth with a napkin. "I found the story about the triplets the most fascinating." Her excitement was obvious. She set her forgotten cinnamon roll down and took a sip of her coffee.

"I thought you might." Drinian tried to keep from sounding anxious. He glanced through the patio door at Dante, and then returned his gaze to Alaina. "It's a marvel really. So many multiple births along this line. It makes me think the women in our line are extremely fertile."

"It's much more likely a genetic trait on the men's side, although if the woman is 'extremely fertile' as you put it, then that will definitely help," Crisalya added, joining them. "What's this about a journal you were reading?"

"Mom wrote of the story she was told from about two hundred years ago. The one Drinian was telling, about the Indian mother who had the triplets, and then died while giving birth."

Crisalya glanced down at Alaina, clearly appalled at Megorah's tactlessness. Glaring at her sister, she kicked her under the table.

Megorah yelped in pain and rubbed at her shin. "What?"

"A little more tact, Meg." Crisalya dug into her breakfast.

Meg's eyes widened and she turned towards Alaina. "I'm so sorry, but apparently, there was more to the story. The elder believed there was a way to right the wrong committed by the mother."

"Really? That makes sense, I guess. I mean, why else would these angels tell Alaina that her pregnancy would right mom's wrong? Although, I wonder how exactly?" Crisalya asked.

"I don't know, but according to what mom wrote, this elder believed that the next child born in their line would receive the gift to see the 'shiny men,' as they called them. Kind of like what happened to Breydon. So the man who sired the triplets took another wife. She became pregnant twice, the first time with twins, the second time with a single child. The first of the twins to be born was found to eventually have the gift to see the 'shiny men' with feathered wings, in addition to the gift of knowing things without knowing why."

"Wait! Did you say the gift of 'Knowing'?" Crisalya started in alarm. "But I thought Dad said that gift came from Grandma Sapphire?"

"And I think dad's right, to a point." Megorah was wide-eyed as she nodded in agreement. "You find out towards the end of the journal that the twins were eventually killed as adults when the tribe was attacked. That would seem to imply that it effectively killed off that line where the gift might have come from. But let's not forget these Indian children all had the same father and mom's family stems from that line."

"There's more, tell her Meg." Drinian encouraged. He leaned back, munching on a piece of bacon while watching her closely.

"Right, many years later, before they're killed, the children all came of age to be married. The last to be born of the triplets married first. Weeks later his wife was found to be pregnant."

"How would they be able to tell within a few weeks if she was pregnant or not in those days?" Crisalya asked.

"Probably the same way I should have known," Alaina interjected. "I was experiencing their gifts within a couple weeks but didn't realize that was what it was at the time."

"That would make sense," Megorah said thoughtfully, then continued her story. "The eldest of the triplets had chosen a wife as well, but the elder refused to allow him to marry until the second born had chosen a wife and married."

"Why?" Crisalya asked, gaping at her then.

"Because the elder thought the only way to fix it was for them to marry and sire children in the reverse order from which they were born, for some reason. But in the end, it didn't matter because the younger brother who'd already married and impregnated his wife ended up dying. And in those days, in that tribe, if a squa lost her mate, she was given to the next son, if there was one. So, the second born took his younger brother's wife for his own."

Alaina glanced across the table at Drinian in alarm. Her eyes widened when she realized why he'd been bringing her the black baccara roses. In his own way, he was courting her, and he anticipated, at some point, he'd be taking Dante's place. Swallowing hard, she set her fork down on the table, barely listening to the rest of Megorah and Crisalya's conversation. An uneasy feeling began in the pit of her stomach as she looked through the patio doors at Dante. What did this mean? Was history repeating itself? Did Drinian believe something was about to happen to Dante? It wasn't until Megorah's next statement that Alaina returned her attention to their conversation.

"Eventually, she ended up having two sets of triplets."

Crisalya's eyes goggled in her head, and she stared back at her sister. "I couldn't even imagine having one set of triplets, let alone two. There are times when I truly wonder how mom and dad did it."

Alaina laughed suddenly as tears welled in her eyes. The realization that she was thirty-six years old and would soon be having triplets, rounding out her household at six children, was already overwhelming. But the thought of another set of triplets was enough to give her hives.

"Megorah, did it say how soon after they found out she was pregnant that he died, by chance?" Alaina asked quietly. Her face had grown pale, and she fiddled with her hands in her lap.

"There was mention of a battle between neighboring tribes a week or so later. I'm assuming that's when he was killed. So from the time that she married the first brother, until when she was handed off to the second brother – like she was a piece of meat – I'd say it was close to a month or so."

Alaina turned towards Drinian to find him staring at her. She stood suddenly, trying to make it look like she'd accidentally knocked over her juice and plate.

"There's no need to be so distressed, Alaina. It's just spilled juice." Megorah pick up the cup and plate from the floor.

"You know what? I'll get something to clean this up." Crisalya grabbed up her own dishes and headed inside. Megorah followed after her, exclaiming she'd come back with a new plate of food for her.

Breathing heavily, Alaina trembled, stepping away from the patio table and further from Drinian. It wasn't difficult to discern his thoughts, for the angel at her side was making them loud, clear, and unmistakable.

Taking advantage of their moment alone, Drinian made his move. Not wanting to take the risk that Dante would be able to catch on, he spoke aloud to her instead.

"Alaina, I think you're meant to be with me, not with my brother. Marry me, not him. I will take care of you, all of you. I can, and would, love you in a way my brother never could."

Alarmed by his words and confused, Alaina became distressed. She fought back tears as she stared down at Drinian's hopeful face. Glancing at her fiancée through the patio doors, she could see he hadn't become aware yet of what was happening on the patio. Looking back at Drinian, she finally found her voice.

"Why? Just because this happened two hundred years ago, doesn't mean…"

"These angels said there was a way to end mine and Brey's suffering. I think you are the way. I think this was more than just some story passed down through the ages," Drinian explained urgently. "Royce is right. It was a way for our ancestors to teach us how to right such a wrong if it ever occurred again."

Shaking uncontrollably now, Alaina didn't know how to respond. She'd just come to terms with what had been happening to her. Now this was being thrown at her. Fighting for control of her emotions, she sat down across from him, breathing deeply as she did so.

"As far as I'm concerned, I'm already married. He and I, we made a promise to each other."

"I know. But I don't think it's meant to last much longer. If we sit down together with him now, we might be able to convince him…"

"Drinian." Alaina interrupted him forcefully. "Do you think Dante is going to die?"

"I don't believe so." He shook his head vigorously. He could see that the thought was distressing to her and wanted to reassure her. "Things were different back then. I think this legend is simply meant to help him understand his role in this. That's all. I think eventually, he will move on. Dante has never really been the type to stay in one place for any length of time."

Alaina whimpered at the thought, her eyes filling with distress. She knew exactly what he meant. He thought Dante would tire of her and want to go back to his work with the CIA. Drinian was claiming he could love her but that his brother never would. Confusion set in, suddenly making her wonder if he might be right. The only reason Dante had gotten involved with her was because he had come to rescue her and her children. He never once expressed his love for her. Not even when he found out she was pregnant with his children. He'd only ever expressed a fondness for kids and lumped her in with them.

Seeing that his words had stung her to her core, he hung his head. Drinian had hoped not to hurt her feelings but it seemed he had done so anyways. He looked away from her into the kitchen and noticed Megorah and Crisalya heading back their way towards the patio. Standing quickly, he left his dishes and turned towards the yard.

"I don't need an answer right away. I've waited this long after all." Unsure of himself he turned towards her, giving her a meaningful look, then he bent low and gave her an affectionate kiss on the forehead. "Please, just think about it okay?" he asked hopefully.

Alaina watched him, as he quickly walked away towards the path that led to the woods. She could hear Megorah and Crisalya coming back onto the patio. Before turning to greet them, she tried to compose herself. Putting on a false smile, she reached out and took the plate Megorah offered, not knowing how she would possibly be able to eat it now.

Sensing Alaina's distress, Megorah sat down next to her and put her hand on her shoulder. Taking a good look at her, she could see Alaina was disturbed by something. Having noticed how quickly Drinian had vacated the patio when they'd returned, she had a strong feeling something had happened between them.

"Alaina, are you all right? Did my brother say something to upset you?"

Thinking quickly, Alaina tried to come up with something that would sound believable.

"No, well, yes actually." She decided it was best to be as honest as she could. "This story has me a little rattled, I guess. You know, about the Indian woman who died during childbirth."

"Oh, I'm sorry, Alaina. We probably shouldn't have been discussing it in front of you." Crisalya apologized, feeling guilty for having a part in upsetting her.

Alaina looked down at the table, and then glanced out at Drinian as his hulking frame disappeared into the woods. Realizing she needed to know more about what was in the journal, it occurred to her that she needed to take a look at it.

"You know? It's okay. I'm just being silly really." Then forcing a bright smile, she inquired, "Maybe, if I had a chance to read what you've read, it wouldn't bother me so much. Megorah, would you mind terribly if I borrowed the journal for a while? That is, if it's okay with you and you're done with it of course."

Surprised and actually somewhat pleased at Alaina's interest, Megorah smiled warmly at her. Reaching out, she took a hold of her hands and giggled.

"I had actually intended to read through it again but if you think it will help you feel better you're welcome to read it. The wedding ceremony might not be until tomorrow, but as far as I'm concerned you are family now."

"Thank you," Alaina replied gratefully.

"We do need to bring the wedding dress down from the attic this morning, so Alaina can try it on later. Meg, why don't you go grab the journal now and then meet me in the attic?" Crisalya interjected.

"That's perfect. The kids are all going with the sitters to the playground, or some such this morning. Now would probably be the best time to try and read it."

Alaina watched them go with trepidation. Staring down at her plate, she winced realizing she just wasn't going to be able to eat any of it and felt guilty for being so wasteful. Pushing the plate away she stared out onto the horizon as she talked quietly with God.

Lord, what is happening? She whispered fervently. *Before this morning everything seemed so clear and now I am so confused again. I thought I understood that I was meant for Dante, for they are his children I carry. I believe you sent me to this family for a reason, for a purpose, and I want to follow the path you set forth for me Lord. But now it would seem there are two forks in the road. Which path do I take Lord? What is it you would have me do?*

Alaina sat for a while, staring out at the mountains where just the night before she had seen the extraordinary swirling Northern Lights. Closing her eyes, she gave the situation up to God, knowing that one way or another, things would happen as He planned.

Feeling a soft breeze waft its way through the patio and brush against her cheek, Alaina felt it lift her hair gently as it whirled around her. The latent memory of a passage in Proverbs 3:5 she'd read many months before floated into her mind, as though the words were being placed there for her:

"Trust in the Lord with all your heart. Never rely on what you think you know."

A sense of calm overcame her. She smiled wistfully, while a tear escaped the corner of her eye and trickled its way down her cheek. Wiping it away, she laughed softly, knowing the words had come from God. *Yes, Lord, I will trust in you. You sent the angels to me, to lead me along the right path, so that is the one I shall take.*

In Jeremiah 29:11 you tell me that you have plans to bring me prosperity, not disaster and that those plans will bring about the future I hope for. I know in my heart that plan is Dante, for with him, I know I have those things. Help Drinian to see that what he seeks is wrong, Lord. Please God, help lead him to the right path for his life and end his torment Lord. For truly he is confused and I suspect the demons are plaguing him with nonsense.

Ending her prayer, Alaina stood and collected her plate. She was about to head back into the kitchen when Dante poked his head out.

"I'm going to head down to the corral with dad for a bit. Will you be okay on your own for a while?" He asked excitedly.

"Of course. I thought I'd read for a bit anyways, and then Meg and Crisalya wanted me to try on your mother's wedding dress at some point."

"It's a tradition. Every woman gets to try it on before getting married. But even if it does fit you can still choose whatever you want. You don't have to wear it, okay?"

Nodding that she understood, she watched him turn around and walk away. She noticed he hadn't bothered to give her a kiss goodbye. It was as though she were an afterthought. Dante seemed more excited about seeing horses than he was at seeing her. That knowledge made her heart hurt a little.

That's when she realized something she hadn't picked up on before. She had fallen in love with him. Turning her back to the kitchen, she stared back out at the mountains. Tears welled in her eyes again as she gazed out at the beauty before her. Alaina had placed her life in God's hands, trusting that He would take care of her and her children, protect her, and guide her along the right path. Now, she would also entrust God with her heart, and have faith, that one day, Dante would learn to love her in the same way.

Chapter 30

The morning moved along quickly. As it progressed, Alaina became extremely annoyed at being repeatedly pulled away from reading the journal. Each time she was halted in her reading, it was for making such decisions about the blasted ceremony. What colors did she want for decorations? What flowers did she want? Or where on the estate she wanted to have the ceremony.

Currently, she found herself in the middle of trying on Lilyandhi's old wedding dress. Megorah and Crisalya brought it down from the attic early in the morning, stating they wanted to air it out in the library upstairs. By noon it was ready to try on, so Alaina sat waiting for the sisters to pull it off the mannequin.

"Did I miss it? I was trying to hurry." Hialey appeared somewhat out of breath as she entered the library.

"Nope, we're just getting it off now," Crisalya said in greeting.

"Cool." Glancing around the room, Hialey noticed Lylia was missing.

"Where is Lylia? She hiding again?"

"Why would she be hiding?" Alaina asked curiously.

"She always seems to make herself scarce when Dante's home." Megorah shrugged. "But I think she'd said something about getting Frappuccino's for everyone from The Coffee Haven."

"If I'd known that, I could have just brought them. I was at the shop this morning after all." Crisalya sounded cross.

"I think it was just an excuse to get away from the house for a bit. Especially since the sitters came to take all the kids to the park today," Meg replied.

Alaina sat listening to the exchange, bothered by the comment Megorah had made. Noticing Hialey watching her carefully, she tried to perk up, but her attempt to change her mood hadn't been missed by her.

"What's up, Little Star?" Hialey quipped, plopping down next to her on the twin sofa. She was wearing what looked like a uniform. Her navy-blue shirt had the word Hialey's embossed on the left side of her chest, and the black slacks she wore were straight legged and form fitting, showing off her tiny figure.

"I was just wondering why Lylia would avoid Dante, I guess. Is there bad history there or something?"

"I think she just avoids being around him, for the same reason she avoids my husband." Hialey picked at her fingernails. Seeing they were chipped, she realized she would need to redo them before the dinner tonight.

"She avoids Breydon too?" Crisalya glanced over at her sister for confirmation. Seeing her bob her head in the affirmative, she became thoughtful. "I guess I'd never picked up on that before."

Megorah paused. Holding the dress across her arms, she allowed it to dangle there. She sighed as she stood there, looking longingly down at her mother's dress. There had been several times over the past ten years that she sensed Lylia's discomfort where their abilities were concerned. She didn't seem to have as much of a problem with Dartanian's gift or Crisalya's, for that matter, as they were both rather benign in nature. But when it came to the rest of them, she seemed uneasy about them.

Megorah would have thought out of all of them, it would have been Drinian's ability to see demons that bothered her the most. But for some reason, she sensed Dante's ability to discern thoughts was the one that really disturbed her. She had a feeling it had a lot to do with the story she'd been told about the accident that happened when the boys were three years old.

"I've picked up on it, but it's Dante's gift that bothers her the most," Megorah said finally.

"Why on earth for?" Alaina asked, more out of curiosity than alarm. "Drinian mentioned something a few days ago about Dante being able to manipulate people because of his gift. Does that have something to do with it?"

Handing the dress off to Crisalya, Megorah stepped over the skirt and came to sit down in the chair next to Alaina. She sat for a moment in silence pondering how much detail she wanted to go into.

"I don't need to know all the details. I'm just trying to understand." Alaina glanced around the room at everyone.

"Okay ... that's gonna take some getting used to," Hialey said with disgust.

Alaina could tell she was only teasing though, for she grinned at her then literally hopped away in order to get a better look at the dress.

"Boy, I haven't seen this thing in quite a few years. Not since I tried it on. It hung on me like a tent, and it was a little too short by a couple inches.

"I believe Lylia is under the mistaken impression that Dante will know what she's thinking about at all times. That's not how his ability works. He, and now you Alaina, can only discern thoughts from people when the angel attached to you deems the information is relevant." Megorah tried to ignore Hialey who was now preening before the dress in such an exaggerated manner that she couldn't help but smile even as she tried to squelch it.

"Dante hasn't really explained too much yet." Alaina giggled as Hialey tripped and fell. Spinning on her bottom, the petite little woman eventually twisted her legs into an Indian style seated position on the floor.

"More often than not, the information is meant to aid you in helping someone else. It can also help you have a better understanding of an issue you're dealing with, or a person you're with," Crisalya said, trying to be helpful.

"Having that information *can* give you an advantage over someone else, which is why, I think, Lylia gets intimidated. But it's more than that, I believe." Megorah sighed. "You have to understand, Alaina. Dartanian put Lylia off for a couple years because he was waiting for Dante to come home."

"He put her off. What do you mean?" Alaina was confused.

"Dartanian and Lylia dated for over two years before he finally asked her to marry him. Then he waited another six months before agreeing to a date for the wedding," Crisalya said, by way of explanation. Getting tired of holding the dress, she moved to sit down in the chair nearest the window.

"Why so long?" Alaina started to ask but then it dawned on her why he'd keep putting her off. Seeing that she'd figured it out Megorah nodded sadly.

"You see, we'd all made that pact about not telling anyone unless we all approved of the person. Since Dante was away and couldn't be reached much of the time, there was no way to get his approval."

"And because of that, they waited a long time before even getting married. Dartanian was hoping to tell her before they got married but couldn't due to the fact that Dante couldn't be reached," Alaina finished the rest for her, filling in the blanks.

"Yup. In the end, they got married anyway without her knowing," Hialey quipped.

Alaina's eyes grew wide in surprise. She looked around the room at each of them. They were all staring back at her meaningfully.

"Are you really telling me, she didn't find out until after they got married?" Alaina asked, already knowing the answer, but still floored by it.

"Yes. It was just by pure happenstance that Dante arrived home two weeks later. When he did, he took one look at Lylia and said he didn't want Dart telling her," Megorah said.

"Wait, why?" Alaina sat up abruptly, alarmed by this bit of news. Megorah and Crisalya shrugged, seemingly becoming uncomfortable with the conversation.

"I wasn't there," Hialey chimed in excitedly, "because I hadn't met Breydon yet, but according to what he told me, Dart was furious, because Dante wanted time to 'feel her out,' as he put it. They got into a *huge* fight, like mega huge knock down drag out fight." Hialey hopped up off the floor and jumped up on the sofa with her arms outstretched for affect. "It only got broke up because Rafe stepped in and nearly clobbered them both."

"Nearly?"

"Yes, it was the first-time Dad ever lost a fight to one of the boys." Crisalya's response was quiet. She was clearly still troubled by the memory.

"You have to understand, Alaina. Dante wasn't really trying to kill any of them," Megorah said softly.

"Kill… What do you mean? Wait… Are you saying Dante beat on his own dad?" Alaina exclaimed in shock.

"They were all pretty beat up, but dad had to be taken to the hospital. It took Breydon, Chase *and* Drinian to get Dante to finally stop in the end. Even then, it took a lot to pull him off." Seeing the stricken look on Alaina's face, Megorah quickly tried to explain. "Oh, Alaina, there was just so much rage in him. I don't think he ever fully got over the accident that happened fifteen years ago … and then finding out the baby wasn't his. He was still just so angry and hurt over Elizabeth and her betrayal. You know?"

"Accident?"

"You know, Meg… I think it was more than that," Crisalya said, clearly missing Alaina's confused state. Hialey didn't miss it, though. She stopped her antics suddenly and stared down at her from where she still stood on the sofa.

Hialey watched Alaina glance back and forth between Crisalya and Megorah in bewilderment. The realization that Alaina was completely in the dark about Dante's first wife hit her full force.

"Baby. What baby?" Alaina asked aloud, though her face was drawn and she stared down at the floor. Stunned, she began to realize there was so much about future husband that she didn't know.

Hialey gaped at Alaina in distress. Her hands flew to her mouth, smothering her squeal of shock. Trying desperately to get Megorah and Crisalya's attention, she began waving her arms frantically in the air.

"Of course it's more than that," Meg bantered with Crisalya, surprisingly oblivious to both Hialey's and Alaina's emotional distress. "He says he doesn't, but I really do think he really resented being sent away for fifteen years and finding out we were never told about him."

"I don't blame him. Frankly, *I* resented not being told about *him* as well. Course, it didn't help finding out he couldn't have children after Elizabeth died. Meg, I'll *never* forget that day she died. April 19th of 2000." Crisalya shook her head sadly as she bantered back, clearly in her own little world. "I think it really hurt finding out it wasn't his baby."

"Guys!" Hialey finally shouted, having become fed up that they had been ignoring her frantic movements. "Hello! Been trying to get your attention here." She watched while Alaina's face flushed with anger and resentment.

"Who *exactly* is Elizabeth?" Alaina demanded.

All three women went silent. They each looked at the other, quickly coming to a unanimous conclusion … that Dante had never told Alaina about his first wife. They sat for a while, without saying anything.

Anger surged within Alaina at the knowledge that Dante had kept something so important from her. She couldn't understand why he hadn't told her about it, and it hurt that he felt he couldn't trust her with it. Bombarded with thoughts from each of them, it was becoming difficult for her to sort them all out. Taking a moment to calm herself, she concentrated on each one individually, eventually deciphering out the events of fifteen years ago on her own.

Sighing heavily, Alaina stood, walking towards Crisalya. Standing before her, she looked down at Lilyandhi's wedding dress. Reaching out she touched a hand to the soft ivory velvet that made up the dress. It was exquisite in every way. Though she hoped it would fit, she wasn't expecting it would, as it appeared too small around. Still angry at Dante for keeping something so important from her, she took hold of the dress, lifting it gently in her arms.

"Let's do this already." Alaina's face was flaming from the embarrassment of being so unaware but she bravely faced Megorah. "I don't think it's gonna fit. The length looks okay, but I think it will be too small because I'm just too fat." She chuckled humorlessly.

"Alaina, I'm so sorry. I assumed you knew about Elizabeth." Megorah watched as her future sister-in-law struggled to fight back her tears. She could sense the hurt and sadness within her.

"It's okay. I was married before too, after all. Let's just get this over with." She smiled weakly as a tear fell from her cheek, barely missing the dress. "I'm sure Dante had his reasons for keeping it from me." Though she couldn't fathom what they would be.

- - -

Thirty minutes later, Megorah was still thinking about Dante and Alaina as she left the Blackthorne Horse Ranch to head to her office. She almost wished she hadn't made the appointment with Ms. Rohann today but knew she couldn't put it off. Veta had a need just as much as Alaina, and one Megorah felt took precedence for the moment.

Sighing, and very distracted as she drove down the long drive, she almost missed seeing Lylia coming up the drive. Pulling up next to her, she slowed to a stop as Lylia waved at her.

"Oh no! I missed the fitting didn't I?" Lylia cried out while leaning out the window.

Megorah couldn't help but feel Lylia wasn't acting quite herself. Her show of disappointment seemed forced, as did her excitement for the impending wedding ceremony.

"It's okay, Lylia. I know you tried."

"Did it fit?" Lylia asked almost pensively. For some reason, she actually appeared hopeful that it would.

"No, unfortunately not." Megorah knew she'd been unable to masque her disappointment. Alaina had been right. It had been too small. They couldn't get it to close in the back for they'd been short by a mere inch of fabric.

"Oh, Meg I'm so sorry. I'd really hoped it would."

Eying her curiously, Megorah replied, "You really did, didn't you? You really wanted it to fit her, so she could wear it."

"Yes, I've always felt guilty that I didn't wear it for Dart. I know how important it was for you that somebody would, and it fit me the best out of everyone so far, though it was still a little big."

"I didn't think you liked it." Megorah was more than a little annoyed.

"Don't get me wrong, Meg. It's a beautiful dress. It just didn't suit me, and it just didn't feel right somehow. I kept getting this nagging feeling like I wasn't meant to wear it. I know that probably sounds silly but I just can't explain it. I really am sorry about Alaina," Lylia said regretfully.

"It's all right. Hialey's gonna take her to the Bridal Boutique to find a different one."

"Have they left yet?" Lylia inquired anxiously.

"No, not yet."

"Good, because I did get those Frappuccino's for everyone. It's the mocha one you like, right?"

Nodding, Megorah reached out and took the Frappuccino from Lylia as she handed it to her, noticing it was a large once again. Taking a sip, she sighed and leaned back in her seat.

"Thanks, Lylia. That was awfully nice of you. I have to get going now or I'm going to be late for my appointment."

"I'll see you tonight then," Lylia called after Megorah as she drove away. Turning back in her own seat, she breathed a sigh of relief. She was awfully glad she'd missed it. Lylia just didn't think she could stand sitting in a room with Alaina right now. Knowing she had the same ability Dante had disturbed her a great deal. She couldn't wait to get back to their home near the bluff soon, partially because of it. But Dartanian wanted to be close to everyone right now, what with Dante arriving home. Yes, because it was all about her blasted brother-in-law, she thought bitterly. She was still upset over finding out he was having triplets.

Putting the vehicle into gear, Lylia continued down the drive to the house. Bracing herself as she got out of the vehicle, she headed with the drinks into the house to locate the rest of the women. She figured she would just pass the drinks along, and then head on to her room to read for the afternoon, until Kayla got home from the sitters. She wanted to delve into more of Lilyandhi's journals that Rafe had brought down from the attic. There was something she was missing in them. She was sure of it. Lylia wanted to figure it out, if for no other reason than to try and help Drinian. The poor man had been clearly suffering especially bad as of late, and she hoped she'd find something in them to give him some hope. Maybe, just maybe, she could help at least one of the Blackthorne children get rid of their so-called gifts, for they seemed more like a burden to her.

Striding into the house from the living room patio, as her three-inch heels punched temporary holes in the carpet, she ran into Hialey coming down the stairs with Alaina. Greeting them warmly, she stretched out her arm, waving the drinks about for them to see.

"Mihapmak! Gosh ... I'm sorry I missed it. But here, a peace offering. Caramel for you Alaina, since you're pregnant, and Mocha for you Hialey, because I know it's your..."

"Favorite! Yes! Mocha frappe *is* good," Hialey squealed, grabbing her drink from the carrier.

"That's very kind of you." Alaina eyed Lylia warily as she took the extended drink from her. Though they were in the same room, she noticed the woman didn't seem to be able to look her in the eye for some reason.

"Oh, it's nothing. The one time I was pregnant, I always seemed to crave those things. I practically lived at The Coffee Haven then." Lylia chuckled good-naturedly, rolling her eyes.

"The dress didn't fit, so I'm taking Alaina to the Bridal Boutique. Want to come?" Hialey asked while sipping at her Frappuccino happily.

"You know, that's sweet of you to offer, but Kayla's with the sitter, so I was hoping to do some reading this afternoon. Mind if I catch you later?"

"That's fine. Might be easier just the two of us anyway. Get too many opinions and then there are just too many opinions, if you know what I mean?" Hialey said cheekily. "Let's go, Alaina. It's just you and me, Chica!"

Alaina followed after Hialey's energetic form, wishing she had a little energy herself. Thanking Lylia again as she passed on by her, she happened to look back and noticed she was staring at her. Stopping suddenly, she turned around and stared back, trying to determine what the look on her face was for. If Alaina wasn't mistaken, Lylia appeared almost distressed.

"You know, Alaina, I really am sorry. I'd thought the dress would fit you. I really thought it was meant for you." Lylia stared at her intently.

Confused by the statement, Alaina's curiosity got the better of her.

"That's an odd statement. 'You thought it was meant for me.' What do you mean?" Alaina asked while holding the cold drink in her hand. Though it tasted really good, her stomach was starting to become unsettled, and she wasn't sure she'd be able to drink it.

Unsure as to whether she should say anything or not, Lylia paused before speaking. Deciding in the end, it wouldn't hurt, and that it might come out anyways, she continued. "Their mom, Lilyandhi, told Megorah when she died that one of the Blackthorne brides would wear her dress one day when they were wed. I was so sure it would be you when you arrived." Lylia spoke almost regretfully, her shoulders falling as if in defeat.

Alaina could sense sadness in Lylia. Cocking her head at her thoughtfully, she couldn't help but pose a question.

"Did it ever occur to you that maybe it *was* supposed to be you?" Alaina asked tentatively. She couldn't help but find it curious, that the one person who the wedding dress seemed to almost fit would refuse to wear it.

"It occurred to me," Lylia spoke, hesitating as if she was unsure about opening up to her. After a moment, she continued. "But then once I had it on and looked in the mirror it just didn't feel right. I don't know how to explain it. I just knew somehow I shouldn't be wearing it. But sometimes I wonder…"

Lylia stopped suddenly, realizing what she was about to say. Hoping that Alaina hadn't picked it up, she tried desperately to think of another subject for distraction. Fortunately, Hialey had come back into the room looking for Alaina at that moment, saving her.

Alaina watched Lylia slip away up the stairs. Allowing Hialey to drag her somewhat unwillingly off to the Bridal Boutique, she couldn't help but worry about what it was Lylia was about to say.

Chapter 31

In the end, finding the wedding dress did not take very long. The Bridal Boutique, it turned out, did not have a huge selection of dresses in her size. After trying the fifth one on, however, Alaina finally got fed up and made Hialey choose for her. Fortunately, Hialey had a good eye and good taste, for that matter, so when she picked out one Alaina hadn't tried on yet, she made her put it on.

Being pale in complexion, the ivory dress seemed to suit her color better than white, and it was of a much simpler design, which suited Alaina just fine. She wasn't much for things that were too fancy or frilly anyway. After paying for the dress, Hialey dropped Alaina back at the house. Anxiously running up the steps with the dress in tow, she realized she might actually still have an hour or two to read before the kids got home. Grabbing the journal from her bed stand, she took it into the library and curled up on the twin sofa to read. She'd brought a pad of paper with her to write down notes as she read.

The further into the journal she went, the more she realized that there was a pattern emerging. Numbers and symbols started popping out at her at regular intervals. Thinking there might be significance in this, she decided to write them down.

While looking down at her pad of paper, Alaina realized the first numbers looked like they could be a date. Murmuring to herself, she sat there pondering the date in question.

2000_4-19//15//2015_(30)^(4-19=3)(5-18=2)(6-16=1?l)

"Four, nineteen, two thousand. April 19th of 2000. Why does that sound familiar?" She said to herself, glancing at the paper. Suddenly, her eyes grew to the size of saucers, as she dropped the book in dismay. Shaking, she stared down at it, recalling it was the date she'd been raped fifteen years ago.

But that wasn't the only reason why she'd become so alarmed. She'd recalled hearing that same date mentioned earlier in the day when she was trying on Lilyandhi's wedding dress. Crisalya had said Dante's wife had died on April 19th that same year, hadn't she? Could this really be a coincidence? Pulling the pad of paper closer to her, she noted the two forward slashes encasing the number fifteen. Unclear as to what that meant, she moved on to the next number.

Two thousand fifteen.

It looked like another year to her. Taking the two years and subtracting them would come out to fifteen.

Sitting back on the sofa, Alaina sat there in stunned silence. Was it possible the numbers were prophetic somehow? Dante *had* once told her that Lilyandhi had the ability, at times, to foresee things that were about to happen. The year twenty fifteen was exactly fifteen years from the two thousand date and they were currently in the year twenty fifteen. Leaning forward with excitement, she began writing down her theory. Though she was unclear as to what the underscore and thirty meant as yet, she noted that four, dash, nineteen was listed again.

There was a nagging thought at the back of her head. Alaina began to wonder if there was possibly significance to that date in this year as well. As the thought occurred to her, she began experiencing an unsettling sensation in the pit of her belly. Unconcerned, she knew that the nausea was merely a symptom of her pregnancy. Glancing down at her belly, she laid her hand there, sighing as she did so. Closing her eyes, she realized she was tiring quickly and simply sat there, resting for a moment.

Her memory of the day when she'd seen the babies on the ultrasound was still prevalent in her mind. Smiling, she recalled how the technician had told her she was only a month along.

A month along. Thirty days.

Gasping, she grabbed the journal along with the pad of paper and left the library. Running up the stairs to her bedroom, she tore into her closet and dug through her purse. Her heart raced as she pulled out the checkbook that Dante had given her. Yanking the register out, she turned it over to peer at the calendar.

Dropping to the floor, her eyes opened wide as she counted backward from the day of the ultrasound. Exactly thirty days from May 18th was April 19th. And on that day, or more accurately, very early that morning, Dante had pulled her from her home. She'd gotten pregnant that morning, that very day.

Stumbling from her closet, the checkbook register in hand, she wobbled towards the bedroom door. Alaina couldn't believe it, but it was almost too much of a coincidence. She'd become pregnant on the same day, fifteen years from the day she'd been raped and Dante had lost his first wife, in an accident. All dates listed in Lilyandhi's handwriting.

Breathing heavily, Alaina walked in a daze down the long length of the hallway, clutching at her belly, beginning to feel faint. Finding herself standing just outside of Megorah and Chase's bedroom, she cried out suddenly in surprise as she experienced a spinning sensation, which had her tumbling to the ground. Unconscious, she dropped the journal, paper, and calendar.

Having heard what sounded like someone moaning in distress as she'd been reading, Lylia bookmarked her spot in her journal in order to go and investigate. She had just stepped into the hallway from her room in time to witness Alaina landing with a soft thud on the floor. Running over to her in a panic, she glanced around frantically, unsure of what to do. She didn't see Dante.

Running down the hallway towards the front of the house, she called out to the living room below. "Hello? Is anyone down there? Dante!"

Hearing Lylia calling out in distress from the front of the house, Breydon popped his head out of the kitchen. Rushing out towards the living room, he peered up toward the upstairs landing at her.

"Lylia, what's the matter?" Breydon called back in concern. Dartanian's wife was not the sort to be shouting through the house.

"Oh, thank heavens, Brey! It's Alaina, I think she fainted or something. She's unconscious on the floor in front of Drinian's old bedroom. I don't know what to do," Lylia exclaimed, clearly panicking.

Alarmed, Breydon called back to her. "Did you see her fall?"

"Sort of, I was coming out of my room when she hit the floor."

"Did she hit her head?"

"I don't think so. She fell on her side."

"Stay with her. And don't move her, just in case," he called up to her. "I'll run and get Dante. He's down at the corral with Dad."

Seeing Breydon disappear, Lylia ran back down the hallway towards Alaina. Staring down at her slack face and limp limbs, Lylia cringed inwardly. She couldn't imagine ever going through what Alaina was, and had to assume the fainting was the result of the three abilities she was experiencing.

Kneeling down next to her, she stared at the woman with wide eyes as she whimpered. Cocking her head as she watched her, Lylia nearly missed seeing the journal lying beneath Alaina's head. Pulling it out from underneath her, she realized it was the missing journal that Drinian had given Megorah. Finding the checkbook register and pad of paper, she chose to distract herself with the notes Alaina had been making.

As she read through them, she became increasingly curious about the content. If any of Alaina's notes were right, it meant that she may have very well stumbled upon Lilyandhi's missing prophecy as well. That prophecy was the very thing Lylia had been hoping to find for some time now. Hearing voices and running feet coming up the stairs from the kitchen, Lylia quickly hid the journal and notes by tossing them in Drinian's old bedroom behind her. She'd just bent back down over Alaina as Dante's worried expression came into view.

Dante shouted Alaina's name at the sight of her lying on the floor. He ran towards them as Drinian and Rafe followed close behind. Taking her up in his arms, he pulled her onto his lap and held her, tilting her head back so he could see her face.

"Breydon said you saw what happened. That it looked like she fainted?" Dante asked, turning towards Lylia.

"Yes, kind of like what happened the day she arrived," Lylia said softly, staring openly with apprehension at her future sister-in-law's unconscious form.

Drinian was watching Alaina intently, but hadn't missed the look on Lylia's face.

"Are you all right there? You seem upset." Drinian stared up at the ceiling then, as if he were seeing something she couldn't.

Shaking her head, Lylia looked back up at him. "No, well yes I suppose I am," she said honestly, catching herself. "I heard a noise in the hallway and came out to check. When I opened my door she looked dazed as she fell. If it helps, I don't think she hit her head." Her face flushed as she spoke. Forced tears welled in her eyes instantly. "I'm so sorry Dante, I was so stunned I didn't think to try and run down and catch her when I saw her falling." Turning towards Rafe, she used a pleading tone. "Do you think the babies will be okay!?"

"I'm sure they'll be fine, Lylia," Rafe said, trying to placate her. "But son, I think you need to see to your fiancée, don't you?" He turned his attention towards Dante, giving him a meaningful look.

"Need help reviving her?" Drinian asked as his brother lifted Alaina and began carrying her down the hall to their bedroom. Both Dante and Rafe turned abruptly and stared at Drinian in surprise.

"Why would I need your help?" Dante growled with displeasure his eyes narrowing. He had picked up on the implication his brother was making, even without the discerning knowledge of the angel next to him.

"You never know, one brother might not be enough," Drinian said in an offhand manner as he shrugged.

Rafe was appalled. "Drin, that's enough!"

Reaching down towards Lylia, Rafe easily helped her from the floor. He could see the shock on her face at his son's offensive statement. She'd paled noticeably, staring at Drinian in alarm.

Dante glared at his brother, and then turned his back to him, as he strode the rest of the way to his bedroom and slammed the door behind him.

"What's gotten into you?" Rafe asked, eying his son suspiciously. He watched Drinian shrug and walk away. Turning towards Lylia, he let go of her hand. "I am so sorry Lylia, he shouldn't have said that."

"It's okay Rafe." Lylia still cringed inwardly at her brother-in-law's crass statement. "At times I don't think he can help it. I get the feeling the shadows make him say and do things that tend to be inappropriate." Pulling herself up to her full height, she inhaled deeply and smiled. "I'm okay. I think I'll just get back to my reading for a while until Kayla gets home." Turning back suddenly, she handed the checkbook register to Rafe. "Would you give this to Dante? I think she may have dropped it when she fell."

"Of course."

Lylia watched as Rafe walked down the hall after Drinian, and then disappeared around the corner. Making sure no one was coming, she quickly opened the door of Drinian's old bedroom, reached in, and grabbed the journal and notepad. Returning to her bedroom, Lylia curled back up on her bed and began reading. Being a speed reader, she managed to get much further into the journal then what Alaina apparently had. As she read, she started to see the same correlation that Alaina had when she was reading it. The numbers popped out at her. She couldn't help but wonder how Meg could have missed it. Or had she seen them but not said anything?

Running her hand along the numbers Alaina wrote on the notepad, Lylia could also see what Alaina had. The fifteen-year time period seemed noteworthy somehow. If her theory about her own pregnancy was correct, was it possible something significant had happened on May eighteenth as well? Alaina had said the angels had told her, that her pregnancy was 'one' of the first in a series of events that would fulfill a prophecy.

Lylia suspected what she had in her hands, in that moment, was the very prophecy the angels had been referring to. Her excitement mounting at the possibility, she might have stumbled upon the very thing that could help Drinian, she made a difficult but hasty decision. Until she knew more and had figured out more of what the numbers meant, she intended to hang onto the journal. Feeling only slightly guilty for the deception, she justified her decision based on the notion that she needed to know the significance of the May eighteenth date first.

Chapter 32

Alaina became aware of her surroundings again, shortly after Dante had laid her in his bed. As she woke, she realized she was being held and could feel his hands running along her back, causing her to shiver. Looking down at her, he chuckled and kissed her brow affectionately.

"Lylia said you looked like you fainted. Are you all right?" He peered at her curiously. "I can call for Chase if you need me to."

Turning away from him, Alaina sat up in bed as she shook her head. Not sure she wanted to share with him about what she'd discovered just yet, she chose instead to change the subject and ask a question of her own.

"Why didn't you tell me about Elizabeth?" She could see Dante tense noticeably, then he sat up himself.

Dante heaved a frustrated sigh and rested his elbows on his knees. Glancing over at her, he could see the hurt in her eyes and winced inwardly.

"I take it you found out from one of my sisters?" Seeing her nod, he turned away and growled in irritation. "It's a sore subject."

"So I gathered. So much so you beat up on your dad and Dart pretty good, from what I understand."

Rubbing at his forehead and running his hands through his hair, Dante, rolled his eyes to the ceiling.

"Those were two separate issues, Alaina. You can't do that. You can't come in on the end of something and expect you know everything."

"I never said I did know everything. And from the sounds of it, I really don't know anything about you. What I did find out came by way of someone else telling me, rather than you."

"What exactly did they tell you?" He asked irritably.

"They said you were married once before, fifteen years ago, and that on April 19th she died in a car accident. They said she was pregnant at the time, and it turned out that it wasn't yours. And they said when Dart wanted to tell Lylia about your gifts, you refused to allow it. You got into a huge fight, resulting in your dad getting sent to the hospital when he tried to stop it."

Alaina relayed what she'd learned as she leaned down towards him while trying to look him in the face.

"My sisters have really big mouths."

"Did you expect with the ability to discern thoughts that I wasn't going to find out at some point? Why would you keep this from me, Dante? You know everything about me and I know nothing of you."

"You know enough."

Hurt by his indifferent statement, she turned away, feeling very vulnerable. Crestfallen, she stood suddenly in an attempt to hurry away.

"Where are you going?"

"To the bathroom. I need to shower."

"That's right. Run Little Star, run as fast as you can," Dante jeered. He watched her back disappear into the bathroom.

"Don't you dare," Alaina hollered as she came charging back out. Pointing at him angrily, she flung back at him. "Don't you dare mock me!" Tears sprang from her eyes.

Yanking the blankets out of his way, Dante jumped from the bed and glared back at her. His eyes threw daggers at her, as he stood with his hands on his hips, taking an aggressive stance. He made a formidable sight, standing as he was, glaring back at her.

"You know you're one to talk. You want me to open up my heart and let it bleed, and yet, you won't tell me what happened to you fifteen years ago."

Her eyes flashing anxiously, she nearly stepped back, but then stood her ground. Squaring her shoulders, she placed her hands on her hips and glared right back at him.

"What could I tell you that you don't already know, Dante? I'm guessing you figured it out weeks ago. Am I right?" She paced before him. "These people here, your family, they know you. They know what you can do. I, on the other hand, was at a disadvantage."

"A disadvantage?" Dante repeated incredulously.

"Yes! In either event, stop trying to change the subject. Because the topic at hand was why you hadn't told me you were married before. Why were you trying to keep it from me?"

"I would imagine for the same reason you won't tell me about what happened to you." Dante was exasperated.

Stunned, Alaina looked back at him in understanding. As she choked back a sob she watched him struggling to rein in his own emotions. She could see the hurt in his eyes that she knew was mirrored in her own.

"Of course," she said quietly in defeat. "Because it's just too…"

"Painful," Dante finished.

They stood there in silence, staring back at each other.

"Wow, look at us … two damaged people who managed to come together," Alaina said finally, breaking the silence.

"Yeah, when do you think we'll actually start trusting each other?"

"I don't know, Dante. I'm not going to stand here and say what you went through wasn't damaging because I've no doubt it was. But speaking for myself?" Alaina paused, taking a deep breath and wiped at the tears in her eyes. "I've had more than one man break my heart. Frankly, I'm not sure I can go through that again, and I think it would kill me … if *you* were to ever break it."

Turning from him, she ran to the bathroom, hoping upon hope that the angel next to him had not shared with him what had just been running through her mind at that moment.

Her heart throbbed as the thought kept repeating itself in her head.

"Because I love you more than I've ever loved any of them."

Stepping into the shower, she allowed the water to run down her body. Her mind reeled at the words that had floated through it, knowing the truth of them. Sobbing, she stuck her head under the water, ignoring the searing heat, succumbing to her misery.

- - -

Dante stared at her, his mouth agape, as he watched her backside disappear through the bathroom door. Too stunned to move, he simply stood there like an idiot, suddenly grinning from ear-to-ear. He knew she'd thought she'd got away before the last thought she'd had escaped from her. He was awfully glad he had been made privy to it because he would never have known how she truly felt about him if he hadn't.

Stretching his arms, Dante marveled at how they had gotten where they were. He knew why it was so hard for them both to say how they really felt. They had both been hurt so badly in the past. Someday, he would want to hear those words of love out loud from those sweet lips of hers. But for now, he was okay with just knowing that she loved him.

Pulling socks and underwear from his dresser drawers, he then grabbed a clean pair of jeans and a shirt from the closet. He'd give her some privacy for now, for Dante sensed that she might need it. Taking his clothes down the hall, he borrowed the shower in the boy's room in order to clean up. After dressing, he headed out into the hallway running into Hialey on the way.

Already in an extremely good mood, he bantered back and forth with Hialey on the way. Her unique personality and fun little quips eased any tension he might have had left. As he stepped down into the kitchen, though, he sensed he might have walked into a war zone. He could not only see, but sense, that Megorah was in a foul mood and it seemed to increase in his presence.

Moments later, she exploded with unsaid accusations, both alarming and surprising him at their intensity. As he watched her stalk off, he stared in shock at Royce and Crisalya.

"Can someone please tell me what is going on here?" Dante asked.

Crisalya looked at him with pain in her eyes. Throwing down her towel, she stalked out onto the patio and into the yard as well, with Hialey following shortly thereafter.

What the heck was going on in this house?

- - -

By the time Alaina finished showering, Dante had already left. Deciding she needed a little extra makeup to cover her tear-stained face, she took a few extra minutes getting ready. Choosing one of her newer loose skirts and a simple blouse, she threw on some sandals and was about to head downstairs when she saw the black baccara rose she'd left on the counter; the rose that Drinian had given her. She looked at it sadly and then picked it up in her hand.

After reading what she had in the journal of Lilyandhi's, she supposed she could see how Drinian could think they were meant to be together. For as much as Alaina wanted to be able to help him, and Breydon for that matter, she just knew that she could never go through with what he was asking of her. The angels Woreash and Maleeka had made it clear that God had another plan for her, and that was the path she intended to take.

After seeing the look in Dante's eye earlier, she couldn't bear the thought of being another Elizabeth, for she loved him too much. Alaina already made her decision where Drinian was concerned. It was high time she built up the courage to tell him. After all, she was Alaina now, not Astraia. And Alaina was a much stronger person than Astraia ever was.

Taking the rose with her, she headed out of the bedroom and walked slowly down the stairs. Glancing at her watch, she stared at its face for a moment, attempting to read the numbers as they faded in and out in front of her. Not having her glasses was becoming more problematic by the day.

Finally registering what the time was, Alaina realized the rehearsal was to have started nearly a half hour ago. Anxious to get to the living room, she figured everybody would be standing there waiting for her. But as she came down the stairs, she didn't hear anyone, and the lights were out in the living room.

Confused by everyone's absence and not paying attention, she nearly missed seeing Drinian standing just outside the kitchen doors. Cocking her head, she eyed him curiously, realizing he was eavesdropping. She was standing within a few feet of him, but he hadn't heard her approach.

Alaina was about to greet him when she recognized Dante's voice talking with Royce on the other side of the door. They were in an in-depth discussion about the woman Veta Rohann, and she could hear everything they were saying.

Her eyes opened wide in surprise as Drinian's panicked thoughts were relayed to her as he listened just outside the door and she started to realize what had happened. Understanding dawned on her then, as she gazed at the back of his head, a mix of shock and dismay roiling within her. Alaina was sure now that he'd never picked up on the numbers. Because if he had, he would realize that she wasn't the one who could help him. She was simply the start of it all.

Alaina overheard Dante ask Royce a question that took him a long time to respond to. After a moment, she could hear Royce's voice again on the other side of the door.

"Rafe taught you all some extremely good morals and values as you were growing up, especially where women are concerned," she could hear Royce finally say in response. "Never hit or hurt a woman, always ask first, never push them if they're unsure and most importantly never cheat on your wife or girlfriend."

"Yes, that's true." Dante could be heard to say in response. "Even if it wasn't one of the Ten Commandments, I'd still never cheat on Alaina. I love her too much even if she doesn't know it yet."

Alaina's heart leaped with joy and tears threatened at the corners of her eyes. She didn't catch anything else that was said after that. Too overjoyed with the news, she was simply grateful to know that he loved her. Even if he wasn't ready to say it aloud to her just yet, it was nice to know that when he did say it, she'd know he meant it.

Watching as Drinian listened in on Royce and Dante's conversation, Alaina could tell he was hearing everything they said as well. As he turned around suddenly, she found she was blocking his path. She knew he was wondering how long she'd been standing there by the expression on his face. Somehow Drinian guessed she'd also heard everything that had been said.

"Quite a lot going on in this house tonight wouldn't you say?" She asked quietly, not wanting to attract the attention of the men in the other room.

"So it would seem," Drinian said cautiously, standing straighter than normal.

Alaina nodded her head in agreement along with him, as she stood staring at him for a moment, trying to process everything she'd just learned and heard. She didn't know next what she would say. What she did know for sure was that her heart was only for Dante.

Chapter 33

The women converged upon Alaina the moment she awoke the next morning. Surprising her with breakfast in bed, they kept her company as she ate, while reassuring her that Breydon and Dartanian were more than capable of tending to her children until the time of the wedding.

Drawing Alaina a bath as she was finishing her breakfast, they added scented crystals to her bathwater. Dimming the lights in the bathroom, Crisalya set out makeup, a hair dryer, and curling implements while Megorah and Lylia lit candles set up all around the bathroom. With orders to strip and bathe as they left her alone in the room, they turned on soft music as they went.

After a very relaxing bath, Alaina was stepping out of the tub as Hialey arrived with a navy-blue box with the word "Hialey's" embossed in silver on it. Trailing behind

371

her was the rest of the women, each carrying something in their hands. Wrapping herself in a robe, she met them in the bedroom with a questioning look.

"You know the old adage," Megorah responded to her curious look, as she laid the wedding dress on the bed. "Every woman must walk down the aisle..."

"Or stairs as in this case..." Hialey said on a side note.

"With something old..." Crisalya continued for her sister, as she held out a small silver wrapped box.

"Something new..." Megorah stated as she gestured towards the dress on the bed.

"Something borrowed..." Lylia said quietly as she handed her another small package wrapped in white lace and a silk ribbon.

"And something blue," Hialey exclaimed with animation, as she shoved the medium navy-blue box into Alaina's arms.

Smiling at them all, she sat on the bed and opened the first package, which was clearly marked as being from both the Blackthorne sisters. As she lifted the lid of the small neatly wrapped box, she gasped as she peered down at the exquisite antique necklace, lying on a thin ivory velvet pillow.

"This is beautiful," Alaina exclaimed, as she gingerly lifted it from its box. The delicate and fancy teardrop necklace featured sapphire gems that had been handset and linked to a sixteen-inch adjustable delicate gold chain.

"Told you she'd like it," Hialey said with a wide toothy grin.

"You could say this goes under the category of borrowed as well." Megorah watched Alaina marvel over the necklace. "It was our grandmother Saphire's, and it was worn on her wedding day."

"Yes, and it's been worn by every Blackthorne bride since," Crisalya added, prompting Hialey and Lylia to nod in agreement. "But only if you want to, of course."

"I'd be honored to." Alaina gushed while gazing at the delicate antique necklace. "It's such an unusual setting and the cut of that sapphire. I've never seen anything like it." She admired the scrolling ribbon-like quality of the setting, which came to a V where the largest of the tiny teardrop sapphires dangled. Within that gem, what looked like a tiny cross had been carved into its center.

"According to Dad, Grandmother Saphire's mother wore it before her, on her wedding day, and so on. We're not even really sure how old it is exactly," Crisalya said. "Much of Grandma Saphire's history is still a bit of a mystery to us, but we understand it's been in her family for many generations."

"Yes, and it is real and we're estimating close to two hundred years old," Megorah said. "Dad had it appraised out of sheer curiosity years back when I first got married. It's worth nearly a million dollars, but it has more sentimental value really than anything."

Gaping at them openly, Alaina quickly placed the necklace back in the box as if it had burned her fingers. "Oh, I could never wear that."

"Of course you can. It's just a necklace." Hialey knew full well why Alaina was reacting the way she was. "I had the same reaction as you. Couldn't imagine having something worth so much wrapped around my neck. But in the end, as Lylia told me when I got married to Breydon, it's not about what it's worth, but the tradition and sentiment behind it."

"Did you say that really?" Megorah inquired of Lylia, sounding more than a little surprised.

Nodding, Lylia continued, "From what I understand, every woman who has worn the necklace has been loved without question by their husband, who also happened to be men of great faith." Lylia shrugged. "I'm not a superstitious person but I figure, why break a chain like that?"

"Okay. But we're putting that on me at the very last minute," Alaina agreed nervously. She set the box on the dresser carefully, taking small steps as she backed anxiously away from it.

Moving on to the next box given by Lylia, she was almost afraid to open it, when she realized it had actually been wrapped with a delicate white lace cloth. Pulling gently on the silk white ribbon, Alaina opened the box and pulled out a lacy handkerchief that had a sky-blue thread intricately woven throughout it, along the edge. At first glance, it appeared ivory in color, until she realized it was simply off-white as the result of age.

Glancing at Lylia questioningly, she watched as the woman's blue eyes flashed with pain. At the same time, Hialey's expression brightened with a note of recognition.

"It is the only thing I have of my birth mother, so please be extra careful with it," Lylia said. She visibly wrung her hands together.

"Your real mother?" Hialey inquired. Her eyes became saucers. "You never told me it had been your birth mother's when you loaned it to me on my wedding day."

"I thought you didn't know who your real mother was?" Megorah said in surprise. She glanced between Hialey and Lylia in confusion. Aware that Lylia had loaned her sister-in-law an item on her wedding day five years before, Megorah had not known what the item was.

Sighing sadly, Lylia grimaced as she sat on the bed next to Alaina. "I still don't," she said finally, after taking a deep breath. "As the rest of you well know, after we were married, Dartanian looked into my parent's story about how I came into their hands. You also know the doctor had already passed away, but what you don't know is that Dart managed to locate the nurse, who had been present at my birth, shortly before Hialey and Breydon's wedding."

"You never said anything," Crisalya said softly.

"I know, I'm sorry. It was just so new at the time. After discovering what we did, I was in shock. We learned the record of my birth had no names listed other than Jane Doe and Baby Doe, and the nurse had grown senile with age." Lylia paused in frustration. "But at one point she did become somewhat lucid. Dart was able to get a much different story than the one the drunken doctor had given to my parents when I was sixteen."

"What did she say?" Hialey asked, her interest clearly piqued as she set down next to her on the bed.

"The woman who birthed me came into the emergency room the same night my parents did. She was bedraggled, drenched from head to foot from the rainstorm and her feet were scraped and bloody from having apparently walked barefoot quite a distance to get there. She was in labor, very weak, and she was having complications," Lylia explained. "She had nothing on her and gave no name but was very adamant that I was in danger. She begged that I be given to the Minnosa's since they'd lost their baby."

"And your parents consented to that? Without knowing where you'd come from or who she was?" Alaina asked.

"My parents didn't know. The doctor and nurse just switched us." Lylia explained, eliciting startled looks from everyone and a gasp from Hialey. "My parents wouldn't have known if it hadn't been for the accident I was in when

I was sixteen. My blood-work didn't match to the records and because I have a rare blood type, I couldn't possibly be their child." The sadness in her voice was obvious.

"And this?" Alaina asked, lifting the handkerchief in her hand towards Lylia.

"The nurse had it. She said it was clasped tightly in the left hand of my birth mother when she died. For whatever the reason, the nurse had kept it all these years."

Opening the handkerchief up, Alaina could see the letter V had been carefully hand stitched with the same pale blue thread into the center of the lacy fabric.

"Lylia, are you sure you want to entrust this to me today?" Alaina asked in concern, almost afraid to even hold it in her hands.

"Yes," Lylia said emphatically. "I've been thinking about this, Alaina. I'm really sorry I reacted the way I did when you first arrived and you found out you were expecting triplets. Instead of being joyful for you I was jealous. I was so very jealous of you and angry at God for blessing you and Dante, with that which I've wanted so much; children and a large family." She admitted as tears threatened in the corner of her eyes.

"It's okay, Lylia..." Alaina began.

"No, it's really not," Lylia interrupted, shaking her head adamantly. "It's one of God's Commandments even. Those laws He laid down for us to follow were so important they're mentioned in more than one book of the Bible. By desiring what you have, which doesn't belong to me, I sin, and I am so sorry. I've already asked for God's forgiveness but I wonder if you can forgive me?"

"Of course. I do understand Lylia, the wanting of something you believe you cannot have. I would imagine we've all felt that way, at one point or another, even though we know we shouldn't." Alaina held the delicate handkerchief out for Lylia to take. "But this is clearly very dear to you and I wouldn't want…"

"Please, carry it for me," Lylia insisted. Reaching out she closed Alaina's fingers over the lacy fabric. "If there's one thing I'm sure of, my mother desired desperately to free me from whatever hell she had endured to that point. Or she wouldn't have refused to give her name and insist the doctor switch me with the Minossa's baby that died. For me, this handkerchief is a symbol of freedom from the past and a fresh start at a new life," Lylia finished while gazing upon Alaina intently. "When we give our lives to God and He washes away our sins, He gives us a chance at a new life. I suspect, in her own way, that is what my mother was trying to do for me."

Peering at Lylia first, and then down at the handkerchief, Hialey said softly, "I wish I had understood the significance at the time you gave it to me. It makes so much more sense now, why you loaned it to me on *my* wedding day."

"Yes, I just get the feeling that we all have something from the past that we've gained freedom from," Lylia said, speaking from the heart. "Alaina, I could choose to look at that handkerchief as nothing more than a tangible remnant of an unknown past. But what were the odds it would one day find its way to me? That nurse had it for as long as I'd been alive." She began to shake her head vigorously. "No, there was a reason it found its way to my hand, just as you found your way into Dante's life, and by extension, ours. Of that, I am certain."

Clasping the delicate handkerchief in her hand, Alaina's eyes began to mist, for she understood what Lylia was trying to say. Gazing down upon the lacy fabric, she sniffled softly. Her marriage with Dante marked the beginning of a fresh start, a new life with him, and freedom from her own sins of the past, for which she had recently repented.

"If it's all right with all of you, I'd like it to become part of a Blackthorne tradition of sorts," Lylia said with a nervous laugh. "From the looks of it, I'll never know where I came from and my parents who raised me have been gone for some time. They were each orphaned themselves, which means you all are the only family I have," she said softly, and with meaning. "It obviously meant something to my birth mother, or she wouldn't have held so tightly to it."

Seeing the approving nods of everyone present, Alaina smiled brightly. "Of course, but from the sounds of it, though, you were even more important to her."

"I agree," Megorah said quietly. A troubled look furrowed her brow. "Dart wasn't able to get any more out of her, I take it? The nurse didn't say why your mother felt you were in danger?"

"No. That was all she said. Then the nurse reverted back to her confused state of mind again."

Deep in thought, Alaina took a leap of faith, making the decision to befriend the woman before her. "Lylia, I know it might not be the same thing as being their mom yourself, but with three babies on the way, I know I'm going to need all the help I can get," Alaina said earnestly. "So if you think you'd be so inclined...?"

"Yes!" Lylia cried, jumping up with excitement. Her face beamed as her eyes sparkled with tears.

Laughing at the joy she saw in her eyes, Alaina hugged her and then moved on to the last box. The intensity of the last few minutes had left her feeling surprisingly drained.

"So, what's this?" She moved to lift the lid.

"I know there is blue in the necklace, but I figure it never hurts to be doubly covered," Hialey quipped. "That is your something blue, and you might want to wait to put it on until you're about to put on your wedding dress." Hialey grinned. Her almond brown eyes lit with mischief. "As you may well have learned, I own an upscale, classy, but demure lingerie shop."

Peeking into the box, Alaina blushed when she saw a sky-blue lingerie set inside. "Yes, I think we'll wait on that as well," she said with a nervous laugh, as the other women giggled.

"I'd say it's high time we get to work, everyone." Crisalya noted it was getting close to noon. "Shall we start with the manicure and pedicure first? Or hair and makeup?"

"That's really not necessary..." Alaina started to say but was interrupted.

"Honey, every Blackthorne bride gets pampered on her wedding day," Lylia exclaimed while grabbing the small bag she'd carried in with her. "I say fingers and toes first. That way they can be drying as we do makeup and hair."

Chapter 34

Feeling grateful that his brothers were seeing to the children for him and Alaina this morning, Dante stepped out of the shower, dried off with a towel, and wrapped it around his lean hips. Searching through the cabinet in his father's bathroom, he eventually got fed up and stuck his head out the bathroom door.

"Where do you keep your shaving cream?" He inquired, still surprised and yet pleasantly pleased his father had offered up his bathroom and bedroom in order to get ready for the wedding.

Looking up from his newspaper at his son from his seat near the balcony doors, Rafe frowned slightly. "I ran out this morning but there should be a new can under the sink."

"You know, if you just let us in your room more often, I might actually know where you keep things, without having to interrupt you."

Glancing back at the newspaper, Rafe grinned at Dante's obvious attempt at making him feel guilty. "Nice try. Besides, I have my reasons for not allowing my children in my bedroom. One day you will understand," he said mildly.

Propping the bathroom door ajar so they could converse and still hear each other, Dante located the shaving cream and began to shave.

"Does that mean one day you'll actually give an explanation as to why?"

"Won't have to."

"How do you figure?" He asked in confusion while wiping across his face with a towel, having already completed shaving. Being part Indian was advantageous, in that he rarely had much facial hair to deal with.

Standing, Rafe laid the newspaper on the coffee table in front of him and stepped around the chair, so he could see his son. "Because one day, along with the house, this room will be yours." He gestured towards the room at large.

Pausing in the bathroom doorway, Dante eyed his father intently. "You're only sixty, Dad. Shoot, you barely look fifty." He harrumphed softly. "You're not intending on leaving us anytime real soon, are you?" His concern was evident in his tone.

"It's not my intention. No." Rafe chuckled softly. "But I will not live forever, Son. One day God will call me home as He did with your mother, and it will be your turn to be head of this house. There is still much I need to teach you, and I feel like I am running out of time." Shoulders slumping, his head turned. He stared out the balcony doors, his demeanor that of a man troubled by some unknown dilemma.

"I'm home now. For good," Dante said reassuringly.

Turning back towards his son, Rafe's posture changed instantly. He stood erect, as though having made a decision. "And I am grateful for that. There were times I worried God would not bring you home to me. Fortunately, he has been watching out for you."

Cocking an eyebrow at his dad, Dante snorted. "I'd wager God wasn't the only one watching over me," he said with a knowing glance his dad's way. Tossing the towel in the nearby hamper, he reached for his tuxedo lying on the bed and began to dress.

"It's a father's prerogative." Rafe grinned, and then turned towards the large walk-in closet next to the bathroom, in order to get his own tuxedo. "One day soon, you will understand."

"I already do," Dante said quietly. He stared at the small ring box in his hand and then looked back over at his dad.

Sighing softly as though relieved, Rafe stopped and walked towards his son instead. "I am glad to hear you say that."

"I already think of them as my own, Dad; Sayleena and the boys."

"Good. That's as it should be, and it shouldn't change when your children are born."

"I understand. I do."

"Take care, Dante," Rafe warned, his tone becoming serious. "It would be very easy to want to treat them different from your biological children."

"I know. I'll be careful." He ran his free hand through his damp hair. "Dad, how did you and mom do it? The three of us boys, all at once? How did you…"

"We did it together as a team. So don't panic, Son. Just take it day by day," Rafe urged. Taking him by the shoulder, he smiled. He could see the worry in his son's eyes. "You may remember I told you this once before when you married the first time; keep God first in your life, and in your household, and you will not fail. As for the rest, you can do this. If you can survive nearly five years fighting for our country and ten years in undercover special ops, then you can overcome this. You will do this and you have an advantage that your mother and I didn't have at the time."

"Really? What advantage is that?"

"You have a family, five brothers, and two sisters, some of whom are married. They have their own lives but they will help where they can I am sure. As will people from church, I would imagine, and I'm still here," Rafe said in answer. "Besides, I'm betting if Lylia has her way, she might well take up residence down from the nursery, just to see those babies every day."

His father's grim tone as he chuckled caught Dante's attention. Feeling guilt once again, that he'd been blessed with children and his brother Dartanian had not he frowned in frustration.

"Why do you suppose this is happening now? After all this time and so many years, to suddenly have children..." He shook his head. "Lylia isn't wrong. What are the odds of two people, who aren't meant to have children, getting pregnant?"

"God clearly has his reasons." Rafe watched with a grimace as his son clumsily attempted to tie his bowtie. "Psalms 127:3 says, 'Children are a gift from the Lord; they are a real blessing.' I'd like to think the two of you are being rewarded for your faith. If any of what Alaina said the angel's spoke of is true, then..."

"You doubt what she said?"

"That's not what I'm trying to say, and I think you know that."

Nodding in understanding, Dante replied, "I feel a little like Joseph must have felt, having found out his bride was expecting God's son. I mean, I know there's a distinct difference here, of course, as Alaina's not having the Lord's child, she's having mine but..."

"We are all God's children, but from the looks of things they will be gifted so I do understand where you're coming from," Rafe said with earnest.

"You really do, don't you? You were where I am now, forty years ago," Dante said as though making the correlation for the first time.

"Yes, and then Lilyandhi and I had three more within the span of four years."

"Bite your tongue," Dante exclaimed in alarm, the notion of raising a family of nine sent chills up his spine. His father smiled back at him, then laughed aloud.

"Your mother once told me, when she was pregnant with you and your brothers, that she dreamed I would have a dozen children to call my own one day." Thinking back on that day over forty years before, Rafe recalled it had been after a picnic along the river. Lying beneath the oak tree out back, they'd napped together. As they woke late in the afternoon, she had shared her dream with him as he held her. Flexing his arms, Rafe realized, in that moment, how much he truly missed having his wife in his arms.

"Seriously?" Dante asked. He turned to look at his father in surprise. Seeing him nod he inquired, "What happened?"

"She stopped getting pregnant after Crisalya," he replied with a shrug. "Then years later she got sick. And, well, you know the rest." Rafe's last words were spoke softly before he looked quickly away towards the bedside near the fireplace. Sadness clear was in his eyes. She'd passed away right there in his bed nearly twenty-two years ago. The memory of it was still very prevalent to him.

Walking towards his dresser, Rafe pulled a small box from within it. Staring down at the intricate silver design on the exterior of it, he made a conscious decision. "Give me that, I'll make sure it gets taken back to the jeweler." He reached for the ring box in his son's hand. Taking it from him, Rafe watched his son do a double take as he placed the box from the dresser in his hand.

Glancing down at the box, Dante opened it and then looked back up at his father in surprise. "This was mom's wedding ring, wasn't it?"

"Yes,"

"You're giving it to me for Alaina?"

"Yes," Rafe said, finally disappearing into his closet. Grabbing his tuxedo, he took it to the bathroom to hang then began donning his clothes himself.

"Why?" Dante asked when his father returned from the bathroom. "You never gave it to me for Elizabeth."

"Alaina is not Elizabeth."

"Meaning?"

"Meaning, Elizabeth never believed as we do, Dante," Rafe replied. "She did not believe in God as she claimed. I think if you were truly honest with yourself, you know that is true."

Rafe watched his son sigh heavily.

Nodding his head in grudging agreement, Dante placed the box in the pocket of his tuxedo pants for safe keeping.

"Alaina, on the other hand, does believe in God. She is choosing to follow the path He has laid before her, rather than one she has made for herself. As far as I am concerned, that makes her so much worthier of that wedding ring than Elizabeth ever was."

"You knew even then?" Dante asked, clearly referencing the day he'd married his first wife.

Rafe inhaled a troubled breath and frowned, appearing deep in thought. "Her words contradicted her actions more often than I cared to hear and see. But I hoped for your sake that I was wrong, for I could see how much you loved her. My intention was to pass the ring on to you after a couple years, in order to give as an anniversary present, if I'd seen a change in her, but..." Rafe's voice trailed off at the implication.

Understanding his father's words, he became thoughtful.

"I think I'm in love with Alaina," he said finally. "How is that possible? I always said my love for Elizabeth was infinite. Even with her betrayal that never changed. And I swore after she died that..."

"The lines of infinity go both ways. A man can find love again."

"You didn't," Dante accused. "And you always said your love for mom was infinite."

"Yes, I did," Rafe said quietly. His eyes seemed to squint and his head tilted back ever so slightly. as though he were trying to look back to the past within his mind. "And I still maintain that."

Looking at his father as he recovered from his past musings and stood before him in his tuxedo, Dante realized how truly lonely his father must have been all these years since his mother had passed.

"If, as you say, a man can find love again, then why didn't you ever re-marry?"

Pausing as he peered into the mirror above the dresser, Rafe adjusted his bow tie. Then turning towards his son, he eyed him, appearing almost uncomfortable.

"Because I was never open to it, Dante." His voice was laden with restrained emotion; his words intentionally evasive. Clearing his throat, he continued. "But you clearly are, or you would never have fallen in love with Alaina."

Hearing a soft knock on the bedroom door, Dartanian's voice could be heard calling out to them.

"Time to bite the bullet and hoist on that ball and chain."

Grumbling as he opened the door, Rafe scowled at Dartanian. "Rather a poor choice of words, wouldn't you say?"

"He is, after all, taking on a wife and six children; three babies at that," Dartanian drawled while grinning. He knew full well he was irritating his dad.

"Let's have a little more respect for the sanctity of marriage, shall we?" Rafe said, throwing on his tuxedo jacket and heading out the bedroom door. "Come on boys, let's get moving. We don't want to keep the pastor waiting any longer."

Striding into the hallway, Dante and Dartanian watched and waited as their father closed the bedroom door tightly behind them and set the lock on the keypad.

"Suppose he's ever gonna stop calling us boys?" Dartanian ventured, glancing towards his brother.

"Nope. Besides, it's better than you little…"

Halting his son's words, Rafe stopped abruptly, glaring as he spoke. "Let's keep the language PG shall we?" They started back down the hallway again together. "Besides, you know full well I never called you that, unless you were in serious trouble and my temper got the better of me." As a rule, Rafe made it a point not to swear, for he did not want to perpetuate the belief that such vulgar language was acceptable in his house.

Exchanging glances, the twins grinned back at each other.

"I don't know about you Dante, but I think I must have been in trouble quite a lot." Dartanian scratched at his brow, his eyes twinkling with mirth.

"I'm just glad he never found out I was the one who wrecked his 1969 Corvette Stingray convertible when we were twenty."

"You mean that cobalt blue beauty he painstakingly refurbished himself for nearly six months, over twenty-five years ago?" Dartanian replied in alarm, as Rafe stopped without warning at the top of the stairs. Glancing towards his father's rigid back, he noted his hands were balled into fists.

"Yup. The very one." Dante anxiously adjusted his tie and carefully stepped around his father in order to move further down the stairs. As he passed him, he could see the dark feral look in his father's eyes and could almost imagine steam billowing from his ears.

"And you're telling him this now! Why?" Dartanian asked, carefully stepping his father's rigid form.

"I promised God as I was doing devotions this morning, that if he blessed our marriage, I would admit to and repent of all sins before I wed today," Dante said uneasily. He watched his father's face turn red. "And the pastor's here now, so I figured..."

"Dante Billius Blackthorne..."

Cringing outwardly as the expletives flew from his father's mouth and carried down the stairs, Dante shrugged. "It was worth a try."

Patting his brother on the back with sympathy, Dartanian chuckled and they moved into the living room. "From the looks of dad, you'll be lucky to get wedding pictures without a black eye."

As they moved into their places near the pastor, who gave them a questioning look, Dante peered over his shoulder. Seeing Rafe step into the living room from the foyer, he watched as his dad strode quietly towards him, while the rest of the family looked on with concern. Hearing the music start as Sayleena giggled from the top of the stairs, Dante worried at what his father might do.

"I am sorry, Dad. Don't suppose you can forgive me?"

Cocking his head towards his son, Rafe's gypsy blue eyes fairly glowed as they bore into his sons.

"What makes you think I hadn't already forgiven you for your transgression twenty years ago?" He said loud enough for everyone to hear.

Startled, Dante eyed his father closely as he watched his expression squirrel into a grin. "Are you saying you've known all this time?" He gaped at his father.

"The father knows everything," Rafe said quietly, tapping at his brow with one finger.

"Then what was all that about?" Dartanian gestured towards the stairwell. Alaina could be seen coming down the stairs.

"I just realized that he used the last of my favorite razors," Rafe quipped, taking his place next to Dartanian.

"Are you kidding me?" They both exclaimed in unison.

Shrugging, Rafe sighed, "I bought out the last two hundred of that brand of razors five years ago, just before they were discontinued."

Watching as his sons exchanged looks and gawked at him, Rafe merely grinned and nodded towards Alaina as she strode towards them, beaming openly. "The Father knows everything. Always remember that, Dante."

Chapter 35

The front living room of the Blackthorne house had been somewhat tastefully decorated with tons of pale yellow and off-white streamers. They extended from each corner of the room, curving across and coming to a point near the fireplace. On the mantle, on either side of the Van Gogh painting hanging above the fireplace, were small glass bowls with yellow floating candles. And though it was nearing summer, purely for show, a roaring fire had been started and maintained throughout the ceremony.

The lamps which normally resided on the end tables had been removed. The tables were pushed towards the fireplace on either side. Each end table had been laden with arrangements filled with dozens of Plumeria flowers. Their soft, creamy white and yellow petals brightened the room without the need for too many candles, other than the ones required for the ceremony itself.

In order to allow for room for the couple and the pastor to stand, the coffee table had been relocated to the entryway. Two of the chairs on either side had been

390

pushed back some to allow space for family and children to stand. To Sayleena, Saruman and Storman's delight, they received the best seats in the house, for they were allowed to sit on the couch during the brief ceremony.

Giggling happily as her mommy kissed her new daddy, Sayleena clapped with excitement and ran towards them once they'd been pronounced man and wife. Grabbing them both about the waist, she hugged them exuberantly as she squealed with delight. Running back to the couch, she grabbed her brother's arms then whispered in their ears. Completely oblivious to the tension amongst some of the adults, they ran from the room into the kitchen in search of the wedding cake.

Unbeknownst to everyone, standing on either side of the couple after they'd been pronounced man and wife, were the angels Maleeka and Woreash. They'd come suddenly and without warning in a flash of bright white light. Their four wings, though normally unseen even by the eye of other angels, were outstretched and aloft as though ready for flight. Pulling their broadswords from their scabbards they drew them in an arch over Alaina and Dante's heads. As the swords came together with a loud clank, the angels reached out with their other arm and gently rested their hands on Dante's shoulder first, then Alaina's.

"By God the Father, your union has been blessed." Woreash looked upon Dante and Alaina. Glancing over at Maleeka, he smiled brightly as they held them there together briefly.

"They each spoke their vows with great meaning. Their feelings and intentions are quite clear in God's eyes."

"Yes, so it would seem for He would not have sent us otherwise."

"One of the first of six in order to fulfill the prophecy." Maleeka smiled back at his friend. "Five more to go," he said with a sigh. He twisted his sword in the air with a flourish and brought it back down to its scabbard.

"No, Maleeka." Woreash cast a knowing glance towards Drinian, who was looking with envious longing at Dante's new bride. Presenting the same motions with his broadsword, he sheathed his at the same time. "Technically, there are only four, for one is half-way there."

A brilliant flash of blue light behind them gave them pause, drawing their attention from their charges. As quickly as it came, it was gone, but left behind was the once tall, broad figure of the angel Rokon who slumped to one knee before them. Appearing both winded and wounded with one wing dragging the carpeted floor of the Blackthorne living room, he spoke with haste. "You're only half right." His broad chest flexed and shook as he heaved a ragged breath. "This chaos effect spans further than we thought. Make haste, dear brothers. Trouble brews in Loveland, for though there may only be four left to go, instead of six ... there are actually seven."

Alarm spread within the two angels as dozens of angelic guards fell within the walls of the Blackthorne home. Each bedraggled and worn to the bone from a war waged from somewhere outside its walls.

"Where have you come from?" Woreash demanded.

Rokon struggled to stay upright as another guard attempted to mend his wing. "You ask the wrong question. Ask not from where ... but from when."

Epilogue

H*old* the phone people!

So let me get this straight.

Lionel Radford is dead. In a shear streak of irony, he gets killed by Alaina's late husband Dylan, who as stated, managed to get killed in the process, making her a widow and placing her in danger cause of his stupidity. This opens up a window for Dante, who happens to be a cousin to Kahner RavenCroft – the same man who married Lionel Radford's former wife, Sable – to step in and take his place.

How convenient!

Oh, oh, oh, but it gets even better because apparently both Dante and Alaina are so weak willed that they make a bad choice in the heat of the moment – just like Kahner and Sable RavenCroft did – and she also ends up pregnant like Sable did.

But not with just one kid. Oh no. Three!

Three babies?

Hello! Sound familiar people?

And what the heck was with Drinian? I mean, I get that the guy's being tortured by shadowy demons and all, but seriously? To think he was going to just step in and take his brother's place? That Alaina was going to just drop the attractive safe guy who doesn't see shadows for a guy who does, of whom she doesn't even know?

Right. Like that was going to happen, because I guarantee Dante wasn't going to allow that. I can't say as I know the guy personally, of course, but shoot, if I were him, I sure as heck wouldn't. Sheesh!

And not to make light of a person's death, but... I guess Kahner's new wife, Sable RavenCroft, now has one less person to worry about coming after her. Although, I wouldn't write off his brother, Kobi Radford, as a concern yet, because I guarantee you ... that man is mad as all get out right now.

-And looking for blood...

-Revenge...

-Or whatever you want to call it. In my mind, it's all the same thing. Regardless, we won't find out anything more on that front until much later.

I did find it interesting that Agent Ricardo Pegueros popped up again in this story. It turns out he really did know a guy who reminded him a lot of Agent Toni Starck, or Kahner RavenCroft as that's his real name. Yuppers, it seems he's met, and worked with, both cousins. Though, I gather he has not made the correlation that they are related...

-Yet.

It makes a body wonder whether Pegueros's knowledge of the both of them is going to come back and bite both the RavenCroft's and the Blackthorne's in the heinie later on. I guess we'll have to wait and see.

Oh, and what do you figure is with this prophecy that the late Lilyandhi Blackthorne supposedly made before she died anyways? It sure sounds like there might be something to it. It's awful coincidental that the numbers within it corollate with the same day Dante's first wife died, and the same night Alaina was apparently raped fifteen years before.

But you know what I really can't help but wonder? Whether it's possible both the RavenCroft's and the Blackthorne's might be linked by more than just blood and their extensive lineage but also somehow by the same prophecy. The fact that both the eldest children of each family have recently found a woman and sired triplets within the same month and around the same time seems a bit too serendipitous to me.

On a side note…

Angels are supposedly real? Hello! If you're a cynic like me then you're probably laughing out of your tuckus right now. Then again…

Hhmmm. I must admit I'm a bit lost for words, which is saying a lot for me because, as you can see, I usually have all kinds of things to say.

(Vortigern scratches head thoughtfully.)

I don't know people, Kalabernus AND Dante are seeing, hearing and being tortured by these shadowy demonic-like creatures. Even as an agnostic, if I'm to classify the shadows as demons, wouldn't it stand to reason that there could be an opposing force to balance it out? You know, like angels?

Hhmmm. It's something to ponder. If they are real as the author would have us believe then what do you suppose the angel, Rokon meant by what he said?

"…Ask not from where … but from when."

Cryptic much?

I have no clue either and I've read through most of this collection so far. Though admittedly I'm still waiting on Ms. Christine to piece together the finale from the notes I found.

I guess, if you're looking to find out more, then I'll see you in the next one.

A Note from the Author

Thank you for taking the time to read my story. I truly hope you enjoyed it. And if you wouldn't mind... Please be sure to leave a review of Kayos Effect at amazon.com. I'd love to hear from you! I'd also like to welcome you to experience...

Karisma Trouble
An Unfortunate Lineage
Volume III

OR, if you're disinclined toward reading Secular fiction at this time, (and there is nothing wrong with that, of course) you may skip on to...

Total Kayos
An Unfortunate Lineage
Volume IV

OR, if you're ready to skip to the finale then feel free to skip over everything and go straight to it.

Karisma Kayos: Out of Time
An Unfortunate Lineage Finale
Volume VII

Either way, I hope you're enjoying the series so far!

Delaine Christine

CHARACTER LIST OF SUSPECTS

Rathbourne Blackthorne - The father of Rafe Blackthorne and former owner of The Blackthorne Horse Ranch.

Saphire Blackthorne - The deceased mother of Rafe Blackthorne. She was married to Rathbourne Blackthorne.

Rafe Blackthorne - The patriarch of the Blackthorne household and owner of The Blackthorne Horse Ranch in Kalispell, Montana. He was also married to the late, Lilyandhi Blackthorne.

Lilyandhi Blackthorne - The deceased matriarch of the Blackthorne clan. She is the mother of Rafe Blackthorne's six children. Originally of Mandan Indian descent, she was the last of her particular tribe. She has maintained many of the journals left behind by her descendants and authored a few of her own.

Dante Blackthorne {A.K.A, Agent Franclin Kastle} - Is the eldest of the Blackthorne clan, first in a set of triplets, and an identical twin to Dartanian Blackthorne. He was married to Elizabeth Blackthorne.

Drinian Blackthorne - The second born in the set of triplets within the Blackthorne clan. He is six feet, six inches tall and the largest, as well as the most handsome of his brothers. A carpenter at heart, he owns and manages several rental properties.

Dartanian Blackthorne - The third son born in the set of triplets within the Blackthorne clan. He is an identical twin to Dante Blackthorne. The Sheriff of Breckenridge County, he is married to Lylia Blackthorne and father to her daughter Kayla.

Breydon Blackthorne - The fourth in the order of birth. He is the fraternal twin of Megorah Blackthorne (Ryans) and the prosecuting attorney for Breckenridge County. He is married to Hialey and is the adopted father of her two boys, Cody and Seth Blackthorne.

Megorah Ryans - The fifth child born to the Blackthorne family, she is the fraternal twin of Breydon Blackthorne. Megorah marries Dr. Chase Ryans and they have three children together: Katana (12), Ethan (10) and Katie (8). She owns and manages The Ryans Real Estate and Rental Agency in Whitefish, Montana.

Crisalya Howard - The baby of the Blackthorne family. She is an ER nurse, working in the local hospital alongside Dr. Chase Ryans. She also assists her husband, Royce Howard, at the popular local coffee house, The Coffee Haven. They have one son together, Aiden (2-1/2).

Astraia Thatcher (O'Kahner) {A.K.A, Alaina Jordan} - Married to Dylan O'Kahner, she is also the mother of Sayleena (6), Saruman (4) and Storman (4) O'Kahner (Jordan).

Lylia Blackthorne - The wife of Dartanian Blackthorne, she has a daughter named Kayla (3). She also has a teaching degree and homeschools most of the children in the family at The Blackthorne Horse Ranch.

Hialey Blackthorne - The wife of Breydon Blackthorne. She owns an upscale lingerie shop called Hialey's Place. She has two children from a previous marriage, Cody (age 6) and Seth (age 4).

Dr. Chase Ryans - Owns a local family practice in Whitefish, Montana just north of The Blackthorne Ranch, but assists at the local hospital in the ER. He marries Megorah (Blackthorne) Ryans and they have three children: Katana, Ethan, and Katie.

Royce Howard - The owner of a local coffee house and popular hang-out called The Coffee Haven. He is married to Crisalya Howard, the youngest of the Blackthorne clan and they have one son, Aiden.

Dylan O'Kahner - Married to Astraia Thatcher (O'Kahner). He is the father of Sayleena, Saruman and Storman O'Kahner (Jordan).

Woreash and Maleeka - These two angelic beings are merely two of God's many Holy warriors. Their determination to see God's will through is fierce and unyielding.

Agent Jericho Henley - Is an agent claiming to work for Homeland Security.

Agent Ricardo Pegueros - Is an undercover CIA operative who has partnered previously with Agent Franclin Kastle.

Photo by Rosemary MacDaniel

Delaine Christine

Who she is, nobody knows;
A crab, a spider, a cat with five toes?
If you said all three, you're getting close.
The pages within will soon disclose.
So take a small peak into her mind.
Within this series the answers you'll find.

For more about the series
and the author

vortigernblack.com

smashwords.com/profile/view
/DelaineChristine

Or to Contact the Author:
delainechristine15@gmail.com